Too Soon

By

I0678244

S.L. Gape

2017

Too Soon © 2017 S.L. Gape
Triplicity Publishing, LLC

ISBN-13: 978-0997740554
ISBN-10: 0997740558

First Edition – 2017
Cover Design: Triplicity Publishing, LLC
Interior Design: Triplicity Publishing, LLC
Editor: Megan Brady - Triplicity Publishing, LLC

Acknowledgement

I would like to thank my editor, Megan, who has been wonderful to work with. Alea, and all the team at Triplicity, who have accommodated all of my requests to an extraordinary level. Also, Lisa Leigh and Sarah Cain, who once again have been my amazing 'go-to' proof readers.

*This book is dedicated to Phil, the joint-first, best man
I've ever met in my life.
You have been taken from us Too soon.
We all love you xx*

<u>Chapter One</u>

"So that's it? Nine years together, just like that? Worthless? Meaningless? No explanation, no attempt at making this work? Just simply, done? Over?" Brooke cried out trying her damnedest not to get upset. How could this be happening? This wasn't supposed to happen. Not to Brooke and Maria. Jesus, it was 'Brooke and Maria'. They were *the* ultimate 'power couple'. Their friends aspired to be like them, set their relationship as the bar they measured all future relationships against. Truth be known Brooke hated it, she actually *really* hated it, because it put so much pressure on Maria and her. It created a pretence that caused undue stress on them. But stupidly for her, she never really thought it had put enough pressure on them to cause their break up. She just didn't like the fact they were known as this 'perfect couple'. Fuck, how had she been so stupid?

"Please, Maria. We can try therapy. We can get through this, it's us. How can you not want to fight for us? You will tear everyone apart," Brooke pleaded with her girlfriend.

She heard Maria scoff and noticed the roll of her eyes. "Oh, fuck everyone else, Brooke. I don't give a flying fuck about 'everyone' else. Pull yourself together, you look pathetic!" she hissed harshly.

Brooke was shattered, everything was falling apart around her. Truth be known she couldn't remember life without Maria, and she had absolutely no idea what she was going to do.

***

Brooke was twenty-one, fresh into the police department when she had met Maria. The woman six years her senior, was cool, calm, sophisticated and oozed confidence. She was also Brookes' Sergeant. The first time she saw Maria she was instantly drawn to her, in most part due to her charismatic and enchanting personality. Maria was firm, but fair with her team, and gained a great deal of respect from them due to her preferred management style. Maria was destined for big things. She was driven and passionate about the force, and everyone knew she would continue to work her way up the ladder at a fast pace.

Brooke recalled the first time she saw Maria. They were both attending a court case, and she noticed the woman glide into the room. Her long auburn hair twisted in a tight bun; she had an air about her, and on the stand she was polite, courteous and friendly. In the courtroom, it was clear she had won them all over. Brooke knew at that moment, Maria was a woman that she would aspire to be like. Brooke had always had a passion for the police, watching the Bill with her dad as a kid. Then any new police drama introduced on TV would be their new found obsession.

Brooke remembered walking out of the courts with an excellent win under their belts; which according to everyone was in most part due to Maria. As it turned out, she was the epitome of good management and chased Brooke and her partner at the time, down the street to insist they allow her to take them out for dinner and drinks at the end of their shifts to celebrate. She remembered being lost in Maria's dark eyes at the time, with the recollection of simply standing in front of this beautiful woman just nodding like a smitten teenager. This hadn't gone unnoticed, as Maria had often made fun of her and that day over the years.

Brooke shook herself out of it and entered back to the here and now, and the reality of the situation. The situation that…that was it. Her life was falling apart she thought. "I just don't know how you can throw everything away like this" she sniffed, "Is it?" she stopped, she couldn't bear to ask the love of her life the question, but she needed to know. "Is it…" Brooke stopped, trying to compose herself, as she sighed heavily. "Is it because of what's happened? Me? The impact of the accident?" she asked sadly.

"Oh, for fucks sake, seriously? I can't do this anymore. Get a grip, we haven't had sex in forever. Jesus, we haven't even kissed for god knows how long, other than a peck. How can you have not seen this coming? I don't love you. Brooke. We have grown apart, and it's nothing to do with the accident. But seriously, some friendly advice, you need to get a grip and move on. We all go through shit with this job, it's expected, and if you can't cut it then get out. But it looks like you're doing that already!" she said matter of fact.

"Who *are* you? Seriously, where has the love of my life gone? You can, and have been a bitch at times, but I guess you'd expect that in nine years. But this? This isn't you. What the fuck is going on? Just tell me. As you always say I'm big enough and ugly enough to deal with the truth, aren't I?" she spat to the woman.

"You can't handle the truth, darling. Just get a grip, okay? Look, I am going on holiday for two weeks tomorrow and when I get back, I want you gone." Just like that, she turned her back and stormed upstairs and into the master bedroom of their four bedroom detached house. Her house. "Fuck, Brooke, why were you so stupid? Why didn't you force the joint mortgage?" she said solemnly? The tears began to fall. She couldn't do this. How could she? All of their friends were exactly that, 'their' friends. She had nothing. Her career was screwed, her relationship was apparently screwed, she had nowhere to live, and she couldn't speak to her friends. Plus, it wasn't fair to involve them. What was she going to do? She couldn't let this happen; she *would* stop this! They *could* make this work, she knew it.

Brooke ran up the stairs and down the hallway to their bedroom. Through the door she could hear Maria talking, so she stopped silently to listen outside the small crack. "I know, baby. Yes, I know, but we were together a long time, babe. You need to remember that. She could come after me for half of everything if we're not careful. Yes, yes I know, Paula." "Wait" Brooke whispered. "Paula? Their Paula? It couldn't be? Paula *and* Jasmine?" No, it's their best friend, of course it wouldn't be.

"I know, baby, but this time tomorrow, we will be starting a wonderful life together as a new family. We'll be on a plane to Florida for two weeks, Jas will have the best time, we can begin our perfect little family. And then when we come back, she'll be gone, baby, and you can both move in. I know it's going to be hard, babe. I know." Brooke heard, before noticing the change in her voice. "*So*? What about them? Paula, honestly, I don't care. I've spent years of my life acting like everything is perfect, yet behind closed doors it never was. I have lived a lie forever, and now, I want *my* happy ending with you

4

two and fuck everybody else. We can make new friends. I don't care anymore!" she spat into the phone.

Brooke slid down the wall, as she took in the extent of not only the damage but the content of what she was hearing. Her girlfriend and her best friend, *their* best friend were having an affair? She was sleeping with Paula? The love of her life's heart belonged to someone else now? A fucking straight woman? Maria hadn't wanted children, ever! She steered clear of straights. They were 'headfucks' and came with too much baggage. Those were her words, HER words! Maria's, that's what she said about straight women. "How could she?" Brooke said quietly shaking her head and containing the sobs on the brink of exploding from her right now.

"Oh, hey. Erm, how long have you been there?" asked Maria fearfully as she came out of their room.

"Long e-fucking-nuff," Brooke said, standing and shaking her head with venom. "Paula? Really, you're fucking having an affair with Paula? Single mum, straight Paula? Are you fucking kidding me right now?" Brooke scowled as she faced the woman, noticing the height she had over Maria and using it as a tool to desperately try and maintain the strength to not break down. She wouldn't! She wouldn't give her the satisfaction.

"Look, Brooke, I didn't want you to find out this way. I don't know what to say. It just... well, it just happened. I was feeling under pressure and you were too busy with your career and so she was there, a friend I could turn to. She got me, Brooke. I can't help it, she was there when you failed your duty as a girlfriend" she said shaking her head.

Brooke had never had a fiery temperament or been a violent person, but in this moment she wanted to punch something *or* someone. Brooke couldn't believe what she was hearing. This dumb bitch is blaming her for being driven and wanting to make something of herself? "Oh, I'm sorry. I guess I missed the chapters where I was supposed to be the stay at home trophy wife whilst you climbed the ranks, and do a fuck all with my life. Yes, those were clearly cut from the script. Why? You are fucking unbelievable. You know what, Maria, knock yourself out. You've lost a little bit of attention, and the key words in that sentence ARE a 'little bit,'" she said emphasizing the 'are', due to other things in life not revolving around her. "And so you threw it all away for someone that shows a bit of interest. It will never work. You will get bored with the 'straight women' dramas, as you so frequently put it. And a child? Fuck me, you're so clueless. And you're the most self-absorbed arsehole there is. You can't even enjoy time with our own nieces or nephews" she said frustrated, walking off. She stopped and turned around again to face her. "Our own nieces and nephews! You're a selfish cow, and you know what, I'm glad to not be wasting any more of my life! You go have an amazing family holiday with Paula and Jasmine in Florida. Make out that the straight single mum, the kid, and the dyke are the perfect happy family, because I can assure you, it will be a disaster waiting to happen. And the only loser in all of this is that poor little girl. I'll stay elsewhere tonight whilst you're packing for your *dream* holiday and return to collect my stuff in the coming two weeks. Don't worry, Maria. I'll be gone before you get back, and there will be absolutely no evidence that we ever had a life together" she spat, running down the stairs before Maria had a chance to see her upset.

Brooke stormed into her kitchen and held onto the island, watching as her knuckles turned white from the pressure of squeezing so hard. She silently screamed, careful not to let Maria see the effect this was having on her. She opened her bag and retrieved her brush, gently combing back her thick blonde hair and tied it into a high ponytail, looking at herself in the mirror. How could you be so stupid? Brooke was unsure who the question was for, her or Maria, as she wiped the one escapee tear and dabbed her eyes dry with some tissue. Brooke breathed in deeply before spraying some of her favourite perfume. She grabbed her keys as she walked out of her house and pretty much the only life she had known in her adult life, as she slammed the door shut behind her.

Chapter Two

Brooke didn't know how or when she arrived to Brighton pier. She did know she had been driving a while, and wondered if there was anyone here that she could crash with for the night. She wanted to avoid going to any of their friends' houses in order to dodge speaking of the situation she was in. Suddenly, Brooke was fully aware that due to having never been to Brighton, there was nobody here that she knew. She wondered if that was why she had subconsciously arrived to the beautiful buzzling place. It was a full two or more hour journey to a place that looked like it could be the edge of the earth right now. Brooke silently sat in her car, watching the waves breaking on the shore, as the fairground rides were whizzing and whirling around in the background. She listened to the laughter in the distance from this vibrant place, from people, unlike her without a care in the world. Brooke had always wanted to come here, and had tried to arrange it on a number of occasions with Maria. Unfortunately, the response was always the same: 'it wasn't her thing'. Brooke sighed heavily, resting her head against the headrest, allowing her thoughts to assess the uncertainty that faced her. The uncertainty of what lay ahead. Unsure of what to do, or how she was going to deal with this amongst everything else. Feeling a panic attack about to start, Brooke closed her eyes and tried to control her breathing in a bid to avoid it. Slowly counting to ten, Brooke took deep breaths and waited for it to pass.

When Brooke had finally calmed herself down, she pulled out her phone and opened the safari page, searching for the booking.com website. This enabled her to locate what she was looking for. A room for the night with parking. Brooke was typing in her card details to confirm the booking, but stopped herself before pressing confirm, having had a slightly different thought. Could she do it? That wasn't really in her nature, Brooke thought, before pressing go and re-searching upgraded rooms and adding another day. "Fuck you," she said out loud. Brooke opened her purse again, pushing her own bank card back inside and retrieving their joint credit card, silently praying Maria hadn't already cancelled it. Entering in all the details, Brooke pressed confirm on the superior deluxe sea view room for two days, smiling when it went straight onto the *thank you for your booking* page. "Well, it's probably the same cost for two nights to Brighton as two weeks in Florida for your piece of skirt. But hey, you can afford it, right?" she said to herself, starting her car back up and putting on her sat nav.

Brooke reluctantly walked inside Brighton Mall, as she wasn't in the mood for shopping. Truth be known she rarely was. Shopping wasn't her thing, but she couldn't possibly spend three days in the converse, skinny jeans and t-shirt she was wearing. She looked at the map, working out where Pull and Bear, River Island and Zara were. Those shops would be fine she thought, she just needed some underwear and a few outfits, and she was set. In true Brooke style, she was done in half an hour, walking back to her car, happy with her purchases. At least that was one less thing she needed to worry about, amending the address in her sat nav and making her way to the hotel.

Brooke checked in with the young guy with bleached blonde hair on reception, noticing he was very young, and incredibly polite and pleasant, wishing her a wonderful stay. She smiled politely, before leaving the reception and heading to the lifts to make her way to her room.

When Brooke walked in and took in the sights around her, she immediately dropped her bags at her feet. "Wow! Thank you, Maria," she said whistling softly. She walked forward and took in the expanse of the room, with floor to ceiling windows looking out over the sea front. A super-king bed on one side of the room, with the world's largest 'L' shaped sofa on the other. She had a study area equipped with her very own Apple Mac and chaise longue against the end window with a Juliette balcony. She made a mental note to make use of that at some point in the next few days.

Brooke sighed, fell onto her bed and lay there for a few moments, reliving the day. Her head was whirling. She had a terrible headache and needed some aspirin. The difficulty was trying to not think back to the times they were together with Paula and Jas. Not too long ago they had been at the park, feeding the ducks. Brooke had always been intent on having children, in reality it was a silent argument the pair regularly had, especially of late. She thought back to the day as she rushed off with Jas to the pond, recalling it vividly. Paula and Maria sat on the bench in the distance. Brooke hadn't thought anything of it, but why would she? She questioned herself. But now it was different, and it was hard to not wonder if they sat and laughed about her. Poor Brooke, poor simple Brooke, stupid little Brooke, she thought. "Come on, pull yourself together. You are not doing this to yourself. You can't change this, and if she changed her mind, you wouldn't be able to forgive her or trust her. You aren't that person," she said to the room.

Brooke had never been one to cheat. She was always very open in relationships. Granted they were practically teenage flings as opposed to relationships, but she was always very open and honest with everyone. She could drive herself insane trying to work out everything, but she knew it was done, and they were done. And like Maria had said in 24 hours' time, the 'new readymade family' would be on their way to the holiday of a lifetime in Florida, and she would be nothing more than a 'period' in their lives.

Brooke could hear the vibrating of her phone in her bag, but chose to ignore it. She got up and opened a bottle of wine and water from the mini bar. Before taking two aspirin with the water, she checked her phone. Thirteen missed calls from a mixture of Maria, Paula and a couple of her friends, *their* friends. Is that it? Has she told them all? Do they all know? She could go weeks without speaking to them, and now interestingly, they were all creeping out of the woodwork. Brooke fell back on her bed again and allowed the tears she'd held back all day to run free.

***

Brooke lay there in silence and thought back to their meet. "So you guys both done well today in court. It's hard on your first time, but it's all about gaining the trust. The police will always have the lack of trust from the general public. Those asshole solicitors will always make you out to be in the wrong: bullying, harassment, victimisation, discrimination. That's how they will get into the jury's heads, so being likeable has to be a prerequisite," Maria had said to the two young rookies.

"Well, I think Brooke has a natural likability about her. So I personally think she will pull that off fairly easily, in and out of court," John had said. She remembered inwardly cringing, partially because she had been in the force a few months now and hadn't come out yet. Secondly, because she was really struggling that he was blatantly flirting in front of their superior. When John had excused himself, Brooke sat there in silence, resting her chin on her fist.

"So, it seems you have an admirer," Maria had said to her. "You into him?" she asked, keeping her eyes on Brooke as she took a swig of her beer.

"Apparently so, and no. I'm not," she said raising her wine to her mouth to take a long sip. She could feel Maria's intrepid glare.

"So what's your type, Brooke?" her manager purred. She remembered the flutter in her tummy, how incredibly turned on she was and how Maria could make the whole world disappear with her intent stares. Brooke held her own, or at least she thought she had.

"I wouldn't necessarily say I have a type. If they can make me laugh, feel alive, keep me on my toes, but not in a negative, game playing way, and treat me well. Then, I guess those are the important things," she said maintaining eye contact.

"Nothing else, Brooke? Hair/eye colour for example? Specifics?" she said, still not looking away. Brooke recalled telling her friends at the time she was in a sexual game of 'stare out' since she couldn't put it any other way and neither was prepared to back down.

"I don't know, Serge. I guess if the sparks are there it doesn't matter what they look like, as long as they are single," she whispered, looking up through her eyelashes. She knew she was playing the game.

"I've told you, Brooke, its Maria, whilst we're out tonight," she confirmed.

"I'm sorry, Serge. I mean, Maria." She licked her lips before pulling in her lower lip and biting it. She had intentionally smirked at that point to her boss, making a point of flirting with the woman, despite knowing she shouldn't have been.

"Your friends coming back, Brooke, but I can assure you, this is unfinished business. I will punish you for being such a flirty little minx," she said with a lop-sided grin, just as John arrived back at the table with no opportunity for Brooke to respond.

Brooke recalled the electricity between them. She had always had a thing with authority, and this was no different. She was highly attracted to her superior, and she was having all sorts of fantasies of her, especially since seeing her in her formals in court that day. Brooke shook the thoughts from her mind. *Come on, Brookie. Pull it together*, she thought. She walked to the lounge area and picked up the remote control, switching it onto a music channel. She was looking for some form of dance station to prevent the possibility of dealing with love songs. Brooke was happy that she had located an hour long show of old school classics, listening to the music as she got undressed. She opened the doors to her bathroom and was stunned. Jesus it was the size of her bedroom at home! *Home,* she thought. She didn't have a home anymore! Brooke ignored the thought and walked into the giant, grey, marble room, fully lit with spotlights all around the base and ceiling. On the right-hand side there were double sink basins and a partitioned wall with toilet, and on the left-hand side there was a double wet room. Directly in front of her was a double Jacuzzi bath with pink LED spotlights built into the marble floor all the way around the proximity. Mesmerised by the sheer beauty of the perfect room, Brooke walked adjacent to the Jacuzzi along the main wall and ran her fingers over the marble with the built in TV and music player. She had never been one for extravagance, invariably opting for basics. As long as they served a purpose she was more than happy, in her mind. The money saved could go towards additional enjoyment. But in this moment, she was completely overjoyed with her room. She was pissed at herself for taking it out of their account, and was reminding herself that the key word in that sentence was 'their' account. Not Maria's solely, and she was fully aware that there would be no expense spared on the holiday to Florida. Maria was a firm believer that money could buy you everything, and she was very driven by money and stature. It was always for show, everything always had been. Brooke inwardly smiled at the irony of her stay in Brighton, knowing full well that's why Maria would have never come here. It wasn't big enough, impressive enough, classy enough.

Brooke pondered over the variances of cleaning options, and finally chose the shower in this instance. She figured she would go to the bar and have dinner and a drink with her book, and then with the whole day tomorrow she could treat herself to a lengthy Jacuzzi bath and movie. Brooke switched on the water and allowed the steam to fill the room before stepping in and letting the hot water flow over her head and body. Brooke had hoped the hot water would have washed away some of the hurt and the pain she was feeling, but it seemed not.

Brooke re-straightened her blonde hair, put some lipstick and mascara on, and looked herself in the mirror, checking herself out. She opted for the new white, skinny jeans, navy fitted-shirt and brown rider boots. Brooke ignored the puffy eyes as she acknowledged her five ft. nine svelte frame. She was incredibly grateful that it afforded her the luxury of being able to pull the outfit off without having even tried it on! Staring at herself as she looked… searching her soul for the answers she knew she would never get and scared of what the future held, she put her bank and key cards in her pocket and shoved her phone into the back pocket. Leaving her room, she made her way down to the hotel restaurant.

<u>Chapter Three</u>

"Good evening, Madam. Have you got a table booked?" the guy at the entrance asked her.

"Oh, no. I'm sorry I haven't, I wasn't aware… it's okay…"

"Don't worry, miss, that's fine, and will you be dining alone this evening?" he asked.

Brooke could feel her eyes well up. "Um…," she said.

"It's okay, miss, don't worry. I have the perfect table for you," he said and smiled warmly to her, gently ushering her by the arm. He stopped to pick up a menu and took her out to the beautiful atrium. Putting Brooke slightly in the corner, slightly hidden by a pillar and a beautiful palm tree, he was right. It was the perfect table.

The evening was drawing in, and the seat the employee pulled out allowed her to be hidden from the other guests and completely facing the incredible sunset. The young guy placed the napkin on her lap and poured some water, handing her the menu. "I was just covering out front, so I will be your waiter for the evening. Will you be paying upfront or putting it on the room? If the latter, what is your room number please?" he said tapping on to his iPad.

"The room is fine, it's seven one two," she said.

"Oh, um, okay, Ma'am, the specials are…"

Brooke addressed the young boy, seeing his name badge. "Gareth? If you are going to be my waiter this evening, would you please do me a big favour?" she asked seriously.

"Of course, madam," he said courteously.

"I'm twenty-nine, not fifty-nine. Please stop calling me 'miss, ma'am, madam' or any other such title. I'm Brooke, my name is Brooke. Please just call me Brooke?" she said to him pleadingly.

Gareth looked taken aback, "of course…Brooke." He smiled sincerely and left the table.

A few moments later, he brought a bottle of pink Moet to the table and a number of papers and magazines for her. "Ermmm, Brooke, I hope you don't mind, I thought you looked like you could use this," he said holding up a bottle of Moet. "If you would like me to return it for something else I can do. I also got you a number of papers and magazines. I didn't know what you liked, so I got a variety. I thought you looked like a 'Hello or Vogue' type of girl." He smiled softly and handed her the reading material.

"Actually, I'm more of a lesbian mag or gossip type of girl. I'm not rich or proper, and I'm never normally this extravagant, i.e. room 712. But I've had a pretty bad day and well, I got in the car, ended up here. And as they say, the rest is history. I've always wanted to come to Brighton, and I guess subconsciously my mind brought me here. Thanks for the mags and the Moet. I will most definitely take that. I feel I need it, and thanks for your help. And the table, it's perfect." She smiled warmly.

"You're very welcome, Brooke." He smiled back to her. "Whilst, this is against company policy, and you don't look like today's the day, but a few of us from here are going out with my friends tonight. We're going to hit a few bars, mostly gay bars, but if you would like to join us the offer is there. You look like you could use some friends, or some shots right about now," he said, gently touching her arm. "Anyways, no answer required, we'll be at the back entrance to the left of reception when we finish about 11ish. Meet us there and we will be walking straight up. Anyways, madam," he smirked winking at her. "What can I get you to eat?" he asked.

She smiled back. Gareth was nice and she thought he had kind eyes. Looking at the menu again, unsure of what to eat, Brooke looked up to him with an uncertain expression. "Umm, I'm not," she paused as she saw Gareth's hand go up to stop her.

"Brooke, at the risk of doing a number of things this evening that would potentially get me fired, I don't want to be intrusive. But from the few short moments I've known you, you appear to be incredibly humble and sweet." He smiled an assuring smile, adding "And whilst, I don't know what your day has encompassed, nor am I seeking to know, you are going to do one of two things without eating this evening. One, you will get drunk and feel even worse tomorrow when you wake and the realisation all of this wasn't a dream and you are hungover as well as everything else. Or two, you're going to end up making phone mistakes. I can only assume that somewhere in this upset and pain in your eyes, there is a woman lurking. So drinking on an empty stomach in my opinion always results in texting or calling the stupid idiots that cause this hurt. Whilst I have no right to make such unprofessional and presumptuous statements, I would urge you to please have something to eat, even if it's just a couple of starters?" he pleaded.

How could she say no to the only person apparently kind enough to care? She could feel the tear slide down her face.

"Thank you, Gareth. I don't know why I met you this evening, but I feel it is an omen. I'm sorry I'm putting this on you, I shouldn't be," she sighed. She looked at the menu again. "Okay, I'll take the hummus and the scallop starters then," she said smiling to the guy.

"Odd, but great choices, Brooke," he said opening and pouring her a flute of pink champagne and leaving her alone.

She stared out to sea, watching the night come in, the waves still heavily breaking on the shore line. The lights on the pier lit up the skyline and made a very picturesque setting, She wished she was sharing this with Maria. She shook her head brutally at the realisation that nothing would ever be shared with Maria again.

Brooke retrieved her phone from her back pocket, opened up the messages and read through each of them. Mostly they were apologies from Paula and Maria. Empty apologies trying not to break up the 'gang', trying not to look the martyr, as she left her high and dry in this shitty period of her life. *How could she be so callous?* she thought. She texted her friend Fran back who'd asked if she was okay.

Hey I'm fine, thanks for asking. Who told you? She sent back the message, trying to find out if the entire group knew.

Well neither, I caught them and told them to stop as I wouldn't be party to it, she sent back.

Brooke read the message and couldn't breathe. She dropped her phone on the table as she tried to steady her breathing once more. Her phone beeped again and she saw the incoming message from Fran again. She opened it up and read: *They didn't tell you I knew did they? Shit, I'm so sorry, Brooke, I'm so sorry* ☹ *xxx.*

"Sorry? Fucking sorry?" she whispered to herself. Her life was falling apart and she didn't honestly know what to do anymore. She held her head in her hands as she once again collected her thoughts and tried to understand the repercussions of the day's activities.

She went to her phonebook and dialled Mitch's number. "Hello, gorgeous. You okay?" he answered quickly. "Brooke, you okay, babe? Brooke? What's happened? I can hear you crying. What's up? Talk to me, Brooke," the concern revealed in his voice.

Brooke sniffed a little. "She's left me. She's been having an affair with Paula, Mitch! The three of them are currently packing for their dream holiday to Florida in the morning to start their perfect life together. I have two weeks to leave my house, my life and just get out. What am I going to do, Mitch? My friends knew about it, and I now feel so alone. How could I have been so stupid?" she sobbed into the phone.

"Babe, where are you?" he said to her.

"In a hotel in Brighton," she sniffed.

"What the fuck are you doing in Brighton?" he said concerned.

"I don't know. I just ended up here."

"Oh, babe. I will get a train there now. I can't drive, I've been drinking with the boys, but text me the details and I will be there in a few hours," he said.

She loved her partner, Mitch. They had been in CID together for the last few years since her promotion. He was hard on her at first, pissed that such an inexperienced copper had moved up the ranks so quickly, and was sure that she was completely inadequate and incompetent. He was certain she had gotten there because of who she was shagging. It only took a couple of days before he realised how wrong he was and how deserved she was of the position. Ever since then, they had become fantastic friends. Sam Mitchell, 'Mitch' as they all knew him, was not a fan of Maria. Personally he didn't see the compatibility. In his opinion, Brooke and Maria were complete polar opposites. Luckily, Maria's drive had meant that she was connected to them for a short two months only, before her next step up, which allowed him to think what he wanted about her.

"I'm okay, honestly. I just didn't really know who else to contact. I didn't want to call Dad, he would be able to tell something was up, and he's already concerned about me. Seriously, I'm fine," she said sniffing slightly.

"You're not fine. Please tell me where you are? I'm concerned you're going to do something," he said.

Since the accident, it seemed everyone thought she was going to kill herself. That was not the case. Since her mum died when she was thirteen, it had been just her and her dad. She would never be so cruel and selfish to do that. "Don't be so ridiculous. Yes, I'm devastated, and yes my world has pretty much fallen apart, but really? As if I'd kill myself?" she said just in time for Gareth to arrive with her starters, looking terrified.

"It's okay, they are being melodramatic," she said partially covering the mouthpiece. "Honestly, I'm fine, Mitch. I just needed a friend, somebody who's not been laughing behind my back for god knows how long," she said solemnly. "Listen. I am in the restaurant and I've been asked to go out with some of the staff for drinks, which I might do." She knew she wouldn't, but also knew he'd feel rubbish for not being able to get here to see her. "I have just gotten my food and I have some magazines. I'm looking out onto the seafront as the sun is setting. I'm good, I promise. I'll check in in the morning okay? I love you, Mitch. Thanks for being a good guy," she said to him sincerely.

"You too, babes. Please send me the details of the hotel so I can at least check in and I won't be worrying. Okay? We'll speak tomorrow, yeah?" he said to her.

"Okay, will send it now. Speak tomorrow." She did as she was asked and texted him the hotel information. When the food arrived she was happy she had taken Gareth's advice. Her hummus and scallops starters looked incredible, and her stomach was now informing her that it had gone too long without food. The scallops were delicious, and the pita breads which came with a variety of hummus flavours and olives were exactly the kind of comfort food she needed.

***

Brooke didn't notice Gareth come and sit down beside her as she was completely lost in her thoughts staring out to sea. Equally, she hadn't even noticed the plates being cleared away until hearing a cough and turning around, noticing at last the friendly face sitting next to her.

"Hey, you okay?" he asked her.

"I'm so sorry, I didn't know you were there," she said fretting.

"Brooke, no need to apologise, I'm really worried about you. Listen, I've called my sister. She's a year older than you and I asked her to come out tonight, too.

She is going to pick us up. I don't want to leave you alone. I heard you on the phone to your friend, and I can't leave you. I must insist you come out. My sister is cool, and I think you'll like her. And I think generally girls are normally better at this kind of thing. My advice is always going to be 'drink through it, or jump off one and onto another', but honestly, I don't think either is going to work for you this evening," he said.

"Look, Gareth, that's incredibly sweet of you but seriously, I'm fine. I won't be good company and I don't want to go out," she said seriously.

"Brooke, I'm afraid you are outvoted. My parents brought us up to never leave someone in distress, and I've just spoken to your friend Mitch who called the hotel and told me that I was not to take no for an answer. I'll look out for you, and won't make you drink if you don't want to. But, I just want you to have some time with others rather than being alone in a hotel with nothing but your thoughts. So, unfortunately, you have one of two choices. You come with Chrissy, me and my mates for a couple of drinks and some friendly company, or I'm going to call my mum. She will force you to come back to our house and well, I'm not going to lie, she's pretty much going to keep you there until she nurses you back to full health," he said to her seriously.

"Why are you being so kind to me?" she asked Gareth.

"Because, you are blatantly not from around here and you look like you need a friend," he said kindly.

"You truly are my knight in shining armour." She smiled sadly.

"Shame we both bat for the other side," he said winking to her and leaving the table once more. "You have twenty minutes, if you need to go and get anything from your room, maybe take your phone back?" he said, "Then I'll meet you out back."

Brooke sighed. She wasn't in the mood for this. But she was glad that someone so wonderful and kind-hearted had taken her under his wing, and forced his sister to come out, to make her not feel uncomfortable. She made a mental note to return the favour to Gareth. He was a true gentleman and clearly a credit to his parents. Leaving the table and writing a note *'be back in 5 save my drink'*, she ran up to the room getting what she needed and applying a little more of her favourite perfume. Brooke held her phone in her hands. He was right, could she be trusted with it? Especially if she ended up having more to drink. But she is a detective. *'Is'* being the operative word, she thought. Brooke had seen a lot of things over the years. Did she really want to be wandering around a city, knowing nobody without a phone? Her gut told her she had nothing to worry about with Gareth. She had no issue in following that feeling either, but she never left without her phone. It was a trait of the job, and her relationship. If Maria couldn't get hold of her, she was always pissed. She put it back in her pocket and left the room once more, making a quick diversion.

Brooke came back to the table and saw Gareth there. "I know you aren't feeling great and stuff, but you really shouldn't leave your drinks unaccompanied," he said seriously.

"Sorry, dad. I'll behave moving forward," she said smiling, the first smile he'd seen all night. "So, I've changed my mind. I would rather pay my bill upfront," she said. "Is that okay?"

"Yes of course, I'll grab it now for you and then we can go. Chrissy is outside," he said.

A few minutes later Gareth had arrived with the bill. She'd worked it out from the tariff an approximate amount and had the money ready. "Hang on, this can't be right," she said, realising it was lots cheaper than she had worked out. "Where's the Moet?" she asked.

"Oh it's on the hotel," he said. "You paid enough for the room and I figured you needed it," he said, smiling softly.

"No you can't do that," she said to him.

"I can do what I want, Brooke. I'm the restaurant supervisor." He smiled.

"What? Really? Why didn't you tell me? How come it says waiter on your name badge?" she said to him confused.

"Because tonight I am a waiter. I wasn't meant to be working, but one of my staff has called in sick today, so I'm covering," he said.

"Do you believe in fate?" she asked him.

"I do, Brooke, and I believe that for one reason or another we were meant to meet tonight, and I think we will be very good friends," he said to her. "Unless of course you make me wait any longer." He raised his eyebrow.

Brooke stood up, still giving the money she had accounted for to him and kissed his cheek lightly. "Thank you for being my complete saviour on the day I needed it most," she said. Gareth smiled shyly and looked at the money.

"Brooke, you gave me 80 pounds too much," he said.

"No I haven't. That's inclusive of tip," she said and downed the last part of her champagne and walked past him.

"Wait, no, I can't. I won't accept this," he said running after her.

"Well, I don't believe you have any choice. If it makes it any easier, it's my girlfr...my exe's money," she said sadly to him.

He stood there looking at the beautiful girl in front of him, unsure of what to say and do. "First rounds on me then I guess," he smirked and ushered her carefully out of the hotel into his sister's car.

Chapter Four

BANG, BANG, BANG, BANG. *Shit, what's happening?* She was lost. Where was she? Her head was spinning. *What's going on*, she thought. She recognised her room, and sighed as she recalled the reasons she was here. She looked down at her clothes from last night, including one boot still on. God the tight, fitted-shirt was really not the best of ideas to sleep in.

BANG, BANG, BANG, BANG. *Fuck.* She wasn't dreaming. *What the hell?* She picked up her phone. It was seven thirty-one a.m. *What the hell?* She couldn't remember a great deal, and that concerned her as she unlocked the door to face Mitch.

"What the fuck are you doing? I thought you were dead," he said pulling her into a tight hug.

"Whilst I may feel half dead due to the copious amounts of alcohol I drank last night, and the middle of the night wakeup call, I'm completely alive and well. What are you doing here,? How did you know where to find me? And how the hell did you get here?" she asked.

"I didn't drink any more. I got up at five, and you told me your hotel and erm," he stopped, looking embarrassed. "I pulled the 'you know who I am' card," he said pulling out the police badge from his pocket.

"You didn't?" she cringed.

"I know, I know. I was genuinely concerned though, babes," he said. Brooke loved Mitch because he was always there when she needed him. He had been her rock in the last eight months, even attending some of the therapy sessions with her. His six foot three muscly frame had always made her feel protected, and his Italian heritage showed. He was the epitome of tall, dark and handsome. But as much as he hated to admit it, he had more in common with Maria than he thought. Both of them were devoted and married to their jobs. He was a shit hot detective and would someday go all the way. His goal was to make it in the force in Canada though, and had often dreamed of settling there. Purposely, disregarding the constant 'bounty hunter' jokes. He could see his future was a detective or homicide over there, and Brooke genuinely thought he'd make it.

"Thank you," she said hugging him tightly.

"Dude, you need to brush your teeth" he said punching her playfully.

She loved the sibling type banter they had. "I know, I feel like my mouth is a camel's armpit at this moment in time," she said.

"What the fuck? Are you still hammered? You're aware that camels don't have armpits right?!" he laughed.

Brooke shrugged, walking off into her bathroom, thinking she was possibly still drunk and shut the doors behind her.

Reappearing fresh faced, fresh smelling and snuggled in her complimentary bathrobe, her wet hair fell naturally as she walked back out to her room. "There's my gorgeous girl," said Mitch, handing her a freshly made coffee.

"You are the best," she said, taking a sip and laying back down on the bed. She had just gotten comfortable as she heard the door knock, looking over to Mitch who was pulling out his wallet and striding to the door. He opened the door to let the concierge in with the room service tray and handed him a note, before bringing the tray over to his friend and handing her the glass of freshly squeezed OJ. She looked down at the platter inclusive of bacon butties, chocolate croissants, and a variety of cakes, cheeses and what appeared to be a mushroom, ham and onion omelette. "So, you just pretty much ordered everything from the menu?" smirking to Mitch. She took a fork and carved a small piece of the omelette off, chewing it slowly. Nope, that wasn't going to do it. She took a bite of the chocolate croissant. Nope that wasn't going to do it either. She inspected the rest of the dishes. She couldn't face the bacon buttie as the grease would definitely send her into a spiral of vomit. "Hmmmm." She picked up a slice of toast and put some strawberry jam on it. Hopefully sorting her out, she thought as she bit into the breakfast and switched on the TV. Although the TV was far away in the lounge area of the room, it was still big enough that they could see it perfectly.

"So, your digs are pretty darn awesome." He smiled, biting into the bacon buttie.

"I know right? I thought I'd treat myself. Actually, no. I thought 'we'd' treat me.'" She smirked, having another bite of toast.

"Here-here, chica." He held his glass of OJ to his friend; already feeling better that he was here.

They talked for a while as Brooke filled him in on the blow by blow account of the situation. They had gotten rid of the food and she was now snuggling into him as she relived the detail. She outlined her concerns, and just trying to work out how she had missed it all. Mitch was fantastic as ever. He listened, offered advice and help, and promised he would be there, support her and look after her 110% through it all.

She didn't know what she was going to do. It was all still so raw at the moment, and right about now, Brooke didn't think she'd ever know what she was going to do. They had planned to go out and just relax for the day, due to Mitch saying he could stay until five in the morning before starting his shift at nine the following day. But Brooke had told him to go home that evening. Mitch was adamant he didn't want to, pretending it was because he wouldn't be able to drink. She knew him. She could read him like a book, and knew it was just because he didn't want to leave her. Brooke also knew it was selfish, but she didn't want to argue with him. She didn't want to become reliant on drink, and that meant that actually he was right, plus she didn't want to spend the night alone tonight.

***

They spent the day on fairground rides, eating candy floss and sugar dummies, and paddling in the sea. Mitch, in true 'boyfriend' style, hooked ducks, dunked basketballs, played donkey derby and hoopla until his best friend and partner could hold no more teddy bears and had to beg for mercy. "No more, please? I'm embarrassed, and we won't both fit in the bed tonight," she laughed. It was the first real laugh he'd heard all day, taking the four-foot banana and three-foot monkey from her and putting his arm around her.

"I love you, kidda," he said sincerely, "and I won't let nothing happen to you. I mean that personally, and when you're ready professionally," he said carefully. Before allowing Brooke to do anything about the reference to work he'd made, he'd already started again.

"Okay, it's four p.m., I say we go home, get in PJ's, hire a load of horror movies, get a six pack each of corona and a large, spicy-chicken pizza," he said knowing it was her favourite.

"I don't want you to feel obliged to sit with me. You should go out, considering you're only here for the night. Go see the sights; meet a beautiful woman," she said solemnly.

"Babes, I'm thirty-eight; and I can barely manage shit when I've had a full twelve-hours kip, so that's not going to happen. And I already met a beautiful woman. I just want to make sure my girl is okay. Alright?" he said looking down into her eyes.

"You know what I mean. A woman that you can have some fun with," she said seriously.

"Babes, there's no girl in the world I could have more fun with," he said, gently kissing her forehead. Even with Brooke's tall frame her partner still towered above her. And in this moment the positioning his height was giving him was making Brooke feel the safest she knew she could possibly feel.

"Thanks, Mitch," she said, tip toeing to kiss his cheek, smiling embarrassed.

They arrived back at the hotel and Mitch walked over to the reception. He asked them to order the pizza and garlic dough balls to the room before making their way back upstairs. As they got back up, Mitch opened his bag and threw a shirt and boxers to Brooke.

"Hey, what's that?" she said opening the clothes out.

"Well, I know you always say you love wearing my big ole shirts and boxers when we're relaxing. So I figured if any time required boyfriend comfies, then that time was now," he said kindly as he got comfy on the bed looking through the movies on offer. Mitch was adamant it was horror movies, telling her that any type of chick flick would only end in disaster. In reality he was completely right.

Brooke picked up her phone and noticed a few new messages. Fran was asking if she was going to fall out with her over this, but she didn't want to think about that right now. A message from Maria basically telling her to stop being childish and ignoring her calls/texts. Unbelievable, she thought. She smiled at the messages from both Gareth and Chrissy checking in with her. In actuality she hadn't had too bad a time. Chrissy was lovely. So kind and exactly like Gareth. She had simply been there as a friend, even though they had only just met, offering great advice and sensible words back to her. She was careful to not let Brooke drink too much and was supplying her with water regularly. Brooke vaguely recalled Chrissy getting her in to the room before leaving. She texted both siblings back, apologising and thanking them for their kindness, before putting her phone back down and laying back on the bed, waiting for their food and movie.

***

"So, you know what you're gonna do yet? Or where you're gonna go?" Mitch asked as he handed her a slice of pizza.

"Not yet, no. I don't know where to start. I guess I will just need to find somewhere else to live. I'll just have to rent somewhere I suppose, whilst I look for somewhere to buy. Unfortunately, I have no idea at this moment in time. I will see what happens tomorrow when I get home.

I have two weeks to play with, plus I'm in therapy on Wednesday aren't I? So I will see what's said then" she sighed. "I know you're only worried, but can we not talk about it right now?" she said sadly.

"No worries, babe," he said, handing her a dough ball and opening another beer for her.

***

When Brooke woke up the following morning, she picked up the piece of paper on the pillow.

Gone to work, gorge. Speak to you tonight. Take care of yourself, love M x.

Brooke smiled at the caring gesture, picking up her phone to check the time. It was only seven thirty. She sighed as she took in everything once again, letting the tears fall freely. How was she going to manage? They had everything together, which would need to be split between the two. *Why* hadn't she forced the joint mortgage? Granted, she had money in the bank, enough to put a substantial deposit down on her own place, but she just didn't know how or what to do. Sighing heavily, Brooke got herself out of bed and went to the bathroom.

Knowing it was almost time to leave, she ran a bath, pouring some of the complimentary bubble bath in. Putting some easy listening music on and returned to her room to pack away the clothes back into the store bags she had.

A while later, Brooke was relaxing in the Jacuzzi enjoying the tranquillity it was offering. She had enjoyed her stay in the hotel and wished it was under different circumstances. But she was adamant she would come back someday, when things were different and actually explore and enjoy the place.

Brooke took one last look around the place before leaving the room, knowing she was now having to go home and face the reality of her life falling apart. She checked out and left a little note for Gareth saying thank you once more, before making her way to the car. She hit home on her sat nav and listened nonchalantly to the voice directing her home, the home that was hers no longer.

Chapter Five

Brooke sat in the car on her drive just looking at her house, too afraid to walk in. She really didn't know if she could do it. But what choice did she have? What was she going to do? There was no alternative, she needed to sort things out. There was nine years of joint purchases that would require splitting, and she was fucked if she was going to walk away with nothing. Breathing in heavily, Brooke grabbed the carriers and walked inside, inside to the empty ruins of her life. She had come home many times when Maria was working nights, or at least thought she was working nights. But this time it felt different. This time it felt final. Brooke threw the teddies Mitch had won in the small spare room, pondering on whether that would be where her friend's daughter would be taking up residence. Brooke had often thought that one day Maria would change her mind and that would be a nursery of their own. She stared off distantly feeling the pain once more.

Brooke didn't actually know where to start, so she decided she would do what she did best first, organise and plan. She got in her tracksuit and went to the lounge and put on a movie. She knew it wasn't a good idea to watch a chick flick, but she loved them and she loved *The Proposal* regardless of how it could result in her feeling.

With the movie in the background, Brooke was searching the internet for places to move into. She had found an apartment that she could have a viewing on tomorrow morning and would be able to move in straight

35

away if she liked it. She figured if she paid the six months' rent and deposit up front, she would probably be able to get things moving quicker still. In reality that would be the best option. Brooke was inexperienced at things like this and didn't even know how long the process would take. Realistically could she be moved in before Maria and Paula returned? Brooke arranged viewings with three properties. A flat, an apartment, and a small terraced house. Next she opened a word document and began writing a list. Before making plans for tomorrow onwards, she would go through each room and dissect it. She planned to remove and box up everything that was hers and ultimately get dibs on "their" things. If she didn't want Brooke in her future then she didn't need to be reminded of any of their past together, she thought. This was probably the only positive of the breakup, which allowed her to take some of the things that they had bought together over the years. Brooke considered changing her number also. Maria was being awful, sending nasty texts about growing up. But in reality, would she really continue with that when she was effectively 'living the dream'?

Brooke began googling local storage units near to her, finding some a couple of miles down the road that should be perfect for a reasonable price. She decided it wasn't fair to get her dad involved, as he was already stressed enough about everything. She certainly didn't want to end up moving all of her stuff into his house or garage. Tapping her biro against her temple, *what else is there,* she thought? She didn't do this. This was all new to her, and she didn't know what should be on the checklist of 'being dumped and your whole world being turned upside down'. Equally, she was lucky in that she had a bit of time to play with, but also knew she had a lot to do with the house. She wanted to ensure everything was done and gone by the time they returned.

***

Brooke didn't know whether or not to ignore the front door bell that was ringing. She didn't want to see or speak to anyone. But if it was Mitch, he'd start freaking out again. She sighed heavily and walked out to the hall and opened it, seeing Kate. "My darling girl, I've just heard. Babes, I'm so, *so* sorry," she said, hugging her tightly. Brooke couldn't stop herself as she collapsed into the embrace "Kate, what am I going to do?" she said, crying into her shoulder. "I just don't know what to do." Kate had been a friend of both of theirs, but ultimately she had always been closer to Brooke. They spent many a night together indoors chilling whilst Maria and Jo went out.

"We'll get through this, babes," as she handed over the bag of wine, chocolate and ice cream to Brooke, who was smiling sadly to her.

They walked into the lounge as Kate spotted the details on the laptop, picking it up and searching through. "Listen, why don't you move in with us for a couple of months? We have the space. Then you can buy a place without wasting money on renting," she said seriously.

"Thanks so much for the offer, but I don't want to do that. I need to remove myself from it all, and I don't want to put you and Jo in that position either. But thanks," she smiled.

"Jo and I were stunned. We had no idea, and Jo is very annoyed with her truth be known! You know the offer is there, but I get where you're coming from. I want you to know I will be here 110%, just like you were with me. I have brought a bag over so I can stay tonight, but there's no pressure if you don't want me to. I have my stuff and we can go tomorrow together. If you don't want me to stay, I will still come with you tomorrow to look at these properties. And then we can come back and make a start on this list," she said to her friend, tapping the computer screen.

"Thanks," said Brooke. She needed this, she thought. Kate would completely get her sorted and wouldn't spend days slagging people off. She was blunt, but like Brooke, organised and focused. At this moment that's exactly what she needed, to get her and keep her on track.

Kate stayed for a couple of hours and then left, arranging to pick her up at nine thirty in the morning to go look at the properties. Brooke didn't know how long breakups, the sadness and all these things generally took, and she hated wasting life. But she didn't know how to kick herself into touch. She needed a run, she thought. She would go running to let off some steam, and then she would just go to bed.

An hour later she returned home, dripping wet and her lungs burning. At some point she had started crying, and that just pushed her further and harder. However, she was now regretting doing that. She got a shower and walked over to her bed, 'their' bed she thought sadly. She gently stroked the beautiful white 'hotel collection' bed linen, wondering if she had been in her bed already. Had they shared nights together, made love in her own bed? She let the tears fall as she grabbed her water and her iPad and walked into the spare bedroom.

Brooke hadn't slept at all. She was tired and grumpy and completely surprised that nobody had mentioned how bloody uncomfortable their spare bed was. She got up and acknowledged her growling tummy, recognising that aside from half the bar of galaxy that her and Kate had shared yesterday she had not actually eaten anything else all day. Making her way downstairs, Brooke got some fruit from the fridge and began cutting it up and making a fruit salad. She poured over her flavoured yoghurt and spooned some granola over the top as she sat at the breakfast bar in her kitchen. She switched the TV on, not paying any attention to whatever was playing. In her mind she was just trying to organise her thoughts and make a plan of what needed to be done. She went to the fridge and saw the appointment card for the therapist Wednesday night at 5pm. She was very happy it was *soon*, as she could feel herself losing control again. She needed to try and get back on track, she thought considerably.

***

Kate arrived at nine thirty as planned and took Brooke to the three different places. As ever, Kate was positive regardless of what she may have actually thought. However, she was constructive when required. The house was no good and honestly, she knew it wouldn't be. It was just the fact it was coming into summer and she didn't want to be stuck without a garden for the whole summer. The flat was probably the best of the three, and was cheap enough too, but she didn't want to make a decision just yet. The agent had confirmed that if she was to pay six months up front, they could turn it around for her to get the keys in a day, which made her feel a bit better. Kate took her to lunch after the viewings and was discussing the properties they had seen, but Brooke noticed she was barely touching her food.

"So, come on then?" Brooke said to Kate seriously, putting her fork down.

"Come on what?" she said, not looking up.

"I know you, Kate. You haven't been yourself all morning. You were fine yesterday, so something has clearly happened. You have brought me to our favourite restaurant, so I can't help but feel there is something you are trying to broach with me," she sighed. "Just say it Kate. I can't be arsed no more with all the games. What is it? Has Jo come out and told you that she knew all along? What?" she said angrily.

"God no. No babes. I promise none of us knew about it," she said, grabbing her hand and for the first time, looking into her eyes filled with sadness. "We did find out a couple of the others knew, more than just Fran unfortunately," she sighed heavily. "Look, Brooke, Maria called last night and she spoke to Jo. I couldn't be a part of it, and Jo was pissed off and told her so as well. However…" she sighed heavily. "She told Jo…"

Silence, she could tell Kate was trying to work out the words to say. This is exactly what she didn't want to happen, people to have to be put in the middle of their lives.

"Umm, I'm sorry, Brooke. She told Jo that she was going to ask Paula to marry her on holiday," she said with tears in her eyes. Brooke couldn't decipher if she was going to be sick or pass out. She felt the tears finally release, unable to ascertain who the sobs were coming from, Kate or herself. Brooke soon realised they were hers and didn't even care what people in the restaurant must have thought. Kate was there hugging her, feeling the tears of her friend. She couldn't believe how much of a selfish bitch Maria was for putting their friends through this.

When the tears eventually subsided, she pulled back from her. Kate wiped away Brooke's tears and apologised to her again. "What are you apologising for, it's not you. None of this has been you, and I can only thank you for being there for me. I need to go, Kate. I need to get home and make a start on things," she sighed heavily.

They pulled up at Brooke's house and Kate got her bag out of the boot. "What's that?" asked Brooke.

"Slacks. I'm not wearing a Ralph Lauren shirt and white jeans to empty your house." She smiled softly, taking her best friend's hand. Kate was always pristine, and her long wavy brown hair coupled with her attire always reminded her of Kate Middleton.

"Look, you don't have to do that. You took me this morning," Brooke said back to her friend.

"I called my boss when I found out yesterday and asked for an emergency week off work. She was fine, and I will do some bits in the evenings. You never left me alone when I was going through this, so now I'm here to repay the favour." She smiled kindly.

***

A couple of hours later, there were suitcases separated into winter and summer clothes. Vacuum bags filled and boxes all over the hallway. Brooke was impressed at how much they had accomplished. Kate had blasted Kisstory through the house, singing into her brush and frequently asking Brooke to remember various holidays they had had over the years. Brooke managed to smile at some of the memories they were sharing, filling herself and Kate with hope that she would get through this eventually.

Brooke had managed to sort her storage for a couple of days' time and load her car with what she could. Kate was going to come and fill her car too. So it was just a case of making sure that the next few days were filled with packing away everything that wouldn't be needed until she found her own place.

Brooke was relieved knowing that she had almost finished the bedrooms, due to it being mostly just clothes. It was only really the breakdown of '*their*' stuff. She didn't feel up to or ready to do that just now though. The feelings were still too raw, and she knew she would end up being a bitch and taking everything, and that wasn't Brooke. Eventually she would end up feeling rubbish, which she didn't want. She'd rather concentrate on her things for now, and then when she had some time, sort the rest out later.

***

"I'm shattered," Brooke said to Kate, just as she heard the front door go. She didn't want to be around people. Kate had been great and she could manage this, but she wasn't in the mood right now to see people.

"Chill, baby. I'll go and say you are sleeping," she smiled, touching her friend's arm warmly. She sat at the top of the stairs which were hidden from the front door.

"Hey you, what are you doing here?" she heard Kate saying.

"Hello, beautiful. I wanted to see how my two favourite girls are? Would it be okay for me to come in, ya think?" she heard Jo's voice. Brooke walked down the stairs.

"Of course it is," she said walking to Jo who put down the bags and embraced her in a big hug. Jo pulled back and held Brooke's face in her hands.

"Cards on the table, how you really doing, sweetie?" she asked her. Brooke couldn't control the tears again and Jo pulled her back into the embrace, whispering to her it would be okay over her quiet sobs. Jo waited until she could feel Brooke's sobs subside. "I'm sorry, Brookie. I wish I could take away the pain. It *will* get easier, but for now you just need to know you have the support of your friends. Whatever you need we're here for you." She kissed her cheek. "On that note, my beautiful girlfriend here can go and assist you further, in packing," she said looking around her at all the boxes, and then lifted the bags she brought. "I, my friend, am going to pinch your kitchen and make you two lovelies some dinner, which will be ready in an hour's time," she said, kissing Brooke on the cheek and kissing her girlfriend on the lips before walking off to the kitchen.

Kate and Jo were turning out to be amazing friends. Whilst they were all quite close, she was unsure how people would be because of the taking side's aspect of a breakup. Jo was smitten with her beautiful girlfriend, and they were totally compatible in every way. Jo's cropped dark hair perfectly accentuated her features and face shape, and the two together made an incredibly good looking pair.

An hour later, the girls were issued a ten-minute warning. Kate borrowed some clean slacks from Brooke and both women showered before making their way back downstairs. Brooke had to admit, the house smelled incredible. She was completely indebted to her two amazing friends for what they had done for her these last couple days. They walked into the kitchen and were immediately frogmarched back out with a glass of champagne each, and ushered into the lounge until it was ready.

***

Jo walked into the lounge and kissed her girlfriend raising her glass 'to friends.' She smiled and they chinked their glasses all saying cheers. "Well ladies I hope you're both hungry," she said smiling. She walked them into the dining room and held Kate back to allow Brooke to walk in first, watching her reaction as she walked in and gasped. She looked around to her friends, noticing the embarrassed smile on Jo's face. Kate looked confused and entered the room, taking in the quiet music playing, the rose petals across the dining table and the food lay out. Kate looked to Jo and squeezed her hand slightly, mouthing "I love you" to her girlfriend. "You're not going to cry again are you?" she said. "This was supposed to be a nice evening for us all. I didn't want you to feel shitty because of some foolish woman's actions. You are a beautiful woman inside and out, Brooke. I know Kate feels the same when I say, we are truly lucky to have you in our lives. NOW…" She held up her hand, "before you start again, here is to a nice girly night. I have made Terry's chocolate orange cheesecake and ice cream for dessert so we can go and chill out with some goodies and movies," she said, dishing up the lasagne and garlic bread on to each woman's plate.

Chapter Six

Jo came into the lounge after insisting that she would clean up after the delicious meal. Brooke hadn't properly eaten her normal three full meals the last couple of days. She could tell right now as she felt suitably stuffed after an amazing meal cooked by Jo. "Thanks so much, guys. I will be forever in debt to you both for assisting me in getting through this," she sighed.

"You owe us nothing. We will always be here for you if you need anything. Whether it be friendship, help, advice, somewhere to crash, someone to help you pack up or someone to come cook for you every night," Jo said softly.

"My word, I don't think my body could cope with eating and drinking like this every night." Brooke smiled getting up to the wine fridge and retrieving another bottle of pink champagne. "Here's to the most amazing friends, THE most amazing couple, and two of the most stunningly beautiful women I have ever had the pleasure of meeting," she said.

"Oh she's definitely trying for you to come cook every night now," Kate laughed. "Anyways, enough of all this soppy stuff now, what we watching, and where's our dessert?" she said giggling. Kate was one of these painfully annoying people who could eat everything in sight and never gain any weight. The problem was, Jo was exactly the same. It was infuriating when you thought about it. Neither worked out, they just ate and ate. And whilst Brooke couldn't complain with her lean frame, if she didn't regularly run or work out and just ate rubbish, she wouldn't be lucky enough to hold down her figure.

"No, I can't eat no more, please don't make me, I will literally be sick," Brooke said laying her head on her forearm.

"Well, I'm with you, Brooke. So this little one can wait just a little and we can let our dinner settle first. Then half way through the movie I will grab some for us," she said kissing her girlfriend's hand. "So what are we going to watch?"

Kate flicked through the stations and made a little squeal. Brooke looked up in time to see Jo's glare over to Kate. Checking the TV, she saw *The Holiday* advertised. "This is one of my favourite movies, lets watch this," Brooke said to her friends.

"Ermm, are you sure, Brookie?" Jo said concerned.

"Yes! I love this movie, and I can't avoid anything 'lovey' forever, so back on the saddle I shall sit," she said smiling.

***

"Seriously, how many times have you both seen this? Surely if you know the words, that's evidence you no longer need to watch it?" Jo asked Kate and Brooke. But the two were giggling at her and continued to sporadically blurt out the coming lines. "You two are mental. I'm going to leave you to it whilst I sort out dessert," Jo said, leaving them curled up watching the movie.

"Come here, you'll see better," Kate said patting the corner sofa her and Jo had been sharing directly opposite the TV. Brooke had been on the loveseat over in the corner. Kate was right, it wasn't the best for viewing the TV, but she loved the seat and generally opted for this one where she could relax with her kindle most nights. She moved next to Kate and snuggled into her friend's shoulder as they relaxed and continued watching. A few minutes later, Jo returned with a tray holding three shot glasses, lime, salt, a huge bowl of ice cream, a huge plate with her homemade Terry's chocolate orange cheesecake, and a bottle of tequila. "Woah, baby. Is that wise?" Kate said to Jo, smirking.

Jo handed each girl a shot glass, not responding to Kate with anything other than a wink. They each downed the shot, biting the lime slice as they squirmed, pulling faces. Jo put the plate and bowl on Brooke's lap and gave each woman a spoon so they could all dig in to the desserts.

Jo was an incredible cook. She rarely did it, but when she did it was great. Brooke couldn't cook for shit, and regularly she had requested the help of Jo for dinner parties or romantic meals for Maria. Brooke sighed heavily, suddenly feeling sad again. "Thinking of her?" Kate said, and Brooke nodded solemnly.

"Shot!" Jo shouted pouring three more tequilas.

"Dear God, I'm going to get sectioned tomorrow when I go to the therapist, if I continue this," she said to her friends, sinking the shot.

"How's it going?" they both asked in unison, smiling to each other.

"Yeah, not bad I guess," she said, spooning a big dessert spoon of cheesecake. "Obviously, I don't know how it will go tomorrow, you know? But we have gone down to once a fortnight now. Well, *have* being the operative word. I don't know. I'm not going to lie, I'm afraid about tomorrow. I feel like I may lose control again," she said, leaning in and getting them all another shot.

"So you think drinking three bottles of champagne and a bottle of tequila will help?" Kate said seriously.

"Not like that, but thanks for your concern. Salute." She smiled and handed them both another shot.

"Seriously though, Brooke. You didn't lose control. We've been through this. Anyone that went through what you did would have been the same. Is it the therapist that's saying you lost control?" Kate asked her.

"No, the doctor didn't agree it was the case either, he thought it was, ummm…"

"Hey, you know how you should totally do this?" Jo said, changing the subject. "I mean seriously, you could just disappear off where nobody knows you and befriend a 90-year-old man or a dog?" she said laughing hysterically at herself.

"Dear God, she isn't ever going to get up for work tomorrow," Kate said laughing and pouring another for Brooke and herself. "Baby, we're having one to catch up with you," she said winking.

"No way, give me some. I'm not that bad. Granted, I'm not sober, but I'm not that bad. But this is great, do you not think? She isn't working, and work is paying for her to be off. All this shit goes off, why not disappear? Think about it. Go and rent a cottage? Hire a barn in France? Oh, my God, we could come visit! Or a villa in Greece, up a mountain where you can lay by the pool for a month? Surfing in Oz? Oh no, scrap that, it's too far. But you should look into it. We could get everything done in the next week. Put it all into storage and then speak to your therapist tomorrow and ask if they are happy you have some time off and for you to go?" she said, smiling and downing another drink, taking a big spoon of the cheesecake to escape the taste.

"Brooke? Jo's, got a point. If you can't go back to work for another month, maybe longer, why don't you consider it? You don't need to leave. We aren't saying it's up to you to leave over Maria. Your life, family and friends are here. But things weren't so great before this happened. You were not right after the accident, by your own admission. Not working wasn't helping, so maybe a break will help you to get back on track? If you didn't want to go alone, we could probably drum up a few of us to do a week at a time with you. Say Mitch one week, us another? You get my point," Kate said to Brooke.

Kate and Jo were looking at Brooke now; whose expression was unreadable. She reached down and poured another shot. "I don't think we're going to be feeling so hot tomorrow," she said to them both and downed her drink. Then she grabbed her laptop.

"What are you doing?" Jo said, inquisitively.

"Well, I guess it's worth a look," she said with a smile. She opened her laptop up and the three women searched through different areas and ideas. As much as Brooke would love a bit of time in the sun, she didn't want to waste her money when she would need every penny to buy a new place. Plus, she didn't want to be in another country. If she did go off the rails or something happened, she would need to be somewhere her friends or father could get to her easily and vice versa. Her friends agreed with her, and once again reassured her that she hadn't gone off the rails, nor was she about to. It was agreed by all that as summer was approaching, the weather would be better all round. So if she could go somewhere near a beach then she may just be able to get the best of both worlds.

"Right. Okay, okay. So we need to find somewhere near a beach then, but, BUT, I want to be far away. I want to have noticeably different accents," she confirmed bemused. "I want to be near a beach…far away…where they have accents," she said holding her finger up to the air, telling… the room, and the ceiling.

"Scotland? The Scottish have ace accents," said Kate optimistically, turning to face Brooke and crossing her legs under her.

Brooke was contemplating the idea. "Hmmmm, I don't think I would be able to understand them. Plus, in reality, it's longer to travel than sodding Greece. Hit me, baby," she winked to Jo holding her shot glass.

"Do you think this is healthy?" Jo said holding up the half empty bottle of tequila, pulling a silly face.

Kate and Brooke were laughing uncontrollably as they downed another shot. "I've got it. Wales? Not too far, not too close, accent-ish. Perfect, right?" Kate said to Brooke.

"Baby, you do realise there's no such word as 'accent-ish,' yeah?" Jo said, laughing at her girlfriend. "I still think a little cottage hidden away, like in this movie," she continued.

"Jo, whilst you have been incredible this evening, the rose petal laden dining table, the cooking, the cleaning, the cake, and the drink. But me being trapped in a cottage in the middle of nowhere with not a single person around would actually tip me over the edge," Brooke said, kissing her friend on the cheek. She shook the bottle in front of her, in a bid to ask if she wanted another.

51

"Got it!" Kate said looking up to the pair, smiling. "I'm a freaking genius ladies. I'm a freaking genius!," she said again. Having got their full attention, Kate turned the computer around to reveal the screen with a gorgeous log cabin, on a slight cliff overlooking the sea. It looked fabulous, Brooke thought. She lifted the laptop and had a look.

"Why don't you ever find things like that for us?" Jo questioned, looking over Brooke's shoulder.

"So it's in. On? Whatever! Anglesey, in North Wales. It's a caravan site, not like your haven, Butlin's type places, but like people who own them. They have caravans or log cabins. I love this though, so I went for that. You can have it for six weeks starting the weekend after next for just over £1500. I know it seems like a lot of money, but in reality you will have all the facilities there. You can just relax on the balcony, have BBQ's and wine looking out over the sea. Oh, I bet they get wonderful sunsets, too. Oh, you can rent a boat! How lovely? We will be able to come up for a long weekend if you like, too," Kate said, getting overexcited.

Kate was right. Brooke was reading over the details and it sounded exactly like what she needed. It could be the answer to the R&R that could potentially get her back on track. "Okay, the only thing is I think this is too big for me. A two bed one would be perfect and a little cheaper, which would be better now that I need to buy my own place," she sighed. "Do they have smaller cabins?" she asked Kate, who took the laptop back off her and started tapping away again. Jo and Brooke watched the four Hollywood A-listers dancing around the lounge on New Year's Eve as Kate searched for two bedroom cabins.

"So, they don't have any smaller cabins, but on the same site they have a two bed caravan, and it's also gorgeous, see?" she turned the laptop again. "They have this terrace and balcony area all the way around again, with their own outdoor furniture and barbeque. It's got a launderette on site because the caravans don't come with them, like the log cabins do. It's got the balcony area that also faces the sea. Look here, there's a picture of people sitting on the balcony overlooking the sea and the sun setting. Brooke, I don't want you to go, but can you imagine having this for six weeks? Just think, on the nights there isn't sunset and the weather is rubbish, the sound of the rain on the tin can roof will be splendid," she said dreamily.

"And the award to soppiest salesperson and romantic woman of the year goes to…Drum roll…The love of my Life," Jo said standing up, toasting another shot to Kate, shaking her head.

"Does it sound shit?" she asked seriously. "Sorry, it's the drink," she said, solemnly putting the laptop back on the sofa.

"Hey, beautiful, I'm only kidding. I love you. I love how you are so caring and looking for everything. I love how romantic you are and soppy you are. You are perfect to me," Jo said, stroking Kate's face sincerely.

"I love it. I love it. I love it. You're right, it's perfect. It's everything I want and need, Jo. Go get another bottle of champers opened and grab my purse from my bag in the dining room please?" she said.

Jo did as she was told, thinking that they really didn't need anything else to drink. She took the tequila and put it back in the kitchen. She opened the new bottle and

53

handed Brooke her purse to allow her to book her mini vacation. "Done," she said smiling, just like that.

"Yay!" cheered Jo and Kate as they grabbed her in a group hug.

"I feel happy, and I know I'm going to regret it tomorrow, but still," she said and shrugged.

"Why do you think that?" Kate asked her seriously.

"Guys, I'm the least spontaneous person on the planet. I will wake up sober and be terrified, and be freaking that I haven't planned it properly, et cetera," Brooke responded, trying desperately to not let the negativity overpower her in this good moment.

Chapter Seven

Brooke woke up with the headache from hell. What were they thinking? Seriously, who the hell drinks tequila indoors? She felt horrific as she attempted to lift her head off the pillow, but the room was still spinning. "Stupid, stupid, girl," she said to herself. God, she thought she was going to be sick. Brooke allowed the thoughts of a McDonald's big mac and fresh OJ rush in and out of her mind. That was it, a big mac. That would definitely sort her out. Brooke was proud of herself for having such a great idea, sure that this would remove the nausea she was feeling. Grabbing her phone, she checked to see if it was time that they did normal food yet, disappointed that it was still ages yet. Throwing her head back onto the pillow and silently screaming to herself, she picked up her phone again and looked into her emails. "Shit…shit…shit, bollox! What have you done?" she said, as she leapt up in her bed and saw the confirmation for the Anglesey booking. "You idiot! What the hell?" she said again to herself.

Brooke got out of bed and threw on her running gear. She must be insane to go for a run, but she needed to clear her head. Randomly, running always cleared her hangover. Considering the amount she drank and ate yesterday, she would need to do it. Putting some money in her running shorts, Brooke put on her iPhone and left the house in silence…silence, but like a bomb had hit it!

***

An hour later, Brooke walked through the door having had admitted defeat about twenty minutes earlier, following a diversion in the trees to be sick. She couldn't remember the last time she had thrown up whilst running, and was pretty certain she'd happily spend the next week detoxing.

Brooke heard the TV in the lounge and walked in to find Jo and Kate laid on her couch, both of which were nursing coffee and sunglasses. "Hello, ladies," Brooke said, walking in to the room.

"Shh, shh, shh. Pain, ouch, please don't make noise," Jo said to her friend.

"So, no big mac meals and fresh OJ's?" She smiled, holding up the bags of food and drinks.

"You didn't? You did. Oh, my God, if the room stops spinning, I'm so going to get up and kiss you," said Kate. "Although," she said, lifting her glasses slightly over her eyes "is that sweat? Do you have sweat on your face and body? Did you run? Baby, she ran? What is up with her? Why is she our friend, baby? BABY?" Kate said in one breath.

"KATE, please. Do...not...shout...if she wants to run, good for her. Now both of you shut the hell up and give me a big mac with no gherkin and a freshly squeezed OJ, before I kill one of your skinny asses," Jo said.

"Moody!" Kate said raising her eyebrows. "You're insane for running, but I'm over it! I don't know what we will actually get done today. Is the gherkin already out of here?" she asked Brooke, getting a big mac out.

"Yes! One big mac, no gherkin for our fabulous chef Ramsey over here. A big mac no cheese, for the psycho exercise hater. Then a normal BM for me, French fries with BBQ for you, French fries with ketchup for grumpy and French fries with curry for me. Lastly, three extra-large freshly squeezed OJ's from the most amazing café on the planet, and diet Cokes each," she said, handing out everyone's food and drink.

"Wait," Jo said, slowly lifting her head from the couch and taking her glasses off. "This isn't a McDonalds OJ? Oh, no you didn't? You went to maccies and the cafe? Oh, my God, I need it. I need it now," she said, snatching her OJ from Brooke's hands and downing half of it in one go, making loud pleasurable noises.

***

Brooke couldn't remember the last time she had a hangover so bad. They had not really had a very productive day. It was filled with too many breaks for food, drink or vomiting. Luckily they had managed to get a few more boxes stuffed though. On a plus, Brooke was so focused on feeling ill that she didn't actually feel the pain of having to separate all the belongings that were sure to bring back memories for her.

It was almost time to leave, and Brooke stepped over and around the boxes in her bedroom, which she had now moved back into since buying new bedding. Tying her hair up, she put her Nike hoodie on and left for the therapist appointment.

Chapter Eight

"So, why do you think that this is related to the accident, Brooke?" her therapist Martin said.

Brooke had been referred by the police after the accident. He was a nice guy and managed to get her to positively analyse things. For as long as she could remember she had over-analysed everything. Her mother dying, her relationships, albeit they were hardly relationships. The being gay thing. Even down to losing out on promotions. No matter what happened in her life, if there was anything slightly negative attached to it, she analysed, and analysed, and analysed until she had pretty much tore herself to pieces.

"Honestly? Why wouldn't it be? We were happy before it happened, now she's gone and done this?" she said seriously.

"But, Brooke, you were happy a week ago, weren't you? How do you know she was happy? Do you even know how long this has been going on for?"

"Well, no, but…" she started.

"But what, Brooke? Now, the way I see it she told you it wasn't to do with the accident, and so what if it was? Could you have changed it? Do you think that would have been right for you in the long term? You had a critical accident, and eight months on you still aren't back in work and she looks elsewhere? I'm not trying to sound callous now, Brooke. What I'm merely stating is, if someone isn't prepared to stick by you through this incredibly difficult period in your life, then surely that's something that needs to be considered on your part. Okay. Say the tables were turned, talk me through how you would have reacted? What would have happened, how would you have dealt with the situation?"

Brooke considered this for a moment. She didn't know how to answer. "Uhmmm, well I would have been there for her. I would have been by her bedside morning, noon and night, and I would have done anything I could to get her through it," she said.

"Why?"

"Why what?"

"Why would you have done everything you could have?" he said seriously.

"Well, why do you think? Because I love her. I love her and she's my girlfriend. We have been together forever, and that's what you should do."

"So there are a series of statements there. Help me to ascertain which is the way you are feeling. Is it because you love her? Or because that's what's expected of you? If it's the latter, is that because it's you, Brooke? Do you think that's people's expectations of you personally, or of you as a girlfriend?" he said.

Brooke went silent. She didn't know the answer and she could feel the start of a panic attack. She uncrossed her legs and grabbed the seat with both hands trying to concentrate on her breathing.

Martin leaned forward. "Okay, okay Brooke. Look at me, focus on me. In my eyes, in my eyes, okay? Breathe? It's going to be okay. Control it, Brooke. You know how to do this, Brooke…," he said patiently to her. "Okay, so tell me about this caravan, this break you want to have?" he asked her.

***

She gave it a couple of minutes before responding, "You don't think I should go, do you?" she said to her therapist.

"On the contrary, Brooke. I think it could be a good idea. I personally don't think you should put any pressure on yourself though. Therefore, don't think, 'I'm there for six weeks? I have to stay for six weeks? I don't like it but I still have four weeks, et cetera?' Do you understand? See it for what it is. Go and have fun, meet new people, learn new things. If you don't like it, come home. But give it a chance, and try not to overthink. Now, I genuinely don't feel comfortable with us not having a session throughout this whole time, so what I suggest is we continue our fortnightly appointment. However, let's do it via telephone call, or skype, or whatever form of media activity you wish to use." He smiled. "I trust you are happy with this?"

"Martin, will I be okay?" she asked worriedly.

"Yes, but you need not worry, Brooke. Worst case scenario, you don't like it and you come home. But in actuality, I think this could be the best thing for you."

"Is that reverse psychology?"

"A psychologist using reverse psychology, why ever not," he grinned. "Listen. Spend time finding you, work out if you want, go back to the police. Uh uh uh," he said holding his hand up to silence her. "And if you don't, don't worry. Just because it may have once been the only thing you knew, doesn't mean it still is. Fill your time, meet friends and go exploring. Take lots of books and relax in the sun on the beach, or on your veranda, just reading. If you like to paint or sketch, then do that. You will have ample opportunity and I'm sure the scenery will be spectacular. But don't fight the feelings, Brooke. Let them flow naturally, because that's the only way you get to the route. You have my number, so if you need to talk or you feel you need additional sessions, then by all means call me and we can arrange. Is that okay?" he said to her confidently.

"Yes. Yes, I think so. I can do this. Can't I?" she said, more as a statement than a question, and more to herself than her therapist. She smiled shyly to Martin before leaving his office.

As she got into the car she could feel the fear starting. She could hear the negative thoughts telling her she wouldn't be able to do it, that it would all go wrong. "No, be strong, you *can* do this! You *can*," she said out loud.

She parked her car in the shopping mall car park and wandered off in search of some holiday bits. She was glad the weather was picking up and the stores were ready with all the top new trends. She was happy that she was able to walk quickly into a number of stores and get some bikinis, some summer evening wear and daytime wear, and a few pairs of sandals and flip flops. She felt ready, equipped and for the first time since the drunken night last night, she felt excited.

***

"So, are you excited then?" Kate said to her friend whilst she poured some wine into her glass.

"Yes, I kind of am. I have gone through the decision three hundred times. Should I, shouldn't I? It's been hard packing all my stuff up, our stuff, my life. But I couldn't have done it without you guys. Today has made me feel better though, getting rid of it all and putting it all into storage. I guess that's what has made me just realise that's it. That part of my life has closed. It's a new chapter and I don't know what it will involve, whether it is the force or a new career or what. But for now I need a break from this place, from work, from Maria and Paula. From women and well everything. I need this time and I need me back. And I think this will do it. I *hope* this will do it. I just want me back," she said seriously.

"You will get you back, Brooke. The amazing, wonderful, gorgeous, sparkly, you" said Jo. "Thanks for coming to ours tonight. Here's to a lovely evening, with no tequila. Seriously this is the first day that I have been able to manage a drink," Jo finished.

They had decided to order in Indian and stay in with a bottle of wine to celebrate the house being sorted. Jo and Kate had offered to put Brooke up for the remaining days so she wasn't sat in a house that was technically her ex's. Especially as there was virtually no evidence that she had ever been there. Brooke was glad her friends had offered. To cause less stress, she had contacted the site and managed to get the van a few days earlier. She spoke to the woman in charge of the site and explained her situation. The owners sounded lovely, which had further settled Brooke. Interestingly, she was ready for her break away.

Chapter Nine

"You sure you have everything?" Kate said, hugging her friend tightly. "We'll see you in three weeks okay?"

"You betcha," Brooke said, hugging Jo and dumping the last of her 'goodie' bags in the car.

"And hopefully, Sainsbury's will have restocked after you have officially done them out of house and home on alcohol and junk food. I mean seriously, who the hell even eats Bombay mix anymore?" Jo said, laughing.

"You never know, she may meet a beautiful woman and decide to make an Indian meal for her. And then you'll have Bombay mix on the table whilst they chat and wait for the food to be served," Kate said seriously, eyeing Jo and Brooke. "Too soon?" She smiled like butter wouldn't melt.

"Baby, way too soon."

"I'm off," Brooke said, kissing her friend once more and shaking her head at Kate's remark.

"Hey, we have a gift for you," Jo said, handing a big bag over.

"What? Why? You didn't need to do that." Brooke was seated in her car seat as she peeked into the bag and saw a huge, soft, cuddly teddy bear. Looking up she laughed at them both. "Thanks, you guys."

"We didn't want you to feel lonely. He's incredibly soft, and we're sure he'll keep you warm at night," Kate said, wrapping her arm around her girlfriend.

"Oh, great, he's a he? So you think me sleeping with a male teddy bear at night will make all the pain go away?" she said seriously. "Really?" She was watching her friends' concerned faces, and couldn't keep the straight face any longer.

"You cow! Go. Just leave, get off our property now," they were shouting.

"See you in a few, beautiful." She smiled, waving from her window at her friends behind her.

***

Brooke was pissed when she arrived. The four-hour journey took seven hours due to an accident on the motorway, so she was stressed and in desperate need of a beer. She found the site entrance but was driving around aimlessly. She had no clue how the hell you were supposed to know where your place was, because there were no fucking names or door numbers! How the hell were you supposed to know? Of course they all knew, because they all sodding lived here! So, why the hell *wouldn't* they know where they were supposed to go? She opened her phone a further time to check the email again. Surely they must have emailed instructions or directions she thought? "Nope, nothing. Nothing at all. Clearly I was supposed to bring my fucking crystal ball to find a sodding caravan that all look identical with no numbers!," she said, driving further around the complex looking for anything. She finally saw the three log cabins. Thinking out loud, Brooke said, "Why the hell didn't you book the cabin? There's only three of them, and one already has someone's clothing on the line. So in reality there were only two options. Then it would simply be a case of trying both doors with the key that fit, easy as Cinderella! But no, you decide to go for one of the forty caravans," she sighed.

For the love of God, please get me to this sodding van or I'm sleeping in this car after severe alcohol consumption," she said as she hit her head off the steering wheel. "Ow, that hurt," she said in to the air.

"Err, hey, are you okay?"

Shit, that was a voice. That wasn't my voice. That was someone else's voice, Brooke thought. *Ohhhh this is never good.* She lifted her head. *Amazing,* she thought, facing the most perfectly toned, washboard stomach she had ever seen. Sighing heavily, Brooke looked up to the woman in a wet suit pulled as far as her waist with a bikini top on. She was holding a surfboard in her arms, and as Brooke looked up she could see the woman desperately trying to stifle the laugh. Amazing, already making an idiot of herself before she has even got in to her new home for the summer.

"So what's up? Other than you clearly having sense of direction and alcohol problems?" She smirked.

God, kill me now, Brooke thought, smiling slightly. "I'm sorry. I'm not normally so dramatic, but it's been a really long day. REALLY long, and I've never done this before. I've never even been inside a caravan. I had no idea that I wouldn't have been given directions, and none of them have numbers. So I've driven around like five times already. And truthfully, without pulling the whole woe is me card, I'm pretty sure someone's messing with me and there isn't in fact a 22. Sorry, I'm over talking. I don't normally do this," she said, sighing heavily again.

"Rough day indeed." She smiled the biggest, softest smile. "Well do you want the good news or the bad news?" announced the woman, who had clearly been surfing, as Brooke tried to ignore the droplets of water falling from her.

"Well let's continue the theme of the day and hit me with the bad news first." She smiled sardonically.

"You're at the wrong caravan park. You need to go out on the main road, take a left after about a mile and a half, and then you will see the Somerville estate site. That's where you are," she said, seeming incredibly sorry.

"Amazing! Just great! Well thanks for your help. Before I leave, I may as well ask what the good news was?" she said, assessing the driveway to see if she could three-point turn. "Hey, hold up. How do you know what park I'm at? I only said twenty-two, not the site," she said, looking confused and noticing the glint in the girl's pure green eyes.

"Sorry, I couldn't help myself," the surfer laughed hard.

She was pissed at the apparent joke after the day she had had, but those eyes. You couldn't help but forgive them. She shook her head tutting, "So, you see a poor girl upset, sad and distressed and you make fun of her? This will be an amazing six weeks," she said, smiling a little. She felt at ease already, and was glad of that fact. "Now please mystery surf woman, it's taken me forever and a day to get here. Please show me where my room is?" she said seriously.

She watched the woman lift her eyebrow smirking. "The good news is, that's your palace, princess. In front of you. Therefore, you park up here and you're good to go," she said, smiling and walking off. She shouted behind her without even turning around. "And FYI, the mystery surfer's name is Chloe, in case you were wondering," she said. Then Chloe turned and disappeared, surfboard in hand.

Brooke watched Chloe leave. Her long dark hair, wavy from the water, bouncing as she moved.

At last, you have found your home she thought. She parked her car up and went to unlock the door, deciding not to move a single bag until she had opened and got into the right place. After today's traumas, she was clearly very pessimistic. Luckily for Brooke, she was good. It was the right place, and she was home free. Walking in, Brooke was amazed by the size of it, regardless of the fact it was sold as a static and not a tourer. She didn't actually understand what that meant, and couldn't help but assume it would be a small room with a bed, settee, fridge, mini oven, and a toilet and sink in the corner. It wasn't like that though. It was a small house, a small flat. It had a full kitchen, a full lounge and dining room, a full two bedrooms and a full bathroom. She was completely astounded. It was lovely and so cute. She walked to the end of the lounge and opened the blinds to reveal the patio doors. Opening them out onto her balcony, she took in the most spectacular sea views. Brooke sighed, and for the first time in nearly two weeks she realised it was a sigh of happiness. She couldn't believe it. This was all completely perfect she thought.

Chapter Ten

Brooke unpacked her suitcases and found homes for everything. She was so glad that there was a lot of cupboard space in her kitchen, because the goodies and alcohol were filling every spare bit of space. Everything was great, and she was already feeling completely relaxed. She went to the fridge, which didn't feel cold yet and opened a bottle of beer, deciding she'd get a shower and change into some slacks.

"Hmmph. why doesn't it switch on?" she looked around the cubicle to see if there was an on/off switch that she needed to switch first, but there wasn't. She tried the basin taps and they weren't working either. "Oh, for God's sake. Why is nothing ever simple?" she said, resting her head against the door.

Brooke found the cupboard with the boiler in it and figured maybe she had to do something in there? She switched the light on in the hall to look better, but that wasn't working either. *What the fuck? Why is nothing working?* This was all becoming very annoying and her tolerance levels were shooting down quicker and quicker. Brooke was starting to feel as though she was about to cry. It had been far too long a day and she had no idea what the hell was happening. She grabbed herself another beer and poured some olives into a bowl. She went and sat on the decking area lighting a citronella candle before she opened her phone and googled caravan water supply. She would find out how to switch the shower on if it killed her! Reading through all the details, Brooke clearly didn't have a clue what she was looking for, putting her head in her hands.

"Shit." Brooke nearly fell off the chair when her phone started to ring. "Jeez, that scared the shit out of me," she said, smiling into the phone as she stood up and looked at the view. "Heeeey? How are you?" she said to Kate and Jo who were both on the line.

"Are you there? Is it lovely? How was your trip? Are the people nice?" Kate said in one go.

"Babe, she can only answer one question at a time. I take it you got there okay though?" Jo asked. "Are you okay though, sweetie?" she asked seriously.

"Yeah, I'm all good. It's like a little flat, big and really cosy, and I have the best view. Oh, actually, are you on the home phone or your mobile?" Brooke said to her friends.

"Mobile, why?"

"Cool, we'll switch to FaceTime." She changed and waited for their faces to appear. "Hey. So look at my view," she said, turning the phone around to the sea. As she was turning her phone around she caught sight of 'surfer girl' in the log cabin next door to her. She nodded her head and raised her beer to Brooke, smiling softly. Brooke could feel herself get flustered. She quickly spoke into the phone, "Isn't it gorgeous?" she said, trying her hardest to ignore the girl. Seemingly, her neighbour laid on the sofa reading her kindle.

"Oh, my word, it's stunning. See, I told you I was a genius," said Kate laughing, taking a drink of wine that completely took over the whole screen.

"So, is the inside nice?" Jo asked her seriously "and, are you okay? Did you get there okay?"

"No! Nightmare trip. Massive dramas, as per…," she said, sighing. "Loads of roadworks and accidents. Oh, and when I arrived, there's no numbers on these things, so I drove around five times, before this surfer girl…" She stopped and looked out of the corner of her eye. She was still sat on her balcony. "Ermmm yeah, sorry. So some girl heard me having tantrums in the car." She stopped and sat in the chair facing Chloe's balcony, smiling as she continued. "Well she came to my rescue, after firstly winding me up and thinking it was funny to tell me I was at another camp site miles down the road," she said, smiling sardonically and lifting her beer back up to the 'surfer girl'. Chloe turned to look at her upon hearing the words, shaking her head.

"Ooohhh, is she cute?" Kate asked anxiously. "Ow, what did you do that for?"

Brooke dropped her phone, quickly grabbing it and leaving her feeling mortified. They were neighbours, but would she have been able to hear Kate's comment? Or just Brooke's? She needed to change it back from FaceTime quickly. She pressed the button and held it back up to her ear, as she could hear the squabbling between the two of them.

"Hey, where did you go? I was only asking if she was cute. You are a normal young woman and you can pay attention to another good looking woman," Kate said stubbornly.

"I took you off FaceTime, but I'm still here. And really?" said Brooke.

"Still too soon?" Kate said.

"Yes!" Brooke and Jo shouted to her.

"So I take it she's there, which is why you quickly changed out of FaceTime?" Jo asked.

"Ermmm, yeah kind of," Brooke said.

"Ohhh, I told you. It's not too soon at all. So, is she cute? We aren't on speaker any more are we?" she said.

"Kate, I love you. But seriously, you are uninvited if you continue. It hasn't even been two weeks since my world was turned upside down. So yeah, just a little bit too soon. But in answer to your other question, yes gorgeous. But so is her husband, and I'm sure her very soon to be born child will also be," she said, getting up and going to get another beer from the fridge.

"Oh I'm sorry," Kate said solemnly.

"I know you're only being sweet. Shit, it's still not cold," she said.

"What's not cold?" Jo said to her.

"The fridge. I don't know what's happening. I was on my phone googling it, but I need to have a look on my iPad to see if I can find out what's up," she said, sitting back down.

"Oh do you have Wi-Fi?" Kate asked.

"Fuck, no! Arghhhh, seriously, I don't know what's up. My fridge isn't working and nor is my shower. I have switched them on, so I don't know what else I can do. Why does everything go wrong for me?" she said, rubbing her temples. "I'll wait until I get off the phone and continue googling. If I can't figure out how to turn everything on, I will have to call the owners. I will have wasted all that money on the food and drink and it's too warm to keep outside. Although I guess I could drink all the booze tonight," she said laughing, trying to make light of the situation and not concern her friends.

"Just call them, Brooke. Seriously, it will make it so much easier," Jo advised.

They spoke for a little while longer about nothing in particular before Kate insisted she go and call the owners before it got too late. At least that way they could all relax knowing she was settled.

Brooke eventually agreed and said her goodbyes as she finished the last part of her beer. The sky was incredible, and she loved sunsets, which was interesting because Maria never did. Brooke had always imagined being snuggled up with the love of her life, cuddling and watching the sun set or rise. In reality, she figured every girl dreamed of that, but apparently not. She stood up, taking it all in before it got too dark. As she looked over she could see the 'surfer girl' painting on a canvas. Whilst she couldn't see it, she was transfixed by her concentration and expression.

"So, sounded like you could use a little help?" Chloe said without looking.

Brooke was embarrassed. Could she feel her looking at her? "Err...um...No...Yes," she sighed heavily. "Honestly, I don't know. I've never done this before and my fridge and shower aren't working," she said, feeling stupid.

"Hey it's fine. We have all been there. Seriously, it's no biggie. I don't mean to sound like I'm belittling you now, but have you switched it on?" 'Surfer girl asked.

"Yes, I have switched all the sockets on. I just figured it would take some time?"

"No, have you switched the caravan on?" she said, smiling slightly as she finally turned around to look across to Brooke. It wasn't a condescending smile, and she wasn't making fun out of her on this occasion it would seem. It was more of a friendly smile.

"Are you fucking with me again?" Brooke said questioningly.

"Wow, you are not gonna let me live that down are you?" she said seriously, feeling a little bad. "I'm actually not, no. I'll come over and show you if you like?" she said.

"I'm not, no. I figure I have rented this place for six weeks, I will need to drag it out for at least three of those." She smiled. "I'd really appreciate that, if you would be so kind?" Brooke said shyly.

Chloe smiled. "Okay, well that's less than a week's holiday, so I can live with that."

"What do you mean?" Brooke asked as she followed her eyes on the 'surfer girl' who was walking along the side of her veranda to come over to Brooke's place.

"Well, I'm only here on weekends so, in reality I will probably only have around six days to deal with the ribbing. As I said, less than a weeks' vacation. I'm sure I can put up with it," she smirked, wondering if that was a look of disappointment on the girl's face. Shaking it away, she didn't know this girl from Adam, and she certainly couldn't read her.

"Oh, umm….? Sorry? I don't know your name?" she asked.

"It's Brooke."

"Okay, Brooke, I'll come now. But would you mind coming and helping me?" she said, pointing to her front door.

Brooke looked at her confused. "Ummm, yes? I guess so," she said, questioning.

"Sorry, it's just..." She looked at her watch. "Well, I'm unsure when my 'drop dead gorgeous hubby' is going to get home, and this soon to be born baby is causing havoc with my getting up and down the stairs," she said smirking, rubbing her tummy. Brooke couldn't help but think about today when she had her wetsuit up to her waist. God, she didn't have an ounce of fat on her, and she had the perfect stomach. She really hoped she hadn't been offended when she heard those comments. No, of course she wasn't, she was totally making fun of her again, she thought smiling inside.

"Funny. Yes! You're funny," she said, pointing to her. "Hmmm, hilarious. Hurry the hell up, I need a shower," Brooke said, shouting to her as she went to get them both another beer.

"Bossy, I like it," she said, laughing.

Brooke opened the door as she reached the 'still not cold fridge'. She pulled two beers out and removed the lids as Chloe walked through the door smiling. "Heeeeeey, Brooooooke." She smiled, drawing the new name out.

"Hey, Chloe. Beer?" she offered quickly turning away from the girl, feeling herself getting embarrassed.

"Ohhh, bribery. I knew we'd get on," she said, taking the beer. "So, what have you switched on then?" she said to Brooke.

"The sockets I wanted to use like at home. Oh, and I turned a switch on and off by the boiler, not like at home," she said confused.

Chloe smiled softly. She put her beer down, pointing her hand a full three hundred and sixty degrees around the place. "But this isn't home. Well, not like we know it," she said. Chloe switched the light and then ran the tap, and neither worked. She turned to Brooke, who looked embarrassed and sorry for herself. God she felt awful. She rubbed her arm softly, bending slightly to meet her eyes "Hey, it's okay. It's no biggie. Come with me," she said, leading them outside. She took Brooke around to the side of the van and pointed to the little mini gates below the decking. "See this? So this is the gas and water. You need to switch these taps on first," she said, pointing it out to Brooke. "It can be tricky, but you just need to put your hand on the taps and turn them all the way around," she said.

Brooke looked horrified. "I have to put my hands in there? What if there are spiders? Look there's webs in there." She pointed, looking seriously to Chloe.

"Whilst you're completely adorable, you are a complete girl," she said. "You need to know how to do this. What if I'm not here next time?" she said seriously.

"Well to be fair I wasn't planning on turning it off if I'm here for the whole six weeks," she said pointedly.

"The full six weeks? Not just sporadically. What are you a teacher or something?" she asked Brooke.

"No. Umm... No I'm not! It's okay, I can figure it out. I'm sure," she said sadly.

"Hey, Brooke," she placed her hand softly on her bare forearm, alerting both of them to the contact. "I'm sorry, I really didn't mean to offend you. I'm genuinely sorry," she said seriously.

"It's okay, it's me. I'm sorry to have been rude, especially when you have been nothing but helpful and kind to me," she said.

"Well, I wouldn't go that far. I've 'allegedly' made fun of you all day by all accounts. You won't let me forget it for another three weeks," she winked, aware she still had her hand on Brooke's arm, before quickly removing it. She knelt down on the floor and switched both taps on, closing the gates again and making their way back inside.

"Where's your bedroom?" Chloe asked, causing Brooke to choke and spit her drink back out.

"Erm, sorry?" she said, embarrassed and wiping her mouth. "Sorry about that." *Shit, you idiot*, she thought.

"Calm down. Just because I've found out you're gay doesn't mean that I'm going to try and sleep with you after an hour!" she said pointedly. "Your bedroom," she opened the fridge which was still dark and lifeless, pointing it out to Brooke, "is where your electrics are, which we still need to switch on."

My God, why was she such an idiot. Seriously, what other reason would she ask about the bedroom? Brooke was cringing because she felt so stupid. Sighing quietly, she turned on her foot and walked off to the bedroom with Chloe following behind her. Chloe grabbed her phone from her back pocket and turned on the flashlight. She pointed out the fuse box at the back of the wardrobe to Brooke and flicked it on, illuminating the room. Brooke was grinning like a Cheshire cat, and she had an incredible smile thought Chloe.

"There you go, should be fine now." She left the bedroom, switching on the kitchen light and opening the fridge, which was now noisy, bright, and cooling down. "Sorted," she said, opening the front door.

"Chloe," Brooke said, grabbing her arm. As they both looked down at her hand, Brooke looked embarrassed and removed it quickly. "I'm sorry again. Seriously, you actually *have* been nothing but nice to me. I have had a rough couple of weeks, which is why I'm here. Seemingly, it has impacted my social skills." She stopped and shook her head before sighing heavily. "I'm not ever normally like this. I just wanted to thank you. I think you seem pretty cool, and earlier when you said we'd get on, well I feel the same. I could really use a friendly face, even if it is only two days a week. I get I haven't really made a great first impression, and I probably sound like a sad loser. I hope I haven't offended you," she said, looking down at her bottle, peeling off the label.

Chloe didn't know what had happened to this girl, but whatever it was, seemed to have done some damage to her. "It takes a lot more than that to scare me off, Brooke. Thanks for the beer. I owe you one," she said kindly. "Oh, before I go," she stopped and turned around again. "If you fancy putting those 'seemingly affected' social skills to use, a couple of my girlfriends are coming up for the weekend tomorrow. We will just be kicking back tomorrow night on the patio with music, wine, and a BBQ. If you fancy joining? It would be the perfect practice for you. They'll be pissed." She smiled. "Plus, you won't really be able to sleep with the noise," she said smirking. "I hope you can make it! Good night, Brooke. I hope you sleep well on your first night, and if you need anything, just knock on," she said, smiling sincerely before leaving.

"Chloe, before you go," Brooke said.

Chloe stopped and turned around to face her. "Yeah?"

"You said before, about me being gay? How did you know that? Nobody can tell I'm gay," she said seriously.

Chloe stood on the step, smirking at Brooke, wondering how she proceeded with this response. "Um, well your friends wouldn't have asked if a girl was cute if you weren't gay," she said, grinning to Brooke.

"Oh…*Ohhhh,*" *she said* embarrassed.

"Don't sweat it, Brooke. I already had an inkling," she said softly. "Good night."

"What's that supposed to mean?" Brooke said seriously.

"A conversation for another time," she said, and left Brooke standing there, wondering what she meant.

***

Brooke finally got out of the shower. She was cringing as she was replaying the stupid things she had said and done in front of Chloe. She couldn't help but think she must be in there on the phone taking the piss out of her to someone, causing her to feel silly and embarrassed all over again. Why had she asked Brooke to join her and her friends tomorrow? Was it so they could all make fun of her? Were they all like her? Would they be like school ground bullies together, making her feel even worse? I bet they would. They will all be laughing at her behind her back, just like Maria and Paula were probably doing. Brooke felt the tear fall from her cheek. She wouldn't have gone anyways, and now it had confirmed it. She was right to not want to be around people like that. Brooke walked back into the lounge and turned the TV and lamp on. She was annoyed at herself for assuming the worst of Chloe, when in fact the woman had actually been very nice to her. Brooke pulled the caravan curtains too and noticed the candles illuminating the patio next door. She pulled the blind over slightly, looking at the illuminated patio with Chloe standing in front of a canvas, painting an incredible sunset. She stood barefoot in her jeans, with an oversized t-shirt on. Her hair, still curly from the water, was now dry and pulled up into a high ponytail. Chloe turned to the table and grabbed the beer, causing Brooke to quickly drop the blind and close the curtains, praying that the woman hadn't seen her. "What's up with you, seriously?" she said out loud, flicking through the channels on the TV in a bid to find something to watch.

Brooke noticed a message on her phone, assuming it must have come in whilst she was in the shower. It was from Maria, causing a knee jerk reaction from Brooke as she immediately sat up to read it.

Heard from Kate and Jo that you have gone on holiday for a month. Where are you, Brooke? I have noticed a number of things that have gone which I wanted, so when you return I suggest you contact me immediately so we can establish who gets what! I wanted you to hear it from me and nobody else, but whilst we were away, I proposed to Paula and she said yes. They will be moving in. Can you please post me your key? I suggest when you come home you don't just turn up, I don't want to make Paula and Jas feel awkward!! Enjoy your holiday, M.

Brooke lay back down on the sofa as she swallowed the words; swallowed them as hard as the lump in her throat, before the uncontrollable sobs began into her pillow. How could anyone have been so heartless? Why was this happening to her? She had been with Maria for nine years and she had never seen this side of her.

***

Brooke woke up disorientated, and her face was damp from the wet pillow. She looked at her phone and saw it was after eleven, realising she had obviously cried herself to sleep. She stared at the ceiling as she recalled the text that had come through, listening to her heavy sighs and her tummy growling. Brooke had only eaten a few olives this evening, but it was too late to eat now she thought. Switching off the lamp and TV, she grabbed water from the fridge. She checked to see if the doors were locked and made her way into her bedroom.

After finishing getting ready for bed, Brooke went to the carrier that Kate and Jo had given her that morning. Retrieving the teddy bear out, she slowly and sadly wrapped her arms around him tightly. Brooke switched the light off and put her bedtime playlist on her iPhone, shutting her eyes and all thoughts of the last two weeks out of her mind.

Chapter Eleven

Brooke woke up with the sun shining in on her, feeling the headache already permanently placed in the centre of her forehead. She hadn't even had a lot to drink. It clearly must have been the stress of the last couple of weeks, and she prayed that this place would ease that. She hated drugs, but at the moment, aspirin was quickly becoming her new best friend. The one good thing about day one, is it was after eight, and she couldn't remember the last time she slept this late.

Brooke opened her blinds and patio doors again. It looked like it was going to be a gorgeous day, and she wanted to find the beach and see what it was like. She was confident it wouldn't be up too much, given she was in the UK and not Greece. But she hoped it was good enough to at least go running on in the mornings, and to maybe have a few days chilling in the sun with a book. Brooke was desperate to get some more information about boat rentals as well, following Kate's revelation last week, thinking that would be kind of cool.

No time like the present, she thought. Getting her running gear on, she put her ear buds in and pressed play on her running playlist. She grabbed twenty pounds from her purse and put it with the front door key in her shorts, zipping it up as she left her caravan. Brooke assessed the paths on either direction of her, unable to remember which way she'd came in from, more so due to the getting lost. She decided to try right. Her dad had always taught her if ever you get lost, always go right. How can it be wrong, it's right? She smiled to herself thinking of her dad's words, and made a mental note to call him later today. She set off on a slow jog, paying close attention to specifics and any resemblance of the allegedly 'close by' beach.

It had only taken about ten minutes before Brooke reached the point she had been looking for. A small pub and restaurant, a couple of shops, and the beach. Interestingly though, it was actually nice. Surprising Brooke, she made another mental note to definitely make an effort to come and watch the sunset properly from this point, at least once whilst she was here. Brooke noticed the boatyard opening up, feeling great that it should be opened before the end of her run. Setting off along the beach, Brooke began running again, getting closer to the water but not quite close enough that her trainers got wet. Suddenly, for the first time in nigh on two weeks, she felt like she was in her element, amazed at the beauty surrounding her. Brooke loved running and more so along the beach. Right now in this moment, she had nothing but positive thoughts for the next six weeks.

***

Brooke collapsed on the sand, unable to remove the smile from her face. It was a great run. She loved scenic running, and it was so much more intense and energetic running on sand. Trying desperately to ease her erratic breathing, Brooke noticed the dark cloud over her closed eyes. Squinting as she opened them, she saw the silhouette of a body and lifted her hand to shade her eyes.

"You okay there?" Chloe said, noticing the damp clothing pulling to Brooke's body.

"Oh, hey. Yeah, all good," she said, feeling content. "Dying, I needed a breathing break, or maybe just a 'let's not die' break," she said giddily.

"Well, yeah, I'd really like you not to die," she heard Chloe say.

Brooke sat up and turned around to face the 'surfer girl'. "So what, you go surfing all day every day or something?" she asked. "Plus, I thought you only come up on weekends?"

"Very inquisitive aren't you, Brooke? What are you a cop or something? No, I don't surf all day every day, and yeah this weekend is a one off for me being here a little bit longer. Girls coming remember?" she winked, and just like that ran off into the water with her surfboard.

Brooke walked back up to the boat shop, grabbing herself a bottle of water and a few different flyers from the snack area.

"Hey, you alright there?" she heard, turning around to face the voice. She was faced with a guy about her own age, maybe a little older, wearing board shorts and a vest. His arms were both full with tattoo sleeves and he had a piercing in his lower lip. His short, dirty blonde hair was styled nicely, and Brooke noticed he was incredibly good looking.

"Oh, hey. Sorry. I was just looking at what you do. Am I okay to take some flyers?" she asked.

"Yeah, for sure. You here for a holiday? How long you about for?" he said, looking at her.

"Yes, I'm at the caravan site. I'm here for six weeks actually. I don't know if I'm going to stay that long, but ultimately that's what I have booked. Hence the reason for picking these up," she smiled, wiggling the flyers in the air.

"Wow, that's a long time. To be fair, some folk live up there, so you will be fine and get to know them all I'm sure. You should definitely do some activities whilst you're here though, since clearly you are active," he said, pointing down to her sweaty running gear. "We have surf lessons every Saturday and Sunday morning, and they are always a big hit. If you have a couple in the first couple weeks you will be able to go surfing most days," he said to Brooke, looking out to the water where she could see Chloe and a couple of guys sitting on their boards chatting. "Don't worry, not much happens this time in the morning, but later on in the day, and in the next few weeks we get some time to surf," he said animatedly. "We also rent boats, kayaks, and boogie boards. You name it we have it or we will get it. Oh, and if you fancy trying a spot of fishing, we have two fishing trips a week too," he said to her animatedly.

"Okay, great. Thanks for your help. I will look over the boat details in this flyer and see if it's of any interest. I'll leave the fishing thanks, not really my thing," she said, scrunching her nose up. "And I do fancy the surfing. I don't know if I'll be any good, but it looks fun," she said happily.

"Okay cool, wait here a minute," he said walking off, before returning with a book. "Right, so tomorrow we have a nine slot with the kids. There's five of them so far, but that will probably increase throughout the course of the day. Or three at ten thirty with the adults. Again, same thing applies, this time of year we normally start getting a little busier, or they just come to have some fun," he laughed. "It's twenty pounds for an hour, but we normally suggest three hours. And if you block book you can get it for fifty quid. Alternatively," he turned the page, "you can come in on Sunday at ten thirty, as we have nobody there at the moment. That may change, but they are often pretty quiet. And I'll tell you a secret," he said with a glint in his eye. He pointed up to a sign on the wall and said, "so we offer private lessons for thirty-five pounds, but if you book for Sunday morning you may actually end up being the only one anyways and can get away with paying the twenty. I mean, I can't guarantee you will be the only one, but it's a possibility," he said, smiling kindly.

He seemed nice Brooke thought. As it turned out, the people she had met so far all did. "Will the instructor have to come in just for me though?" she asked seriously.

"Not really. Casey will have to be here anyways, as people can just show up at the time to book on, so don't worry about that," he said. "So you wanna book? If you take it and like it, you never know you may be onto Kite surfing by the end of the six weeks," he said seriously.

She was never good with posture. So chances are she would probably fail miserably at surfing, but he was sweet for being so optimistic. "Okay great. As long as Casey won't be annoyed that he's coming in just to teach an unteachable to surf, I'll do it. Can I pay when I come? If not I can come back later, I just don't have enough money on me now," she said.

"That's fine, bring it Sunday. What's your name?" he said.

"Brooke, Brooke Davis. Do I need to bring anything else with me? And how much to rent the equipment, wetsuits etc.?" she said excitably.

"It's included in the cost. Bring a drink and a towel I guess, but everything else is fine. Great, all booked in for you. I'll see you Sunday at ten fifteen then Davis," he smiled, giving her a ticket with the details.

Brooke felt quite good considering everything that had gone on. She had had a great run this morning, the guy in the boatyard was really helpful and sweet, and she had some surfing lessons to look forward to. Arriving back to the van she made herself some cereal and sat on her decking, flicking between her newspaper and Google, searching for things to do in the area. Although, since she would be here for six weeks, she knew she didn't want to do everything in one go. So she would make a plan of some of the things that would be worthwhile, and then she would be able to make some arrangements and a timetable. She felt proud of herself and her plan.

***

"Hey, how goes it?" Chloe asked.

"Oh, hi," Brooke placed down her kindle and leaned up on her elbows to face Chloe. "I'm okay thanks, yourself?"

"Yes, I'm good thanks. I'm looking forward to my friends coming later," she said, smiling widely. "I hope you can make it. Did you have a good run?" Chloe was hoping that Brooke would come over this evening. She liked the girl, and she totally seemed like she needed a friend or three. Additionally, she seemed like she could do with letting her hair down.

"Yes, my run was great, thanks. I needed it. I had a look in the boatyard and got some flyers to maybe try some stuff," she said, apprehensive of telling Chloe about the surfing lesson. She liked her. She seemed kind and nice, but she didn't want the surf pro to make fun of her.

"You should totally try surfing. You could be a pro or get into kite surfing by the end of your time here," she said excitably, as she knocked on her board.

Brooke was smiling at her. She was very animated and very likeable. "Well, I um... Well, I don't think I'd be any good. I'm not good at things like that. But we'll see," she said, suddenly feeling exposed and insecure.

Chloe noticed a change in Brooke's mood. She nodded sombrely. She couldn't read the girl, and she didn't know if it was just because she had gone through a rough patch in her life or what. "Okay. Well if you fancy a go, let me know if I can help. I will leave you back to your book. I need to go and get ready and go shopping. I... I genuinely hope I see you this evening, Brooke. It will be fun. Bye," she said, turning around and putting her board on the decking before going into her cabin.

Brooke wondered what it was like inside, if it was like the one that she almost booked? She wondered why Chloe seemed intent that she go into hers that evening and spend time with her friends. She didn't know the first thing about Brooke so why did she seem so keen? She shrugged off the thoughts and returned to her book. Unable to concentrate with all the things swimming around in her head, she picked up her phone and texted Kate, revealing her feelings. Suddenly she was feeling weird and didn't know if she wanted to stay any longer. *What is the matter with me*? she thought. Checking through the messages, she found Paula's history and read through the messages. The last one was only a week before Maria had ended things, calling her 'her lovely,' asking if she wanted to come over for dinner one night. Brooke could remember about a year ago when suddenly Paula and Jasmine started becoming a bigger part of their lives. It was just before the accident, and she assumed it was because she was lonely. They had set up profiles on dating websites, even babysitting when she went on dates. She had spent more and more time with them, at their house. Was that when it started? Was it because of the accident? She sat there, still letting all the unanswered questions come over her. She wiped away a seldom tear, suddenly feeling so alone and regretting coming here altogether. *Shit.* Why had she looked at those messages?

"Oh, my God. Are you okay? Brooke? What's happened?" Chloe said quickly climbing over the decking.

"Oh, um… I'm fine. Don't worry," she said, wiping a tear with her hoodie sleeve and focusing in on Chloe, who was kneeling down in front of her looking into her eyes with concern. Brooke first noticed the light pink lipstick she was wearing, as it plumped up her lips perfectly and complimented her olive skin. Then she noticed her long dark hair, which for the first time wasn't wet or wavy from the surf, but in fact straightened. She was incredibly pretty and smelt divine in whatever perfume she was wearing. There was an ever so slight floral and fruity scent to it. It was soft and feminine, and she wore it incredibly well. *Shit.* What was she doing? She stood up quickly, too quickly that she ended up head butting the girl.

"Ouch," Chloe said standing and moving backwards, rubbing her chin.

"Shit. I'm so sorry," she said, immediately moving to Chloe and moving her hand to check her chin, whilst rubbing the top of her head. "I'm sorry. I'm a klutz, I know. Can I get you anything? Do you need some ice?

I'm sorry," she sighed, looking down to her bare feet and fidgeting with her fingers.

"Brooke? Brooke?" Chloe asked, waiting for the girl to look up to her before continuing, reluctant to get too tactile with her. When Brooke looked up to her, there was sadness in her eyes. She didn't know if it was whatever had upset her before she got there, or the fact that she had hit Chloe by mistake. Chloe didn't know what to do or how to handle it. She didn't want to upset the girl further, but equally she didn't know the girl so how could she stop her from feeling rubbish. "Right. Come on. I don't know what's going on, and its none of my business, but you can come shopping with me? It's only for groceries, basically booze and some meat to barbecue before the girls get here tonight. You will be able to see where the asda is at least," she said, looking at Brooke.

"Ermm, I really don't want to go anywhere. I'm fine, honestly. I just..." Brooke didn't even get a chance to finish her sentence.

"Oh, I'm sorry. You thought this was optional? NO," she said, sternly looking at Brooke. "You just head-butted me, it's the least you can do. Go get some shoes on. I can't drive alone; I may be concussed with your big head nearly knocking me out," she said gratingly.

"I so don't have a big head," she said seriously, as she began rubbing the top and already feeling a lump forming. "It's me that will be concussed with your big ass chin," she said, folding her arms, which made her feel like a stroppy teenager. This caused her to start laughing as she uncrossed her arms. "Sorry," she said, shyly noticing Chloe's smile. It was huge and it went all the way up to her big green eyes. She was very good looking, and looked great with her hair down and straightened.

Chloe was wearing grey skinny jeans, sandals, and a tight fitted t-shirt that accentuated her amazing body. Brooke didn't have a bad body by any means. She needed to keep in shape because of her job, but it wasn't nothing in comparison to Chloe's. She really hoped she could surf, because if that was the product of it then great!

"Earth to Brooke?" She heard, "Shoes! Now!"

"You're very demanding aren't you?"

"Yes. Hurry up please. I need to prep the food and make sangria before they arrive," Chloe said, pushing Brooke inside. She grabbed her belongings and put them inside before she locked up. She went to Brooke's fridge and got a beer out for her.

***

Brooke was looking in her wardrobe, wondering if she should change. Yes? No? Why would she? Seriously, what was going on? She was feeling shit because of the messages she'd read, and now as a result of that she'd ended up in this situation. Putting on her converse, Brooke grabbed her purse and left her room.

"Seriously, I don't need babysitting," she said, walking out to the living area.

"I didn't say you did. You may have concussed me, and therefore, I do! For you, now come on," she said, handing her the beer and leaving the van.

Brooke locked up, feeling very weird. She didn't know this girl at all. She'd met her a day ago and she couldn't really be bothered making small talk. She didn't appear to have a choice though. On a plus, the distraction would probably help. So she took a sip of the beer and decided to just go with it, despite the fact she hadn't really been given a choice.

"So, pop quiz? You really okay?" Chloe asked, checking each way as she crossed the junction out of the site.

"Speed fan, huh?" she said back, looking out the window still.

"Avoidance? Smart! I still want an answer. I am genuinely concerned," she said sighing. "I don't know you from Adam, Brooke, but I think you seem really awesome. And if you are here that long and we're gonna be neighbours, I'd really like us to be friends. I go home in a couple of days and I want to know that you'll be okay," she said seriously.

Brooke was surprised, and she couldn't remember anyone being concerned for her. In fact, that was a blatant lie. She met Gareth in Brighton, and he was caring and kind. Kate and Jo had been there for her too, and they had cared. "Look, thanks for your concern. But honestly, I am fine. You don't have to worry. I have 'clearly' come here to get away from the shit that's going on in my life, but I'm good. I was just over thinking some stuff when you came back. Stupidly, I shouldn't have been for obvious reasons. For example, you can't change the past. And thinking about it will only impact your future, I think," she said solemnly. "But seriously, I feel better since being here. I've made plans to do things and local places to visit et cetera. But you don't need to worry. Seriously," she said, looking over to Chloe.

"Okay fine. I don't know you well enough to know whether I'm buying that or not yet, but we'll get to know you tonight. And then I'll be able to make better judgements. We're also going on an all dayer tomorrow if you fancy it? Seriously, before you start, there is no movement on this evening, Brooke. I saw you upset, so there's no way I am not going to force you into it. Plus, as I said yesterday, you won't have any opportunity to do anything else because of the noise," she said, pulling into a parking space and leaving the car, walking off. Just like that, make a demand and then walk off. Brooke walked hurriedly to catch up to Chloe.

***

"Are you a veggie?" Chloe asked, as they were walking around the aisle.

"What? God no. I couldn't give up roast dinners," she said. "Why do you ask?"

"Just wondering what to feed you tonight," she said, bumping shoulders with her and walking off quickly again.

"Oh, my God, are you actually purposely trying to annoy me?" Brooke said to Chloe as she caught up to her again.

"Yes!," she said. "Do you like spice and all meats? Kebabs? Jacket potatoes? Et cetera?"

"Why would you want to piss me off? And yes I like all of that, but honestly, I'm fine. I don't wan…"

Chloe stopped and turned to face Brooke. "I thought we'd established this already? I didn't want to piss you off. I am trying to stop you thinking about whatever you shouldn't have been thinking about by preoccupying your mind BY pissing you off." She smiled. "Great news about the food. Do you like sangria?" she said lastly. "We just need to go to the drinks aisle."

"Are you a therapist or something? That's a great deal of effort with the whole reverse psychology thing. You could have just been nice. And yes I like sangria," Brooke said seriously.

"Good God, no," she said, laughing and putting some bottles of champagne into the trolley. "Come on, we're done. Anything you want before we leave?" she asked.

"Nope. Apparently I'm all good," she said, smiling slightly, and noticing the look of upset and/or concern on Chloe's face.

Brooke instantly felt bad and smiled half-heartedly. "Let's go party, I guess?"

<u>Chapter Twelve</u>

Brooke had an enjoyable day. She was an absolutely appalling cook, but she had helped prep the food with Chloe, taking instruction where given. And truth be known, she'd actually quite enjoyed it. She checked her eye, which was still a little red, but luckily was barely noticeable. It was still hurting like hell, but as Chloe had told her it was a *'war wound'*.

She didn't feel comfortable about going at all, which she had told Chloe a number of times. But would she listen? Of course she wouldn't. She'd sent her on her merry way with a glass of her sangria, which was delicious. Strong as hell, but delicious, and she could already feel the effects of the alcohol.

"Oi, oi," she heard shouts and a horn tooting, and then loud, girly shrills. Clearly Chloe hadn't been wrong in the fact that they would be too loud for her not to come. She smiled, recollecting the bottle of champagne she bought for her neighbours Mr and Mrs Willis on the other side. She now understood why that was necessary.

Brooke straightened her hair and put some lip-gloss on. She was only going next door so she didn't need to dress up. Although, she wondered what Chloe's friends were like as Chloe had appeared to have made quite an effort. She was cursing herself, unsure of what to wear. It was a BBQ and beer on a veranda in a caravan park. What did you wear to something like this? They rarely went out. Whether it be because of working, too tired because of working, or just simply because Maria couldn't be bothered. She sat on her bed and sighed with her face in her palms, looking directly into her wardrobe. "Hmmmm," she said out loud as she heard the door go. It would only be Chloe. Shit, what if she had brought her friends already? She sighed heavily and wrapped her towel around her body. She should have put some clothes on by now really.

Brooke opened the door to find Chloe holding another glass of sangria.

Chloe nearly dropped the glass that she was holding when Brooke opened the door in nothing but a towel and her long blonde hair falling over her shoulder. "H...Hey, erm..." *shit, pull it together*, Chloe thought as she coughed. "Sorry, too much sangria. I figured you may be having second thoughts, and my friends really want to meet you. Apparently they want a new face to have fun with rather than being bored with me all evening." She smiled widely. "I brought you this Dutch courage. Please hurry?" she said, handing Brooke the glass. "We don't bite, unle...doesn't matter."

Brooke wondered what Chloe was about to say as she handed her the glass and ran off. She obviously didn't want to leave her friends, or the food that she could already smell seeping through the van. It smelled delicious, and Brooke had a sense of pride over the fact that she had actually contributed to the preparation. Clearly not a great deal, but it was something all the same she thought, smiling. "Right. Come on girl, get your ass in gear."

She went through the different outfits she had. She knew she wanted to go smart casual, but not too much of one or the other. She pulled out a few different pairs of jeans and went for a dark blue pair of skinny Levi's and a coral light jumper with a low cut back, revealing a fair amount of her tanned skin. Brooke put on her casual flip flops to dress it down a bit and checked her reflection once more, running her fingers through her hair. She grabbed her phone, sliding it into her back pocket. She grabbed a bottle of rose before locking up and putting her key into her front pocket.

She smiled as she heard the squeals coming from next door. Geez, the neighbours would love them she thought. If Maria was here and they had rented this, she would have gone around and complained to the occupants. She shook the thoughts away again. She really needed to stop this, it was too much.

The door was opened to the cabin, so she knocked before entering. "Hello?" she said as she entered.

"Hey, you look great," Chloe said, before quickly turning back around to her chopping. There was a blond girl with a glass in her hand, looking suspiciously at Chloe.

"Hey, you must be Brooke? I'm Emily. We've heard all about you." She smiled. "We're so glad you could come over. These nights are always great fun," she said warmly.

"Hey, I hope not all bad. Nice to meet you Emily, beautiful ring," Brooke said, pointing to the huge diamond engagement ring on her wedding finger. "Chloe, I brought over a bottle of wine. I don't know where you want it."

"Thanks," Emily said shyly. "Come on, come meet the others whilst she's prepping," Emily said, linking her arm in Brooke's.

Chloe took the wine and smiled 'thanks,' then looked straight back down to the peppers and onions she was cutting.

***

Emily and Brooke walked outside together and saw two more girls who were chatting away animatedly. "Hey guys, this is Brooke, the girl from next door that Chloe invited. Brooke, this is Carla and Natalie," she said, pointing to each of them.

"Hi, how are you? Thanks so much for letting me crash your night. I did try to get out of it, but I think your friend thinks I need babysitting," Brooke said, smiling widely.

"Sounds like Chlo," said Natalie. "But seriously, we're glad you could make it. It's nice to have someone new in the mix. Chloe said you're here for like six weeks or so?" she added.

"Yes, well I think… Maybe… I don't know. I have booked it for six weeks, but we'll see how I get on. I have some friends coming up for a long weekend in three weeks, so most definitely up until then," she said smiling.

"Whatever they say, it's all lies!" Chloe came out with some candles and the jug of sangria.

"So my lovely lady doesn't get bitten when it gets dark," she said, ruffling Carla's long black hair, laughing, and lighting the citronella candle, placing it close to Carla.

"Really?" Carla said, straightening her pristine locks and rolling her eyes.

"So how do you manage to get all that time off work? Geez, I'd love to come spend six weeks here, with all the downtime, especially through summer. It's like the greatest place. They even have their own weather. *Sorry*, what's it called again…micro climate?" Natalie said excitably.

"That's a bit nosey isn't it, Nat?" said Chloe, as she lit the barbecue and topped everyone's glasses up.

"Sorry, I get a bit carried away. I didn't mean to pry," she said, taking some more of her drink.

"Hey, no worries, ask away. I'm not saying I'm going to answer, but ask away all the same," Brooke confirmed smiling. "The reason I'm able to do it, is I'm not working at the moment," she said, taking more drink, and now feeling uncomfortable with the noticeable silence. *Great, Brooke, nice way to kill the mood*, she thought.

Brooke's phone lit up and Mitch's face filled the screen as the music started to sing, 'Whoa, Ohhhh, Ohhhh, oh, I get a good feeling.' She silenced her phone, apologising.

"Is that your boyfriend?" asked Carla.

Brooke couldn't help but laugh. "Mitch? God no," she said.

Carla had grabbed her phone, looking at the grinning face. "Really? He's hot. Is he single?" she said, smiling at Brooke.

"Annnnd she's off," said Emily, rolling her eyes to Brooke.

"Well not all of us are lucky enough to have met our mister rights. I can't help it if I'm not as lucky as everyone else and still on my conquest," Carla said sulkily.

"Hey, no worries. He's very much single, yes, and a great guy. But he is in Oxford, which is kind of far from here. Plus, he doesn't have much time, truthfully. But how's about if I get him up here whilst I'm here? I'll let Chloe know, and you can come up again? If you're able to?" Brooke said, smiling to Carla.

"Really? Oh, my God, I *love* you. You're fab, and you need to come out with us tomorrow. She's cool. So why aren't you guys together if he is so great?" Carla added.

Just as Brooke said, "I've just come out of a nine-year relationship," Chloe at the same time outed her.

"She's gay," she said, suddenly looking completely embarrassed.

Everyone went quiet. "I'm sorry, that wasn't my place to say," Chloe said.

"And I'm gay," Brooke said smiling. "It's fine. I'm more than comfortable with who I am. I have been gay for sixteen years, so I have no issue with being outed or outing myself. If people don't approve or don't like me for who I am, then really that's their problem," she said seriously.

"Here, here. I personally think you're great," Emily said, holding up her glass to 'cheers' her.

Chloe got up to check the BBQ, "I'll go and get the food to put on."

"Here, I'll give you a hand," Nat said, following her friend inside.

***

"What's going on, Chlo?" she whispered.

"Nothing. Why?" Chloe said, not looking at Nat.

"I thought you were just perving on this girl. I mean granted, I can see why. She's gorgeous, but there's more? What's going on?" Nat said concerned.

"Nothing. I'm not perving, I'm just concerned for her. Her mates called her and were saying stuff. I...I just think she's gone through a rough time and she's clearly ran away, so I don't want her to feel alone. We've all been there, remember?" she said, finally looking at Nat.

"I don't buy a word of it. But seriously, this isn't you. You can't commit to a piece of toast, let alone a relationship. Whatever she has going on, well it's not gonna end well for either of you!" she said, taking a plate of food and walking back outside.

Chloe put her head against the overhead cabinet. Where the hell had all of that come from? She doesn't even like Brooke like that. For once, she *can* be a friend to a good looking gay woman. She didn't need to try and sleep with everyone. Why hadn't she thought of saying that to Nat when she was there mouthing off? She sighed heavily, shaking her head. "So much for a fun night," she said, loud enough for only herself to hear.

Walking back outside with the remaining dishes, Chloe put the food on the BBQ and turned it down to a low heat. "You okay, Chlo?" she heard Emily ask.

"Yes, yes fine. Just wanted to get that sorted so I can relax and drink with you guys," she said smiling.

Brooke felt there was an atmosphere. She didn't know what Natalie and Chloe had discussed, but Chloe walked inside and seemed fine, and returned not so much. Which caused Brooke to suddenly feel uncomfortable, like she should leave.

"Okay, last of the sangria ladies and then I guess we go onto the champers," Chloe said, filling the glasses up.

"Erm, I'm okay, thanks," Brooke said, covering her glass with her hand.

Chloe was looking at her intently, almost trying to look beyond her eyes. "Okay," she said looking over to Natalie and sitting down again. What was that look between them she wondered? Was there history? But Carla had said they all had boyfriends? *She* said that...*She* said...they had ALL met their 'mister rights'?

"Can I use your bathroom please?" Brooke asked, getting up.

"Yes, sure last room on the left," Chloe said, looking at her phone that was ringing and pointing inside to Brooke.

She walked through the cabin, which was gorgeous. It was beautifully decorated and would be so perfect to come and visit each weekend.

When she returned back outside, the three girls were talking quietly and laughing. "Your phone went off, but I think it was just a text though," Emily said. "We were laughing at the different tones you have going off."

Brooke checked her phone and saw it was Mitch. "Sorry, I don't mean to be rude, but its Mitch again, so I just need to respond," she said.

"I don't know! You've got her in there," she said, pointing to Chloe who had rushed off on her phone, saying, "Oh I gotta take this its Martin and now you're 'ohhh it's Mitch, I gotta take this'. Gone are the days where girls have a nice night without phones," Nat said, laughing and rolling her eyes.

"Oh, I'm sorry I won't..." Brooke started.

"Brooke, she's fucking with you. Ignore her, she's always like this," Emily said, slapping Natalie who was grinning mischievously.

"Okay, right yeah. Thanks, I'll see you Monday then," Chloe said, walking back to the table with the bottle of champagne, ending her call and grinning like the cat that got the cream. She put the bottle on the table in the cooler and went to the barbecue turning over the food.

"So smiley, you gonna share the news or just sit there with a stupid grin for the rest of the night?" Emily asked Chloe.

Brooke was confused. Who was Martin? Her boyfriend? Her mister right? They all seemed to be on the same page except for Brooke. She was confused and the drink apparently wasn't helping.

Chloe put the lid from the barbecue down again, before turning around to face her friends. Leaning against the railing she looked serious, but apparently was unable to hide the smile. "That was Martin," she said, grinning widely.

"Yes, we all established that," said Nat.

Chloe poked her tongue out at Nat and rolled her eyes, ignoring the sarcastic comment from her friend. "Well, one of my pieces has just sold, and well...sold...well. Like really well," she said, smiling. "But I've sold something," she said, smiling widely.

"My God, that's amazing news. Look at you, the little highflyer," said Emily, standing to hug her friend.

Carla and Nat got up and followed suit, hugging their friend. Brooke noticed the wink Nat gave Chloe. She couldn't put her finger on it, but there was something there, she was sure of it. Nat popped the lid on the champagne. "Congratulations, Hun," she said, filling a glass and handing it to Chloe before filling the others.

"Ermmm, I'm okay. Actually, I think I'll go back to my van and let you guys celebrate," Brooke said.

"What? Wait. Please don't go. I'd really like you to celebrate with me…us," Chloe said, correcting herself and looking at her intently.

"Come on. How can you leave that adorable little face?" said Emily, grabbing Chloe's jaw.

Brooke looked at Nat, trying to gauge her expression, before her phone went off again. She looked down and saw Mitch was calling her again. *Shit*. She didn't text him back. "I'm sorry, he really will be worrying about me, and I should take this," she said solemnly.

"Brooke, take your champers and we'll see you when you've finished. Go into Chloe's room so you can get some privacy," Nat said sternly, although she had a slight smile on her face.

She didn't dislike Nat in any way, shape or form. But, there just seemed to be something about it all, something that she couldn't put her finger on. In reality she was having a good time, and they were all in high spirits now, which created further anxiety that it was maybe just her being self-conscious again and being stupid. She smiled to Nat, taking the glass she proffered.

Chloe smiled as she walked past and mouthed to her, first door on the right. She had no intention of going to Chloe's room, figuring she'd sit in the lounge/dining area.

"Hello, gorgeous," she said into the phone. "I'm alive and well and just having dinner with some girls from next door. Yes…I *know*…me, making friends? Who'd a thought?" she said, laughing.

"Really, you are as bad as Kate. Seriously! Yes, it's too soon. And FYI, I am trying to set you up. They are four straight girls, but I do believe only one of them is single. Anyways, I don't mean to be rude, babes, but... I don't want to ignore them. I only met them a short while ago, so I'll call you later? What time are you finishing? I can call you when I'm home. Mitch, I'm a big girl. I'm literally next door to my place. NO, I will not! I am not giving you anyone's names. Mitch, behave. Seriously, dude. I met the one that owns this place the first minute I'd arrived, and she helped me. I have seen her and spoken to her a few times. She helped me get this place set up, and now her girlfriends are up for the weekend okay? Nothing's going to happen. They are all lovely, and one of which is all up for hitting you up. So chill the fuck out and get Brown to get you a weekend off in the next five weeks. I love you, but I'm going and I'll shout at you later, okay?" she said sternly.

Brooke said goodbye and hung up. She stood at the dining table and sipped some of her champagne, sighing heavily. Why was she so weird these days? Ever since the accident she had lost herself. Before the accident, Brooke was so extroverted. Everybody commented on her bubbly and outgoing personality, but now she couldn't establish who she was anymore.

"Penny for them?" Brooke heard, turning around quickly.

She smiled slightly to Nat. "Oh, hey. Sorry I was just..." She stopped.

"Thinking, I saw. Are you okay? You seemed a bit quiet, which is weird. Because although I only met you this evening, I don't get the impression you are naturally like that? I kinda figured you were assessing us. I always do that when I'm meeting new people, ya know? Weigh them up and find out what they're like first. But then you just seemed a little off. Is everything okay with the phone call you just took? We might all be a bit mad, but you can talk to this lot about anything," Nat said to her, concerned.

"I'm good, honestly. I just feel a little odd, I guess. I am here with people I don't know and feel a bit out of my comfort zone. I don't mean that to sound rude, so I'm sorry if it does," Brooke said worried.

Nat stood in front of Brooke holding her shoulders, and Brooke was forced to look into her green eyes.

What was it with this group of women? Were they the 'green eyed girls', no pun intended?

"You didn't offend me, and you couldn't if you tried. We have all been saying you seem cool. We all really like you, and we all hope you can spend some time with us this weekend. We're only here for a couple of days. Come on. Stay. Have a drink with us. We can all eat shit, have fun, drink champers and cocktails, dance, poker, and all the other random shit we all end up doing on our random nights," she said, looking into Brooke's eyes, pleadingly.

"Oh. Hi, is everything okay?" Chloe said, walking in to find Nat holding Brooke's arms.

"Yes, just making sure our new friend is okay," Nat said. "Fortunately, she's staying to play with us all. To help you celebrate," she said, smiling to Brooke and leaving them.

"Everything okay?" Chloe asked her.

"Yes, fine. You? Congratulations by the way.," she said quietly.

"What's happened? Have I done something? Has one of my friends said something?" she asked seriously.

"Noooo" Brooke said shaking her head. "I just…ummm. Feel…a bit out of sorts, I guess. I'm fine.

It's just been a while since I was with new people. Well with anyone actually, and I just feel like I'm imposing. I just wanted to go home and then let you and your friends celebrate as you are," she said solemnly.

"But my friends have all said they really like you. And I... I mean, we all want you to be here to celebrate with us too," she said, maintaining eye contact.

Brooke noticed the long eye lashes surrounding the big green eyes. She didn't know what to say or do in that moment, but she felt wanted for the first time in such a long time. So much so, that she didn't feel like she wanted to leave any longer. "Well, I guess I'd better hunt down the tablets for the morning, because I have a feeling I'm going to be a little hung-over," she said half-heartedly.

Chloe smiled slightly, "I'm pretty sure it's going to be more than a 'little' hangover. Thanks, Brooke," she said.

"Oi, idiot, our foods burning here?" Nat said, shouting into them.

"Shit, my food!" she said, running back outside with the plates in hand. Brooke picked up the cutlery and dips that Chloe had left behind and followed her outside.

Chapter Thirteen

Brooke was drunk. The last time she was this bad, she booked this place! But the point was, she was with friends again. Albeit with new friends, but friends who made her feel normal and liked, and back to her normal self. She was laughing. Genuinely laughing, like real, actual, belly laughs. And she needed to realise that people did like her. And more importantly, didn't all judge her.

"Seriously, are you going to stop eating?" Emily asked Carla. "You have to answer the question."

"Rihanna. Ohh, no Cheryl Cole, or Vasquez or whatever the hell her name is now," Carla said, taking another bite of a cold chicken kebab. "Oohhh, maybe Brooke can tell me who Mitch's ideal girl is and she can be my 'cross the fence girl,'" she said, causing them all to laugh hard. Carla almost fell off her chair, thinking she was so funny.

"My God, she's obsessed. She isn't going to let this go, I hope you realise this. Brooke, okay it's on you. Hit us," Nat said to Brooke.

"I know, I'm getting that. I'll need to call him and tell him," she said. "Hmm, I've never really thought of it," Brooke said.

"Don't say Mitch!" Carla said, clearly very intoxicated now. "It would literally break my heart," she sniffed.

"How can she say him? He's not bloody famous, you loon! Secondly, how would it break your heart when you

haven't even met him yet? You might not even like him,"
Emily said laughing.

"How do you know he's not famous? He could be
for all you know," Carla said soberly. "For all we know
they both could be, and that's why she's hiding out here
with little old us."

"Dear god, she's really gone now! She's already got
him rich, famous and they're married," Emily laughed,
topping her and Chloe's glass up. "Come on then,
Brooke. Who's yours? Or is it your 'famous' friend
Mitch?" she said, giggling again.

Brooke couldn't help but laugh, unfortunately unable
to control the snorting of her drinking through her nose.
My God she was really making a habit of that. "Sorry,"
she said, holding up her finger and shaking her head. "I
don't know it's hard. Okay, I have it. Ryan Reynolds. I
love him in the proposal," she said.

"Oh, my God. I love that movie. I love Sandra
Bullock. Oh, actually, I want to change mine. Beautiful.
Stunning. She is an older woman. Hmmm, yes. I will say
Sandy B," Carla said, finding herself hysterical. "I need
the bathroom – game pause, game pause," she said.

"So is that your thing then, blondes?" said Nat.

"No, not really, brunettes actually…blondes are
about as much my thing as males are, but there's just
something about him. I guess the looks and humour are
my thing. Is she okay? I thought I was drunk?" asked
Brooke.

"This is the norm for Carla," said Chloe, pouring half
of Carla's glass of champagne into her own glass and
topping her half empty glass with water. "This is a trick
we regularly do and it sorts her out," she continued.

"Okay, okay, I'm back. I'M BACK," Carla sang loudly. "Oh, I love this song, *'How will I know, if he really loves me.'* Come on, sing with me," she said, singing louder now.

Brooke looked around at them all laughing and rolling their eyes at their very drunk friend.

"Okay, next question?" Nat asked.

"No, we haven't finished. Chlo hasn't said hers," Carla said, taking a sip of her champagne. Nat watched Brooke intently, assuming she'd realise. But the girl, for all her beauty was very much the tortoise in the race, in relation to catching onto things. It caused Nat to smirk at her at the irony of this whole 'gaydar' rubbish.

"You know mine. Anyways, we should probably start a new game," Chloe said.

"No, I don't know who yours is. You have to tell or you have to dare," Carla added.

"Car, we aren't playing truth or dare. You are aware of this, right? We are all in our 30's," Chloe said, laughing with Emily as they both shook their heads at their friends.

"Yes, come on, Chlo, who's yours?" said Nat, smirking again.

Emily and Carla were looking at Chloe, but Nat was watching Brooke for some reason. She looked away before throwing occasional sideways glances back over to her.

"Come on then, I think we should do favourite sexual positions," Carla announced, clearly getting bored of the waiting for Chloe to announce.

"Oh my word, she's going to get me kicked off the site. I am not doing sexual positions, or crushes, or

109

longest relationships, or perfect threesomes, or anything else. I think we start poker," Chloe said.

"I don't get it. Well I get the wanting to stop this game, I think some of us," Brooke pointed to Carla, "are getting a bit carried away, but why won't you say who it is? Are they that bad?" she continued smirking. "PS, I don't know how to play poker."

"Bets!" Emily and Nat shouted, standing and high fiving each other.

Brooke was looking between them completely confused. "That means they want to play and gamble properly rather than pennies, because you don't know how to play. You should play. It's good fun, and nobody will rip you off. Lastly, no. It isn't that bad at all. I'm not afraid to say it, who my cross the fence person would be," she stopped smirking. "Do not judge me, I am well aware of the age gap," she said. "No ridiculous comments about cradle snatching, you two," Chloe added, pointing to Nat and Emily.

"Oh come on already?" Brooke said laughing, before she had said anything.

Nat was watching Brooke. "Okay, it would be Justin Bieber. I can't help it," she said, listening to them all laughing. Nat had heard it on many occasions, but she watched a laughing Brooke, who had seemingly missed the obvious. But then the realisation was just kicking in. Brooke looked over to Nat, serious, who smiled at her.

"Come on then, cards it is?" Nat said, grabbing the cards and starting to shuffle.

Brooke had practically downed her champagne. She was normally pretty good with her gaydar, but they had all been talking all night like all the girls were straight. All of the talk confused her from the comment Chloe had made on the first day about wanting to sleep with her because she was gay. But she had experienced that loads, where straight women wanted a go just to experiment. Emily topped up Brooke's and her own glasses, when Brooke's phone went off again. It was Kate this time with a text message.

"Do you have a different ring tone for every person?" Emily asked seriously.

"Yes I do. And text tone," she said. "Oh, and picture," she said, showing the picture of Kate.

"Is that Kate Middleton?" Carla said snatching her phone from her hand "God, I'm drunk."

"No, it isn't Kate Middleton. But we all think she is very much likened to her, and her name is Kate," she laughed.

"Is that your girlfriend? She's gorgeous, cute couple," Carla said, causing silence around the table. Carla looked up from her cards, suddenly very aware of the lack of noise. "What? Did I say something? What have I missed?" she looked around. "Oh, shit. That's why you're here. You have split up with her. Fuck. I'm so sorry," Carla said, throwing her head in her hands.

Brooke stroked the girl's head, "Hey, hey, you haven't said anything wrong. Kate is one of my best friends, and like Mitch she will be checking in on me. I only arrived last night, remember," she said seriously.

"I'm sorry, Brooke. I really am. I would never mean to hurt you. I really like you, you're great," she said with a childlike smile.

"Ditto, it's okay. Look, I'm going to safely remove the elephant from the room, or world," Brooke said, pointing to the outside darkness. "My girlfriend of nine years split up with me two weeks ago. She didn't initially tell me why, just that it wasn't working and that she wanted me moved out of the house within two weeks. As it turns out, I went upstairs, stupidly, in a bid to try and save it and heard her on the phone to one of my best friends...our best friends. Straight friend with a kid. She doesn't... didn't like, neither straights nor kids. Anyways, in a nutshell, she's left me for them. Flew to Florida for two weeks, and I had to move out within that time so they can all live together in a perfect world when they come back home tomorrow. Oh...and the icing on the cake...she proposed to her whilst they were there...she didn't want marriage or kids...her career was allegedly too important!" she said. "Anyways, now that's out of the way, how do I play poker?"

Brooke was regretting saying it already as she faced her new friends who were all looking at her with pity, sorrow and sober looks.

Brooke sighed inwardly. *What should she do?* she thought. "Okay shall we ditch strip poker and play spin the bottle instead?" she said, feeling her lip twitch.

Emily was the first to laugh. "I knew I would fucking love you. FYI, I'm not playing strip poker or spin the bottle. And secondly, her loss is our gain. She sounds like a fucking bitch!" Emily said standing up and hugging Brooke. There it was again, the look between Nat and Chloe.

"Hey, it is what it is. And FYI, I also have no intention of playing either game, but as I had so wonderfully dampened everyone's evening, I figured I should probably pull it back with some laughter and stupidity," she said, as she picked up her phone to a call from Kate. "Sorry again, I'll be two secs. Hey, gorgeous. I'm fine. I'm not ignoring you. I'm at my neighbour's place with her friends, drinking, having a barbecue, and now about to start playing poker. I know I don't play poker, and yes *STILL... TOO... SOON*. I love you, and Jo. I'll call you in the morning, K?" she said, putting down the phone.

"Sorry to be rude, but are we going to play or shall I leave?" Brooke asked seriously.

"NO!" they all shouted in unison. They went through the rules of poker for Brooke after she'd collected her purse. The 'big blinds,' as they were calling them, were for a pound a go, which they had explained about. In reality, it was far too late in the day and she was far too inebriated for all of this, but she wasn't in a position to bail now. Equally, she also wasn't too stubborn to admit that she had actually had a great time.

"Okay, so I wanna know something, Brooke," Nat said.

"Sure, shoot. As I've addressed many a time this evening, I'm not necessarily going to answer, but by all means ask," she said grinning.

"Oh, don't worry, it's not a difficult one. So you have tones for everyone in your phone. If you took my number, what would mine be?" Nat asked smirking.

"Hmmmm, that's a difficult one," she said, sitting back in her chair.

"If it was my phone, it would be trouble," Emily said.

"No, that would have to be for Chloe," Brooke said, laughing.

"Oi, unfair and completely unjust," Chloe said, feigning disgust and sadness.

"Really? You made fun of me and told me I was staying in another campsite when I was clearly stressed to hell upon arrival, given you witnessed me head-butting the steering wheel out of frustration," she said laughing.

"You didn't," said Emily, shocked, but badly stifling her laugh.

"What? It was funny," she laughed, eventually. Plus, she was talking shit about me to her friends *and* I helped her switch on the van, so I paid my dues," Chloe laughed and shrugged her shoulders, seemingly proud of herself.

"Okay. It would be... either Poker face by Lady Gaga, as I couldn't work you out at first, or wild one by Flo-rida. I'd have Chloe be Trouble by Pink. Emily, without a doubt, Bad Influence by Pink, as I think we could be very bad influences on each other, and not in a sexual way. And Carla, wow, something lovey, searching for love, I don't know right now," she said, laughing.

Nat stood up. "I'll give you that. I couldn't have done it better if I tried", she said, high fiving Brooke, "and, so right for Carla," she said laughing.

***

They had moved the game inside the cabin. Carla was now passed out on the couch, whilst the others were at the dining table, still continuing drinking.

"So, do you think you'll stay here the full time then?" Emily asked her seriously.

"Honestly, I don't know. I was unsure yesterday when I got here. I received a text from her, and then tonight I have had a good night. The fact of the matter is, until Chloe leaves and I won't have anyone around that I've met, I don't know how I'll be. Sorry, that sounds like I need you to be my babysitter, and that really isn't the case. But ultimately, had I arrived on Monday for example and had got used to occupying my time without meeting anyone, I might feel differently. I have had a lot of shit happen in the last nine months, so I just feel completely unsure of everything. I guess the point I'm clearly struggling to make is, if I was here alone for a week before meeting 'the weekend crews,' I may have given up and just gone home. But now that I have met people, it's going to be weird being alone again, all day every day. I'm sorry, I'm speaking rubbish as I have had way too much to drink it seems. Sorry," Brooke said, sadly.

"Hey Brooke, you know what? You're completely cool. I don't know what happened to you, well outside of what you said tonight. But you shouldn't say sorry all the time. You shouldn't change the person you are, for anybody. Because ya know what, you are pretty bloody awesome in my opinion," said Emily. "Every time you speak of her or refer to her or certain things, you become the absolute opposite of who you have been all night," Emily continued.

"Here, here. I agree with her. So tell me to mind my own, but what's the history behind all this? You can have six weeks off and you mentioned that it's not just the last two weeks since this dumbass skipped on you. So what's the deal with the last nine months?" Nat asked seriously. "Again to reiterate, please don't feel obliged, we only just met tonight and I get that," Nat added.

Chapter Fourteen

"You don't have to tell us," Chloe said, watching Brooke, who appeared to be struggling.

"I'm sorry, Brooke. I didn't mean to upset you," Nat added.

"It's okay, it's just weird. I speak to my therapist about it, and to Mitch, but not anyone else. Not my dad, nor my friends. Maria used to just tell me to get a grip. I guess I've heard it so much for the last eight months that I have started to genuinely believe myself that I am just being melodramatic. It just leaves you feeling very exposed. But chances are, I'll never see you again and for the first time… maybe it's the drink, but for the first time, I feel like I don't want to hold back," she sighed."I am making it all sound a lot more dramatic than it actually is," she said smiling sadly, as she noticed the three girls all watching her and hanging on her every word.

"You genuinely don't have to tell us," Emily said sincerely, taking hold of Brooke's hand.

"It's fine, I actually feel okay. I'm sure that won't be the case tomorrow but hey ho, maybe it's the best thing for me." Brooke took a deep breath "So, you know Mitch my friend that called earlier that you asked who he was?" she said to the girls, who all nodded in response.

"Well, he's my partner. As in, work partner. I am a detective in the police force. We have worked together for a number of years. Maria, initially was our boss. He hated…hates her actually, but hated me more," she said, smiling slightly. "You know how it is. He works his butt off for the promotion and then gets partnered with the boss's bitch. Well, luckily for me, he realised he wasn't the only one to work his butt off. I needed to prove myself also...more, if I'm honest. And when she got another promotion, we got on much better, amazingly in fact. He's like my big brother. Anyways, we had been working a case for a long time, and got a tip off that something was going down about eight months ago. We unfortunately got into a bit of trouble, and long story short, I got shot," she said, placing her hand across her stomach and right side. "Well, Ermmm, it was quite bad. I was in a coma for two weeks. When I eventually came around, I had partial paralysis and had had to have my uterus removed due to the bullet. So that was pretty shitty, because I had always wanted kids," she said, looking off into the distance.

She coughed slightly, and avoided looking at any of them, allowing her to just continue. "So, yeah it took a bit of getting used to. Initially, Maria was fine, helping me where she could. But thinking about it now, soon after she was becoming shorter, outbursts of 'pull yourself together' and 'well I never wanted kids in the first place' type comments. Oddly, I never felt anything about it all though, ya know? I guess I've just been a bit lost. Maybe that's when she and Paula started the affair? Anyways, I went through a fair bit of therapy, group counselling from people in the force that had suffered something bad. However, three months ago, after a lot of hard work, I was able to go back to my job. It's all I've ever known and wanted to do, so I was completely committed to start walking again and get my life back on track. And of course, to try and deal with the psychological effects of not being able to have kids of my own one day. So I returned to work, and my second day in, I had this God awful anxiety attack. Clearly something had obviously clicked inside me and took me back there, and I ended up back in the hospital again. I was a state and I was signed back off with long term sickness, undergoing therapy, counselling, group counselling, meds et cetera, et cetera," she said, downing her newly refilled glass. She looked up at the girls and wondered how she would be received after the full spill out of her BS.

"So, it was your girlfriend that's made you think this was no biggie?" asked Nat pointedly.

"Well, I guess I am not being very fair to Maria, she never actually sai…" she didn't get a chance to finish.

"No, *no*, don't you dare! You said you hadn't spoken to anyone but Mitch and your therapist about this. A therapist sure as hell wouldn't make you feel this was nothing, and Mitch called you earlier to see if you were alive, so I'm guessing he certainly wouldn't. So your opening words were that you were being over dramatic? Correct?" Nat said irritated.

"Yes, that's right?" Brooke said apprehensively.

"So, you don't tell anyone? And you feel this is no biggie? Excuse me for my bluntness, Brooke, but your girlfriend, your ex, is a controlling, abusive, selfish bitch! That's abuse…she's mentally abusing you. She has done this to you, been unsupportive and done nothing to help you. For the record, so you know, being shot is bad, *and* big. Being in a coma is bad, *and* again big. And paralysis? Losing your chance of having a baby when you want that? Losing the career you have always wanted? These are all *big* things for anyone to deal with! Oh and let me guess, she is nowhere to be seen when you're at home every day alone with nothing but your

118

thoughts. She doesn't attend counselling with you? I bet not. People like that do not deserve people like you. You didn't over dramatize this at all. I'm sorry," Nat said putting her head in her hands. "I'm sorry, I shouldn't have been so outspoken, and I'm sorry you have gone through this," she added, looking up to Brooke and taking her hand.

"Geez, what a way to kill the night. It's like the Brooke and Nat show," Brooke said smiling a small smile. She squeezed her hand and danced her empty glass up to the girl. "Shall we have one for the road?" she said, "try and pick this party back up? I will say something that I'm kind of happy about and is cause for celebration. Sorry to take your limelight, Chloe," Brooke said as they all looked up to her with anticipation. "Well, this is really no big thing, but to me it really is. Last month, I was taken off the medication I was on, anti-depressants and stuff. And also dropped from weekly therapy to fortnightly. Even when all this happened, you know, the whole 'affair' revelation. I didn't need the tabs again, and my therapist signed me off to come here, even thought it was a good idea to do it. I think that's pretty good," Brooke said bashfully.

Emily got up and grabbed another bottle and opened it, topping them all up. "Oh, my God, that's excellent news… that is amazing, and that just goes to show the character you are and the strength you have," she said sincerely, and clinking all of their glasses.

"Now strip poker," Brooke said, laughing to them all.

"I told you all lesbians are perverts," said Nat to Emily, causing Chloe and Brooke to feign hurt feelings.

Luckily, moments later they were all laughing together and attempting to move on from the recent revelations.

<u>Chapter Fifteen</u>

Brooke woke up sweating from another nightmare. She tried to calm her breathing, looking at the time. It was three forty-seven, and she'd left at a little after one. The only thing she hated about summer was the stupidly early mornings, knowing she wouldn't get back to sleep, as the sun was starting to creep into the van. She sighed heavily and grabbed her hoodie and iPad, going out to the kitchen and switching the kettle on. She slipped her feet into her slipper booties and opened her patio doors, taking in the sky, which was changing colours over the water.

"Couldn't sleep either?" Chloe said, whispering over to Brooke.

"Hey, what are you doing? It's not even four a.m.," she said, noticing the girl at her canvas painting.

"Back atcha. What you doing up at this time?" she asked, leaning on her balcony so she could speak quietly.

Brooke smiled slightly "True. I had a bad dream." She cursed herself for the last comment. Why the hell had she said that? She sounded like a child, not a grown ass woman. Causing her to feel stupid, but before she had even realised, Chloe was there whispering to open the door.

"What are you doing?" Brooke asked, opening the door.

"Gosh, it's chilly this time in the morning. I'm making sure you're okay. Oh great, kettle has just boiled.

You like hot chocolate?" she asked, holding up the mint aero and galaxy varieties to Brooke.

"You don't need to do this," Brooke said.

"Oh, I'm sorry I missed the part you asked me to? Seriously, do we have to do this every time we talk? I won't be doing it after tomorrow as I won't be here, so it doesn't matter does it?" Chloe asked.

Brooke just looked at the girl, who had her long dark hair pulled up in a high ponytail. Her hair was still severely straight, and she was wearing a pair of checked pyjama bottoms, a fitted white v neck t-shirt and a thick hotel style robe, which was opened. "Mint please," Brooke said and walked off, leaving her to it. She walked back on to her veranda and picked up her kindle, continuing to read it and lying partially on the garden furniture.

Chloe came back out, shutting the doors behind her and handing her a cup of hot chocolate with a couple of mini marshmallows floating on the top. She put a plate with some cookies on the table too, handing one to Brooke and keeping one for herself.

"Thanks. Bit late or early for sugar isn't it?" Brooke laughed.

"It's never too late or early," she said. Chloe sat on the same couch facing Brooke's body with her knees up in front of her, allowing her to rest the hot drink there. Taking a bite of her cookie she asked, "So what was the dream about?"

"Oh, nothing really, it's fine," she said, taking a bite of the cookie and resting her head back on the chair. She looked out to the oranges being introduced to the scenic morning sky. Listening to the very faint chirps of the birds starting to awaken, she realised that there was no other noises around them. Chloe just sat listening and looking out to the other side of the sky and didn't push her, which made Brooke feel something she hadn't felt for a long time. That made her feel trust...and even a little wanted...like someone cared, and was bothered about her. More importantly, it made her feel like she could and wanted to speak about it, rather than just being told to go back to sleep or get up and go downstairs. "I have them frequently. I see the guy's face, and he comes up to me with a gun. I try to fight him and scream and shout, but I'm stuck and I can't make any sound. He always points the gun to my face, only to show me a baby he is holding, and he turns and points the gun to the baby instead. That's when I wake up. I generally can't get back to sleep, or maybe I don't want to," she said distantly, before taking another sip of her hot chocolate "Thanks for the drink, it's just what I needed. I must get some, it's lovely," she said.

"I know it's not the same, and I hope you don't think I'm speaking out of turn, but you can still be a mum. Granted you won't be able to carry, but one positive of being a lesbian is there's two chances for carrying," she said, smiling sadly. "Or you could adopt. There are so many children that need care, love and attention in this world," she added. "I'm sorry you had a bad dream, and I'm incredibly sorry this terrible thing happened to you," she said as her eyes watered.

"Hey, you're supposed to be here picking me up," Brooke said, forcing a smile and slapping Chloe's leg playfully.

"I don't know if I can though," she said. The words seemed to have a deeper meaning and Brooke didn't know what that was. She would put that away for later to analyse.

"So did you get him? Is he still on the run or is he in prison?" Chloe asked seriously.

"He's dead. Mitch shot him and he didn't survive."

"Oh right, good," she said, nodding thoughtfully.

"Where were you shot?"

"Sorry?"

"Where abouts? Where did the bullet go?" she confirmed looking into Brooke's eyes.

"Erm, here," she pointed to her side. "And came out here," she pointed to her back. "Nobody's ever seen it. Only me," she said distantly again.

"What do you mean nobody's seen it? Surely your…people, must have seen it?" Chloe said.

"No, we were due to be going on holiday, which obviously got cancelled. I couldn't walk, the doctors fixed it and then it was taped up. I stopped swimming and started running more regularly. Obviously, when I was able to do so, and well I guess Maria was getting what she needed elsewhere. As time went on, I didn't want her to see it. I remember having had the dressing off for a full six weeks and she had still never seen it. It made me get incredibly paranoid and self-conscious that I just made an effort to get unchanged or showered when she wasn't around or was in another room. She wanted to go on holiday and I refused. I didn't want to be in a bikini, although she thought it would help the recovery. Martin, my therapist agreed, but nobody had ever got me through that initial time. I don't know how to describe it, but I guess that initial introduction to a new part of me, that was a constant reminder of the part of me that was taken away. They replaced what should have been a beautiful part of me with this horrible, disgusting part of me," she said, wiping a tear away.

Chloe discreetly wiped away the fallen tear from her own face. She didn't know what to say. What do you say to someone going through this? What should she say? 'Oh I'm sure it's not that disgusting? Or 'oh it will get better with time?' Of course it wouldn't, and she felt so completely inadequate. She sighed inwardly, punching herself for not filling the silence. "I'm sorry, Brooke," was all she could muster up. "I wish I could take it all away, I really do," she added, rubbing her shoulder compassionately.

***

"No way! She's a *bitch*, and she completely trashed that relationship. She cheated for God's sake. Seriously, you have completely gone down in my estimation," Chloe scoffed.

"Yes, but she felt unloved and like she was not having any attention paid to her, it's no wonder. Look at the way she has treated her in the therapy session, she's awful," Brooke responded.

"OH…*MY* GOD, are you kidding me?" Chloe said aghast.

Brooke started laughing and threw the pillow to her face. "Jesus, the irony of it," she said, removing it again. "Stop looking at me like that." She hit Chloe with the pillow from the corner sofa they were laying on. Brooke was lying along one end with her feet resting over the top and Chloe was lying at the other end. "Okay, yes. Granted, I get your point. I guess I really struggle to move away from how HOT she looked in flash dance and clearly can't see anything bad said about her. I must add though, Tina did ignore her, and she was too busy with other stuff. Do you disagree?" Brooke said, pointing to the L word TV show which was playing on the TV in front of them.

"I do disagree, yes. You can't start looking elsewhere when it gets stale. You work at it. You don't fuck about with people's feelings and lives. In actuality, Bette was just as busy and preoccupied. But the reality of it is, life gets in the way. It won't be hearts and flowers all the time. You have to work at it. But that wouldn't make good TV, would it?" Chloe said, laughing.

"Okay, so we are clearly at battle on this. I'm 'team Bette' all the way and you're 'team Tina', so take them out of the equation. What's your 'team' out of the remaining cast?" Brooke said trying to redirect the conversation.

"Team Carmen and Team Alice," Chloe responded. "How about you?"

"Team Marina all the way. God that accent. I mean seriously? I just wanted to go rescue her. Don't get me wrong, I was devastated that she wasted time on Jenny, but yeah, I'll forgive her," Brooke said smirking.

"Oh my word, Nat's right, you Lesbos are perverts," Chloe said.

"Excuse me, correct me if I'm mistaken, but are you not a 'Lesbo?' as you so eloquently put it," she said back to her smirking.

Chloe lifted her ringing phone up to Brooke, "*This*…this is normal ringtones," she grinned. "Hey, how goes it? I'm next door…NO. Oh my God, are you for real? I have a routine, regardless how fucked I am. Plus, I was kinda tripping over the whole sale thing, so I got up and painted. Shortly after, Brooke came onto her balcony, also couldn't sleep, and so now we are watching movies in her lounge. Nope. No. Nothing. NOOOOO. Yes, I will be back now and get the kettle on. Is everyone up? Okay cool. Who wants brekkie? Okay, yeah for sure. I'll ask her now," she said, looking over to Brooke rolling her eyes. "She's a grown ass woman, I can't force her. Oh dear God, I will ask her. If she says no you can come and drag her over yourself, K? Great, see you in a sec. See ya," she said, hanging up.

"So what are you forcing me into? And what was it sex or kissing they thought we were doing?" she said seriously.

"Hey look, they will just expect it is all. I'm not there…we're both gay, it's really no big deal. I'm sorry if they have offended you," Chloe said.

"On the contrary, I'm….well, I guess I'm kind of flattered," she said shyly.

"Brooke?" There was silence. "Don't worry, it doesn't matter. Look, they want you to come over for breakfast before we go on the all dayer. We need to line our stomachs, and I need to go as it's me cooking. You coming?" Chloe asked, standing up.

Brooke wondered what Chloe was going to say. Although, a big part of her knew it was not a good idea. "Well, I don't really know if it's a good idea today, since I already crashed last night."

"We all want you there, so come. What are you gonna do instead? Stick around here all day alone? Come on, come get brekkie, something substantial as opposed to the cookies we've had," she said while smiling.

<u>Chapter Sixteen</u>

"I can't believe you guys have talked me into this again," Brooke said downing her third shot. "I mean seriously, it's not even 3p.m.," she said, holding up the empty glass squeamishly, looking at the girls who seemed to be taking it in their stride. "I mean, Carla, what the hell? How can you do this again? Especially after last night?"

"The joys *and* irritation of Carla. First to fall, first to say I love you, first to crash and first to start again. She's like a teenage drinking machine," Nat said to Brooke.

"So, how is my Mitchell? You speak to him about me yet?" Carla said smiling. "How did you meet him?"

Natalie and Chloe looked at each other and then Brooke. "Um we work together. More importantly, the first thing you should know, is his name isn't Mitch," she said, grinning at Carla.

"What? You called him Mitch," she said confused.

"Yeah. Sam Mitchell. We all call him Mitch," she said. "So how do you guys all know each other?" Brooke asked trying to avoid getting back into the story she had already relived the night before.

"Well, Nat and I went to school together," Chloe said. "Then I went off to Uni, and she went travelling around Asia and we lost contact. A few years later, we got back in touch and at the time, Nat was seeing Emily's brother and Emily and Carla were friends. To cut a long story short, Nat was out with these two, and I bumped into her on my way from a blind date." She stopped as they all chimed, "a horrific blind date," and began laughing.

"Anyways, I stayed with them, grabbed a beer, and I guess the rest as they say is history. That was what eight years ago, right?" she looked at them.

"Yeah must have been," Carla added.

"Wow, so how old are you all then?" she asked. She had put them all around her age, but that didn't quite seem right.

"Chloe and I are thirty-three, Carla and Ems are 30," Nat said to her. "How about you? How old are you?" she said, taking another mouthful of her beer.

"Twenty-nine. I'll be thirty in a few weeks," she said distantly, taking another drink trying not to think about her impending birthday.

"Still a baby compared to us old farts," Chloe said, holding her drink up and noticing the saddened face.

"Not that you look older in any way, but I did think you were older than that. You kind of ooze that maturity I guess," Carla said.

"Oh my God, Carla, that's the most positive insult I have ever heard," Nat said, reprimanding her.

"What? No! I didn't mean to be offensive. Maybe it's just because she sounded so adult-like with a grown up relationship and everything all sorted and that," Carla added. She was suddenly aware of Chloe, Natalie and Emily's glare just as the realisation set in of what she had said.

"Fuck, I'm sorry. I didn't mean it..." Carla said, clearly upset.

"Hey, it's okay. You don't need to keep pussy footing around me okay? It is what it is. I can't change the past, so I have to deal with it. The sooner people act normal and stop worrying what they can and can't say, then I will be able to ease myself into a sense of normality again," Brooke said softly. "I'm sorry, I didn't mean to put a dampener on things.," she said sadly. "Look, thanks so much for the kindness and hospitality, but I'm not really feeling it anymore. I'm going to leave you guys to it. I'm sorry," Brooke said again, and ran off before they had an opportunity to do or say anything.

***

"Chlo, it's not your fault. She's obviously just had a lot go on in a very short space of time. Don't feel bad. Like she said, she doesn't need babysitting, and she can't have people keep pussy footing around her to further enhance the fact that everything in her life has just crumbled. Look, she probably just felt normal for a short period, and then people are like 'sorry this and sorry that' and wary of what they can and can't say, you know? That must be fucking hard for anyone. She's in the middle of nowhere, out of her comfort zone, and will just need some time to herself to assess things. Ultimately, that's why she would have booked this. It's nobody's fault, so just give her some time and she'll be fine," Nat said.

Nat was right. Travelling had completely matured her younger self. She had become so wise, and always knew the right things to say and how to make sense of everything. Unfortunately, it didn't stop Chloe feeling completely shitty about the whole thing. The alcohol consumption had made her feel the emptiness of Brooke leaving. What the fuck was she doing? She couldn't be doing this. Chloe picked up her phone and went to the messages.

Hey you, long time no speak. Fancy meeting up one night this week? Dinner at mine? Cx.

"Who are you texting?" Emily asked her. "Are you texting Brooke?"

"What? No. I don't have her number. I only met her two days ago. No, not important. Another drink?" she asked them, leaving without getting an answer.

"What's her problem?" Carla said, huffily.

Nat and Emily looked at each other, knowing full well what her problem was. Chloe's phone went off and Nat picked it up showing the notification to Emily. "Unbelievable. Penny! What the fuck is Chloe playing at?" Emily said to them.

Nat put the phone back down before Chloe returned. "Thanks. Your phone went off," she said, taking a big gulp of her drink.

Chloe was basically just topping up from the night before, and she knew it. She also knew texting Penny was a stupid arse thing to do, but being attracted to a girl with this many problems was much more of a stupid arse thing to do! She picked up her phone and opened the message.

Hey sexy. Yes, it's been a very long time. I do believe it was about 3 months ago when I had the pleasure of a quick fuck in Flames? I can make time for you any day this week. When are you thinking? Px.

Shit, she hated the crudeness of this girl. Why oh why had she texted her? Chloe sighed heavily.

"Regretting it already, huh?" Nat whispered to Chloe.

"I'm fine, Nat. Okay? I'm just fine. Come on let's get out of here," Chloe said, downing her drink.

"And here we go again..." Nat said to the girls, downing her drink and following Chloe out of the bar.

131

<u>Chapter Seventeen</u>

Brooke had been awake since six, but she didn't want to go on the veranda this morning. She was too concerned she would bump into the girls, and she was embarrassed of how she had reacted with them all the previous day.

Putting on her bikini, Brooke threw on a pair of jean shorts and a t-shirt and locked up her caravan as quietly as she could. She didn't know why she was being so quiet since she had heard them all come in after eleven, which meant it was almost twelve solid hours of drinking. They must have been in some state if they had had three shots before three-forty p.m., which was around the time that Brooke left them.

She arrived at the boatyard at ten a.m., five minutes earlier than advised. She was actually looking forward to the surfing lesson, hoping that she was going to be alone still. "Hi, I booked a surf lesson for this morning a coup..." Brooke started to the same guy from Friday.

"Hey, Davis. How you doing? Well you'll be glad to know you are still flying solo today, which means Casey will be able to give you full attention." He looked her up and down. "I reckon a small will do," he said, grabbing a wetsuit. "Changing rooms are over there. Go get suited up and then we can grab your board and get you surfing," he said smiling, to her.

Brooke was surprised he remembered her name, as he must see people all the time. And more importantly, she hoped Casey would be kind to her. All she needed was him to be an arsehole. *Come on, Brooke, be positive and shake this bullshit off,* she thought.

Brooke put the wetsuit on, leaving it at her waist, the way Chloe had the other day. Chloe had looked cute, but also cool the way she wore it that way. But it wasn't the same with Brooke. Granted she had a toned stomach, had always liked working out, and had no choice with her job, but it was different for her. The scars were there, and they were evident when she wore it that way. Brooke gently touched the scar and sighed heavily. She rarely looked at that part of her any longer. She hated it, and it was ridiculous to think that something could hold so much weight over a person. Sighing heavily, Brooke desperately tried to diminish the negative thoughts slowly forcing their way into her mind. She pulled the suit up and zipped it all the way to the top, then grabbed her belongings and returned to the young guy.

"You look awesome," he said. "Right, all done?" he said, waiting for the nod of the head. "Awesome. Okay, lockers are over there. Feel free to put your stuff away and I'll get your board. Pink, white or blue?" he asked

"Erm, white," she said, putting her belongings away and walking back over to him. "Okay come with me." He smiled.

They walked outside and he gave her the white surfboard. "Right, you're all set. You excited?" he said kindly.

"Erm, nervous actually."

"Don't be. The surf is awesome today, and you'll love this I guarantee you. You and I are gonna be surfing buddies this summer. Yo, Case," he shouted, smiling sincerely to her.

Brooke looked over to where he had just shouted. *Shit*. Chloe was there. *Oh God*. She was cringing inside. Oh no she was coming to say hi. She was going to watch her make a fool of herself, and she didn't want to do this any longer she thought.

As Chloe walked closer, Brooke could feel the look of discomfort on her face. Brooke looked down at the sand, praying that she wouldn't feel the need to stop and chat.

Nope, clearly not that lucky Brooke thought.

"Hey," Chloe said awkwardly.

"Casey, Davis, Davis, Casey," the guy from the boatyard said, and walked off.

"Casey?" Brooke looked up to Chloe.

Chloe sighed lightly, "Chloe Casey. That's Joel. He calls everyone by their last names," she confirmed.

"But he said you were a guy?"

"He what? When?" Chloe said questioningly.

Brooke thought back. He did. She was sure. Or did he? "It doesn't matter, maybe I just assumed and seemingly he never corrected me."

"Okay. Come on, let's do this," Chloe said, walking off. "We'll go down to this part, where I'll go through all the starting points of how to get on, how to stand, where to position yourself. And then, we will get in and have a go. Okay?" Chloe said, turning back to Brooke who was walking quickly to catch up.

Really? She is going to act like we have never met? I know I was a bit abrupt to up and leave yesterday, but she doesn't need to be so rude about it, Brooke thought, sighing heavily.

"Okay, you ready to start?" Chloe asked her.

"No," Brooke stated sternly.

"Right? What's up? You need to go to the toilet or something?"

"No. Look, I don't fuck about. Life's too short, and too much has happened. Granted, I know it was a bit of a blunt exit yesterday. And you may have thought I over reacted, but I can't act like nothing's happened. I'm sorry if I've offended you. Okay? But, I guess everything just got a bit much. For a very short time, I felt ordinary. I wanted to be me again, and I was me again, but it just got a little bit too much," she said seriously.

Chloe felt awful. She hadn't wanted to hurt her. She was trying to not make her feel bad and protect herself, if she was totally honest. "Brooke, I didn't want to make you feel uncomfortable, and I am not mad at you. Why would I be? We all got it yesterday, we understood the reason behind it. I felt bad that it was my fault. But ultimately, you are paying for this lesson, and I want to make sure you benefit from it. I'm sorry that I made you feel uncomfortable."

"It wasn't your fault. It was nobody's fault. I just guess the whole weekend has probably taken its toll. And honestly, I just didn't really acknowledge that my birthday was coming up. I guess with everything else...well, I don't know, must have just swallowed it up. The alcohol, the hangover, the being out of my comfort zone with new people and in new places, then when my age was raised. I suppose the reality set in that I'm going to be alone. That for the first time in nine years, I'll not wake up with the woman that I thought I would spend the rest of my life with. But then, I had the thought of me being alone, waking up here with no family, friends, partner...nothing. I don't want to sound like I'm a serial dater, or can't be alone, because it isn't the case at all. It's a long time to be with someone, and I just need to figure out how I go on alone," she said seriously.

"I know. I apologise either way. How about we just leave it there? We had a great time with you. They all love you and were upset they might not get to see you before they leave. They were concerned they upset you. Anyways, hopefully you can see them before they go. Come on, let's teach you to surf," Chloe said, smiling.

***

"You know, a professional teacher wouldn't keep laughing at me," Brooke said, mounting the board again and shaking the water from her ears and nose.

"I'm sorry I really can't help it. You were great on the sand. You got the posture right, and you got the strength and pace right on the paddling. Granted, you were paddling on the sand, but you had the upper strength right in terms of the jumping onto the board. So when you are in here acting like you've never been taught the basics, I can't help but laugh," Chloe said, stifling it again.

"Because it's easy on the sand. In the water, it's an entirely different scenario," she said.

Chloe couldn't help but laugh again. She was straddling her board in the water as the waves were rolling under her.

"Seriously, will you stop it?" Brooke said, splashing Chloe. "You are so infuriating." She lowered her front back onto the board and started paddling away from Chloe, giving it another try. "I'm going to raise a complaint against you. You're a rubbish teacher, Casey," she shouted behind her, listening to Chloe's giggles still.

Brooke would do this if it killed her. There were ten minutes left in the lesson, so she had to pay attention. She was a total water baby and always had been. Prior to the accident, she spent five times a week at the pool. She could do this, but more importantly she *would* do this.

Brooke paddled out slowly, gently rolling over the broken waves. *Okay, so this looks like a good wave to go for.* 'Ride,' she corrected herself with the right terminology. She paid attention to it like Chloe had taught her. It had the low and the high breaks in it. It didn't look too big, but she was still a little cautious and apprehensive, so this looked okay for her. She turned around and saw Chloe facing her. She smiled a sincere smile and gave her two thumbs up. Brooke looked back and saw the wave coming, so she pointed her nose to the tip of the board, paddling deep, strong strokes into the water. She felt the foot of the board start to rise, when she heard Chloe shout, "Now!"

Brooke quickly put her palms under her shoulders, lowered her right hand, twisted her body slightly, and dug her toes into the board as she pushed up and jumped onto the board.

She was up. "Yes!" she shouted. She was up.

"Bend your knees, bend your knees," Chloe yelled.

Brooke was up, but she could already feel the unsteadiness. She bent her knees, focussing on pushing her weight onto her left foot that was in front. She was trying to bend her body and position her arms correctly to allow her to steer the board, but she was down as quickly as she got up. It felt like the longest two, maybe three seconds of her life. Brooke remembered to lean away from the board so she didn't hurt herself. She remembered the advice from Chloe about going under the water, and covered her head, holding her nose as she started to surface. Brooke pulled herself back onto the board. She hadn't surfed as such, but she stayed upright, and she was completely captivated by the whole thing. And for the first time in a long time, she felt in control and happy, even if it was only for a matter of seconds.

"Hey you, that was awesome," Chloe said, paddling next to Brooke and high-fiving her. "You did great," she added animatedly.

"Well, I didn't stay up too long, but it felt great," Brooke said happily.

"Most people wouldn't do that on the first lesson, Brooke," Chloe said. "You gonna try again?" she added.

"Ahhh, I'm sure you're just saying that. No, I'm good. The lesson is over, and I kind of want to end on a high. It's been a while since I've had something to feel good about, so I want to leave now. I can keep practicing, have some more lessons maybe and go from there. Thanks for the lesson. But why didn't you tell me that you were the instructor?" Brooke asked.

"Well you didn't ask. I asked if you wanted to learn and you didn't seem keen. Had you let me know, I would have told you it was me and advised that you didn't need to pay. I would be able to do it for you outside of my teaching hours, for nothing," she said.

"Yes, this is true. I felt pretty stupid, and saw that you were an avid surfer so I decided I didn't want you to make fun of me. So I kept it quiet. I didn't think for a moment it would have been you teaching me. Anyways…," she said, leaving it to hang in the air. "So, do you only instruct on a Sunday? You didn't leave and come down to do it yesterday." Brooke asked.

"Do you really think that I would make fun of you? I would never make fun of anyone, unless it was a mutual banter-esque thing. I would never purposely make someone feel like shit though, that's not my style. I love teaching surfing, and I love surfing. I bought my place when my ex and I split up as a bit of a 'go to'...a 'hideaway' I suppose, and one of the first things I did was learn to surf, and I loved it. Now, I love sharing that thrill, passion and love with others. Yeah, it's not for everyone, I get that, but I want people to buy into it like I do. I wouldn't make fun of someone for trying something, whether they were amazing or crap," Chloe sighed. "Sorry, Brooke. I don't mean to be rude, but please don't judge me. I could almost understand if you had known me longer than a few days, but it isn't fair to tar everyone with the same brush. The reason I didn't do it yesterday, is because I knew the girls were up for the weekend, and because the kids' lesson is nine a.m. and I knew I wouldn't be in any fit state. I wouldn't risk the safety of anyone, but least not children in my care, so they got a cover for me. Otherwise, I do it every weekend at nine and ten thirty Saturdays and ten thirty Sundays." She continued, smiling small, "We should probably get out, I need to go and say bye to the girls before they head off."

"I'm pretty shit at all of this, as you've now realised. I don't know what's got into me, and I don't know why I have suddenly felt so sorry for myself. You're right, I shouldn't have judged you, and I had absolutely no right. Thanks for today. I loved it, and I really hope I can get the same out of it that you do. Are you not leaving with the girls then?" Brooke said, paddling back to the beach.

"No, I'm going straight to work from here in the morning," Chloe said, paddling alongside her. "I generally tend to do that so I can make the most of a full weekend."

Chapter Eighteen

Brooke needed to call Kate and Jo. She knew they would love this place, plus they would be happy to hear her buzzing, as the adrenaline was completely flowing through her body. She grabbed an apple from the fridge and went to the veranda to call her friends, hearing the door knock. "Maybe not, then," she said, turning back to the door.

"Hey, what are you guys doing here?" Brooke said to Carla, Nat and Emily.

"We weren't going to leave without saying goodbye," Emily said, walking in.

"Are you okay?" Nat asked.

"Yeah, I'm good. I apologise for yesterday, you guys. I am good today though. So, you leaving now?" Brooke asked.

"Yes, and no need to apologise. We had a ball with you this weekend, and we will get back up before you leave. If not, you need to come across and see us one weekend. We're only an hour away, so you can totally do that, right? Also, we have got you a gift," Emily said, moving forward with a bag.

"Oh, you guys, I didn't ge..."

Nat didn't give her a chance to finish, holding up her hand, before letting Emily continue.

"Well, it's only a small token. We saw it and thought of you. We hope it makes you smile and think of the positives," Emily finished.

Brooke opened the bag and pulled out a metal picture, with the words written in different directions: *Life is short. Break the RULES, FORGIVE quickly, KISS slowly, LOVE truly, LAUGH uncontrollably, and NEVER REGRET anything that made you SMILE.*

"I love it. It's perfect. I *will* get through this and then when I do, you guys can all come down to Oxford and visit me in my new home and see this hanging up," she said, smiling genuinely. She hugged Emily, Nat and Carla, making promises to see them soon and to try and set up Carla and Mitch. Feeling a pang of emptiness, she closed the door to the girls, wishing them all a safe journey. Biting in to her apple, she picked up the phone to call Kate again.

"Hey, how are you? We were getting worried," she said concerned.

"Sorry, Hun. Been a bit of a mental couple of days actually. So how are things? What have you pair been up to this weekend?"

"Not much. Jo worked late and went out last night. I've just been relaxing really. Erm, Maria and Paula came round yesterday. Paula was being sheepish, which annoyed me a little bit. Maria was acting like nothing had changed, which to be fair, pissed Jo off and she told her so. They asked us round for dinner to celebrate, the weekend after next. Jo said no, we were coming up to see you, and then booked the weekend off," she laughed. "Anyway, enough about us, what you been doing?" Kate said to her friend.

"I'm good. I've been surfing this morning," Brooke said, waiting for Kate's reaction.

"What the hell? You've been surfing? Where did you do that? Oh my God, check you out. Did you like it? Oh, please be careful. There was that film. The true story about that girl who lost her arm to a shark. Oh, and that film we used to watch, what was it called with the hot girl…Ohhhh Blue Crush. That was about surfing and she had an accident. Shit, I'm sorry. I am making this all negative. I'm sorry, I'm completely rubbish aren't I?" Kate said, sadly.

"Yes, you did rant a little about all the negatives, but I know it's only because you care," Brooke said.

"So did you do anything today? How was Friday night? You never called me back," she said.

"Oh I know I'm so sorry, you got some time to spare? If so, I'll make a brew, get comfy and fill you in on it all?" Brooke asked.

Brooke and Kate spoke for over an hour, and she went through every last piece of information, even down to the mini break down yesterday. She filled in her and Jo, who had returned home half way through the conversation.

"It sounds like you're having fun, kid," Jo said happily. "I'm genuinely happy for you. I know it won't happen overnight, but I think you're heading in the right direction. Continue with the surfing lessons, because every time you talk about it, you can hear the enthusiasm in your voice. I think you will need something like this," Jo added.

"I know. Chloe told me this morning that she had bought her place next door as a bit of a hideaway when she split up with her ex-girlfriend. She put all of her time and energy into surfing, and now she has the most amazing passion and love for it. I really hope that I get the same. I literally stood up for a second or two, but I was actually moving. So technically I was surfing," she said, excitably. "Sorry, I know I keep going on about it," she said solemnly.

"Hey, don't be so stupid, we love hearing you like this. We hoped this is what you would achieve from going there. We didn't expect it to be so quick, so another major positive. We love hearing you happy," Jo said.

"So, ermm, what's Chloe like? She seems to have taken you under her wing," Kate said.

"Yeah, she has. I genuinely had a great time on Friday, and as I said before, it's the first time I've ever spoken about the accident. And she was great yesterday morning. She's nice, and she's been nice to me, but she leaves tomorrow," Brooke said.

"Why, what did she do yesterday morning?" Jo asked seriously.

"Oh, I woke up after having a nightmare around three thirty a.m. and decided to go and watch the sunrise. I knew I wouldn't get back to sleep and she was up and painting," she said, getting interrupted.

"Painting?" said Kate.

"Yes, she's an artist and an art director. She couldn't sleep either. When I said I was up because of a nightmare, she came over and brought hot chocolate. We just sat up talking about the nightmare, then watched some L wo... erm some TV," she said quietly.

"So, she looked after you when you were feeling low? That's really nice," Jo said.

"You watched the L Word with a cute lesbian?" Kate said. "Ow! Seriously, you have got to STOP doing that," Kate said angrily to Jo.

"I've never said she was cute, Kate. Really are we going to do this every conversation? It's only been two weeks. Nine years of my life lost, and after two weeks,

144

no. She's been a nice person and restored my faith in the human race, but that's it, okay?" Brooke said.

"Babes, we care about you, but you will have to ignore my lovely partner. She just wants to see you happy again. She isn't trying to force you into things, but we love you, and you are very special to both of us. You are one in a million and deserve someone who will treat you that way, and we just want to see you happy. Because regardless of these last two weeks, you haven't been happy in a long time. And for a slight moment in this conversation we have been able to hear the old you back again. Don't get annoyed with her, she loves you. We both do. I'll have *another* word with her, and let her know that it's STILL TOO SOON, right Kate?" she said.

"I'm sorry. I didn't mean to upset you. I won't bother saying it anymore," she said sadly.

Jo intervened and changed the subject. "So, what are you up to today then, lovely?" she asked.

"Oh, nothing. I have started a new book. I'm going to get something to eat, read my book for a bit on the balcony, and then relax I guess. I am going to go and do a bit of sightseeing tomorrow too, so have a bit of a chilled one I guess. I want to go into town and get a dongle so I can watch some movies since I brought some DVD's, but when I had a look yesterday I didn't really fancy anything. Plus, I can watch some box sets then as well," Brooke said.

"What are you going to eat? Have you got food there?" Kate said concerned, causing Brooke to laugh.

"I'm not that bad, Kate," she scorned. "Yes, I have a few microwave meals in the freezer, so I will have one of them. And then I am going to go to asda when I'm out and get some more bits that I can freeze. I will pick up a chicken to roast, and get a couple days of food from that. Plus, I'll get some soup and frozen baguettes to live off," she laughed.

Eventually, the friends said their goodbyes, leaving Brooke feeling good. Really good in fact. She'd really enjoyed catching up with them, smiling as she recalled the day's events. She picked up the picture from the girls, smiling as she read the words again, and placed it on top of the TV. She wanted to be reminded of the girls she had met and the words. She needed to start fighting again, she needed to become her again, and she would. She knew she would. Something had transitioned in her. She couldn't quite explain it, but she felt the fight again. For the first time in a long time, Brooke felt sad in a good way, and suddenly there was a little bit of hope for her.

***

Brooke got changed into a tracksuit. Even though it was still quite warm out, she felt the need to get into big oversized clothes. She was looking through the DVD's she had brought with her, trying to decide what she should watch. She wished she had downloaded some before she left. She didn't think for a moment that she wouldn't have WIFI. Seriously, who doesn't have it these days? Between that and the lack of signal, she was struggling completely. She was glad she had downloaded a load of books before she left, but they wouldn't take long to get through at this rate.

Brooke turned to the lesbian section of the movies she had brought with her, searching through them, trying to decide which one to watch, stopping as she heard the faint knock on the door.

Too Soon

"Hey," Chloe said, as Brooke opened the door.

"Hi? Is….everything okay?"

"Yeah, yeah all good. Apart from the silence now that the girls have gone," she smiled. "I've made a roast dinner, since I was craving one. I have made enough for you, and I remembered you saying you didn't like to cook. But that you loved roast dinners so, um, I figured, after your surfing lesson this morning you may have built up a bit of an appetite. Sorry, I'm waffling. I wondered if you wanted to come across and eat together, maybe watch another couple L words. If not, it's fine. I will plate it up and bring it over, and you can have it here." Chloe asked.

Brooke was looking at Chloe, and watching her as she was fidgeting. "Is it a date?" Brooke asked seriously, unable to control her mouth.

"What? God no! Erm... sorry, I didn't mean to sound rude then. Look, forget it. I just wanted to make sure you ate. I'm sorry, Brooke. I'll bring you over a plate," she said leaving.

"Sorry, Chloe. Wait?" she grabbed her arm. "I'm sorry. I'm so fed up with everyone insinuating things because we are both gay. I just saw you fidgeting and…well, clearly I jumped to conclusions and didn't want to be in a difficult position," Brooke said, sighing and shaking her head.

"Brooke, I like you a lot. You're fun. But I've been where you are. And truth be known, I've avoided relationships for the past three years because of it. I wouldn't put you or me through it, and I know you are *nowhere* near ready yet, even if I were interested. Likewise, the girls left giving their views on you and me, and honestly, that's the reason I was fidgeting. I felt like you needed a friend, and just because we are both lesbians, I don't see why we can't be that. That's all there was to the invite. I'm gone tomorrow until next week, but it's annoying me that everything feels so uncomfortable just because of other peoples' assumptions. I mean, it's infuriating. I don't feel like I can treat you the same way I'd treat Carla, Ems or Nat, because of what people are assuming," said Chloe.

Brooke grabbed her arm and pulled her inside. "Okay, no more. Neither of us. We have got on really well. I want to continue surfing and I'd like to do that with you. Plus, I want to be friends so we can chill and go out and have a laugh and stuff, the way normal friends do. So here, take these?" she said, handing her a couple bottles of wine. "So...moving forward, that's it. We say it like it is, we have fun, and we aren't afraid to ask each other out or to do things." She smiled.

"I have to drive tomorrow, so I hope you're planning on drinking these, but yes, I'll raise a glass to that. Come on, get the DVD's, lock up and I'll meet you over there," Chloe said smiling.

***

"What are you thinking?" Chloe said, handing her another glass of wine.

"I am thinking that I can't remember the last time I ate such a good roast. That I feel sick because I ate so much. That I'm coming here every Sunday, and that Jo would love you," Brooke said, laying on the sofa watching the L Word and sipping more of her wine.

"Is Jo your ex?" Chloe asked.

"God no. No, Jo is Kate's girlfriend. They're coming up in a couple weeks, and I'm so excited for them to see it. Jo loves to cook, and she's the reason I'm here," Brooke said, smiling off into the distance. "Kate helped me pack everything in the house up before I came here, and then Jo turned up and made this amazing meal. Nearly a bottle of tequila and a few bottles of champagne later, we got to watching The Holiday. I love it, have you seen it?" she said, rolling her eyes.

"Yes, I love it. But I love any Christmas movies or chick flicks. Combined, well its perfection," Chloe said.

"Well, she thought I should do what they do. Anyways, after looking into it, the three of us, in our drunken states, had booked this place. Interestingly, we originally looked into a cabin just like this," she said, taking in the gorgeous surroundings.

"No way? You would have been next door, but one to me on the other side. Clearly we were destined to meet," Chloe said smiling. "Here's to new friendships," she said, holding her glass up to Brooke.

Chloe hoped she didn't say too much. But as Brooke said, they needed to stop over thinking everything based on what their friends were saying. Let them get on with it, she thought as she picked up her beeping phone advising of a text coming in. Looking at the screen smiling, Chloe assumed it was the girls, finally remembering to text they had got home. She squirmed when she saw Penny's name.

"Problem?" Brooke said, giving her a sideways glance.

"Ermmmm, no…yes, probably," she sighed.

"Well, I figure I owe you about six sessions over these last few days, so spill. I'll get us another drink," Brooke said, taking the glasses to Chloe's fridge.

"Oh. Seriously it's nothing, and it's stupid really," Chloe said, before noticing the annoyed look on Brooke's face. "Alright, already!"

"So, I am, um, friends with this girl Penny. I met her a while back and, well you know? We had fun, whatever, but then she didn't let up. The girls can't bare her, think she's controlling, think she's insane, and make it known. So anyways, Saturday I texted her, pissed. Oh God, Chlo. What the fuck were you thinking?" she said to herself, putting her head in her hands.

Brooke handed her a refilled glass. "Well, you must like her if you called her. It's kind of far for a booty call, isn't it?" she said, watching her.

"Yes," Chloe said, running her fingers through her hair, closing her eyes tightly. "You're right. But I was drunk, and I felt a bit bad for you after you ran out. Sorry, I'm not trying to put this on you by any means. So I was pissed, and I figured it would be a good idea to arrange a night out. But Nat went mental at me and then of course, it spurred me on more. I was annoyed and agitated over the whole 'lesbians can't be friends' thing. People think that I'm gonna hit on you and fuck you up further just because we're both gay," she said, sighing, before realising she had said too much. Chloe sighed heavily, "Jesus, and you think you are bad at this? I made that all sound like it was your fault and that wasn't the case at all, so I apologise. But they all make it like I'm some kind of predator and I fuck with people's lives. I never had any intention of that with you. Jesus, I don't have that intention with anyone. I am always completely open and honest with people, but it's like I intentionally go out to fuck with people's heads. Sorry, I guess I've had too much to drink," she said, taking another drink.

"Please stop apologising Chlo. Listen, do you like this girl? Or did you do it as a response to your friends questioning your motives with me? Or do you just want a quick, no strings shag?" Brooke said bluntly.

Chloe choked on her drink. "Wow, blunt or what?" she said, wiping her mouth.

"Look, Chloe, if this last month has taught me anything, it's that things aren't always what they appear, and clearly life's too short. The last nine years have flown past, gone in the blink of an eye, and that's a third of my life! Gone like that," she said, stopping and clicking her finger and thumb in a snap. "Your friends will be looking out for you, and seemingly me. But seriously, you're what? Thirty-four? If you only want this girl for a quick fumble and she likes you, then don't do it. If she's in it for the same, go for it. At the risk of sounding completely crude, if she's a good lay, you are both single and on the same page, why not? But don't fuck about with her. More importantly, don't fuck about with you," she said.

"What's that mean? And thirty-three not thirty-four," Chloe retorted.

"Okay, answer me seriously. Is this the only girl you...well, have fun with, whatever? I don't know the terminology these days since it's been a while, and clearly I'm out of practice," Brooke said.

"Erm, I don't really know how to answer that. It makes me sound like I sleep around, and I don't. Well I don't think I do. Not in the way it's sounding anyhow."

"I'm not trying to trip you up, just trying to make a point."

"Well, if I like someone then I may have some fun. But I make it clear I don't do relationships," Chloe said seriously.

"Okay, so she's potentially not the only one. Yet you made contact with her. *Her* specifically? Your friends made a statement, something which you apparently didn't like. You were being reactive, and it seems to me from what you're saying you have specifically gone to this girl. Either to piss your friends off or just as a reactive action to something that's happened," Brooke said seriously.

Chloe was analysing what she was saying, annoyed that she clearly had a point. How could she not? Chloe wouldn't have been cringing when she responded to her otherwise. "Okay, so why was I being reactive? What's the point on that?" Chloe asked somewhat confused, and somewhat fearful of what the reasons could be behind why she had done it. More importantly, why she was so reactive, seconds after Brooke had left?!

"Hun, I'm your friend, not a shrink. You need to either work that out by yourself, or you need to give Martin a call," she laughed.

"Who the hell is Martin?" she questioned.

"My shrink," she said, smiling again.

"Oh? Seriously, there are so many names! Do you really have a shrink?" Chloe asked inquisitively.

"Well, I guess it depends on what your definition of a shrink is? If it's a psychiatrist, then no I don't. If it's any form of 'head' doctor, then yes, I go to a therapist. I think I mentioned that the other night," she said. "Anyways, enough about me, what are you going to do about this girl then? If you don't mind me asking?" Brooke said.

"No, I don't, and honestly I don't know. I know she's not wanting to be anything more, so it's not like I'm leading her on or messing about with her. But…" Chloe sighed heavily. Ohhhh…I shouldn't have done it, end of story. I'll have to sort it when I get home tomorrow night," Chloe sighed. "So what are you up to the next couple of days?"

"I have made a plan of a few things I fancy going and seeing and doing. I want to spread it out over the next couple of weeks though. I'm probably going to relax tomorrow, as that will be my first day alone. And I'm going to go find asda again. I need some actual food, and because everything I eat goes in the freezer, I couldn't bring anything with me. That and find a phone shop. Apart from that, chilling with a book." She smiled.

"Why does all the food need to go in the freezer? And what do you need a phone shop for, is your ex giving you hassle?" she asked concerned.

"No, no not at all. I want to get a dongle. Having no Wi-Fi is killing me, and I want to have access to more movies and TV shows so I can get on Netflix et cetera. The food is all in the freezer because they're ready-to-eat meals. I told you I can't cook." She smiled.

"Oh my God, they are so unhealthy, full of salt and sugar and who knows what else. You should really learn to cook, at least some basics. I love to cook, and I'll happily teach you some things if you like?" Chloe offered.

"Hmmm, maybe. We shall see," Brooke said reluctantly. "Look, it's late and you have to be up early and travel tomorrow, so I should get going," she added.

"I know, but I was just relaxing and enjoying some normality to try and ignore the prospect of work. Listen. On a different note, take this," Chloe said, walking over to a drawer. "Here is my Wi-Fi password. I will leave it on this week, and you will be able to get it from next door. It's really pointless of you paying for a dongle when you can just use mine." She smiled.

"No, Chlo. I couldn't do that," Brooke said.

"Why not? It's being paid for anyhow. If I didn't have a password, you wouldn't know and would just get on anyways. So please just do it?"

"Thanks, that's incredibly kind of you. I tell you what. To thank you when you get back, I'll treat you to dinner? I won't cook, don't worry. But I'll order in or take you out to say thanks. If you fancy it, that is?"

"You don't have to do that, it's no biggie, honestly."

"I didn't say I had to. I want to. And…thanks for today, *and* this weekend. Seriously, it was great meeting you and your friends, and now I can look forward to seeing a friendly face again next weekend," she said smiling.

"You too, Brooke. Another surfing lesson I hope," Chloe said, waving bye as she watched the girl leave her place.

Chapter Nineteen

Brooke woke up late with a fuzzy head, rolling over looking at the alarm clock. *Wow, nine twenty. I am having some decent lay ins these days*, she thought. Smiling as the idea hit her; she got out of bed and freshened up in the bathroom before getting changed and leaving the van hurriedly.

"Hey you, must have been good if you're back again? Casey's not back until the weekend though I'm afraid," said Joel.

"It's okay, I'm not here for Casey. But you're right, I really enjoyed it. I was wondering if I could hire a board for an hour though. I want to keep at it whilst the lesson yesterday is fresh in my mind. I'm not going to lie, I'm not holding out much faith without a teacher, but I figured I could try." She smiled.

"Best way to do it, as you say it's still fresh in your mind. You can hire a board for sure, go out there and give it a go. I'd say if you are going out alone, stick to this area," pointing out an area to her. "See how you go, and if there's any problems you can't overcome then lemme know when you come back. I'll be able to tell you where and why you're going wrong. Then you can work on that next time you have a go," he said.

Brooke suited up and grabbed the board, heading off to where she had been directed. "Wish me luck," she said.

"Good luck, Davis," he winked, and went back to measuring a couple of kids with a board each.

Brooke looked out at the waves, recalling everything that Chloe had said the day before. She could feel the nerves starting to bubble inside her. "Breathe, Brooke." She breathed in deeply, running over Martin's words. *It's just a thought, a bad thought. It's the anxiety creeping in, focussing on the negativity and your fears. You can do this. What's the worst that's gonna happen? Shit dummy, why did you have to go down that road?* She shook herself off once more and made a run for it.

Brooke spent the first ten minutes paddling her board in and out of the waves. She wanted to get the confidence she had yesterday with Chloe. Not Chloe, an instructor who provides support. Right. It's time Davis. She started making deep strokes into the surf, seeing the wave start to break. She focussed on what Chloe had taught her, taking a deep breath and jumping back on the board. "Come on Brooke, bend, turn, lean, bend, turn, lean." She was up! Again for a very small amount of time, but she did it again.

"You're doing awesome, Davis. Good going," she heard the words being shouted from Joel from the shore. It was all she needed to build the confidence and give it another go.

***

Brooke was still buzzing. She felt like a total adrenaline junkie, which was so far from the truth. But more importantly, she actually felt like she was slowly taking control of her life back. She'd put all the shopping away that she had got from asda, even going as far as cooking herself a meal. Something she had actually prepared and cooked alone, no readymade meal. Granted it was only a paprika, 'roast in the bag' seasoning that she put her chicken in and roasted with some fresh salad, but in her world this was cooking, she thought.

It had been a fantastic day, which had nicely occupied her mind and allowed her to have some fun without noticing that she was alone again. Opening a bottle of red, Brooke covered the top as she placed it outside with the citronella candle. It was simply perfect she thought, as she admired the view from her decking railings. God it was incredible, and she couldn't wait until Kate and Jo came up in a couple of weeks. They really would love it.

"Hello, love. Nice evening isn't it?"

She turned to see Mr and Mrs Willis on their veranda by the side of Chloe's empty place.

"Hi? Yes, it really is, isn't it? I never knew that any part of the UK could be so…well, so relaxing and peaceful…tranquil and beautiful. I am totally in love with it," she sighed.

"Why do you think there are so many oldies here and not a lot of young people? Well, present company excluded of course," Mrs Willis said.

Brooke hadn't really noticed many people. The people she had seen, aside from Chloe, had actually been slightly older. "Well, I didn't really notice since I kind of only met Chloe," she said, turning to hear the phone alarm go, notifying her that her dinner was ready.

"Well, it's only you two, put it that way." She smiled again.

"Oh, right. Well I am here to relax and hideaway for six weeks, so I'd like to think I won't bring any trouble." She smiled again.

"You a teacher, love? And we weren't alluding to that at all. Chloe has been here for a number of years. And as you noticed, on occasion has her friends here, but she uses this place as her 'muse'. She paints, you know? She's an artist and owns her own gallery and everything. She's a very successful young woman," Mr. Willis said, pride oozing from him as if she was their very own child.

"No, not a teacher. Just on a…sabbatical. And yes, Chloe did mention that she was an artist. And I noticed her painting through the course of the weekend. She appears to be very good. Anyways, my dinner is ready. And truth be known, I'm not the greatest chef. In fact, far from it. I have had to set two alarms so I don't burn it. And it's my first attempt of cooking, so I best go get it." She smiled. "Nice talking to you both," she said meaningfully.

"Well, if you are here for that length of time, then you simply must come to us for dinner one night. And that's not a request. We'll let you know when," Mrs Willis said, nodding her head with a wag of her finger as she returned to her husband and the bench they were sharing together.

What was it with people at this place not requesting that you do things, but merely telling you that you will? She smiled inwardly, feeling intensely cherished and protected for a change.

Brooke grabbed her dinner and laptop, entering in the details of Chloe's Wi-Fi. She relaxed at finally being able to get online, and she definitely owed her a very big dinner for this.

Chapter Twenty

Brooke had spent a couple of days visiting some different areas in and around Anglesey, namely places of interest to her from a historical and cultural point of view. But she was amazed at how many more doors it opened up, and the things to see and do here. Better still, she had managed to maintain the surfing too. She was clearly not, nor ever going to be a pro, but god she was loving the buzz of it. Through her practice she had learned to stay up a lot longer now, which had equated to the revelation that she wouldn't need any more lessons, which she was made up about.

Joel and Brooke had been getting along great, having coffees after her morning surfs. He had even offered to take her out to look at a couple of boards so she could buy her own. Due to Joel working at the boatyard, he wasn't really in a position to allow her to take the board without hiring it. And in reality, Brooke didn't feel comfortable making him feel that he had to. That was theft after all. But he was incredibly cute and helpful and had 'scoped out' some decent boards for her to buy. He even offered to take her so that he could make sure they *cut it*, and agreed he would pick her up and take her to pick one of her own.

***

Brooke was waiting at the bottom of the road when she saw the old beetle pull up. She didn't really know what she'd expected to see Joel driving, but she didn't really expect this. He was a genuinely nice guy, and had really helped her out with the surfing. He often watched her and gave her helpful advice and tips when she got out of the water.

"Hey, how's it going, Davis?" he said, smiling and throwing the water bottle and empty McDonald's bag on the back seat. "Sorry for the mess. As you can see, I rarely use it," He smiled.

"Hi, no worries. Thanks for doing this. I'm so excited," she said back to him.

"Anytime. I told ya, we'll be getting you kite surfing in no time at this rate," he said matter of factly. "It's only about half an hour away and then we can grab a bite, if you have time?" Joel asked.

"Yes, of course. The least I can do is buy you lunch for taking me and helping me buy my own board, and I have no other plans. I am going to go back home, relax and watch a movie or two once we've finished. So, I have nowhere else to be than here." She smiled.

"Sounds good, I am back at work at two so we will be back with enough time for you to...*movie yourself out.*," he said, smirking back at her. "So, what brings you up here for all this time then, if you don't mind me asking?" he said, looking over to Brooke.

"Well, it's a long story, but the short version is my girlfriend left me for another woman a couple of weeks ago. One of our friends actually, so I needed some time out. An opportunity to figure me and my life out again, I suppose," she said, smiling slightly.

"Wow, sorry to hear that, chick. And what? Work is okay that you have this much time off, or are you working from home?" he said, questioningly.

"No, I am currently not working. I'm on long term sick. I am in the police force, and there was an accident, so I am currently going through therapy to work through it. Truth be known, I don't know if I want to go back into it. But I genuinely don't know what else I would do," she sighed, realizing the easiness of talking to Joel.

Brooke liked Joel a lot, because he was unassuming and easy to talk to. And she noticed how he was listening intently and completely un-judging of her and her words. To be honest, there was no reluctance with him. She was easily telling him the situation, and she didn't know if it was Joel or this place calming her enough to do that. Martin constantly told her the more you bottle it all up the harder it is to get out. He always likened it to honey. *"Brooke, if you have a bottle of honey and use it frequently, it slithers out smoothly. If you leave it, not using it so often, it hardens and is virtually impossible to get out."* She smiled at the memory of Martin and his analogies.

"You okay there? Hope I didn't offend or upset you," he said seriously.

"God no. On the contrary, I was just thinking how I'm finding it easier to speak openly about it all, and how easy I am finding it to talk to you. It's not really something I'm used to, honestly. You are clearly a positive influence on me," she said, smiling over to him.

"Hey, I'm fairly open minded, as you probably guessed. I live life as I see it and don't mess about. I guess I call a spade a spade. Life's far too short for otherwise. But I really like you, and if you want or need a friend to talk to whilst you're here, then by all means call upon me. But do me one thing, Brooke. It's all well and good escaping and thinking things through, but don't get over involved with it. Don't over think and let it drive you insane. You can think... *that's* great, and *always* helpful. It allows you to see things you never really saw before, like negatives you know? But don't dwell. *Never* dwell, because this place can be very lonely for the non-residents, and that's dangerous. But I'll stop lecturing now. This is a goooooood day for you, Davis, you wait and see," he said, drawing out the word *good,* as he pulled up and smiled to her.

***

"Oh my God, I can't believe that's my board," Brooke said excitably, looking out of the window at the board strapped to the top of Joel's Beetle.

"I told you it would be a good day. Now you wait until you first ride it. It's sweet, honestly. You will have this totally rad connection with it, and well when that happens, you won't ever love another as much as you love that sweet little lady." He smiled, taking a bite of his sandwich.

"Do you believe in fate, Joel?" she asked him seriously.

"Of course I do. Life is for the taking. Too many people are hung up on what might have been, what could have been, what will be...Why? I believe in living for the moment. If it is meant to be, the universe will make it happen. I had it all mapped out for me. My future, my destiny, who I'd marry, where I'd work. That wasn't for me...My parents aren't so thrilled by that fact, but why have me, why bring me onto this beautiful planet if you want to live your life through me? I had money...excessive amounts, a trophy wife, a FTSE 100 chasing my tail, and I didn't learn anything about life. I was miserable, and the only ones who were happy were my parents. Now, much to their dismay, I work in a boatyard. Geez, I sell surf lessons for a living, and I scrape by month to month. But you know what? I'm up each morning watching the sunrise on my board, and spend my mornings surfing before I start work. I spend the whole of sun up counting the things I'm grateful for. I thank the world for those things, the things that are good in my life. Yeah, I know people think I'm some kinda wannabe 'aussie surf boy' or a 'soap dodger,' but you know what? So what? I'm excited by life, I'm in love with life and the beauty of this planet, and I couldn't be happier. Life is my drug these days," he said sincerely. "So, in answer to your question, yes, I totally believe in fate. Why do you ask? Come on we need to leave," he said, putting his rubbish in the bin and leaving their table.

"Sure," Brooke said, following him. "I don't know. It's weird I spent two decades dreaming of the police force. Twelve months ago, I got up happy, excited, embracing my day, and looking forward to it. A month ago, whilst I was undergoing some issues in relation to work...I was okay, I was happy, I thought I was happy...I think I was happy. I waited for the love of my life to come home. I got up and made her fresh OJ's to take to work. I read recipes and tried to make her dinner, and went and shopped so she didn't need to do that on top of work. I'm not trying to make it sound like everything was on me, because it wasn't. I wasn't working, so it was only right. Everything was wonderful, again I thought. Then, two weeks ago...geez I'm at a stage where I feel I have nothing...no job, no home, no love of my life, no friends, nothing. Done! Kaput! Game over! Ya know?"

S.L. Gape

she said, turning to face him as he concentrated on the drive home.

"Yeeeesss, I'm with you so far, but guessing you aren't ending it there?" he asked, looking over when he could.

"Well, on a drunken night with friends, I booked this place. The following morning, I could honestly say I had never felt so alone. My friends were so positive about it all, and I simply couldn't say to them I'm too afraid to go. So I didn't. I muddled through. I mean I was feeling low and alone anyhow, right? So I came, but I'm changing in just a short week. I can feel myself changing, but I can't work out why. Everyone always talks about fate and, 'everything happening for a reason', but what is that reason? Why am I doing things I'd never dreamed of? Why am I pushing myself beyond my boundaries when I can't do it with the important things? Like, my life, my job? And most importantly, why the hell am I up here all alone and feel less alone than I've felt in the last twelve months?" she said questioningly.

"Wow, Davis, your heads sure been busy whilst you've been up here," Joel smiled. "Look, you're not gonna figure this all out quickly, but you know what? You've now found each and every single piece of the puzzle, and it's all about putting the pieces in the right places. Try to work on one part at a time rather than it all together, and don't force it. You can't over analyze it. Don't push too much too soon, when it's ready to be seen it will be. Keep at the surfing because I think you'll find that helps. And something else, you said you were in therapy right?" Joel asked.

"Yes, why?" Brooke responded.

"Well, if you've spent the last three, six, nine months trying to figure all this stuff out with a trained professional and haven't quite got there yet, I would put that on the back burner. Maybe the reason you weren't able to figure all the stuff with work was because there were underlying issues you were contending with. So live free, enjoy *life*, surfing, happiness and freedom, and take each day as it comes," he said honestly. "Then every so often, another piece will surely fall in to place!" He smiled, as he pulled into the car park.

"You really are incredibly deep aren't you? Thanks for today Joel, it's been great fun. You've made an incredible impact on my life already, and I feel I've made a friend for life," she said, and kissed his cheek.

"This is very true, Davis," he said, winking to her. "So, I'm gonna take the board for today so I can wax it up for you. Then, tomorrow it will be ready for you guys to get acquainted," he said, smiling a slanted grin. "Right, Davis. I gotta shoot, thanks for my lunch. I'll see you tomorrow, yeah?" He waved, and just like that he was rushing off with her board in hand.

<u>Chapter Twenty-One</u>

Brooke's alarm went off, and she rolled over groaning, looking at the alarm clock. "Oh my word, what was I thinking?" she whispered to herself.

She hated dark mornings. It was her least favourite part of winter, however, this was not a dark morning, this was a dark night. It was actually the middle of the night. She rolled back over and hid her head under the cover. She hadn't made plans, so she *could* just stay in bed and nobody would ever know. And therefore not disappointing anyone. "Argh." Why did she have to feel guilty god-dammit?

Brooke got showered and dressed before putting the Krispy Kreme's carefully into the bag. She added the polystyrene cups and lids, then the flask of coffee and fresh OJ. She checked if she needed anything else, and she could see the faint pinks and oranges beginning to appear in the distance from the lounge, and cursed herself for being late. She was never late... it was her pet peeve, she thought as she locked up and ran down to the beach. God, she hoped this was worth it.

Brooke reached the beach, and dropped the bag on the floor as she bent down with her hands on her legs. Seriously, she was a runner! How had she become so unfit in a matter of a week, her chest burning and everything? In reality, it was more than likely that she felt this way because she had sprinted the whole way down here to ensure she didn't miss the sunrise and join Joel in attempting to...'*Appreciate life and all that's good*' as he called it. Granted, this was new to her, and seriously an alarm going off before four a.m.? Sheesh…who does that? But the guy was quickly becoming her Mr. Miyagi.

Joel was clearly very trusting as he had left the boatyard open, allowing Brooke to go and retrieve her board. Appreciating the smoothness of it, she smiled to herself, then grabbed it and her bag and walked over alongside Joel to join him. "So, you said you sat on your board watching sun up, mister?" Brooke said, slapping his arm playfully.

"Davis, what are you doing here? And I am on board, it's under my butt isn't it?" he asked.

"You said this was the place to be? The thankful, worshipping place to be, I do believe? So I figured, with all your help yesterday…the least I could do was repay the favour. So…" she dipped her hands into the bag to pass over the gifts, as she noticed the slight glimmer of sun on his face, illuminating his chiseled features. "Fresh OJ…coffee, *and* doughnuts…oh, and sun up," she said, smiling partly to Joel and partly to herself as she embraced the American terminology he'd used yesterday. I hope you don't mind me coming down and intruding," she finished seriously.

"Free country, Davis. Plus, you can come join me anytime if you bring this delightful spread," he stated, as he took a mouthful of OJ and picked a doughnut out of the box.

"How can people not love this planet when you have this beauty to look at?" he said, mesmerized by the sun rising before them.

"It sure is beautiful," she murmured. She was envious of the way Joel looked at the world. Appreciative of every aspect, even the simple things in life. Brooke had never really been like that, but in this moment she felt that Joel's energy was rubbing off on her.

"So, Davis, tell me what you're thankful for. Three things, anything you want?" he said, looking over at her.

"Wow, spotlight or what?" She smiled. "Ummm well, I can't let this go unnoticed. I love sunsets. However, I'm never really normally around for sunrises, so this will have to be the first one. To friends, that's become a huge thing," she said, banging into his shoulder, and reaching for a doughnut.

"Oh, friends is a massive thing. If you *have* friends in life, you are the richest person ever. Because they'll get you through everything in some form or another. Here's to new friends," he said, lifting his OJ up to her's. "And, I hope you know that you are more than welcome to come to me if you need to talk. I can't tell you I'm gonna fix all your problems or make it all better, but I can promise I'll be there when I can. Casey is one of my besties and I know you guys have got on well, too. So if you need to talk about stuff, I know I don't understand the whole 'lesbian' thing, but equally she'll always be there, too." He smiled.

"Just because we both like women doesn't mean that we need to speak to each other. I would talk to boys, straights, or anyone else if I wanted to talk about it," she said, lost in the beautiful sky.

Joel was looking at her. "Sorry if I offended. It was just that Casey had told me that you were at hers when the girls were here last weekend and that you'd gone out with them. So, I just figured you two were friends also," he said.

Brooke sighed lightly. This guy had been nothing but great to her, and now she's snapping at him. "I'm sorry, Joel. I shouldn't have been rude," she said quietly.

Joel didn't press any further, as they sat in silence on their boards and appreciated the beautiful morning view before them.

***

When Brooke got back to the van, she got in the shower. Her body was aching, her arms were burning and her tummy was growling. But by God, she'd had the best day she could remember. Her board was awesome. Joel was right when he said she'd feel a connection with it, so much so, she'd spent nearly four hours surfing. But then her body was signaling that it needed to stop, and she knew that she was going to feel the burn tomorrow.

"Ahhh, that's better," Brooke said to herself, as she threw on her sweats and tied her wet hair in a ponytail. She needed her body to feel the benefit of a steaming shower, and now she was good to go…all the way to the fridge so she could grab something to eat.

Brooke opened the patio doors and lit the barbecue that she'd played about with a few days ago to see if it worked. Luckily it did, and was just missing coal, which she'd picked up when she did the shopping. Putting the lid back down she allowed it a bit of time to heat up whilst she seasoned her chicken breast.

Brooke was impressed at how domestic she had become whilst being here. She'd relied heavily on Maria back at home. And although whilst she had been off work Brooke had maintained a clean house, the cooking still lacked massively and they either ordered in or heated up readymade meals. It was always something that Brooke had felt a bit of a void with. She was always jealous when she heard Kate and Jo talk about cooking together, or being in the kitchen together as Jo cooked and the simplicity of just *being*, and talking. Then followed by a meal together, discussing the day. Brooke and Maria never did that, and the more she thought about it, she didn't think even in the beginning they did. Granted, their work schedules often meant that they were unable to eat together. However, even when they were both off or finished at a similar time they didn't do that. They would sometimes go for dinner, and for the most part sit in silence or talk about live cases. Or Maria would sit in the lounge watching TV and Brooke would stay at the island reading. In fact, Brooke couldn't remember a time that Maria and she had ever eaten a meal in their dining room other than having people over. Why *was* that she thought? These were new details she needed to try and analyze, but for now, she would put it to one side and continue on her 'surf' high.

"Holy moly, am I seeing things," Brooke heard behind her as she was placing the chicken breast on the barbecue. She turned around, smiling as she saw Chloe. "Yo, Casey, you're back." She smiled. "And in answer to your question, no, you are not seeing things. I am in fact, grilling. All by myself. It's official, I am the new Jamie Oliver," she said, holding up her tongs and smiling. "So, whilst I am not trying to get out of the obligatory impending dinner offer I made, would you care to join? Save you having to mess about when you have just arrived," she asked.

"I don't want to impose," Chloe said seriously.

"Not imposing! And anyways, least I can do. There was lots of imposing on my part last weekend," Brooke said, turning back to the food. "So, am I getting more chicken?" Brooke said, still not turning round.

"Sure, that would be great. It saves me going shopping this evening. I can go after my surf in the morning. Oh hey, how about I give you a lesson in the morning? I mean, if you're up for it and don't have any other plans? Free of charge, of course, for cooking for me tonight," Chloe said.

Brooke could feel the side of her lips twitch. As she straightened her face and turned to walk back in to the fridge, she looked over to Chloe. "That would be fantastic, if you wouldn't mind? I'll let you get sorted. Dinner will be ready in around fifteen minutes, I think. Come over when you're ready, but if it takes you longer I can keep it warm," Brooke said to her, before going and hiding her new surfboard in the spare room.

"Nope, that's perfect. And no worries on the lesson. We'll have you a pro surfer in no time at all." She smiled, and walked into her cabin.

Brooke put another chicken breast on the barbecue and set about getting the rest of the meal ready. She opened a bottle of red and put it on the table with some napkins, then she grated more cheese and cut up some more onion. Finishing the remainder of the prepping for their dinner, Brooke put the slices of smoked bacon on the barbecue, too.

"Hello," Chloe called, as she came into the van.

"Hey, that was quick," Brooke said, walking back inside.

"Quick worker when it comes to food and wine," Chloe said, handing a bottle of wine to Brooke. "Can I do anything?"

"Nope, all under control. I've opened a bottle of red on the patio if that's okay for you. If so, you can take these and pour us a glass and I'll serve up," Brooke said.

Brooke poured a bit of oil on the ciabattas and took it out to the barbecue to toast briefly before putting the chicken, bacon, onions and cheese on. She put the lid back on for a moment to allow the cheese to melt, grabbing the plates and the bowl of crisps.

"Wow, this actually looks good," Chloe said, passing Brooke the wine, and taking the plate loaded with her food.

"Erm, thanks, I think! But, to be fair it's a bag of crisps, and a chicken and bacon melt," Brooke said laughing.

"I know, but salt and vinegar crisps can't give me food poisoning," Chloe laughed, popping a crisp in her mouth and raising her eyebrows to Brooke.

"Oi? Rude! I won't invite you for dinner again," Brooke said smiling.

"Jokes…so what you been up to the last few days then?" Chloe said. "Hmm, this is actually delicious, and the smoky melted cheese and onion are fantastic," she finished, before taking another bite.

"Thanks. I've been watching cooking shows," Brooke said, laughing and rolling her eyes. "Not much really. Thanks again for the Wi-Fi code, it's been great. I have been relaxing, watching movies, thinking about things, looking for places to live, and just enjoying some me time really. Luckily the weather has been quite good so I've been spending some time on the beach reading too, which is kinda fun," she said.

"Yes, I noticed the slight increase in darkness. You can tell you have skin colouring like my own, in that you just have to look at the sun and get a tan. So I can't say I'm surprised. And, no worries about the Wi-Fi. As I said, I am paying for it anyways, so it's really not like it matters. I'm actually glad you're using it. It makes me feel worthwhile in paying for it," Chloe responded.

"I thought your friends were up this weekend? You wanna take that?" Chloe said, pointing to Brooke's phone that had just started ringing.

Brooke picked her phone up. "It's Mitch, I won't be a minute, sorry. Hello?" she said.

"Bloody hell, she lives. Where the hell have you been? I've been freaking out like you wouldn't believe. What's going on? You haven't contacted me at all. Is everything okay?" Mitch said to his friend.

"Blimey, calm down. I'm good, just been busy. But I am eating dinner with my next door neighbor, so any chance I can give you a call tomorrow? I know I'm rubbish!" she said.

"Yeah, as long as I know you're alive. But I do need to talk to you, so please do call. Anyways, is this the next door neighbor from last weekend?" he said, and she could hear the smile in his voice.

"You are as bad as Kate, but yes, the same one! Is everything okay, mate? And before you start. Yes, she's a lesbian, yes she's very good looking, yes she's single, no I haven't slept with her. Nor am I intending to follow the mass revelation that I had because my heart was broken less than a month ago, so clearly far too soon. Okay? Anything else?" she said to him.

"Bloody hell. Easy tiger, I was only interested. Yes, all is okay. I just needed to speak to my bestie. Also, if you're planning on staying up there, I was gonna come up if that's okay?" he said.

"Yes of course. Kate and Jo are coming up on Thursday, but other than that we're fine. But if you wanna come up then, it's cool. You will just have to sleep with me."

"Great. Well, I was thinking three weekends time if that's okay, but we can discuss tomorrow. Take care, gorgeous, and if you can't be good, be careful," he laughed, hanging up on her.

"Arghhhh," Brooke sighed, rolling her eyes as she put her phone back down.

"Trouble in paradise?" Chloe said laughing, finishing the last part of her melt.

"Of course not," Brooke rolled her eyes. "So, what's your plans this weekend then lady?" she added.

"Same as it always is. Relax, work a little, paint a little, surf a lot and enjoy this place. And you? Anyways, I'm more interested in finding out more info on this cute single lesbian," Chloe winked.

"Shut up," Brooke said, throwing her scrunched up napkin at Chloe. "Pretty much the same, minus the painting," she smiled. "I have come to very much enjoy this doing nothing…so I'll continue to do what I have been doing really. Which is relaxing, reading, watching movies and box sets. And cooking shows so I can show off my awesome cooking skills of course." She smiled, grabbing a few crisps into her hand. "You know, keep up this clearly hidden culinary genius that I seemingly am. Plus, I do believe I owe you a dinner, if you have an evening free?" Brooke said to her.

Too Soon

"Brooke, I told you that isn't necessary at all, as I said, the fact someone is using the Wi-Fi is great. Plus, you have just done me dinner. It's fine," Chloe said, topping up their glasses with more wine.

"You already agreed to it, and I'm not saying it's necessary. But I'm here all the time, so it will give me an opportunity to have a night out. Plus, there's a nice Italian place I would like to try. Alternatively, if you're not up for it I can always ask Joel," she said, taking a sip of her wine.

"Joel? My Joel? Why would you ask Joel?" Chloe asked quizzically.

"You're Joel? Really? Well aren't we predatory over the lovely Joel? Now, my understanding is you were gay and he was a guy, so what's that about? Why could I not ask him to come with me?" she smirked.

"Oh, you're fucking with me. Nice…yeah good going," she threw a crisp at Brooke.

"Flirting now too…blimey, you are too much, Casey," Brooke said, smirking and raising an eyebrow. *Fuck what am I doing?* she thought, putting it away to consider later.

Chloe was weighing Brooke up. She liked her. She was fun, and she had noticed a considerable difference in the few short days she'd been gone. She wasn't so uptight, and apparently she was getting exactly what she needed from this place. "Me flirting? On the contrary, you have cooked me dinner, asked me to go out with you for a romantic Italian meal, the meal of love no less and…*and* you told your friend I was hot. See that?" She pointed to the side of her cabin.

"What?" Brooke said looking confused.

"That? That right there? *See*…that's the writing on the wall," she laughed loudly, apparently finding herself way funnier than Brooke did.

Brooke threw her napkin to Chloe again. "You are a dick. I didn't invite you for a romantic meal. I said I'd take you for a meal to say thank you because I can't cook. I like Italian food and thought it would be a good opportunity to try it. And FYI, I didn't say you were hot, I said you were good looking. There is a *very* big…very real difference. Just so you know," Brooke said back, with a single eyebrow raised to Chloe.

"Whatever you say, Davis," she smiled, picking up the plates and taking them inside.

"Hey, leave that, I will pick it up shortly," Brooke said.

"No way. I am a well-mannered young lady. You cooked, so I'll clean up. So, as it's the weekend, you fancy opening another bottle? Unless you have something else on tonight?" Chloe asked as she started cleaning the dishes, grateful for the diversion. It hadn't gone unnoticed how good Brooke looked. Seemingly, she pulled off the 'girl next door, relaxed' look really well. And Chloe knew that would be an issue, as she had debated declining the offer of dinner, but she just wasn't able to.

"Young? Really?" Brooke smirked. "Yes, open another bottle. Not like I have anything to get up for, is it?" She pushed out her bottom lip.

"You are a child, but you defo need to get up. You have a complimentary surf lesson, remember?" Chloe said, feeling a blush cross her face as she recalled the girl in her bikini.

Chapter Twenty-Two

Brooke opened the door, having heard Chloe's knock.

"Hey, good morning. You ready?" Chloe asked, trying to maintain contact with Brooke's eyes, and ignore that she was standing in front of her with her bikini top showing through her open zip up hoodie.

"Of course." Brooke smiled, reaching all the way up to her eyes.

She turned on her feet quickly, noticing the ever so slight smirk in her smile. Did she notice? Hell, had she been blushing? Chloe sighed inwardly. This was not going good.

Chloe had sorted the Penny situation out when she returned home. She knew that it wasn't a good idea, and it really wasn't fair when someone was more invested than others. The fact of the matter is she was kind of annoying, but an amazing lover, so was bearable? Maybe…well, probably not. But she had served a purpose in the past. And in Chloe's defence, she had spent many a drunken night pushing Penny off of her and explaining that she didn't want anything more. It wasn't fair to keep going back there. Penny on the other hand, constantly battled and argued that it was fine, declaring she had felt the same. Eventually, the drunken sex and sober fallouts resulted in Chloe feeling shitty. She was completely unaware that Penny did seem to want more, and hadn't been truthful. So, she cut all ties. Because the fact of the matter was…Nat was right, it wasn't fair on Penny.

"Yo?" Brooke shouted, removing Chloe from the trance.

"What? Sorry, I was just, ummm," Chloe attempted coming back round, unable to finish the sentence.

"Were daydreaming? In a daze? I've been talking for ages," Brooke said to her.

"You have?" Chloe spun around.

"No, not at all, I was just saying I made you a fresh OJ if you wanted it," Brooke laughed.

"Wow, you really are doing well. I would love it, thanks. Hmmm it's great. But, did you actually just say 'yo?'" Chloe was laughing now.

"Actually, fresh OJ is one of my hidden talents, so that's not anything new. And again, to reiterate, I had been speaking to you for a little while and you were ignoring me, so in answer to your question, I did say '*yo*.'" Brooke waggled her two fingers sideways, like she was some kind of rapper, for extra effect.

"Brooke?" Chloe asked seriously.

"Yes?"

"Did you actually sleep last night or just stay up drinking, because you're acting like you're still drunk?" she laughed drinking the OJ and carrying her board down to the beach.

The short walk was filled with the pair joking with each other and making plans for that evening. Brooke had still not mentioned the surfing to Chloe, and was praying she saw Joel before he had a chance to spill on her.

"So what colour board do you want Davis?" Chloe asked.

"Erm…let's go blue?" Brooke said, seeing Joel rushing in to Chloe.

"Yo, Case. How's it going?" he said, hugging her tightly.

Brooke stood beyond Chloe and looked at Joel putting a finger to her lips and smirking. Joel looked confused, raising an eyebrow, but went with it anyway.

"I'm good, buddy. Missed you as always, but I'm back. And this lovely young lady cooked me dinner last night, so I thought the least I could do is give her a free surf lesson," she said.

"Ah, right. Well that's ever so kind of you, buddy." He smiled. "I have a feeling this one's gonna be a natural. I told you both last week, I will have her kite surfing by the end of the six weeks." He grinned.

"Here's hoping, just depends how much she remembers from last week," Chloe responded.

"Of course, of course. So how much do you remember, Brooke? Do you think you'll be okay? Or is our best teacher here going to have to provide some private tuition?" he smirked.

Joel was having fun with this. He knew that Brooke was playing with Chloe, but he could also see a lot more than that. He needed the girls to sort this out and let it unfold naturally, knowing this would be far too much fun to miss out on.

"Well, I don't think I could justify private tuition, because this lady leads a busy life. So I guess I'm going to have to ensure I remember everything so I don't get in trouble." Brooke smiled.

"Yes, a busy life indeed. I forgot to call you the other day. How was the hot date?" Joel asked Chloe.

Chloe flashed a look over to Brooke, whose expression was unreadable. "Erm, yeah, good. I'll talk to you about it when I've finished with Brooke's lesson," she said awkwardly, and ran into the store.

Joel watched Chloe run off, noticing the uncomfortableness of what had just happened. "You okay?" he asked Brooke seriously.

"Yep, why wouldn't I be?" She smiled.

"Hmmmm, okay then. Enjoy your lesson, Davis. Don't poke too much fun out of my girl out there," he smirked and walked off.

"Hey, is this one okay?" Chloe asked, holding a bright Blue board with a neon orange Roxy logo in the middle.

"Yes, great thanks," Brooke said, taking the wetsuit from Chloe. "I'll just quickly change into this. I won't be a moment," she said.

"If you have your bikini on already, why not just do it here?" Chloe said.

"Ummm, no, I'd rather not," Brooke said walking off.

Chloe was feeling like she'd said something wrong, and she really hoped that Brooke didn't think she was being weird or something. Especially after what Joel said about the date.

A few moments later Brooke was out in her suit and picked up her board. "You ready to go then?" she said, walking towards the water.

***

Chloe and Brooke were on the boards in the water, and Chloe went over all the basics. Brooke had had an amazing day yesterday, spending nearly four hours surfing. So today she was itching to get back onto it, and it was painful having to sit through Chloe's directions. It was painful even though she couldn't help but feel a sense of appreciation to the girl who had gone out of her way for the extra tuition. But in the same respect, she knew how much fun she could have with it and Chloe, and was trying desperately to hide the smile.

"So is that okay? I've only briefed you, as you did it last week. So I think you should remember it, if you are happy with that?" Chloe asked.

"Well, we shall soon find out?" Brooke said, feigning a worried look out to the waves.

"You'll be fine, since you were a natural. I'll bet you'll be up on the water in no time." Chloe smiled.

"Really? So what are we betting on?" Brooke smiled back to her.

"Well, I was actually figuratively speaking, Brooke," She smiled.

"Ohhhh. Is Chloe Casey, our resident super pro, afraid of a little wager?" Brooke smirked.

"*Really*? You *really* want to do this? Fine, bring it on. What are we betting on?" Chloe asked seriously, which spurred Brooke on all the more.

"Well, you tell me. You're so reactive about the bet. So what do I need to do and then what do I win?" she said still smirking, noticing the annoyance in Chloe's face. Apparently, she was very competitive.

"Oh, you're all confident now, huh? Well you need to stay up for longer than five seconds. I will give you three practice goes, and then by the fourth that's what you need to do. Deal?" Chloe said, challenging Brooke.

"Okey dokey, then. And this is for?" Brooke asked.

Chloe was quiet for a moment, searching the sky. "Okay. Since you are so intent on paying for dinner this evening, I will pay for a taxi as opposed to you driving so we can both have a drink. Maybe find a couple of bars to visit after and make a bit of a night of it?" Chloe asked questioningly.

"Okay yes, I can live with that. Although, for the record, I don't need a drink. I am more than happy driving," she said seriously.

"I know that. And I know it's ridiculous to ask, as it's simply never gonna happen, but what's your end of the bet? What would you like from me?" Chloe asked intently, not removing her eyes from Brooke's.

God that was a loaded question, thought Brooke. Her initial reaction was to respond to it as such, but she couldn't. She didn't know what she was doing, but she knew it wouldn't have ended well. Both women were still staring at each other silently, as neither were prepared to back down. Brooke went to speak and stopped herself. "I'll drive," she said, leaning down on the board and starting to paddle into the surf.

Leaving Chloe with nothing…nothing at all. Other than the sight of her behind paddling away. *A very cute behind in actual fact*, thought Chloe. "No, stop this right now," she said, splashing herself with some water, and trying to scrub off the inappropriate thoughts.

Brooke didn't quite know how she was going to pretend to fall off. She had managed to stay up, had caught on fairly quickly, and had no issue with the bet which she was more than confident she could win. But she had to have some fun with this. Brooke wanted to instil some cockiness into Chloe, otherwise where was the fun? She needed to at least let her think she had a chance of winning. Brooke considered it further as she was getting closer to the break and figured if she went too far forward or too far back she would come off the board, so she attempted that. As it turned out, it worked and she was off before she had even had a chance to fully stand. Looking over at Chloe, who sat there with her arms folded, smirking to high heaven. "Oh, let's see how much you're smirking now, lady?" Brooke said, turning back around, and starting to paddle aggressively into the surf once again.

Brooke waited until the right moment and paddled hard. When she felt the wave reach her, she twisted and popped, or whatever else they called it. And that was it, she was standing up. Her arms and feet were correctly positioned, her front foot directing and her arms balancing. She was surfing over the relatively small wave that was leading her all the way back to Chloe, who she could see was looking at her inquisitively, causing Brooke to laugh so hard she was back off her board.

***

Chloe and Brooke walked out of the water with their boards in hand. Brooke could see the group of little children getting helped into their wetsuits and boards excitedly, anticipating their impending surf lesson.

"So the girl did good?" asked Joel, smiling a little.

"You knew? Oh my God, you did this? You have been having secret surf lessons?" Chloe said aghast.

"Nothing to do with me," he said, hands up. "Just a quick learner. We have loads, so I'll split the lesson and take half?" Joel said, laughing with Brooke.

"Lie to me if you will. I know the truth. She screwed me and you were in on it," Chloe tutted.

"Get over yourself! Believe me, you'd know if I'd screwed you," Brooke said, walking behind the two as she tried to undo her wetsuit. She stopped in her tracks as the realisation of what she had just said had took stock. *Shit*. That wasn't Brooke. She didn't do or say things like that. Chloe and Joel turned round to look at her, and Joel was smirking as he noticed the look on Brooke's face. Mumbling about needing to go to work he ran off down the sand.

Chloe was still staring at the girl, unsure of what to say. In fact, Chloe had been ready to respond. However, upon seeing Brooke's face, it was apparent that she clearly hadn't meant to say it. So Chloe left it.

"Erm, I'll let you go to your surf lesson," Brooke said, as she shoved the board in the sand and grabbed her hoodie, leaving nothing more than the dust from the sand as she dashed off erratically.

Chapter Twenty-Three

Brooke had been beating herself up all day. She had spoken to Mitch, and in true Mitch style he was very blasé about it, and telling her not to worry. Following it up with, 'go with it, drink tonight and get some action. It's maybe what you need'. This infuriated Brooke even more. She didn't need action, and she wasn't even attracted to Chloe! She was a good looking woman yes, but not Brooke's type at all. Plus, it had been days...minutes, in fact since Maria. So why would she do that?

Brooke had wanted to forget about it, and luckily had been given the opportunity when Mitch had filled her in on the situation at work. As it turned out, there were a few changes happening. Maria allegedly had been given a further promotion, which unfortunately meant that they would be having more dealings with each other. Bad, very bad. Worse still, Mitch had advised that there were going to be some departmental changes, and Mitch would no longer be her partner when she returned. Again, bad...very bad. Furthermore, the news didn't end there. He had applied for a senior role in Canada and had been offered the opportunity of an interview. He would be taking a week off in a month to attend and then wanted to come to see Brooke on the way back. This was the worst of all the information she had been provided. Mitch had been her rock. He was like her big brother, and she didn't know what she was going to do without him if he left.

***

It was five thirty, and Brooke hadn't seen or heard from Chloe since that morning. She didn't know if Chloe was still up for dinner, and Brooke wasn't really feeling up to it after Mitch's news. But what was her other option? Stay here alone and wallow in self-pity? Brooke was not a selfish woman, far from it in fact. Jesus, there could only be one selfish person in a relationship, and Maria had done enough for both of them. She was surprised of the thought that had flashed into her mind. She had known it was the truth, but it was unclear as to where this information had suddenly just appeared from. She forced herself up to get ready, realizing it was her that had reacted to what *she* had said. In fact, Chloe hadn't said a single thing, she'd been quite sweet actually. Especially given the nature of Brooke's comments. And therefore, she would stop being a selfish cow…a petulant child, and actually go for dinner with her friend. Her friend who had been there for her since they first met.

Brooke straightened her hair and added a loose clip to one side. She put a little lipstick and mascara on, thankful that the tan she had been getting required no more effort to her face.

Still completely unsure of what to wear, she picked up her phone and quickly dialled Kate. "Hey you, how are you?" Kate asked.

"Hey. Great, fine. Sorry it's only a quick one, I'll call you back tomorrow to speak at length. What do you wear to an Italian restaurant?" Brooke asked her best friend.

"Sorry? What?" Kate asked quizzically.

"What do you wear to an Italian restaurant?"

"Well, whatever you want, Brooke. It depends on the occasion and the restaurant. Some are very fancy, others are very quaint and more café like," Kate added. "Why?"

"Oh, I just don't know what to wear. I'm going now. It's nice, and I chose it as it looked lovely when I drove past it. So what do you think? And please hurry."

"Okay, okay. Well who are you going with and what's the occasion?" Kate asked.

"There's no occasion, Kate. I just need help, please?" Brooke said pleadingly.

"Well, if you tell me who you're going with, then at least I can give some guidance. You really aren't giving me much," Kate said again.

"Oh, don't worry its fine, I'll find something," Brooke said agitated. She didn't know why she couldn't just say she was going with a friend over a bet.

"Brooke, please don't hang up. Do you have your grey skinny jeans?"

"Yes."

"What about the navy, slightly see through chiffon vest with the neon pink rims?"

"Yes, got that too."

"Okay, and what about the baby pink shoes, with the metal heel you wore for New Year's Eve?"

"Yes," she said excitably, envisioning the outfit happily. "Yes I have those, too."

"Knock her dead, Brookie, speak soon."

Before Brooke had a chance to respond…to profess…to argue…Kate was gone. In reality, she didn't really want to argue. Kate had been there for her all the way, and she shouldn't be an ass to her. Brooke knew Kate would be worrying about her up here alone, so the least she could do is fill her with some confidence that she wasn't just all alone and crying into her pillow every day. Even if that did mean she would be sat there thinking that she was hooking up with someone else.

Brooke wondered if Kate and Jo would have told Maria about this. She didn't want her to know anything. But why not? Maria and Paula had done all this, so what the hell if they knew? It was sod all to do with anyone else anymore.

***

Brooke looked in the mirror and realized Kate was right, as she'd always had an excellent eye for fashion. Kate was girly all day every day. Naturally pretty, very much girl next door beautiful, which is probably why so many people likened her to the princess. However, Brooke was much more about comfort, and she would dress based upon how she felt.

Tonight though, was different, and she was feeling shy and a little sad. But she couldn't really put her finger on why. She'd felt ridiculous this morning at what she'd said, especially as Joel was there to hear it. But why should she? Why couldn't she get back to her normal self where she could have a laugh and joke? Everything she said or thought, she heard Maria's voice in her head telling her she was ridiculous and sounded stupid. Brooke knew one thing, she needed to go out and have some fun. And thanks to Kate, her outfit was perfect. The neon pink accentuated her suntanned arms, and she wore some bright bangles to finish it off. She added a long silver necklace and checking herself over, she couldn't deny it. She looked pretty darn good, and felt so. She shook the feeling out of her thoughts as to how long ago it was that she felt so confident about how she'd looked.

Grabbing her purse, phone and car keys, she looked at the clock. It was a quarter to seven. Brooke locked up and knocked on the door to Chloe's cabin. Suddenly nervous for seeing her after this morning…nervous for not saying anything after that and just running off… nervous for having just hidden away and ignored her all day…. And, *oh shit*. Nervous for how incredible Chloe looked when she opened the door to Brooke.

"Hey, I didn't know if you were going to show," Chloe said shyly.

"Clearly," Brooke responded, as she pointed to Chloe. She stood in the doorway of her cabin wearing a knee length, grey pencil skirt, with a black crocheted vest. The vest was very crocheted, very…holey, *stop Brooke*. And heels. The heels she was wearing made her legs look like they went on forever. *Brooke, stop it*, shaking the thoughts off.

"Well, I figured that if you hadn't shown up by seven, then I was going to come and knock on. And if I made an extra effort, then you would be less inclined to pull the whole 'woe is me card' and leave me and my sorry ass at home. Alone, on a Saturday night, with no food in. However, now I don't need to worry. Shall I get changed into something, ermm…less 'work like'?" Chloe asked.

"Have it all figured out, huh? Do you want to get changed?" Brooke inquired, maintaining eye contact with Chloe.

"Well, I actually would have done until I saw the way you looked at me when I opened the door, so you

know what? No, I think I'll leave it. Are you ready?"
Chloe smirked confidently.

Oh hell, this is entering into dangerous territory, she
thought. "I did not look at you in any way. I was
surprised you were dressed like you were going to work.
Anyways, stop flirting, we're friends and going for
dinner. Of course I'm ready. I'm here, do I not look
ready?" Brooke confirmed.

"Oh, you look more than ready," Chloe smirked.
"And I'll ignore the dig about looking like I'm going to
work. I was actually going for smoking hot." She winked.

"You are on fire tonight, hey?" Brooke said, getting
into the car.

"See, that's what I was going for," Chloe said.

"So, we're going to do this all night then?" Brooke
asked Chloe squarely.

"I don't know what you mean," she smirked. "Oh,
Brooke?" Chloe said.

Brooke sighed heavily, turning to her. "Yes?"

"You look stunning this evening," Chloe said,
quickly turning away as she felt the fire in her cheeks.

Brooke was just about to throw a sarcastic remark
back, but noticed the sincerity in her eyes. "Um, thank
you. Same to you," she whispered, and pulled off the site.

***

Brooke and Chloe were quiet on the drive, and
Brooke was beginning to regret not letting Chloe win the
bet earlier, suddenly feeling like she may need a drink to
get through the evening.

They parked the car as close as they could get. "Sorry, we'll have to walk about five minutes. I hope you don't mind?" she asked, looking over to Chloe.

"No, I don't mind at all. I kinda like walking in the early evening. Where is it?"

"Just around the corner, so not too far." She smiled, as she locked the doors.

"So, how did everything go at work?" Brooke said to Chloe on the walk to the restaurant.

"Work? What do you mean?" Chloe looked confused.

"You sold something that we were celebrating last week?" Brooke responded.

"Oh yes, sorry," she laughed. "Yes, it was good. We cashed the cheque and it wasn't a fake. Additionally, they have put my company details out to some prospective clients, so fingers crossed," Chloe said coyly.

"Wow, that's incredible. I'm very happy for you." She smiled sincerely.

"And you? Any thoughts about what to do since being here with some time to think?"

Brooke held the door open to the restaurant for Chloe to enter. "Wow, it's busy. I didn't book. I didn't think I needed to with just the two of us," she said, looking to Chloe concerned.

Someone came over and advised there was a forty-minute wait for a table, and Chloe could see the disappointment in Brooke's face.

"Yes, that would be wonderful thank you. We will be across the road at the wine bar. If I leave you my number could you possibly call me when the table is ready?" Chloe asked.

***

A few minutes later, leaving the restaurant, Chloe spoke. "Now before you start, I have accepted the offer of dinner to which I didn't need. However, since I have obliged, I'm going to buy us some drinks over here and you will leave your car. I can bring you down tomorrow after the lesson to get it," Chloe stated.

"Quite bossy, aren't you? I didn't even notice this bar, so clearly I'm led by my stomach. But it looks lovely," Brooke said. "And thank you, that's a kind offer."

"What would you like to drink? Why don't you take that booth in the corner?" Chloe indicated.

"Well you seem to want to have the control this evening, so surprise me," Brooke said, smirking and walking away.

Chloe was smiling as she watched Brooke walk away, and she was still well aware of the fact that she shouldn't be doing any of it. But...put simply, Brooke was beautiful, and she looked amazing tonight. The brightness of the rim of her dark top made her arms look sexy as hell. Chloe couldn't stop herself from imagining what it would be like to run her fingers down those arms, no matter how much she didn't want to. The problem was, she didn't believe that Brooke was the type to just let go and have some fun. She came across as the type who would be all in. And a relationship was clearly the last thing she needed right now. Equally, it wasn't what Chloe was looking for either. So she needed to back off and start behaving herself, throwing out any of these naughty thoughts crossing her mind.

Too Soon

"Oh, looks very, erm, thick? What is it?" Brooke laughed, as Chloe put down the glasses.

"Flirtini's. I figured they were quite apt?" Chloe grinned, and held the glass up. "To new friends, beautiful women and plenty of flirtinis," Chloe laughed, causing Brooke to shake her head as she clinked their glasses.

"So, you didn't get to tell me about your thoughts on work?" Chloe asked, sitting back into her seat.

Brooke filled Chloe in on what Mitch had said earlier today, elaborating on the fact that there was so much uncertainty to her feelings. The uncertainty was screwing with her head, and any form of decision making she was required to do.

"Do you want to go back? Do you still have the love and passion for the job? Or has it all gone?" Chloe asked.

"I don't know. I miss Mitch, but then I remember things and it freaks me out, and I just think I'll be better off just quitting," she said.

"But you haven't quit, have you? And there's a reason for that clearly. What about a transfer to another station, where there are no memories? Nothing to take you back to that situation? Additionally, no ex-girlfriend?" Chloe asked.

Brooke pondered on that for a moment, "I don't know. I love my station, so I don't know how I would feel," she said, still thinking on it. "Oh, I love this song," Brooke said, as Shania Twain's 'You're still the one' came on.

"Nice diversion," Chloe said, watching Brooke as she was enjoying the song.

"I hope you know I'm joking with you with the flirting. I love the reaction I get from you, watching you squirm and get embarrassed, but I am only kidding with you. I wouldn't want to make you feel uncomfortable," Chloe said to Brooke, seriously.

"I know. I guess I just don't know how to take it. I know you don't mean it, but I don't seem to be able to stop myself from getting embarrassed," she said.

"And you're super cute when that happens…just saying! Hence, why I have no sense of control with it." She smiled softly.

Brooke rolled her eyes at Chloe. "You just can't help yourself can you?" She smiled.

"Actually, that time was no jokes. I hope I didn't offend you today though when I told you to get changed into your suit in front of me. I wasn't…um, being like, weird or anything, I promise." She smiled shyly.

"Look at little miss shy over there. Who'd have thought it?" Brooke laughed. "On the contrary, I didn't think that at all, so not to worry." She smiled to Chloe.

"Ahhh right, good. No more piss taking from you." She pointed to Brooke. "It was just the way you reacted. I was just doing it so we could get in the water quicker. But don't get me wrong, the bikini top on show didn't go unnoticed. But, I wasn't saying it for that reason. Um, as I just said," she added, feeling embarrassed of the over speak.

Brooke could see the awkward look on Chloe's face, but thought best to leave it than make fun of her any further.

"Well thank you for the observation, I guess. I didn't think that whatsoever, the…" Brooke stopped, running her index finger around the rim of her glass. She looked up to Chloe between her eyelashes and sighed a little. "The reason I was funny, is because of the scar. I hate it. I can't bear to look at it, and I don't, ever. But, as I pointed out last week, nobody else has ever seen it either. That's the way I would like to keep it," Brooke said, looking down into her glass.

"Brooke, look at me please? I am not going to question as to why your girl...your ex-girlfriend has never seen this. But regardless of anything else, you are young and this is going to be a part of you for the rest of your life. I'm not saying learn to love it, but you are going to need to acknowledge it at some point, or you will just continue to beat yourself up and cause added pressure. You are a beautiful woman inside and out, and the next woman you meet and fall in love with, will love that part of you as much as they love you and the beauty inside of you," Chloe said sincerely.

Brooke didn't know at what point it had happened, but Chloe's hand was around hers, and she could feel the warmth and softness of her skin. Brooke pulled her hand away and thanked Chloe for her kind words.

***

A while later, Brooke and Chloe were sat in another booth in the Italian restaurant. They had moved onto prosecco and ordered their meals, grateful that they were finally about to get some substance in their tummies.

Brooke had to admit it, she was having a really good time. The serious conversations were not awkward, there had been much laughter, and even the making fun of each other was on an equal par. It was easy, that's what Brooke realised. And there was no expectation of two gay women, two single gay women correcting herself, going out. They were friends and acting as such.

When their drinks arrived they kept the conversation much lighter. Sticking to subjects like school, coming out stories, first kisses and even down to alternative jobs for Brooke. Jobs consisting of sheep herder, surf teacher, busker, and stripper. At that point they were giggling so loudly that other customers were stopping to look around at them.

The women were still giggling when their starters eventually arrived. They realized that they had probably consumed far too much drink. They blamed that on the restaurant, making them have three flirtinis in the wine bar due to the wait time, which ended up being an hour and ten minutes.

"What's your food like?" Chloe asked Brooke, as she took another bite of bruschetta. "This is one of my signature dishes, but my word, this right here is incredible," she groaned, as she took another bite.

"Is this more flirting, or are you just really enjoying that?" Brooke smirked, causing Chloe to choke on her starter.

"Oh my God, I can't believe you have just said that," Chloe whispered, shaking her head vigorously.

"It's actually beautiful, thank you! Seemingly, I have taken a leaf from your book. You know, on the crude, blunt, and flirtatious front," Brooke smirked.

"You, my friend," Chloe said pointing her fork towards Brooke, "are quickly evolving from that introverted and timid young lady I met last week," Chloe smiled. She noticed the slight blush creep across Brooke's face. "Hey, I'm sorry. I didn't mean to embarrass you."

Brooke smiled a slight smile. "You didn't. It's just kind of nice, you know? That for someone who doesn't know me very well, you have noticed a change in me. I have noticed it too, but I figured it was probably just me, being…I don't know, stupid I suppose," she said solemnly.

"Can I ask you something serious? And you can tell me to go to hell. I don't want to offend you, but unfortunately, I may," Chloe asked, moving her plate to a clear part of the table and pouring them both another drink.

"Well, I'm not so sure now you've said that, but you may as well. You don't appear to be the type to purposely set out to hurt people, so I'm sure you are not intentionally looking to hurt me. Knock yourself out," Brooke said seriously, taking more of her drink.

"Why do you still let her control you this way? Had I not seen this new person over the last 24 hours, I would have never known that the person I met last weekend and who spent time with us wasn't who you were. And I'm not saying there's anything wrong with that, as I really liked you when I met you. But I prefer this you, and I can see a…I don't know how to explain it. I can see a comfortableness with you, and the way you're acting. It leads me to believe that," Chloe stopped and pointed to Brooke, "that *this* is you, and I love that. As it's you…you're finding yourself again. But then you say things like, 'you're being stupid'. Why do you let her have this hold over you? You have so much going, and yeah I'm drunk and yeah I know I shouldn't say this. I'm probably going to lose one of the best gay friends I've ever met, but you are incredible. You're stunning, funny, smart, and such fun. And my God, if situations were different, I would be jumping all over you, and would be pulling out all the stops right now. But, it *is* different, and

I happen to like the person you are. But you can't keep letting this silly bitch have this control over you. She's gone. She's someone else's problem now, so stop thinking so much. Stop worrying you're doing stupid things. Because, Brooke, in reality, so fucking what if you are doing something stupid?" Chloe said bluntly, taking a large gulp of her drink and hoping that she hadn't offended her.

There was silence at the table, and although only a few moments, it felt way longer.

"What are you thinking? As I said, I'm sorry if I've ruined your evening," Chloe said solemnly.

"You haven't at all, Chloe. On the contrary, I'm a little bit gobsmacked but a lot appreciative that you've had the balls to actually say what many have probably wanted to say," Brooke said.

Chloe could tell she wasn't finished. But unfortunately their food arrived and they returned to the silence once more. Brooke eyed Chloe a few times when she wasn't looking, wondering how she had managed to get so much about Brooke when she had only met her a week ago?

***

Chloe regretted what she said to Brooke because, although she said it was alright and there was nothing to worry about, they hadn't spoken for the rest of the meal. They hadn't spoken in the taxi and here they were now. It was all very…awkward.

"I'm sorry I put a spanner in your evening. It was lovely and you chose well. The food was incredible.

Thank you, Brooke," Chloe said, and left the girl alone as she walked into her cabin without looking back.

***

Brooke couldn't sleep. She didn't know what it was about what Chloe had said that had got to her, but something apparently had. Looking at her clock, she sighed heavily. It was after midnight and she had been laid in bed for over an hour, recalling everything in her mind. She had really hit home with the words, and that had made Brooke feel good about herself. And that had been such a long time since anyone had made her feel that way. Getting up, she got out of bed and put her flip flops on, before she had an opportunity to talk herself out of what the drink was driving her to do.

Brooke knocked on Chloe's door, looking down at her Calvin Klein boxers and an old work t-shirt. *Massively different to the attire an hour ago, Brookie,* she thought.

"Hey, is everything okay?" Chloe said, not looking like she had managed to sleep any either.

Brooke leaned in and pressed her lips softly to Chloe's, and they felt as amazing as she had expected them to. She took in the faint smell of perfume before pulling back and ignoring every part of her that was longing to stay, and continue what she'd started. "If things were different I'd be all over you too, just so you know!" Brooke said. And just like that she was gone, leaving Chloe with her mind whizzing, her stomach dancing and her lips tingling.

Chloe shut the door, allowing a smile to grow across her lips. She leaned her head against the wall as she put her fingers to her lips, reminiscing seconds earlier.

<u>Chapter Twenty-Four</u>

Chloe couldn't sleep. She tried and tried but couldn't get past what happened last night. She couldn't stop thinking about the kiss. But more importantly, she couldn't get past the fact that she was ever so desperate to go and knock on her door and continue what Brooke had started.

"Argh," she screamed into her pillow. She knew she wasn't going to get back to sleep, which wasn't great. Worse still she had to leave this afternoon due to her meeting at 8 a.m. tomorrow morning. This was causing a great deal of frustration, and there were so many elements to that frustration. But in most parts those reasons were that she couldn't get past the wonder of if something further would happen if she wasn't leaving today? *And,* she was due to have another date tomorrow evening with a wonderful woman whom she had actually enjoyed meeting last week. So why did she feel so rubbish?

Chloe needed to talk, but it was far too late or early. She hadn't quite established which yet. Picking up her phone she sent a text to Emily, knowing she hadn't been getting much sleep of late. Emily was stressed because of the impending wedding and the planning that goes along with it. Additionally, Chloe would get a sensible response from her.

Hey you, hope you're well and wedding plans are coming along well. Fancy dinner Tuesday? I miss you long time, mama. Cxx

Chloe got up, grabbing her phone and pillow. Putting a filter into her cappuccino machine, she set it off and looked over her DVD's. Needing something light and easy to watch, so she grabbed the Friends boxset and randomly picked a disc to watch. She grabbed her drink, adding some chocolate shavings across the top.

Pulling the throw over her and snuggling into her pillow, she blew her coffee and took a small sip, noticing her phone vibrate, shocked that Emily was up at this time. The stress of the wedding had definitely been getting to her. Chloe clearly needed to take her friend out this week and make it up to her. There was a gorgeous little knick-knack store in the village, so Chloe would see if there was something cute she could get for her friend later today.

Chloe looked at the screen dumbfounded, at the realisation it wasn't Em's, but an unknown number. She opened it up, still confused by it.

Couldn't sleep either?

Unsure as to whose number it was, she was racking her brain trying to think who it could be.

Sorry, who's this?

Charming!! Spend a wonderful evening with a girl and then question their identity. Exactly how many women you got on the go?

Chloe was smiling, as she knew that sense of humour. But how did she get her number? Equally, what if it wasn't Brooke? To be fair, it would only be her or Clare, and she was due to have dinner with her again tomorrow night. Smirking to herself, thinking she knew how to overcome this.

Well, I guess it depends on what day you're asking! ;) Nope can't sleep. You can't either huh? What's on your mind?

Floozy!!!! Apparently not, no! Lol...ohh you know! Wondering where my heads at, overthinking shit, under thinking shit. How about you?

You can under think? Wow, good skill. ☺ Yup, pretty much the same. So I figured I'd come get some posh caffeine and watch some TV. You wanna talk about it?

Chloe didn't know if she was right to ask it, but she knew regardless of the answer she was enjoying the conversation. She was loving speaking this way to Brooke, because it was a different portal. And in reality, she felt safer and more confident. More importantly, she was glad she was sober. The problem was she'd gone silent!

Chloe checked the phone again to see if the message had gone through...It *had!* Why had she gone quiet? Chloe sat up and drank her coffee in a bid to stop her fingers from deceiving her and texting Brooke back. The last thing she wanted was to be a text pest. Jumping up, what if she was coming over? She asked if she wanted to talk about it. What if she was coming here now? *Shit.* She hadn't even brushed her teeth. She ran into the bathroom and mouth washed quickly, whilst running a brush through her hair, before stopping and looking in the mirror. "Seriously, what are you doing?" she cringed at her childlike behaviour. "You're a grown ass woman," she said, sighing and returning back to her couch.

Chloe lay back down, squirming as she took some coffee, having forgotten about the mint mouth wash she had just swigged. She wasn't into games, so she didn't want to wait simply because someone, somewhere says *allegedly,* 'you can't text them before they've text you' bullshit!

Sorry if it's me that's messed your head up.

Chloe's thumb hovered over send for a while. She hated this about herself. She had never been a player. But due to always falling so hard, she maintained a high level of *space,* for want of a better word, in a bid to protect herself. And...for a number of years she had removed any possibility of that happening. It worked well, and she liked it that way, but this was different. She could already feel and sense the lack of control on her part. Screw it...life's too short, she thought, and pressed send anyway.

Hey, sorry for delay...you didn't mess up my head. I was debating what I should say.

Chloe's heart dropped. What did that even mean? She was the one who started texting. *Well hey, I don't want to make you feel uncomfortable, so we can just leave it.*

You are misinterpreting what I am trying to say, Chloe. I instigated the texting remember? I instigated the kissing remember? I instigated the flirting on the beach yesterday remember? I was debating if I should say what seemed to be willingly coming out of me. That's what I meant.

Chloe didn't know how to respond to that. She wanted to go back with so much, but she didn't want to force that on her. But equally, she was right, she had instigated all of those things.

Ouch, silent treatment...playing me at my own game, huh?

Chloe felt bad that she made Brook feel that way, but she didn't know what to text back. God what was she doing?

No, I'm here. Tell me what you were going to say? ;)

Why?

Because I want to know silly.

Silly? Silly? Really? Well now I'm not telling you!! ☹

Okay, I'm sorry, you're not silly! You're super cute, and when you went silent I rushed to the bathroom to sort myself out in case you came over....:/ see now I told you something embarrassing? And I feel absurd! X

Well there's an overshare. I figured you may have 'sorted yourself out' after the kiss last night, but not from one text...I'm clearly better than people made me think ;).

Chloe spat her coffee out, re-reading the words on her screen. My word, she was trouble. This was bad, and this was going to end badly. Yet she still couldn't help herself. Putting her coffee cup back down, she slipped further down into her couch, smirking into the phone.

BROOKE!!! I CANT BELIEVE YOU JUST SAID THAT!!! You are very bad, and you are going to be trouble, I can feel it! Well, now you have to tell me what you were going to say, because it can't be worse than that. Ps feeling rejected when you failed on the "X" etiquette... ☹ *x*

Oh give over...you know you are bigger trouble than I! I am not trying to bail right now, but I actually can't remember! No lie, I promise!! Old age, I think. Quickly approaching 30 and all that. I am genuinely stumped, and I am going to make it worse though, because I know it WAS naughty ;)

You are awful... really awful. You and I will most certainly fallout. STILL NO KISSES?? Kiss etiquette, read up on it!!! SERIOUSLY.

Fallout? Really? With no more kisses? ☹ Maybe I don't want to give you kisses. Maybe I enjoy winding you up. Maybe I only want real ones.

Well, you're 2 feet away so come get one.

I don't have the balls ☺x.

Hooooorrraaaayyyyyy at last, the woman understands kiss etiquette!! Me neither ☹x.

You liked the kiss? You want more? X

I liked the kiss... a LOT. I couldn't sleep because of the kiss. The 'kiss' kept me up all night!! I want more...yes...but that scares me! A little. The kiss was most definitely worthy of a 'romcom' kiss ☺x.

Scares me more than a little. The kiss also kept me up all night. Well I'm glad I could live up to your little romantic mind. X

Little? A bit rude isn't it? I am a highly intelligent artist and art director, I'll have you know!! Have you never heard of Vincent Van Gogh, incredibly intelligent gentlemen, also an artist! X

Sweetheart, a man that cuts his ear off isn't so intelligent. X

I'm going to ignore your ridiculously poor attempt at sarcasm and override it with the 'sweetheart'. I like it. I know I shouldn't, but I do. ☺X

Me too. x

Shit. What was that? She was left hanging there. Chloe sighed heavily, unsure of how to respond, or if she even should. Maybe she'd just wait it out to see if she sent anything else? She had already been the first to text back, and she didn't want to seem too full on. "Seriously

Chlo, why are you even bothered? Just leave it." Chloe threw her phone on the couch and got up to shower. It was still far too early to do anything, but she couldn't sit about waiting…ooohhhh text message, she spun around and dove on the couch, retrieving her phone.

So you know this flirting, albeit on text, is wrong right? X

Yup! X

And you also know this is going to end badly? X

Preeeety much! X

And yet you're still proceeding? X

You started it. X

Yup. ☹ x

We will have to end it, because I have to take you to get your car shortly. I'm not so sure either of us will be able to deal with the consequences when we actually have to face one another. ;) x

This is incredibly true. ☺ x

So when do you want to go get it? X

I'm actually not so sure I can. ;) I may need to get a taxi. :/ x

Don't be so ridiculous. How about we go get it and…ummm…if you would like, come back here for dinner. Nothing funny I swear. I have a horrendously early meeting tomorrow, so I'm going home today. We can go for the car, and I want to stop off in a little gift store in town for a pretty little gift. Then I want to stop by to get a joint and come here? We can watch some more l word and have dinner, and then I will be on my merry way, without any chance of drunken naughtiness. X

Wowzers, war and peace. ☺ OKAY, that sounds bearable. No misbehaving though! And no flirting face to face and sober. ;) Shall I come meet you after your lesson and get straight off? X

   Nope, I will want to change. I'll come get you at 11. X

   Sounds like a plan. ☺x

Chloe sighed, feeling pathetic. Suffice to say, the *'patheticness'* was having a rather giddy effect on her though.

<u>Chapter Twenty-Five</u>

"So, take Nat out of the equation. What's the issue?" Emily said into the screen on their facetime chat.

"Everything. How can it not be? I don't do relationships, and she doesn't need a relationship. Nor does she sleep about. I don't know. Nothing...everything. I don't know what to say," Chloe responded.

"Chlo, do you like her?"

"Well, ye..."

"Chlo, for fucks sake, answer the sodding question!"

"Alright, calm down! I've never watched that bridezilla TV show, but I'm getting what people are talking about."

"Listen, love, I don't have time for this rubbish. Do you like her?"

"Yes."

"Do you think she likes you?"

"Maybe," Chloe mumbled, and noticed the annoyance in her best friend's face. "Yes...*yes*. She kissed me didn't she? Jesus."

"So you keep quiet, and go with the flow, and if something happens it happens. Set some ground rules so neither of you get hurt. Just play it by ear and see what happens. Maybe it will, maybe it won't .But you've clearly got feelings for her, and that's been an age since we saw that. Don't spout none of your rubbish to me...it's me. You've called me rather than the others for a reason, remember?" she said forcefully, with her hand up to the screen for added effect.

Chloe saluted, "yes ma'am," smirking. "I love you, princess."

"Whatever. Right. I have to go and choose the food, sack the florist, blame the dress maker for drinking too much at yours last weekend, and threaten to leave my future husband if he leaves one more of my friends out of the 'save the dates'. Hmphhh," she growled into the phone. "I love you, keep smiling, and go have fun for God's sake. She's amazing, and one day she *will* be ready," Emily kissed the screen and was gone.

This was a good day. She was happy. Actually, this was a good week.

***

Brooke opened the door, relieved that she had noticed Chloe hovering outside, which gave her an additional boost of confidence. "Hey there, soldier. You okay?" Brooke smirked.

"Seriously? You wanna do this? My God, you're so infuriating at times. Get in the car," Chloe said, stomping off, which was feeding Brooke all the more.

"Oohh, I like Bossy Chloe!," she said pointedly. "I'm good at saluting. It's a prerequisite of the job. If you slow down and look, I'll show you," Brooke said, laughing hysterically to herself.

Brooke got in the car, laughing all the while at Chloe. "Sorry, sorry. I will refrain from making fun of you any longer." She smiled sincerely.

Chloe opened her mouth to say something and shut it again, rolling her eyes as she sped off out of the car park.

"You're actually loving this aren't you?" Chloe said.

Brooke jumped in her seat, turning to look at Chloe. "Oh my God, I really am," she said, with the enthusiasm of an excitable child on Christmas morning. That look and enthusiasm would win Chloe over every time. She was in trouble and she knew it.

***

"It's beautiful, don't you think?" Brooke said, clearly moved by the beautiful bracelet with the circular words inscribing 'a lifetime of happiness' on it.

"Yes, it is, and she will love it. The words are simply perfect. Thanks, Brooke. I wanted to get her something that she would be able to use as her 'something new'. But additionally, something to make her stop and take stock of the happy parts of this, not just all the stress involved."

"Do you want marriage?" Brooke asked Chloe seriously.

"Ermmmm, I did at one point, and thought I would have it all. You know the whole marriage and kids…but, not so much anymore. How about you?" she said, walking to the till to pay for Emily's gift.

"Yes, completely. But I'm not saying that I wouldn't be fulfilled if I didn't get that. If I met someone I wanted to spend the rest of my life with and they didn't want it, well I suppose it isn't a deal breaker for me. But yes, I want the commitment, the silly piece of metal and silly bit of paper to say I'm hers and she's mine. I want big family Christmases together, and us to set wonderful Christmas Eve family traditions together. To enjoy it as a family, and when the kids go to bed we stay up kissing under the mistletoe. We drink expensive champagne together, and wrap their presents as we make love amidst the wrapping paper and tape. I would love it all. I want to put out mince pies and brandy, leaving cotton wool remnants on the glass as Santa's beard, and hot chocolate dusting around a hoof stencil. So that when they wake up in the morning, it's incredibly perfect for them," Brooke said, sighing lightly. "I know you're thinking I'm a freak, but..."

"Hey, no. You don't get to do that," Chloe said, turning Brooke into face her. "I've told you this already, don't assume you know me. I wasn't thinking you're a freak. I wouldn't ever think that. But I will be honest with you, which you may not like. I was actually thinking that it doesn't sound like it isn't a deal breaker for you. To go to that level of detail, proves you have thought about this lots…and I was thinking you deserve someone who won't take all of that away from you, who will embrace all of that, *with* you," Chloe said sincerely.

<u>Chapter Twenty-Six</u>

"So you're actually going to make me do this?" Brooke said, folding her arms across her chest for extra effect.

"Yes, what's the big deal? Next weekend you can cook me dinner," Chloe said, smirking.

"Whatever. But listen, about that," Brooke turned around, facing Chloe.

"Stop being a petulant child and score the pork like I told you. What about what?"

"You are painful, you know that? Like this?" Brooke asked seriously, carefully cutting diagonals into the pork rind.

"Yes…you tell me every two minutes. I'm starting to think I will stay away from the park until your six weeks are up. No, not like that. How I showed you, crossways," Chloe said, putting her hand over Brooke's to ensure she was cutting correctly. "Erm, sorry," she said, walking back to the potatoes she had been peeling.

Brooke scored the pork the way Chloe had showed her. "That isn't a nice thing to say! So before you got all weird on me, what I was trying to say, was if I haven't completely scared you off, and you do return whilst I'm still here, then my girlfriends are here next week. And well, I would really like it if you could come over for dinner and drinks on Friday and come out on Saturday, if you can make it? I mean, only if you don't have plans and stuff. If you can't, it's no bother," she said quietly.

"I'd love to meet them, but I don't need to spend the whole weekend with you guys," she laughed. "How about I just catch up with you on Saturday after surfing and spend the day with you? Ohh, awesome scoring. That's going to make the best crackling, and I'm kinda hoping you don't eat it." Chloe shoved Brooke playfully.

"I try not to eat too much rubbish, but this here, my friend, you have *no* chance! It's being perfectly halved. And there's no movement on the weekend. These are my best friends, and it's been difficult for them as they have been pulled like a child in a divorce. I've upped and left to the other end of the country, and they have no idea if I'm good, bad or indifferent. And I'm good, exceptionally good actually. Truth be known, I have only you to thank for that. From the surf lessons, to the making sure I'm okay when I can't sleep, to the Wi-Fi, to the forcing me to spend time with your friends. It's been so long since I was single and just chilled with friends. And in reality, I don't have many of my own friends. Everyone and everything is linked to her, and that makes it so difficult. But with you it's different. You're *my* friend, and only mine. I can be myself. And better still, you are friends with me despite the fact that I'm still actually trying to ascertain who I am. Because I don't actually know who that is anymore. So I would like them to meet a good friend who has made a big impact in my life. Please?"

"I'm kinda stoked about meeting your friends, but more so, over the opportunity to be there to see their faces as they realise you are not the person that left their house a few weeks back. Even I've noticed a massive change in you in just this short time, so it will be awesome. Thanks for the invitation. I will very happily accept. You know you really are a good person, and me personally thinks you're best off out of that. But only you can manage that and move past it when you are ready to. Joel said something to me when I first came up here, that you can't force the pain to disappear, you need to allow everything to surface in its own time in order to establish certain things, and realise certain things. He was right. Nobody can force that, but it's hard when you are waiting. More so, when you can begin to feel the dynamics changing. That's what I have found most difficult. I could see the light at the end of the tunnel and wanted to run as fast as I could to get out of it, ya know? But I wasn't ready, because there was still a lot of things that needed to be worked out and surface. Does that even make sense?" Chloe asked her seriously.

Brooke liked Chloe's and Joel's outlook on life. They were both so positive and sensible. "He said something similar to me last week, so I think I get it," she said, distantly in thought. "I guess I'm starting to realise I was in a state of comfort, and had become complacent. I was broken hearted over what happened, but the more time I'm spending thinking about stuff, I am starting to become aware that things weren't perfect. That life isn't perfect. Relationships aren't perfect and you have to work at it. But people have to both commit fully to do that, and I'm just starting to realise that it was very one sided. I am realizing that maybe things weren't as great as they seemed. I guess that's what I think you and Joel mean?"

"Exactly, but as we said don't push it. Anyhow, let's forget about that now and focus on you cooking a nice lunch. So, shall we make some cauliflower cheese?" Chloe asked.

"I will. And thanks…again…for everything. Yay, I love cauliflower cheese. You do realise I will not be able to stand on my board tomorrow right? All this bad food. You are a bad influence." Brooke smiled shyly, ignoring the unintended pun.

***

"You like it?" Brooke asked sincerely.

"It's gorgeous. Really nice, and I told you the crackling would be awesome," Chloe said, smiling at Brooke's infectious excitement over cooking her first proper, full roast.

"So you think I could do it again next week for four? Or is that just a little bit too optimistic? Oh, and these Yorkshire puddings are incredible. I love them, but I'm not going to lie. I was a little bit scared when you said that we would be making them from scratch. But I have excelled in the category of Yorkshire puddings master. Oh, and you cannot tell the girls next weekend I'm making lunch, I want it to be a surprise." Brooke smiled shyly.

"Sure thing, kiddo. And yeah they are delicious. I think next time we need a meat that generates more fat, so they have a bit more of a meaty flavour, as Pork only really gives off a little flavour. Like lamb or chicken, ohhh or beef? We can go pick it next weekend. See what the girls fancy," Chloe said excitable.

Brooke couldn't help but be drawn to Chloe, because she was completely infectious. Especially when hearing her talk about the dinner next week, and giving her positive guidance as opposed to negativity.

"What? Why are you looking at me like that? Sorry, I shouldn't have just assumed that I would come for dinner on Sunday. I can help and then leave," Chloe said embarrassed.

"Woah, easy tiger. I just said dinner for four so you haven't assumed. I just like listening to you. I've never really known anyone to get excited by cooking and doing something nice...well for others, or to help me do something for my friends. It's amazing. Of course you are coming for dinner on Sunday. Can you stay and drink too? Hey, you wanna know something? It's kinda stupid though, actually don't worry. What do you want to drink, diet coke, water, tea, coffee?" Brooke said, not looking at Chloe anymore and quickly hurrying herself over to the fridge.

"Don't do that, I told you already. You cannot make me think you're stupid in any way, unless we are talking about '*silly, stupid*' things, which I actually love. Please tell me? And a Coke's fine, thanks."

Brooke wanted to analyse why Chloe always said things like that, why she made her feel this way. Did Maria do that initially? Had they just become complacent over the years, or was it just a case of Maria had now fell out of love with her? She needed to file that away for later. Ultimately, she had her insecurities, but Chloe didn't actually make her feel stupid, which was an entirely different dynamic.

"Well, you know *these* amazing bad boys?" Brooke smiled widely, holding up half of her Yorkshire pudding. "These are called popovers in the states," she smiled, pouring lots of gravy inside it before warning Chloe she was going to be gross now and biting into the gravy loaded pudding.

"*Really*? Are you winding me up?" Chloe asked, shaking her head at the gravy falling out from every angle, from the bite she had just taken.

"Yep. They pop over the top don't they? Hence the name. But unlike us, they have them more like a scone or a dessert. Weird, huh?" Brooke said, licking her fingers.

"That's so weird. I mean seriously, why would you have cream or jam on a Yorkshire pudding? That's pretty gross," Chloe squirmed, seeming interested.

"Well, have you ever seen their breakfasts? They have like sweet and savoury together. Like bacon, eggs, beans and melon on the side," she laughed. "And although I wouldn't have ever thought I'd say it as I personally dislike sweet and savoury…but I must profess, that my favourite breakfasts ever is bacon with maple syrup and then pancakes with sugar, all together," Brooke said smiling.

"You know, I didn't actually think I could think of you of being gross. But between that Yorkshire pudding thing you just did, and then your revelation on that breakfast, well let's just say my opinion of you has changed. And you are definitely gross," she laughed. "I'm disappointed at the Americans. I feel we need to go over there and introduce them to this," she pointed. "A proper roast, yorkie puds, or popovers, and loads of gravy," Chloe said.

"Well, we would need to introduce them to gravy too. Real British meat gravy, as I don't know what theirs is, but it's white. And they would need to be yorkies as they are made with meat juices, whereas popovers are made with oil. Ohhhh, we could open our own British restaurant, like our equivalent of a toby carvery," Brooke laughed, enjoying the silliness they were sharing.

"Ohhhh, I don't know if Canada is the same, but if it is, we could go with your bestie and live in a Canada outback type place. Like the Rockies or something, hidden away in the cold and have a bar stroke restaurant. The bar side with cosy log fires all around, where they have moose heads on the wall. Not real ones obviously, and then tia Maria and bailey cocktails to warm you up by the fire. We would also have a carvery so the gruff old men can go out and do their manly things. Then they could '*mosey on down, and bring their little women for a wholesome British roast dinner with real gravy and proper Yorkshire puds'*,*"* Chloe finally finished. She was unable to stop the laughter rolling out, as her interpretation of a Canadian drawl made her sound stupid.

"Oh my gosh, that was painfully horrific, yet so funny! What exactly was that supposed to be? Because I'm pretty sure you have just offended every Canadian and American known to man," she laughed, shaking her head at Chloe.

"What do you mean? On the cooking channel they have a TV show called Pioneer Woman, and they're still cowboys like that. Ohh whatever, I will make my millions in my little bar and restaurant and you can go be a bounty hunter with Mitch," she smirked to Brooke.

"Blimey, you have our whole future mapped out and we haven't even slept together," Brooke said seriously, causing Chloe's cheeks to flush intensely.

"Uh, I um..." Chloe sighed heavily, putting her head in her hands. "Um sorry I didn't mean."

"Chloe, chill the heck out, I'm fucking with you again," Brooke smirked, while picking up the dishes and taking them to the sink.

Chloe ignored the fact that Brooke was making fun again. "Hey, I'll do that since you cooked. You go and set up the TV so we can watch one L word if you fancy, then I need to head on out," Chloe said seriously.

"It's fine, leave those. I'll do them later or tomorrow. It will give me something to do. Seriously, it's fine. Just for this once, please? Do you know where we are up to?"

"It will take me two minutes, and I have no idea where we were up to, like eight or nine maybe."

"No, it's all good, come…sit." Brooke pointed to the sofa.

***

Brooke wasn't really watching the TV, because she was aware of the closeness between them and was feeling like everything was spiralling out of control. She didn't know what was right or wrong, or if there even was a right or wrong. She knew it was too soon, but she couldn't establish what exactly it was that was too soon? *A relationship? Sex? Friendship*? She was so confused by everything, but what she did know is she liked spending time with her and was disappointed that Chloe had to leave soon.

Brooke wished that Mitch was there already, because she wanted to talk to someone. And as much as she loved Kate, her heart always led her head and romance always took over logic. Brooke decided that when Chloe left, she would call Jo and speak to her. She noticed Chloe's phone vibrate and saw the name Clare appear on the screen. "Ermm, your phone is going," Brooke said, looking over to Chloe.

Chloe picked up her phone and read the text from Clare, who was checking if they were still on for the following night. Chloe was unsure of whether she should broach it with Brooke. Brooke had clearly seen the name, but just because it was a girl's name and she was a lesbian didn't mean there was something to it, surely?

"What are you thinking?" Brooke asked Chloe.

"Huh?"

"You do this thing when you are deep in thought, where the top of your left eyebrow twitches, so what are you thinking?" Brooke quizzed again.

"It does?" She reached up to her eyebrow.

"Not there, here," Brooke touched very softly, causing a stir within Chloe. "So what's up? Is it the text?"

Chloe sighed heavily. "Yes. I was debating what I *should* and what I *need* to tell you."

"You don't *need* to tell me anything, Chloe. If it's about the girl you're dating, then it's nothing to do with me. We kissed, so what? It's no big deal," Brooke said, way too harshly.

"Wow…erm, okay," Chloe said, surprised and stunned into silence. "I guess I should go?" Chloe said, as more of a question.

Brooke felt rubbish and knew she didn't want Chloe to leave, but she was more afraid of what would happen and what she would say, if she stayed. "Okay," she said quietly, and pressed stop on the DVD.

Wow, just like that, how the day's events had transpired. Chloe wanted to stay and explain, but in reality what would she be explaining? They weren't a couple, they weren't dating even, and Brooke was right. They kissed, so what? It was a drunken stupid kiss. Brooke didn't want more, and wasn't prepared to offer more. And in actuality neither did Chloe. More importantly, in the grand scheme of things, in a few weeks she would be gone back home to the opposite end of the country as Chloe.

"Thanks for dinner, Brooke. All three of them." She smiled slightly, and walked out.

Chapter Twenty-Seven

For the first time in weeks, Brooke was back to feeling sad and lonely again. She laid her head against the couch and let the tears flow naturally down her face. What was happening to her? More importantly, why was it happening? Really…what was she doing? Brooke felt terrible at how she had behaved. That wasn't her, not at all! Geez, they were the actions of Maria, not Brooke. She picked up her phone and opened her messages, re-reading the messages of earlier that morning. Why did she do that? Why? She opened the messages up to Jo and asked her to call her in private when she was able to, and was relieved when she called her within seconds.

"Hi. What's up? Are you okay?" Jo said to her.

Brooke was silent. She needed to speak but she couldn't get the words out. And in most part, that was due to the fact she knew she was holding on to the water faucet that was about to explode at any point.

"Brooke? Are you there?" Jo said again.

"Hmm hmmm," she sniffed.

"Hey, what's up? You're scaring me. Do you want me to come up early? Has something happened?"

"No, I'm okay," she sniffed.

"So what's going on?"

"Are you alone?"

"Yes, what's going on, babe?"

"I don't know what I'm doing. I'm hurting, but I don't know why anymore. I love it here and its hurting me. I kissed her. I kissed her last night. Then she had a message from a girl named Clare. I don't know who she is, and I basically said screw you! I said to her, 'so what, big deal, we kissed'. How awful! But it was a big deal, Jo. I don't know why, but I know it was. I pretty much said you're nothing to me, who cares? And so she left, and I let her leave, and now she's gone. I still don't know what the hell I'm doing. She was nice, and I guess I liked the attention, but now she's left and I'm here all alone and I don't want to be anymore. I don't know why I'm feeling this way and I don't want to. Oh…*and* we spent all morning flirting on text. What's happening to me, Jo? I can't ask Kate as she will just see romance, and I don't want there to be romance. I don't want any of this. But Katie will make me do something that I can't do, that I'm not ready to do. Jo, I feel so sad and I just don't know what to do, so I need someone to talk some sense into me," she said between sobs.

"Okay, let me order a coffee and I will be right there…," she said seriously. "Okay, I'm done. Shoot, and start from the very beginning."

***

"Honey, you are overthinking this, and you need to stop! You're right, today is very unlike you, but with everything that's recently happened, I think it was your fear talking. You need to apologise to her, Brooke. You have had a nice weekend, and to end it that way isn't fair on her," Jo said seriously.

"I know. So what do I say? Jo what's going on? I think I may be attracted to her, but I can't do that, I'm not ready. Should I just sleep with her? I'll never see her again after the next few weeks."

Jo sighed heavily. "Answer me one thing? Is she a bitch? If so, why is she such a bitch?" Jo said.

"What?"

"Well, the woman has implied, seemingly a number of times that she was very hurt, and as a result, won't commit and doesn't do relationships. She lives life, and has fun, and seemingly is kind enough to make sure she isn't messing with people's lives. She ensures they are fully aware of that fact. So what has she done to you that makes you feel it's acceptable to sleep with her when she clearly likes you, and possibly could be developing feelings for you? But then you walk away and hurt her? So to reiterate, what has she done to you?" Jo said harshly.

There was silence for a long time, and Jo didn't push Brooke. She knew she would respond in her own time, and eventually she did.

"I'm thirty next week, and I'm acting fifteen. I don't want to get hurt, and I don't want to hurt her. I don't know what I want…from anybody, if I want anything. It's nine years of my life down the drain. I don't want another relationship. Probably never, but certainly not now. So what happens now?" Brooke said solemnly.

"You are allowed to act out of sorts, considering it's been a pretty rough month, well year, for you. You don't know how to deal with new occurrences within your life, but you aren't a nasty person and you don't behave that way Brooke. Speak to her. You both appear to deal effectively with the forum you were communicating in this morning, so go down that route. Brooke, stop overthinking it. You have got someone showing you some interest, and anyone would positively react to that. It doesn't mean that you are going to get married and have kids. Equally, it doesn't mean that nothing will ever happen either. Speak to her and tell her how you're feeling, and if you don't know how that is, then tell her that. She's a friend, so treat her that way. Pretend you're talking to me," Jo said.

"Thanks, Jo," Brooke said, sighing lightly. "I will text her in a little bit. And thanks, I feel a bit better," she added.

"Good, I'm glad I could be of help. So what are you doing for your birthday? Are you sure you don't want to come back with us and spend a few days here so you aren't alone for it?"

"No, it's nothing. I will celebrate it this weekend with you guys," she said.

"Okay great. Well I'll speak to Chloe Friday, and see if she has any ideas of something memorable we can do on Saturday for it and organise that."

"No. It's no big deal, it's just a number. Jo, I know this is a bit unfair, but can we keep this conversation private please?" Brooke requested.

"If that's what you want, yes. Look, don't worry, we'll have a great weekend and will do something special for your birthday, Hun, and I'll guarantee that. Anyways, lady, as you sound a little more chipper, on a scale of one to ten, score on the kiss please?" Jo smirked into the phone, trying to lighten Brooke's sombre mood.

"Jo! I can't believe you are asking that. I need to go now. I will keep you posted re the weekend. Thanks again," Brooke giggled.

"Spoil sport. Right. I will see you on Friday, lovely. Okay?" Jo said.

"Thanks, I can't wait. Oh and Jo?"

"Yes?"

"It was an eleven," Brooke smiled, and hung up the phone.

***

Brooke finished the last of the clearing away and poured herself a glass of wine. She picked up her phone and went and sat on the veranda, opening up her messages to find Chloe's messages. Just as Brooke was about to write a message, she noticed the grey dots, indicating that Chloe was typing a message. Brooke waited a few moments before she noticed them disappear again, deciding to take action and not wait for Chloe to message her. In reality, it wasn't up to Chloe to reach out to Brooke. She was the one completely out of line in this instance.

Hey you, did you get home OKAY? Listen, I'm incredibly sorry for what I said. I was out of line, and you didn't deserve that. I hope you can forgive me? ☹ X

Hi, Brooke. Yes, I got home a short while ago. It's OKAY, nothing to apologise or forgive for. Thanks again for dinner today and a nice evening yesterday.

Ouch Brooke thought. She laid down on the couch nursing her wine and allowed the one lone tear to fall from her cheek. What had she done? She had mistreated a true friend and now she regretted every moment of it. What was she supposed to respond to that? Or wasn't she? But before she had time to think about it she had another incoming message from Chloe. Already feeling a sense of reluctance to open it, she hesitated at first, but knew Jo was right. This was her doing so she needed to grow up, fix it and stop avoiding.

And Brooke, for the record, I'm not dating anyone. I went on one date last week with a girl, yes named Clare, who I am supposed to be going out with again tomorrow. One date thus far, does not constitute dating in my opinion. I am merely getting to know the girl. As it turns out, this morning I had made the decision to cancel anyhow.

I'm very sorry I was an arsehole, and that I upset you. I didn't mean to. I wouldn't have intentionally done that. I...um...I guess, I got jealous, but I don't know why, because it's none of my business. But that's why I reacted the way I did. It isn't an excuse, nor is it acceptable, but it's the reason. And I can't do or say anything further than sorry and offering you that by way of an explanation. X

She didn't know if Chloe would accept or even wish to discuss it, but it was the most she could do at this moment in time. Brooke sighed heavily and watched the grey dots appear and disappear, then reappear again. She took a large gulp of her wine and laid back down again, waiting for the response to come through. She didn't know if it was what she wanted to see, but she knew that she wasn't going to give up that easily. This was a truly wonderful woman and friend, and there was no way she was going to lose her, least not through fear.

Brooke looked on google for cute 'I'm sorry' pictures. She was scanning through the mixture of puppies, kittens, plane banners and a number of other options, when another message came through.

Why did you get jealous?
Because...I don't know, erm... ☹ Oh I don't know!!
Well I think you do!!

Brooke knew this was all her doing and was deserving of this reaction from Chloe, but she didn't know how to deal with it.

I don't know anything anymore. I left because of shit, I arrived and it was going great here, and still is. I know I have fun with you and miss you when I'm not with you, but part of me doesn't want that. Part of me needs to sort my own head out first, before I can consider anything or anyone else. Then I am getting jealous? I don't know how to deal with that, because this was never supposed to happen. I don't know how to deal with the fact that I seem to be attracted to you and I kissed you and I knew I shouldn't have kissed you. But even through the beer, I knew I wanted to kiss you. I don't like that feeling, because it's making me feel exposed and that scares me. x

Why shouldn't you have kissed me?

She was going to make Brooke pay, and pay she would. She was going to make her say it all and explain it all. Brooke was struggling with the prospect of having to put everything on the line, but like Jo said, she needed to make this better and be open.

Because I don't think I'm ready. Plus, you don't have relationships…and I don't do one night stands, and most of all, because I'm afraid Chlo. ☹xxx

Of me?

No not of you, of what will happen if I lose control. x

What about me? You don't think I'm afraid of letting go? Of what might happen if I do? I don't do this. I haven't because I don't ever want to go through that pain again, but I can't help it with you. I know you aren't ready, and I don't want to push you, but I don't know

229

how to protect myself either, other than just staying away until you have left! X

Is that what you want? X

Brooke's heart was racing, and she didn't know what she was going to do if Chloe came back with yes. And the realisation set in that she was terrified about what that would mean. Worryingly, she was unsure if she was *more* worried about that, than facing that she might actually be attracted to her.

No, but at the same time I don't know if I'm brave enough to face it either. I didn't expect your words to hurt as much as they did, and that's scaring me a lot more. ☹

I will leave early. I will tell Jo and Katie to leave coming up and I can meet them somewhere in between. It's your place, and I was only renting, so it's no big deal.

Apparently not much is a big deal to you!

That isn't fair. I don't want to hurt you, and I was trying to make things easier for you, that's all. I'm sorry I seem to be wrecking everything. I would never intentionally hurt you, because that isn't who I am. Look, I'll let you go. I'm sorry again for everything. I am not normally like this, but I just don't know how I get me back, or when that will actually be! I wish things could have been different, because you truly are an amazing woman. B xxx

You can't keep running forever, Brooke. For one, you run the risk of wasting your life and missing out on so many opportunities. I wish things could have been different also. Look after yourself, Brooke. X

Brooke seemed to have lost the ability to breathe normally, and before she knew it she was sobbing uncontrollably, once again.

Chapter Twenty-Eight

Brooke had gone two whole days without speaking to Chloe, and she felt rubbish because of it. She didn't know how she had managed to spend a full weekend with a beautiful woman where there were no presumptions or expectations, and it was all just entirely natural. So how had it ended like this?

Brooke wished she knew her address, so she would have been able to drive over in a bid to make it alright. But instead she had done nothing but feel rubbish about it all. How had she messed up so majorly? Chloe was right that she'd run away from something that might not have even been anything, and lost an amazing friend in the process.

Brooke went to the safari page on her phone, and saw the 'miss you' images she had been looking at the other night. She found one with a teddy at a steamy train window, with the words miss you written in it. She pressed send to Chloe and threw her phone on the couch, as she walked out of the van.

Brooke needed to go shopping, and the last thing she wanted was to be phone watching the entire time. So she figured she would leave it behind, and if she didn't text back at least it wouldn't mess with her whilst she was out.

A few hours later she returned laden with bags of food, drink and little housey bits, such as candles to give it a little bit of a homey feel. She was desperate to check her phone, but she didn't allow herself to. She couldn't handle the rejection if the phone was empty. Unpacking everything, Brooke had found new homes for the candles and incense. Even though it was only little bits, it gave the place the perfect feel.

Brooke put on a pair of shorts and a vest debating whether to go for another run, when she lit up the screen and saw a message from her dad, a message from Mitch and a message from Chloe. She closed her eyes and tried to talk herself down from the thumping heart that was beating down her chest. She said a silent prayer that it wasn't a *'leave me alone'* text.

You do? Me too! ☹ How is that even possible?

Brooke sighed with relief, completely overjoyed that Chloe didn't hold a grudge. If that was Maria she would have been ignored for a number of days, and then she would have had continuous digs about what she had done. This was a new dynamic for her, and this wasn't Maria, this was Chloe. Nice Chloe…nice, normal, sweet Chloe. Brooke stopped her thoughts, feeling the sudden wave of nausea come over her. She sighed heavily, and pushed those odd thoughts to the back of her mind, as she got comfy and replied to her friend…

I don't know, I really don't. But I was so worried that I had lost you. I don't know who I am or what I want at this moment, but what I do know is I miss not being able to see or speak to you. And I hate fighting with you. x

Me too. I think we're both in a strange place, but in the same respect we are both adults and it isn't doing anyone any good to keep hurting each other.

Maybe we should come to a decision, define what we both want and go from there? X

S.L. Gape

I'm good with that. I don't know exactly what I want, but I know I like you. And I'm terrified for me, for you, and for the distance between us when you go home. I'm terrified for the fact you have so much on your plate, for me not doing relationships, and for you needing time out of relationships. So whilst I can't say specifically, I know I feel pretty low when we don't speak. I miss my friend, and I miss your company. x

I see all that, and totally get where you are coming from. They are all my fears and concerns, added to the fact that I may not be (without sounding like a freak now) mentally stable enough to know what I'm doing. That I'm just maybe living in a bit of a daze and therefore, when I come round, we are too far in, and one if not both of us gets hurt. X

I don't think that will be the case, because I don't think neither of us knows what we want. Except for the occasional kiss and someone to take the piss out of. ☺x

I liked the kiss. x

I'm kinda missing that kiss. :/ x

You are? ☺ I don't know if we would have had another one before I messed it all up, but I kinda wish we had. I don't know how or why, but the universe is apparently trying to tell us something? X

You didn't mess it up, please let's forget it. In other news, you're getting very brave. ;) x

I know! ☺ How are you? Are you still coming this weekend? X

Well there's a loaded question? ;) X

OMG you are so rude at times. It didn't take you long to start misbehaving!! You know what I meant!! X

Says you!! I was merely responding to your misbehaving nature!! Do you want me to? X

I do. x

And do I get another kiss? X A sober kiss this time? X

I'm not so sure about sober, but I am sure I can arrange another one. x

Only one? ;) X

Greedy!!! We'll have to see if you're a good girl. xx

I'm always good, well unless asked otherwise. ;) x

Are you drinking? Stop misbehaving. X

Why? I like misbehaving. X

Brooke read, as she opened the picture message from Chloe of a glass of wine…

My first one, haven't even had a sip yet. ☺ Don't need a drink to talk naughty. x

Hmmm I'm sure!! Sexy nail polish. ;) x

I'm going to respond with a simple thank you to that comment. But I will caveat that with, that it's taken every inch of will power I have to not respond any other way to that comment. ;) X

OKAY, now you are being very bad, and this isn't going to end well!! So, what have you been up to? X

Why change the subject? Very bad is very good. ;) LOL. I've just been working really and sorting some stuff out. I went out to dinner with Ems last night, and she loved the bracelet. Thanks for helping me with that. So when are the girls getting there? X

About midday Friday, I think, and leaving first thing on Monday. I'm so looking forward to it, more so now. ☺ X

How so? X

Well, I've made up with my very best looking single, lesbian friend, who's now put a smile on my face saying she will be here. So I may actually enjoy myself. x

Hmmmm, very best looking single, lesbian friend. She sounds hot! ;) Haha... awesome, maybe you could hook me up with her, you know being we're both single and like to have some fun. x

Ouch, and ouch!! You wouldn't like her, she's pushy, and dirty, very dirty. Likes to misbehave! X

Ohhhh sounds like fun, send me her number. It's been a while, and I could do with a little bit of dirty. x

A while? Really? Didn't get lucky on your date on Monday? JOKES. xxxxx

I'm glad you gave 5 kisses, since I will kick your ass when I see you next!! No, I didn't get lucky, but yes I went. I forced myself to go because of what happened, but I wasn't great company. And I have since respectfully removed myself from the situation. X

You didn't need to explain. And I would like to see you kick my ass. You realise I am a detective? There is no way you'll ever kick my ass! X

Well that sounds like a proposition, and I will accept that bet! You can't use your handcuffs though, well not in that situation anyway! ;) X

BEHAVE!!! No handcuffs, maybe the gun though!! ☺ X

OMG do you have a gun? Wow, do you have a uniform too? OKAY, I may need to stop this conversation, or we are going to have major issues this weekend! X

You are so wrong. Right, subject change! What do you think we can do on Saturday? X

Spoil sport! ☹ I don't know I will have a think. What you doing tonight? X

Currently pouring myself a drink after dealing with you for the last hour. I'm going to just chill and watch a couple of movies and have an early night. How about you? X

Same really, a couple of wines and an early night, dreaming sweet of a recent sexy kiss. x

Really? Well there's no pressure for the next one then is there? X

Chloe and Brooke spent the remainder of the evening speaking to each other, until Chloe finally had to say good night because of work the following morning. Still keeping it a surprise that she would be there tomorrow night, just hoping it would be a good one and not putting any pressure on her. She was glad that Brooke had reached out to her tonight as she had missed their interaction. And whilst she was still completely unclear of what she was doing, she knew that she couldn't turn her back on it. And that meant she had to take a risk on Brooke, even if that meant running the risk of getting her heart broken, once again.

***

Chloe parked her car at the top of the site so that Brooke didn't see it. She walked down to her cabin, careful to not get caught out by anyone. She had a couple of conference calls to dial into, and then she was hoping that her plan for tonight worked. She was feeling somewhat nervous after spending practically all night the day before flirting their asses off, leaving her feeling incredibly uncertain as to whether she would be able to face her now. She would most definitely need a little drink, that much was a given. Chloe also hoped that Brooke didn't get upset by the surprise. She knew that the texting was coming far easier, but when it came to the crunch there was still so many hurdles for her to overcome. Chloe couldn't dwell on that, because she needed to focus on this weekend and having some fun and...well they would just have to see what happens.

Chloe finished up with work and put her stuff away as she opened a bottle of wine. She took a large sip and grabbed a shower whilst she worked out how she would get Brooke over to her place, without giving anything away. Feeling unsure of what clothes to wear, she didn't want to make Brooke feel uncomfortable and certainly didn't want her to feel like there were any expectations. Equally though, she seemed to have taken the uncontrollable turn she had been trying to avoid, and as such she actually wanted to look good. Finally, after far too long deliberating, she gave up and put some yoga pants and a converse vest on, and left it at that. Releasing her hair band, Chloe allowed her long dark hair to fall down. Her head was banging tonight, and this great plan had contributed a large element of that tension.

Grabbing the takeaway menu and her phone, Chloe laid on her bed and dialled Brooke's number. She was still unsure as to which route to go down, but pressed call and figured she'd go with the flow and decipher which way to handle it when Brooke answered.

"Hi, how are you? So what do I owe the pleasure? Oh, please don't tell me you are bailing?"

"Hey you, I'm good thanks. Are you? Erm, yes about that. I am really sorry but I am going to have to leave this weekend. Some things have come up at home and I can't get out of it I'm afraid," Chloe said, feeling a little awful and trying to kerb any laughter.

"Oh, um, right...well I get it. It's fine, and thanks for letting me know. Is everything okay at home?"

Chloe felt awful hearing the disappointment in her voice, so she needed to move the call quickly.

"Yes, just some issues on this end. Listen, there is something else. I have a bit of a problem, erm, can you smell gas at all?" *Shit, what the hell was that?* She had never once thought about gas, and she was totally going to mess this up.

"Erm gas? Here? No why? Let me check outside. No nothing. Why?"

"Well, I have just had a text. Would you mind checking my cabin for me?" Chloe said, shaking her head to herself.

"I don't have a key."

"Oh, there's a spare one. On my balcony there is a palm tree and then three stone type things. If you check, there's a key under one of them."

"Are you kidding me? Do you know how unsafe it is to keep a key there, Chloe? Why don't you leave it with a neighbour? That's ridiculous. What if someone got hold of it and you were in there alone?"

This really wasn't going according to plan thought Chloe. "Okay, well you take it when you leave and you can keep it until you go home. Thanks so much for this, Brooke. If you could call me back when you have been in or if there are any problems?" she said, hanging up before she slipped up.

Chloe downed her wine and giggled to herself. She was rubbish at stuff like this, but she had to give herself a ten out of ten for effort. She heard the key unlock in the door and stood up. It would be just her luck now for Brooke to have her gun!

"Seriously, for a grown woman you're idiotic! Who leaves a bloody key in this day and age? And seriously,

S.L. Gape

'oh I can't come this weekend' but do something for me, charming…" Brooke was mumbling to herself wandering around the room sniffing all around.

"First sign of madness you know," Chloe said from the doorway.

"Holy shit!" she screamed out. "What the hell is wrong with you? You scared the shit out of me! What are you doing here? Jesus, Chloe!" Brooke said, holding her chest with one hand and her head with the other.

Chloe couldn't help but burst into fits of laughter, "I'm sorry, I'm sorry," she said, holding her hands up in surrender.

"What are you doing? Why are you here? Why couldn't you check the gas for yourself? I still can't smell anything? Oh…there was no gas, you were pulling my leg. But why?" Brooke asked confused.

"Well, initially I thought it would be a nice surprise that I could get here and help out and have a night together, but now I'm doubting that," Chloe said with uncertainty. "Oh, and I didn't mean anything by a 'night'. I just meant a chill out before this weekend's antics. Sorry, it sounded great in my head," she said, feeling embarrassed.

"You went to all that trouble for me? Come here early, hide your car and make up ridiculous lies to surprise me?" Brooke said, smiling slightly.

"Well, ermm yes. But it wasn't any big deal. I worked from here this afternoon, and then thought it would be fun and a nice surprise. Additionally, after you were going on all night about wanting an Indian, I am going to treat you to an Indian takeaway. Well, unless you have other plans. If not, take a look and let me know what you want and I will order it," Chloe said. She held up the bottle of wine, in question of whether Brooke would like one.

"Yes, thanks."

Chloe poured another glass of wine and handed it to Brooke, who was leaning against the cabinet with her arms folded. She kept her eyes on Brooke's as she had taken the glass, in a bid to ignore the girl in her running shorts… her exceptionally short running shorts and fitted t-shirt. It also didn't go unnoticed that the girl was smirking at Chloe.

"What's up with you?" Chloe asked quizzically.

"You really will do anything for another kiss, hey?" Brooke said with one eyebrow raised.

"Oh my gosh, I so would not. Seriously, it was nothing to do with that. There are no presumptions this evening and no expectations. Please don't think I was trying to pressure you into anything," Chloe said concerned.

"Woah easy tiger, I was fucking with you," she said, still with her eyebrow raised and a slight smirk to match. "Thanks for the surprise, I really appreciate it. Okay, I'm going to check out this menu whilst you're freaking in the corner," she said, laughing and slowly walking to the couch.

Oh dear. In Chloe's head she was in total control. Whether something had changed with Brooke after the weekend, or she was that excited about her friends, or maybe even that she'd had a drink. Whatever the cause, things had definitely switched. Brooke was most definitely in control now, and she was actually swaggering. She had a sexy swagger that she didn't normally have. And she knew it, and she was doing it now, in those short shorts. Oh my god, she was awful.

Once again the realisation was hitting home that she was getting herself in deeper than she would be able to handle. Of that, she was pretty sure.

***

"Have you decided what you want?" Chloe walked over to the couch, putting her wine glass down and sitting on the couch.

Brooke went to say something, but stopped herself. "I have. Here you go. Do you want to order it? I was going to quickly nip home and get a quick shower, change and lock up etc. I haven't changed since running this afternoon, if that's okay by you?"

"Yes that's fine. Shall I order it now, or wait until you are back?"

"I'll be ten minutes. I don't have to do that much, so just order it now." She smirked, as she embraced this new confident swagger again.

"Right oh, I will order it no...*oh*, seriously? You need to STOP doing that!" Chloe said with her hands on her hips, feigning mad.

Brooke walked past Chloe to the door, and as she passed her she turned around and whispered into her ear, "I don't know what you mean Chloe?" before leaving. Brooke walked into her own place and leaned her head against the door, sighing heavily. She didn't know what had come over her, but she was suddenly feeling the nerves. Taking a deep breath, she rushed into the shower and got ready. Uncertain of what to wear she opted for a similar look to Chloe in some lounge pants and a vest. She breathed in heavily and grabbed a couple of bottles and walked back over to her friend's cabin.

***

"Hey, it's me," she said, entering slowly.

"Well it was hardly going to be the burglar was it? So, um, your phone has been going…a fair few times," she said, walking past Brooke without looking at her.

Brooke picked up her phone and saw four missed calls from Maria. She spun around to face Chloe. "So seemingly Maria wants to get hold of me. She's called four timem;s!" she said pointedly to Chloe.

"Right. Well best call her back, it could be important. You never know, she may have seen the error of her ways. You said she didn't want marriage and kids, so taking off with a mum probably wasn't the best idea she ever had. We can leave tonight, go home and talk to her," she said quietly, turning to pour herself another glass and wondering why the hell she was sounding so needy.

"Chloe?" she said, walking over to her.

"Yep?"

"Turn around. Please?"

Chloe was reluctant to turn and face the girl, but slowly turned to her, keeping her eyes on her drink.

Brooke lifted Chloe's chin so their eyes met. "I don't want to leave this evening. You went to all this trouble, which I'm hugely touched by, and I'm not prepared to jump just because she says so. I spent the last nine years doing that. If it's that important, she'll leave a message, otherwise she can wait. Because I have a nice bottle," she said, holding it up. "A nicer dinner," she lifted the takeaway menu. "And an even nicer woman," she said, leaning in and kissing Chloe's lips softly. Then she quickly moved away to allow her to take back the control of her breathing again. "Okay?" she smiled lightly.

Chloe didn't know what to say. Her head was swimming and she could barely breathe, failing miserably at trying to maintain eye contact, feeling constant flushes over her face.

"Gone very quiet there, Casey?" Brooke was smirking at her again.

"How has this happened? How have you now got the control?" Chloe whispered.

They were looking deeply into each other's eyes, unspoken questions still unanswered, when Brooke's phone went off again. "Seriously!" She leaned her forehead against Chloe's. "Do you mind if I just take it to get rid of her?" Brooke said, walking away.

"Yeah, if dinner comes I'll keep it warm until you return," Chloe said quietly.

"I'm not going anywhere, sweetie. I can deal with it here. I brought more wine over," she pointed to Chloe as she answered the phone.

"Hello?" she snapped.

"Where the hell have you been?" Maria snapped back.

"Excuse me? Who the hell do you think you're talking to? Where I have been is none of your business. I'm busy, Maria. What do you want?"

"Of course you are! Playing games, no doubt! I have been promoted again, but I don't know if your *'best bud'* told you?" she spat. "Anyways, there are going to be some changes, so I need to know when you are returning to work. I have been speaking to HR and we can't continue paying you forever. We have been more than lenient, but now, well...I need to manage the department and my structure, so I will need some indication as to when you are returning," Maria said.

"And you need to know this now? At seven o'clock on a Thursday night? The night before my best friends are coming up to see me for a wonderful weekend? You need to know that now?"

"Oh, get a grip and stop being childish. You are so melodramatic. It was the best thing I've ever done, getting away from yo…"

"NOW listen, Maria, and listen very carefully to me. I may not work in human resources, but I know the basics from being a manager, and you cannot force me to return if I am signed off sick. You should know that more than most! You should also know that working in the public sector means you will no doubt be breaching all sorts of laws. Additionally, do NOT ever, EVER speak to me like that again. Rightly so the best thing you ever did WAS 'get away from me' as you so classily put it. But, I wholeheartedly agree with that position. You are most definitely correct. We are not, nor were we ever, right for each other, and you did nothing but belittle and undermine me for all those years. I am away from you and slowly becoming me again. But if you want me back, you will need to sack me and I'll see you in court. Otherwise, I will make contact with HR in due course. Do not contact me again, or I will contact the department about harassment. Alternatively, I will go to HR about raising a formal grievance about my new line manager victimising me when I am deemed as unfit to work due to work related stress. Work related stress caused by issues arising from being shot at work, which I'm pretty sure will not bode well for you. Now, piss off and leave me to go back to my lovely evening." She hung up and immediately switched her phone off. "*So…*" she turned around to Chloe who looked gobsmacked. "Sorry about that."

Chloe could not believe what she had just heard, but couldn't help but laugh "Wow, quite the little feisty one aren't we?" she said.

Brooke went serious. "I'm sorry, maybe I shouldn't have taken it here. I apologise if you felt that was inappropriate. But I don't really think that I deserve being spoken to like that, when I am away trying to sort my life out. Least not, over things that have been a result of her. And to then be shouted at that I am childish, melodramatic. Although I agree we weren't right for each other, it's still not particularly nice after nine years with someone that you thought you'd spend the rest of your life with, *and* your boss, to scream down the phone that the best decision they ever made was leaving you. I may not be perfect, but I deserve a little more than that. So my apologies that I may have overreacted and been equally as rude to her but…"

"Woah, woah, woah. I don't think you were wrong. Not by any means. I'm biased, Brooke, and I will happily admit that. She doesn't deserve you. She's a stupid, nasty, self-righteous bitch, and I'm incredibly proud that you have finally stood up for yourself with her, instead of letting her continue to walk all over you," Chloe said empathetically. "Please don't let us fall out over this? I feel like we have finally found some common ground and we are… well, at least on the same chapter now. Brooke, don't let her ruin our night, or weekend. Do you not think that's what she was aiming for? Do you not think she knows they are coming up and she is purposely, *still* trying to control you?" Chloe said factually. The door knocked, causing them both to look over at it. "I'll go and get that, I won't bother putting it out," she said deflated.

"Chloe, may I borrow your phone please?"

Chloe looked down at Brooke's phone confused.

"I don't want to turn it back on. I'll only be ten minutes. Will you keep it warm until I return?" Brooke said, taking Chloe's phone and walking outside.

***

"Okay, I love you too. Call me if you need to. Yes, that's fine. She only lives next door so she can reach me if need be. Love you, bye," she finished, as she walked back inside and shut the door.

"Everything okay?" Chloe asked.

"Hi, yes. I know you haven't said anything, but I can't keep feeling shit and feeling like I need to apologise for everything. I feel like she's turned me into this person, and I don't know how to not be that person that takes the blame for everything. I want to just forget about what just happened, continue with our planned night, have dinner, watch some movies and look forward to the weekend," Brooke said, leaning against the radiator, and waiting for some response from Chloe.

Chloe had been thinking about things whilst Brooke was outside. She seemed so insecure about everything, and she couldn't quite work out if that was her or if this was the influence of her ex? Why was she even thinking all this stuff?

"Pour the drinks, and I'll plate up. How do you have it? Do you want poppadum's and dips first?" she asked, walking to the kitchen.

"Poppadum's and dips first is the only way to go. FYI, if we are watching anything other than a cartoon you are going to have to put a jumper or jacket on," she said, kissing her lips quickly and grabbing the bottle, causing Chloe to blush.

"Erm, care to elaborate?" Chloe asked as she put the cutlery and food on the table.

"You know full well, lady." Brooke smirked, and pointed to the revealing vest she had on. "Cheers, here's to another attempt at a nice night." Brooke smiled, holding up her glass with one hand and her poppadum with the other.

"Don't know what you mean, Davis. Cheers, here's to good friends, an amazing weekend and a nice evening. And hopefully a yummy Indian," she said, smiling wide.

***

"Thanks for dinner, that was lovely. I can't move now though, so what do you fancy watching?" Brooke asked.

"I'm easy, so knock yourself out," Chloe said, putting the dishes in the dishwasher.

"Imagine me and you? That's cute and one of my faves? Or a TV show? I don't know?"

Brooke and Chloe laid on opposite ends of the sofa with their feet slightly touching. The movie was easy going, which made it easy to not think and flow with the movie. This was great for Brooke, who was still feeling weird about the whole Maria thing. In reality, she didn't know what to do about it. She couldn't keep her phone off all night, and seriously, why should she have to? She spoke to her father and told him to text Chloe's number if he needed her, or if Maria made contact. She was happy that she had not heard from him, hoping that was a sign that she was being quiet as opposed to him trying to handle it himself.

"You okay?" Chloe asked quizzically.

"Yeah, just thinking about my dad."

"Your dad?"

"Yeah, that's who I called when I asked to borrow your phone earlier. I just wanted to make sure he was okay, and to forewarn him about her," Brooke said, leaning her head against the couch.

"So, is he okay?" Chloe asked concerned.

"Yes. I just know what he's like and really don't want him to be getting rubbish from her, then making the decision to not tell me so he doesn't stress me out any further. He's just so worried about me, and I really don't want him to be. I'm sure he'll be fine. Maybe I should just switch it back on?" she asked, more to herself than anyone else.

"Why don't you switch it on and just block her number?" Chloe asked.

"Hmmm, I could do that actually. That makes sense. I guess it's no different to getting a new number, which was actually always the plan," Brooke said. "Is it too late for another bottle?"

"You can, I'm just gonna have a coffee," Chloe said, watching the TV.

"Oh, okay, we can leave it. It's just me being greedy, sorry. You should have said if you wanted to call it a night."

"It isn't that," she said, still not looking. "I've had a great night, but in the same respect, I am also not the greatest with will power. I don't trust myself watching movies like this, with a beautiful woman who I know I need to keep my hands off. In reality, the more I'm telling myself I need to, the more I really, *really* don't want to. So I'm going to respectfully decline any more drinks and stick to coffee and make the most of a booze fuelled weekend, where I am going to have to pretend that I have never noticed the things I have noticed about you," Chloe said, peeling the label from the bottle of wine.

"What have you noticed about me?" Brooke asked smiling.

"You need to stop that."

"Why?"

"Because it's naughty, and you're naughty," Chloe said, finally looking up to the smiling face.

"Maybe I wanna be naughty," Brooke confirmed.

"You need to stop."

"So tell me already and I'll stop."

"You have a very beautiful smile," Chloe said.

Brooke sighed lightly, "There's so much I want to say and do, Chlo, but you're right. I really don't want you to doubt that though. But until we are both at a stage where it's okay to put ourselves in that position, we are better off being sensible. I know it's too soon, and I really don't want to hurt you. I really hope you believe me when I say that, but I just don't know what to do at this moment. I love hanging out with you because you're so much fun, and literally made everything feel like it's falling back into place. But equally, I know it's not fair on you, especially if it feels like I'm playing mind games. I know I'm suddenly aware of you, like hugely aware, and honestly I'm not particularly happy about that. But

I've quickly realised I just need to roll with it, so I'm living with it." She smiled softly.

Brooke sighed heavily, "I guess what I'm trying to say is, I wouldn't blame you for removing yourself from the situation and me. I think I would."

"Woah, easy tiger! I'm scarily, for me, past the stage of wanting to just sleep with you. I don't know why or when it happened. And I'm not saying that to allude to the fact that something is going to happen, whether it be just sex or anything more, but I'm not in any way, shape, or form asking you to clarify that for me either. Like you, I am enjoying spending some time with you. I have few lesbian girlfriends, so it's actually been a nice change. But in the same respect, I'm a red-blooded, single lesbian and you're a hot, single lesbian. So whilst I'm not assuming or anticipating or even expecting anything, watching a lesbian chick flick, with a beautiful single woman in close proximity whilst inebriated is a task in itself. So what I'm doing is merely removing myself from the situation so that way I won't get wasted and think it's a good idea to try and lure you into bed," Chloe laughed.

"Well, I could easily carry on drinking, so I'm actually glad you're taking the control. I don't think you're far off the mark with where it would end, and like you, I don't know what I'm doing or why I'm doing it. But I really don't want to do something for the sake of it. My head is a mess still, and I just can't work out what to do. But one thing I do know is I like kissing you. GOD, do I like kissing you. But equally, I don't want to do something that may mess things up right now, if that makes sense?"

"Brooke, it's okay. I think we're on the same page. I'm not going to take anything you have said with offense and I think...I hope, that's what you were intending," Chloe said, smiling. She knew this was a risk, and that was exactly what Nat had warned her of.

"Do you fancy a surf in the morning before the girls get here?"

"Yes, definitely. I want to get up early to prepare, because stupidly I said we could have a BBQ. So I need to go through the freezer and get bits out for Jo to sort when she arrives. If I do that before we go surfing I won't be as stressed."

"Please tell me you're kidding? You cannot invite friends up, expect her to drive for hours and then get her to cook?" Chloe laughed. "How about I come by first thing, and prep some food? I have loads of marinades and seasonings here and then we go for a surf?" she said. "If everything is frozen just make sure you get it out this evening."

"She loves it, but okay. We can sort it in the morning. Good night, Chloe, thanks for this evening and the surprise, it was wonderful. Sweet dreams," she whispered, looking deep into her eyes.

Chloe didn't know Brooke well enough to understand what the look meant, or what she was trying to say, but she could see that there was something there. Something more that she wanted to say. "I can assure you I will be having the sweetest of dreams, Brooke. Same to you." Chloe winked.

"Hmm, pretty safe to say," Brooke said, leaving the cabin.

***

Chloe was staring at the ceiling as she heard the phone vibrate on the side.

On a scale of 1-10, how much do you were wish we were together right now? Xx

Smiling at the screen, she was thankful that at least it wasn't all one sided, despite the fear and apprehension that she was still committing more and would end up being hurt.

You turned your phone back on? Good going. Um, 11? Btw, you don't really get this whole 'being good' thing do you? Haha X

Nope, seemingly not!! Me too! ☹ Not even in a sexual way... well, possibly a little. ☺ But I kinda wish we were just snuggling on the couch together after tonight's shit. My God, I am such a lesbian. Only a lezzer would say she'd rather be snuggling than having sex. Xx

I'm pretty sure no lesbian would say that. Or maybe after having had sex they would like to be snuggled. Have you heard from her again? Are you OKAY? X

I'm fine. I'm ignoring, I'm reflecting, I'm thinking (this is hurting, FYI) and I'm trying to stop myself from letting my mind take me to places that I know it shouldn't. X

Such as. ☺x

BEHAVE!! I'm not telling you! X

Spoil sport. x

Hardly, I'm trying to regain control before I end up spiralling out of control. X

Is that what you see me as? X

Nope, I just keep losing control, and I don't like that! It seems that's all that's happened to me for the last 12 months. And I keep thinking about you as opposed to my job, my life, a place to live. x

Maybe you are trying to have control, and that's why you keep losing control? I have a solution☺ that's simple. Let's have sex, then that's one less thing to worry about and you can continue with the thoughts on the other stuff! ;) X

You really are a nightmare aren't you? I don't think that will help me. x

Maybe not, but it would be sooooo good ;). Plus, it would help me, and then it would help you in the sense that you have a kind heart. ;) x

You are mental!!! Stop it, NOW!! Do you think you are going to be able to behave this weekend? X

Yes of course, I can behave occasionally!! And in case you haven't noticed, I'm only naughty in a text form. I think you'll find that you are the one that misbehaves in reality. But I know that we are friends and that there will be no looks, kisses, or touching in front of your friends. Behave like we are nothing, act like nothing has happened. x

You sound pissed with me. I don't want you to sound like I am making all the shots, and I don't want to make you feel shit, as that really isn't the case. ☹X

Chill out, princess. I'm fucking with you... you need to relax a little!! ☺ I am fine with it. Actually, I would prefer it until we have had a chance to establish, understand, discuss or accept what's going on. I really don't want other people involved. I think we need to do stuff at our own pace and see what happens. But I'm really looking forward to meeting your friends and having some girly time with you guys. What happens between you and I, if anything, really needs to start and finish with you and I. x

*You really need to stop that!! ;) Good plan. OKAY,
I'm moments away from starting to lure you into naughty
conversations or come over there, so I'm going to do you
a favour and bow out gracefully. Good night, Chloe. xx*

*And you think that's OKAY to say that before you log
out? What were you going to say? Come on, tell me. I bet
you can be very dirty when you want to. Oh dear God, I
think I'm happy to go now! Good nigh,t little miss
naughty. xx*

*And you have the audacity to say I'm naughty??
Naughty? Me? I don't know what you mean. ;) On the
contrary, you have absolutely NO idea about my
dirtiness, just saying! ;) Good night you. Xx*

*OMG I am taking no responsibility for anything
where you are concerned EVER again!! I can't believe
you are leaving me with a statement like that!! Well, I'm
confident that I'll learn one day just how naughty you can
be, if recent events are anything to go by! ☺ Good night
again Brooke! See you in the morning. MWAH xx*

Chapter Twenty-Nine

Chloe couldn't sleep, and couldn't get past the yearning inside to impress Brooke's friends. Up at the crack of dawn and making marinades for the food, she was confident that whatever Brooke had, there would be a seasoning to suit, given the variety and amount she had concocted. If they needed anything else, she would grab it when she was at the store. Brooke had mentioned that Kate had a sweet tooth, so she wanted to go and get ingredients to make an amazing dessert for them.

Chloe finally finished up in the kitchen. She got into her bikini, pulled her wetsuit half way up and locked up before going to Brooke's, laden with various bags of sauces and spices.

"Hey yo...," she said, stopping mid-sentence with her mouth open. "*Really?* You need to stop wearing shit like that, or the lack there-of!!" Brooke held the door open, shaking her head and refusing to look at Chloe.

"Well sorry, but I'm a surfer. I'm going surfing and this is how I dress when I go surfing. So unfortunately, tough shit," she smiled. "Now where's the food?"

"What? Now? I thought we were going surfing?" Brooke said.

"Brooke, go get that pretty little ass of yours ready, point me to the direction of the food, and I will sort everything out. I will be done by the time you return." Chloe smiled as she opened the fridge.

"Okay, no more talking like that." She smiled wickedly.

God that smile was going to kill Chloe.

"Be two ticks," she said as she ran off.

Chloe pulled the meat from the fridge, checking what was there, and was impressed. She opened the chicken breasts and put half of them in one of the bags full of marinade and the other half in another bag of seasoning. She opened the ribs and rubbed in her dry rub, which smelled amazing she thought. She poured her barbecue sauce into a freezer bag and added a little bit of Jack Daniels to the mixture.

"Hmmm, it smells wonderful in here. What have you made?" Brooke asked, looking over her shoulder.

"You'll have to be patient," she smiled. "When we get back, you will need to go through what more we need and I can stop off at the supermarket. You ready?" Chloe asked.

"Sure am. And why do we need more, don't I have more than enough?" Brooke said confused.

"Well, we just need a few more bits. For example, you have chicken breasts, but surely you aren't going to expect everyone just to eat a random kebab. We need some wraps, flatbreads or something? Or are these ladies 'anti carbs'?" She smiled.

"Ah, I'm with you. And definitely not. They'll kick my ass if I don't have something other than just meat to give them," she said, looking concerned.

"Thought so, and exactly my point. But it's fine, I will sort it out when we get back. The food will be marinating whilst we're out, so when you get back just take the ribs out of the container and put them in the bag full of barbecue sauce."

"Okay, I can do that," Brooke said, feeling proud of herself. "Wait," she stopped, grabbing hold of her arm, "how will I know which one is the barbecue sauce one?"

"Brooke, it's the only bag with no meat in it," she laughed.

"Right. Right. Of course. Come, let's surf." She smiled cutely.

***

"Right, so we're good. We have wraps, baguettes, garlic bread, and two varieties of chicken, BBQ ribs, and plenty of booze. I have my surprise dessert, so I think we are good to go," Chloe smiled.

"What's your surprise dessert?"

"Well, that defeats the purpose of it being a surprise," she said. "Okay, I'm going to head back and get showered and ready. I'll come back later, as I need to do some emails and bits," Chloe said.

"Sure, see you later," Brooke said, clearly disappointed.

"Umm, unless of course..." Chloe stopped. "Umm, well, if you want to come and watch a movie at mine, I can work whilst we watch?" she said, looking for a compromise, so as not to hurt her feelings.

"No, no. I'll be fine, it's okay. I can relax and read my book whilst I'm waiting for them. I'll see you later." Brooke smiled shyly, annoyed at herself for sounding and feeling needy.

Chapter Thirty

Are you coming over?

Chloe read the message on her phone.

Be there in 10. Just on phone to mi famiglia. Pour me a drink please. ;) x

Cheeky and demanding? Loving the Italian. ☺ x

Really? Note to self, learn Italian. ;) Can't have this conversation whilst on phone to mum. :/ x

Brooke smiled as she poured another glass of prosecco, putting a strawberry in.

"What are you smiling at?" Kate said inquisitively.

"Erm, nothing." Shit, she could feel the blushes starting. "Just super happy that you guys are here. Seriously, it's so good to see you." She smiled, and gave them both a hug.

"So, fancy going on to the veranda so we can appreciate this place of yours in its total glory?" Jo said.

"Yes of course, it's so pretty. I can't wait until tonight when the sun sets. It's incredible, you wait. You don't get to see the full way down. But virtually every night so far, it illuminates the sky in the most incredible way, and it's just wonderful. Thanks for coming, you guys. Here's to the most amazing friends. I wouldn't have got through this without you, and I love you both so much," Brooke said, sincerely.

"How much have you drank before we got here? It's not even 2p.m. yet," Kate laughed, giving her a kiss on the cheek. "We love you too, and we are happy you are starting to feel better."

"Hello?" Chloe said.

"Hey, we're out here. Your drink is in the fridge," Brooke shouted.

Jo was quietly watching Brooke, who was seemingly making a conscious effort to maintain a sense of normality to Kate, albeit, subconsciously, nervously fidgeting.

"Hey," Chloe said, walking outside. "I'm…obviously, Chloe, apologies for crashing your weekend," she said.

"On the contrary, we are led to believe that you insisted she did the same with your friends when she first arrived. The first step to getting our gorgeous girl back to that wonderful woman we all love," Jo said smiling, looking at Chloe intently.

"Hi, thank you so much for looking after her. I'm, Kate, lovely to meet you." She jumped up and hugged Chloe.

"Oh, hi? Erm, wow, we're doing this," she said, smiling and hugging Kate back.

"Sorry," Brooke mouthed, shaking her head.

"You'll be pleased to know I am less physical. Well certainly with people I have just met, so I will…offer my hand," Jo said. "Nice to meet you, Chloe. We have heard a lot about you. As Katie said, thank you for looking after this one. She doesn't deserve what happened to her. It's nice that she's not been alone, and has met someone that's been so kind to her," Jo said sincerely.

"It's been my pleasure. Unfortunately, I have been in exactly the same position and interestingly did the same as her. I came to this place, ran away to hide, and met some wonderful people who impacted my life. It's this place. It has this wonderful ability to rebuild you and highlight the positives. I'm glad she's enjoying it," Chloe said.

"Well, something's got her smiling again," Kate said, smirking and sipping her prosecco.

"Katie," Brooke barked.

"What, I'm merely stating a fact. So what's the plan now the party is complete?" Kate said.

"Well, I thought today we could just stay here, enjoy the sun and the booze, have a barbecue and then go out tomorrow," Brooke said excitably. "What do you think?"

"Yes sounds great with me," Jo said, raising a glass.

Chloe was in the kitchen, grabbing some ice, when Jo came in. "Hi, do you want some more prosecco or are you drinking something else?" Jo held up the bottle.

"Hey," Chloe said surprised, turning around. "Yes, that's good, thanks." Brooke was right, they were an incredible looking couple. She could see what she meant about Kate being likened to the Duchess of Cambridge. Incredibly crafted and poised to perfection. Equally their contrariety, connected them exquisitely. Jo was tall and lean, her style accentuating the figure. Her short, dark, cropped hair was contrasting to her femme approach, and Chloe had to admit she pulled it off something wicked. She was stunning, there was no two ways about it.

"So how's she really doing? I spoke to her a few days ago without Kate and she seemed a bit off, but it's difficult for us, because we have been so far away. And I know she is always concerned that she is worrying us. Therefore, she is resistant to telling us the truth. Although, I will caveat that with she seems pretty okay out there today," Jo said, smiling at Chloe.

"Well, to be honest, I have only known her a couple of weeks. But, I have noticed a transition in her. I said it was the thing I was looking forward to most, about meeting you guys."

"What do you mean?" Jo said, smiling and leaning against the cupboard.

"Well, I've noticed a difference to who she was when she first arrived. She spent time with us, and through the beer and the first 24 hours she was so up and down. I mean, don't get me wrong, understandably so. But I've noticed that change in her, that easiness, that happiness. I knew you guys would be worried, so when she said to come out with you both, I didn't have any intention of intruding the whole weekend like she's trying to force upon me. But actually, I was stoked about spending today with you guys, because I wanted to be a part of that realisation from you both that she is quickly becoming who I think she, well…probably is. Does that make sense?" Chloe asked, unsure if she had made herself clear.

"Yes, you put it perfectly. And you're right, she is becoming herself again. And between you and I, she hasn't been herself for well over a year," Jo said.

Chloe didn't know what that meant, since Brooke had only had the accident nine or ten months ago. So why was it longer? Chloe was confused, but put that away for later.

"Hey, what are you guys doing in here?" Brooke shouted at them both quizzically.

"Calm down, we're coming," Chloe said, rolling her eyes at Jo.

The four women spent the next few hours laughing and chatting and just enjoying the day, their time together, and getting to know one another.

***

"Everyone ready to eat yet? I'm getting hungry. Otherwise we are all going to be dying tomorrow and not want to do anything for this little one's big three oh," said Kate.

"Yes, this is true. Plus, I'm a bit bubbled out with this prosecco. Do we have food sweetie? Or is it takeout?" Jo said.

"Yes, we have food." Brooke smirked.

"Great, what am I cooking?" Jo said smiling, rubbing her hands together.

"Actually, I said I'd cook," Chloe said shyly. "You guys have travelled up, so…lady here shopped, and like you, Jo, I also love to cook. So I have prepped and we will have a barbecue. I hope you don't mind?" Chloe asked Jo.

"What? No way. But I may need to come with you so we can work it together, beer and tools," Jo said, following Chloe into the kitchen.

Chloe and Jo were talking about nothing in particular as they prepped the food. Chloe really liked her, but she was unsure at first by the way Jo seemed to be weighing her up. Fortunately, that was over in seconds, and in reality her friends would have been exactly the same, given the circumstances.

"Do you want to make the kebabs, and I'll put the tandoori chicken on and then sort the ribs?" Chloe asked.

"Yes, sounds good. We expecting more people, Chloe? Or do you always aim to feed the five thousand?" Jo was laughing.

"I know. I'm a nightmare. We will have to eat it for supper, and then for breakfast, and then lunch, and possibly dinner for the remainder of the weekend," she laughed. "I won't be a moment, I'm just gonna put these on the barbecue," Chloe said.

She returned and was handed a beer from Jo. "I feel like I've drank far too much prosecco, the bubbles don't do well for me it seems. Plus, I definitely think we should have eaten earlier," Jo grimaced.

"Here, have some of this to tide you over," she said, pulling out some dips and pita's. "Feel free to toast them if you want," she said.

"Hmmm, going all out here, Chloe. Are we trying to impress?" Jo laughed. "What's that you're doing?" Jo asked inquisitively, looking over Chloe's shoulder.

"Smoking chips!" She held them up, smiling. "Smoked mesquite BBQ, the best invention on the planet for that authentic flavour," she laughed. She took a swig of her beer and turned around to face Jo. "And maybe trying to impress, just a little," she held up her thumb and forefinger a small space.

"Cheers," as she held up her beer to Jo. "So how long have you guys been together then?" she asked, turning back around and covering the tray with foil.

"Four years," she smiled genuinely.

"Wow, amazing. You are the cutest couple and it's awesome to watch. Do you think you'll do the whole marriage and kid's thing?" Chloe said.

"One hundred percent," Jo blushed. "And thanks for saying that, it's very kind," she added. "What about you? Do you want that one day? Have you met that girl yet?" Jo asked inquisitively.

"Honestly? I don't know. I thought I did at one point, and I figured that would be the natural progression. However, my ex screwed me over quite badly, and to be quite truthful, I kind of changed my opinion on it. I didn't want to have a relationship again, and I suppose threw out any thoughts of ever having the whole package anymore. I put myself majorly into my work which, don't get me wrong has paid off hugely. But I guess I never really looked back," she said seriously.

"And now?" Jo asked seriously.

"And now what?" Chloe responded.

"Well, you started with 'you didn't know', then you went back to the beginning where you stated you didn't want any of it. So what's happened that's made you start to consider it again?" Jo asked again.

Chloe smiled, "I see where you're going with this, and you can stop right now. Does Kate want the whole shebang too? Have you discussed how and when etc.?" she said.

Jo laughed and poked Chloe in the ribs. "Yes, we have. I don't know if Brooke told you, but Katie is a complete hopeless romantic. So it's all on me," she said, and rolled her eyes.

"Really? And how do you think you'll do it?" Chloe asked passionately, as she bit into some pita and hummus.

Jo smiled. "You so want it all, you just need to find the right woman." Jo started and stopped again, before looking behind her. "Well... can you keep a secret?" Jo finished.

"Yes?" she said, questioningly, ignoring Jo's initial sentence.

Jo checked behind her yet again, and held out her hand to Chloe. Half way down her index finger was the most stunning diamond ring. "Do you like it?" she whispered.

Chloe held her chest and gasped. "Jo, it's beautiful," she said, holding her hand to get a better look at the ring. "So, what? You are going to do it here?" Chloe said, still looking at the heart shaped diamond with two small diamonds on either side of it.

"Well, I'm not actually quite sure. I've been waiting for the right time, and it just hasn't come yet. And that's not a negative, I just need it to be absolutely perfect. Not because it's Kate, but because she's perfect and she deserves it to be perfect," she blushed. "I've been wanting to do if for, gosh six months. And she is seriously, so fairy-tale princess like, that I haven't found the right time. That time where…it has made my heart skip and I just know, does that make sense?" she said, pondering. "Brooke keeps going on about how amazing and beautiful it is here that I figured, well you never know, this place may well be the place that provides me the perfect opportunity." She smiled shyly.

Chloe was just about to say something, when Brooke walked in. "What's the matter with you two? I think your food may be burning, because there's an awful lot of smoke coming from that barbecue," she said seriously.

"Hold that thought? We need to go check the food, before dumb and dumber burn it." Jo smirked.

"Hey lovelies. So, we get lost in gossip and you guys trash the food?" Chloe asked, opening the barbecue, thankful that the food was all okay. She turned it over, placing the tray of ribs on before shutting the lid and joining the others.

"Food's good, no thanks to you pair! What did we miss?" Chloe asked, sitting back down.

"This beautiful lady has been telling me that you taught her to surf, which I must see," Kate said.

"No way. Really?" Jo asked, surprised.

"This is true." Brooke smiled sheepishly. "And I was just saying how beautiful it is, especially the sunrise," she continued.

"Really?" Chloe smirked.

"What are you smirking at?" Brooke asked.

"Nothing," she shrugged, looking over at Jo.

"What are we missing? Why are you smirking? Have you guys been doing naughty things on the beach?" Kate said.

"KATIE," Brooke and Jo both shouted at her unison.

"What? What? Sorry, it was just a simple question," she smiled into her glass.

Chloe checked the food, feeling a sense of urgency to run. Kate was acting like she was pushing them together, and for the first time, she realised the magnitude of the situation. She felt like she couldn't breathe. She needed to go to the bathroom and caught Jo's eyes.

"Watch the food, Chloe and I are just going to her place," Jo said.

"What? What for?" Kate asked concerned.

"That's for us to know and you girls to find out," Jo said, kissing her girlfriend's lips.

"Come on, Chloe," Jo said, walking back inside and out the front door.

***

"What's going on?" Chloe asked, as they walked inside her cabin.

"You looked like you needed a get out. Look, Chloe. I'm not going to have you hurt my best friend. She is a wonderful woman and doesn't deserve that. But equally,

Kate wants everyone to have a happily ever after. Don't panic just because she wants to push you guys together. And yes, you're right, that is what she is trying to do. What you both decide is up to you guys, and it's nobody else's business. I will have a word with her again, but I can pretty much guarantee that she won't let this go. But if you are out looking for nothing but sex, please stay away from Brooke or tell her so. She's not like that, and I can't have this beautiful woman go through being treated like shit all over again. You have been hurt, and your coping mechanism was to avoid a situation where you will never be exposed or vulnerable again. But you're young, and you and I both know that a life with nobody in it to share the basics, the big things, the happy times, and the sad times would be an incredibly lonely life. You will get back on that saddle again, when you meet someone that is worthy of getting back onto it. I don't know if that's Brooke, or maybe somebody else, but it will happen, I guarantee that," Jo said seriously.

Chloe sighed heavily, pouring two glasses of tequila. "Jo, I don't want just sex in any way, shape, or form. I like her. We haven't done anything, and we haven't even discussed wanting to do anything. But I guess the reality just set in that I'm exposing myself, and ultimately, she could decide she wants to take the route I did, and then what? What…I'm left back at square one," she said, handing Jo a glass of tequila. "Probably not the best with the amount we've drank already," she grimaced, "but I really feel like I need one."

"Chloe, you're not the first and certainly won't be the last person to have had your heart broken. But can you honestly, hand on your heart, say that you want to live alone for the rest of your life? To spend your days chair hopping each Christmas between married and coupled friends, due to fear? Surely it's a risk worth taking one day. Look, as I said, I am confident you will one hundred percent meet someone that will make you lose all of that fear. You'll be afraid and apprehensive, but that will add to the wonder of it all," Jo said smiling.

"Kate is clearly not the only romantic, is she?" Chloe smiled shyly. "Thanks for the chat. For the record, I have no intention of hurting Brooke. I hope you know that."

"I know. Anyways, what were you going to say to me about the ring, before the girls came in?" Jo asked.

Chloe smiled. "Funnily enough, what Brooke said. The sunrise is beautiful, unfortunately it will be a very early one. But it would be the most incredible setting. You could take some champagne down there and watch the sun come up with her and do it there," she said expectantly.

Jo was quiet a moment, before a smile spread across her lips. "Okay. I like the concept, and you're right that would certainly be '*romantic*' enough, but there's a few things to iron out," she said sceptically.

"Okay, hit me," Chloe said, sitting back in her chair.

"Well, how do I get her there at four or five in the morning?"

"Brooke's been telling her about it, she must be interested already. Tell Brooke and get her to talk her into it, make her think it's her own choice."

"Actually, I'd rather not tell Brooke if you wouldn't mind?"

"Erm, yeah okay, fair enough," Chloe said sheepishly. She felt honoured that Jo had trusted her with this information, over her best friend.

"Right, so if we speak about this enough this afternoon and evening, I think she will be game. I can mention in front of you guys about going early and watching the sunrise with Joel, since he does it every morning, and then we surf straight after. Chances are she will want to come down to see Brooke surf. If that doesn't work, then we say about how incredibly romantic it is. She's going to want to come either from a romance perspective, or to try and set Brooke and I up." She smiled.

Jo smiled sardonically. "You are getting to know her so well already. Okay, I think you are onto something there, and I think that will work. So how do I do it then? I don't really want to just say marry me," Jo said.

"Leave it with me and let me think about it. I love a love story; I think between us we can come up with a wonderful plan. Seriously though, what are we going to say as to why we came over here?" Chloe said concerned.

"You showed me the place?" Jo said, shrugging.

"I think Kate will say she wanted to have been given the opportunity to come. Oh, I made brownies for a surprise dessert, so we can say we came to get them," Chloe said.

"That would work. Grab the stuff before they trash our food. I'm starved and the tequila is not helping my drunken state."

Chapter Thirty-One

"That was seriously amazing, Chloe. Thank you so much," said Kate.

"That was awesome, I'm not going to lie," Brooke confirmed, rubbing her tummy. "Just far too much again. I am going to be the size of a house by the time I leave here."

"So, I would like to know something," Kate said seriously, looking at Brooke.

"Katie. Do we need to have another conversation?" Jo warned.

"Oh, be quiet! Brooke, since when do you use words like awesome? You seem to have formed this new vocabulary." Kate smirked.

"Shut up, Kate. Maybe it's the surfer in me." She smirked. "What's up with you, smiler?" Brooke asked Chloe inquisitively.

"Nothing," she said, smiling. "Anyways you two, as we prepped and cooked, it's only fair you two go and clean up," she smiled wide to Jo.

"Yes, I agree, only fair," Jo confirmed.

"What are you two plotting? You have been thick as thieves all day," Kate said.

"Dunno what you mean?" said Chloe, holding up her hands.

Jo watched the pair leave with all of the dishes. "Shoot, kiddo," she whispered.

"Okay, what about when I'm surfing I hold up a poster saying 'marry Jo?' Or, write a note in the sand 'will you marry me?' Or, I have another idea, but I think it may be just a little bit too corny. Although I *do* love it!" Chloe whispered, constantly checking behind her.

"I like the enthusiasm, tell me?"

She looked over her shoulder again, and watched the girls laughing and joking as they were washing up, filling Jo in on her idea.

"I think it's the one," Jo beamed. "How will I get her to do it though?"

"Screensaver, new Facebook profile pic. Jesus, Christmas cards if you want," she said excitably. "It may be a bit lame! Sorry," she suddenly felt embarrassed.

"No, you are a genius and she'll love it. I love it," she kissed Chloe's cheek. "Thank you. Seriously, thank you so much."

"What are you two up to now?" Kate said, looking at them.

"Nothing," they both said in unison.

When Kate returned, Chloe and Jo continued. "Do you reckon we do it tomorrow then?" Chloe asked.

"Well, initially I thought yes. But actually, I don't want it rushed. It's already getting to the evening now, and we're all drunk. Plus, it's Brooke's day tomorrow for her 30th, so I don't want to take away from that. So, I'm thinking we have a plan, an amazing plan thanks to you. But tomorrow we make sure it's all sorted and everything is in place and absolutely perfect. Also, it gives us more time to sell the early wake up call to my beautiful wife to be." She smiled.

"Good thinking, all very valid points. So I bought a bottle of Pink Moet for today, but then you said you were all 'bubbled' out. They don't know about it, so you can have that. It saves you having to escape and find excuses.

You have the ring, we have plenty of pens, so literally it's just getting her there. From what I've seen of this one, it shouldn't be too much of a hard task." Chloe smiled.

"This is true. Okay, we need to lay off or they will get suspicious. If not, I think the rest we pick up tomorrow?"

"I'll drink to that. I'm glad we met, you guys are wonderful. And I am truly honoured you have trusted me with this. I'm so happy to be a part of it," Chloe said, feeling herself get emotional.

"What's up with you two?" Brooke said.

"Nothing. We're just bonding and I'm pissed. I think I need to go to bed," Chloe said.

"Are you kidding? The sun hasn't even set yet," Brooke said disappointed. She was aware that she needed to ease up on the drink, or she was going to end up making a fool of herself to Chloe, and in front of Kate and Jo.

***

Chloe woke up with a thumping head. She was glad she stopped drinking when she did, or there was no way she would have been able to deal with a surf lesson this morning. Checking outside, the sky was just starting to go a slightly lighter shade of blue. She debated going back to bed, but then changed her mind. It had been a while since she'd joined Joel for sunrise and 'thanks'. She would grab some coffees and then have a surf with him before she started her surf lessons. She got up and got ready before setting off for the beach.

"Hey, good-looking," Chloe plonked her bottom next to Joel and kissed his cheek. "I got you something. How goes it?"

"Hey, it's been too long since you've been here. I missed you and this." He held up the coffee. "Thanks. Front facing?" He smiled, and pointed by his feet.

"You betcha," she said, as they both turned around on their fronts, head in their hands and watched the sunrise. "What are you grateful for today?" she said lazily.

"Room for one more?" they both looked up when they heard the voice.

"Hey, what are you doing here?" Chloe asked Jo.

"Well, I figured I'd test out this alleged beauty. That and I figured I would try Brooke's theory out of running is the best hangover cure on the planet. FYI, it's bullshit, excuse my language. Hi, you must be Joel?" Jo leaned over, holding her hand out. "I have heard such wonderful things about you, and I must thank you for assisting Chloe in looking after my best friend," she said sincerely.

"Sorry. Joel, Jo, Jo, Joel. These are the ones up for the weekend," Chloe said.

"Hey, nice to meet you, Jo. You should try surfing. Now *that* is the best hangover cure in the world." He smiled.

Jo couldn't help but notice what a beautiful smile he had.

"Well, maybe one day. For today I'm more than happy to just sit and wallow in self-pity, before I'm forced to start drinking again." She smiled sombrely.

"Oh. No, no, no, you came to the wrong place. See, this is our time to be thankful. We appreciate the beauty of this stunning planet and name three things we're happy for," he said. "I know, I know, I don't look like some kind of 'hippy' blah blah blah," he said.

"Actually, I don't think it's fair to say only 'hippies' say thanks. However, I am somewhat surprised. You look like you've just walked off a catwalk runway so yes, I accept. I was wrong to have judged. Thank you for allowing me to crash on this though. I'm already grasping how beautiful this is and will be, so I think this is the perfect opportunity to be thankful." She smiled sincerely.

"Okay then, you wanna go first?" Chloe asked.

"Actually, would you two mind going first? Just while I gather my thoughts?" she said.

"Sure. I'm thankful for my health, and the opportunity to be able to come down here and appreciate this as is, when so many others aren't fortunate enough. Secondly, my job. It's not the be all and end all, but I had it all and was happy to give it all away. Now I get to spend every day meeting people and teaching people to surf and enjoy my life to the fullest. Lastly, I am grateful for love. All different varieties. The soul mate, can't live without each other type, and the love of true friends and acquaintances. That's my three," Joel said simply, and returned his eyes to the pinks and oranges appearing in the sky above the water.

"Wow that was deep. What happened to my board and my coffee?" Chloe laughed.

"I'm grateful for those too, but we have company," he laughed. "Come on then what's yours?"

"Firstly, friends. This place has brought me so many wonderfully, incredible people, inclusive of the newbies that arrived yesterday and our newest addition to our sunrise team." Chloe smiled, staring out at the sunrise. My family. I know they're there when I need them and I love the closeness of us all. Lastly, this place. It does everything for me. Makes me appreciate life, calms me, and gives me the most incredible high when I'm out there riding the waves," Chloe smiled at Jo. "You're up."

"Wow, no pressure after you too. Well, I'm going to have to pretty much steal what I've already heard I'm afraid. Slightly different reasons though, so not all bad." She smiled. "This place. This is one of the most beautiful things I have ever witnessed, and I feel deeply touched to be here with two amazing people. I am also grateful to the positive impact it has had on one of my very best friends. Secondly, friendship. You guys are both incredible and I am hugely thankful to have met you, Chloe. You really are an amazing woman. Joel, thank you deeply for allowing me to be a part of this today. And last but most importantly, love. That beautiful, wonderful, can't bear to be apart, can't keep your hands off each other love. The type that makes you thankful for life every day when you wake up and see her lay there. The way your tummy flips every time she walks into a room, the way you hurt when she hurts. When she's in pain you just want to hold her tight and make it go away, and when she's sick you want to stay by her side, stroke her hair, make her fresh OJ's and stay close by. The type that makes you realise that life would not be complete without her in it. Additionally, finding such perfection in this place, that I will be able to ask said person if she would like to spend the rest of her life with me. Because if tomorrow is anything like this, I'm pretty sure her proposal will be as complete as she makes me feel," Jo said sincerely. She looked around and saw the tears in Chloe's eyes, and Joel was smiling from ear to ear, nodding his head.

"I like this woman…a lot," he said, sipping his coffee.

"It's a surprise though, not even Brooke knows," Chloe said to him.

"Okie dokie," he said, saluting. "So I'm guessing tomorrow morning is the big day?" he asked.

"I think so, yeah, we only really planned it last night," Jo laughed to Chloe.

"This we did! And I think whilst we're sober we should finalise the details before those two appear," Chloe said.

<u>Chapter Thirty-Two</u>

"So when are you going to actually tell us where we're going?" Brooke was whining to Chloe, who was driving.

"Is she always like this? I've never seen this side of her," Chloe said, looking in the rear-view mirror at Jo and Kate.

"All the time," Kate said laughing.

"Hey!" Brooke hit her.

"Seriously, we will be arriving in a few minutes okay?" Chloe said.

"Okay, tell me again. We're here for two hours, then we're doing lunch, and then we're going somewhere else?" Brooke asked.

"Oh my God, she's killing me right now! Seriously, I am going to gag you if you don't cut it out soon," Chloe said, looking to Brooke. She quickly turned her head to face the road as she noticed the smirk across Brooke's lips. Seriously, was she actually thinking naughty thought's when her friends were in the car with us? She was so bad, thought Chloe.

They pulled up to where the power boat ride left from. "Right, princess, we're here, okay? This is your birthday surprise, a little bit of thrill seeking." She smiled.

They were all kitted out with the life jackets and listening to the guide's safety brief. Chloe was so happy that everyone seemed to be excited, due to the fact she'd not run it past anyone. She ran the risk of people alerting they had fears of water or adventure, but luckily they were all good.

***

"Oh my word that was amazing! It was so exciting! I actually thought we were going to go over, and I thought I was going to die. I didn't know there were so many amazing things to see here either. There is so much history and culture," Kate said, like an excitable child.

"Wow, I know. How fun when we sped around that corner? I was like there's no way we aren't going to tip over at this speed. But seriously, it was so much fun. I've never done anything like that before. Thanks so much, Chlo. That was literally one of the best birthday days out ever." Brooke smiled shyly.

"Well, to be fair, is it not the only one? Do we not normally just go out for dinner?" Kate said sarcastically, walking off to the car, stopping Brooke in her tracks.

"Hey, sweetie," Jo stopped, and grabbed Brooke's arm. "She didn't mean to hurt you with that, she's just happy that somebody has made an effort and put some thought into it. You know what she's like. You cross her friends, she won't forgive easily," Jo said diplomatically.

"Yeah, I know," Brooke said quietly, walking off by herself.

"Argh," Jo sighed, putting her head in her hands.

"Very diplomatically put," Chloe said, bumping shoulders with her.

"I love Kate and I love that she is so caring and territorial, but I just wish she would think of how she words things sometimes. Rightly or wrongly, nine years is a long time in a relationship, even if they do make you feel like it was all worthless. Anyone would want to cling on to that little part that it wasn't just a waste of their life. Making her feel like she's wasted that isn't really going to help," Jo sighed.

"Don't worry, we can all look after her," Chloe said. "She's got the best friends. So we can go have lunch, some nice civilised drinks, and then an easy afternoon. We can cheer her up and hopefully try to stop her from thinking about all the 'ifs, buts, and whys.'" Chloe smiled, running after Brooke and throwing her arm around her shoulder. "Yo. Thrill seeker, you enjoy the ride?" Chloe smirked, trying to take her mind off things.

She smiled glumly. "Naughty."

Chloe checked around her, making sure the others were out of ear shot "No. Naughty would be trying to sneak you into the bathroom at the next place to get a kiss," she said, running off, laughing.

"Come on, slow coaches. It's dinnertime," Chloe shouted, running backwards and looking at the disjointed group.

Chapter Thirty-Three

They had a beautiful meal at the Italian restaurant that Brooke had taken Chloe to last weekend. Jo had bought a bottle of champagne, which was perfect for the day and added to the cake that Chloe had arranged to celebrate the impending thirtieth birthday.

Brooke was happy her friends were visiting. She had had the best day so far, and according to Chloe it wasn't over yet. Chloe really had gone all out, and there had been absolutely no reason for her to have done that. It appeared she just wanted to make sure it was a special birthday. Brooke figured it was because it was an important one. But this was all new for her. She wasn't used to someone making an effort for her, birthday or not.

"So what's next then, lady?" Brooke looked at Chloe with her head in her hand and smiling widely, which went all the way to her eyes.

"Patience is a virtue, princess." Chloe winked.

"Where has this princess nickname come from? It's twice today you have called me it," Brooke questioned, looking across the table to Kate and Jo.

"Well you have been acting like one!! 'Where are we going? Why won't you tell me? What will we be doing? When will be there? It's my birthday, so you have to tell me'. See, princess-like." Chloe smirked.

"Actually, I would have gone more for 'brat-like.'" Jo smirked.

"Oh my God, you two are so unfair. I was just merely excited. There's nothing wrong with that. It's not my fault you two are too old to appreciate and get excited by things any longer," she laughed. "I bet you like roll out of bed at midday on Christmas morning, after spending Christmas Eve drinking champagne with your old arty farty friends. Then go to bed late, wake up late, and act like it's a normal day, all boring and so forth."

Chloe raised an eyebrow over to Jo. "Maybe I should cancel this afternoon?"

"I think you should, or maybe us two 'oldies' should go and enjoy it and leave these two whipper snappers to go 'clubbing' or something." Jo smirked.

"No no, please don't?" Brooke pleaded.

"And, in my defence, I do believe I am being pulled into something I have at no point actually commented on. So whilst I am happy to be referred to as a 'whipper snapper,' I have no intention of missing out on this afternoon. As far as surprises go, this morning was exceptional, so I'm very eager for this afternoon," Kate said.

"Charming, now you're trying to turn my friends against me too?" Brooke said to Chloe, poking her bottom lip out.

"I think you'll find, you brought this on all by yourself!" She smirked.

"So, you think they have any idea they are falling for each other?" Kate whispered into Jo's ear.

Jo crossed her legs, watching the women intently while leaning back in her chair. "They have absolutely no idea," she responded in a whisper and smirking to her girlfriend, as they watched the pair 'bantering' with each other.

Chloe collected the car whilst Jo paid for the lunch, insisting on it for Brooke's birthday. When the three women came out, she noticed they were clearly giddy from the bubbles. Chloe was the designated driver and had only had half a glass, despite the whinging of leaving the car and getting taxis. But she didn't want to do that when they weren't going straight home, and she didn't want to risk not getting to the second part of the birthday surprise. Although, she was wondering if she had made a silly mistake. Kate, Jo, and Brooke were all…well, they were all lovely, down to earth women. But they had that air of upper-class-ness about them, liking the finer things in life. They weren't snobby at all, but it was just something that Chloe felt.

"Hey, about time," Kate said, as she got into the car. "Where to Jeeves?" She smirked.

"I'm pretty sure that's the name of a butler and not a driver, but okay," She smiled. "Okay, so it's up to you. We can go and do the last thing, or alternatively, just go home and drink more," she said, keeping her eyes on the road.

"No way. Why don't you want to do the last thing? Has something happened?" Brooke asked concerned.

"No no, not at all. I just wanted to make sure that's all. I…well it's only something silly, it's nothing major. This morning was the main thing," Chloe said quietly.

"Hey, Chlo, I'm sure it will be fantastic. Today has been incredible so far, and we can do this next surprise, and then we can go home and enjoy a bottle on the balcony," Jo said, rubbing Chloe's shoulder from her spot in the back.

***

When they pulled into the sea life centre and Brooke spotted it, she was giddy all over again, and clapping her hands. "I love stuff like this," Brooke said excitably.

"Well, as I said, this morning was the biggie. I, um…well, I…" Chloe stopped and looked out the window, scratching her head. She was suddenly very aware of the people and the silence.

"Come on let's go and get the tickets," Jo said, grabbing Kate's hand.

"What's the matter?" Brooke asked seriously.

"I don't know. I suddenly feel like this was kinda stupid," Chloe responded.

"Why, tell me what you were going to say? Why bring me here, other than I love it? Which I don't think I have told you." Brooke smiled excitably.

"Well, not really," she sighed heavily. "See, the other night when all that shit happened with your ex, well you just seemed to have had a lot of stress over the last few months. And then she went all out to bring it back to the boil. What she did was add to the list to tip it off. So whilst I thought you would be okay and happy as your friends were here, I recalled something you said when we first met. You told me that you love sea life, fish tanks and just watching fish, as you find it very therapeutic. So I figured it would be something a bit different, nice and calming almost, which I thought you may need. Sorry, it seemed a better idea in my head," Chloe said blushing.

Brooke grabbed Chloe's face/ "Don't you dare. Don't you dare feel embarrassed by this gesture, this thought provoking gesture. I can't slag Maria off all the time, because it will bring me down further and I don't want to. But Katie was right earlier. She never put this much thought into anything for me! If it was expensive and looked expensive then great, it was a winner. Everything was for show. I would rather have a five-pound ticket to a car wash that we met in, than a five-thousand-pound holiday to Cabo San Lucas. I would rather have a free, homemade CD, than a thousand pound Cartier watch." She pulled Chloe's eyes to meet her own, brushing over her cheek with her thumb softly. "I would rather have a five-pound entrance to a sea life centre with an incredible woman. A woman who makes a point of booking me this because she remembered I once told her that it destresses me, and she thinks I have had some unpleasant things happening. Nobody has ever done anything like this for me. It's the most incredibly and considerate gesture, and I'm truly touched. Thank you, Chloe. Thank you for this whole day, gosh for this whole month, for everything," she said, kissing her lips softly.

Chloe pulled back looking concerned. "Your friends," she said, looking over Brooke's shoulder.

"Screw my friends." She smirked. Leaning in, Brooke gently brushed Chloe's lips with her own once more.

***

They found Kate and Jo by the entrance waiting patiently, both happy that they hadn't seen what happened in the car. "Hey you guys, apologies for the delay, just felt a bit stupid. I mean, I'm sure sea life centres are not really the up and coming thing in Oxford," Chloe said.

"On the contrary, Chloe. Jo and I do stuff like this all the time. We would much prefer a day off together doing something like this, or a zoo, where we can enjoy at ease," Kate said, looping her arm through Chloe's. "Come on, let's go inside," she said excitably.

Chloe was disappointed with herself that she had pre-judged Brooke and her friends, more so because she had spent over twenty-four hours with them now. They really weren't what she was assuming they were, and that was completely unfair to them. They entered the sea life centre and wandered around easily, making a point at stopping at each area and checking it out.

"So…girl done good, huh?" Jo said to Brooke. She pointed her head over to Chloe, who was walking ahead with Kate, still arm in arm.

Brooke looked at Jo seriously, unsure how to respond. "Yes, she did. Without sounding disrespectful to you guys now as I don't want to offend obviously, but I don't think anybody has ever done something so special for me. And I just can't believe she would do that. Who does that?" Brooke said to Jo.

"Everybody that thinks somebody's worth it, babes," Jo said simply, giving Brooke the freedom to continue if she desired.

Brooke started and stopped, then she looked around and saw the other two ahead, and began again. She explained to Jo that she didn't know if it was fair to say this since she was good friends with Maria, but went on to tell her all about what she had done on Thursday night.

"Are you actually kidding me right now? Please tell me this is a joke. Brooke?" Jo said, clearly angered.

"Look," she whispered, checking that Kate and Chloe were out of earshot. "It's okay. Honestly, I'm fine. Please don't mention it. I don't want you guys getting involved, because that isn't fair. But that's why she did it," she smiled shyly. "She remembered I said it destresses me."

"She's amazing, Brookes. I know she's been hurt and is reluctant to get involved again, but honestly, I don't think she'd hurt you. Equally I don't think you'd hurt her. Least not intentionally. She's a good egg," she said, bumping shoulders with her best friend.

"Thanks, she's really helped me through everything since I have arrived here. I genuinely love this place, but I wish it wasn't so far away. I would love to do what Chloe's done and buy a place on here. I really don't know what I would be like had I not met her," she said sadly.

"Well, fate works in mysterious ways, sweetie." Brooke was just about to respond, but Jo put her finger to Brooke's lips "Too soon." She winked, and just like that jogged off to catch up with the other two.

Brooke watched Jo link her arm in Chloe's spare one, all of them paying close attention and pointing to the different varieties of sea life around them.

Chapter Thirty-Four

"Do you want beer or wine?" Chloe asked, as they got back to her place later that afternoon.

"I'll have a beer actually. I'm a bit wine and bubbled out again," Jo said, with Kate agreeing.

Jo and Chloe needed at some point to get the conversation on to the sunrise in order to get Kate to want to go. Chloe figured she will just have to keep going on about it, as it will be a great deal easier than it would be for Jo.

"Cheers," Brooke held up her glass to them all.

"So, you coming for a surf in the morning?" Chloe asked Brooke.

"Oh, I don't know? I haven't been today, and I want a ride, but I may be too hungover. It is my birthday you know." She smiled.

"Really? I thought you would want to show off the skills you have learnt to these two. The weather is looking awesome, so I'm thinking I'm going to go down and watch the sunrise as it's looking perfect, then go for a surf," Chloe said, purposely avoiding eye contact.

"Oh, is the sunrise as good as the sunset here?" Jo followed suit, acting well indeed.

"An Anglesey sunrise makes the sunset look rubbish, believe it or not. It's stunning, but then I'm a bit of a geek. I love anything like that. I'm the idiot that cries at romantic love stories, so probably not well equipped to answer," Chloe said, looking away and praying this would work.

"Oh, you're a softie," Brooke joked. "Actually, she's correct, it's unbelievably beautiful. Joel got me on it, but you know what else? I wouldn't have known there was such beauty in this country. It's unfortunate you are here in summer where you need to be up around four a.m.," she continued.

Shit, Chloe thought looking at Jo, reverse psychology it is then! "Yeah, I mean it's good, but like anyone wants to get up that time on their holidays? I mean it's only a sunrise. A sunrise is a sunrise isn't it?" Chloe said nonchalantly.

"No way. Yes, it's early, but it's not just any sunrise. It's incredible. On par with overseas, in fact. Kate, it was better than when we went to… hmmm, where was it?" Brooke said, clicking her fingers. "Greece somewhere, and we were on the wrong side of the island, so we didn't get to see a full sunset. But when we did it was gorgeous. Well anyways, it is more stunning than that," she said enthusiastically.

"Oohhh yes…wow really?" Kate said.

"We should maybe take a look, as tomorrow is the only opportunity for all four of us to go," Chloe said.

Jo laughed "Thank you for the offer, Chloe. However, this little one here," Jo said, putting her arm around her girlfriend, "well, you have little to zero chance of getting this one out of bed at that time. Even when we are going on our holidays and she has to get up early, she is miserable. Sorry, but there is no way. I may come, I really fancy it," Jo said, knowing full well that as soon those words left her mouth, Katie would push back.

"Excuse me? Please wait a minute. What do you mean? I can get up. And to be honest, if it's that

289

beautiful, then I do want to get up and go see it," Kate said frowning.

Jo needed to not be condescending, but just get to her enough that she would do it just to prove a point. It was now or never, she thought. "Baby, I love you unconditionally. But if you were to go see that, you are going to need to go to bed now. At six p.m., to ensure you have had sufficient sleep," she smiled, kissing her nose softly. *Please work, please work, please work*, Jo prayed.

"Seriously guys, it's no biggie. I will be there. I just thought you may like to come too," Chloe said lightly.

"Look what you have started." Brooke grinned.

"I'll be there, Chloe. I will give you my number, her van keys, a trumpet, and a bucket of water if I need to. I am only going to have this one opportunity to see it, so please come wake me up," Kate said indignantly. "May I please use your bathroom?" she said.

"Yes, it's the second door on the left," Chloe said; waiting until she left, and Brooke had gone to get drinks. Chloe fist pumped Jo discreetly. "You need to do some serious making up, or she'll be saying no tomorrow." She smirked.

"Nahhhh, she'll be fine. I'll make it up to her before then," Jo said.

"Erm, TMI," Chloe laughed.

"Hello, I wasn't meaning any such thing, cheeky." Jo slapped Chloe playfully.

***

"Do you want a Moet?" Chloe whispered to Jo, so as not to wake the other two.

"It's very late? Should we?"

"Well the way I see it, you either aren't going to sleep because you're too nervous, or aren't going to sleep because you're too excited. Either way I think it's unlikely, so we could have one more, make sure we are good to go and then hey presto, crash...wake... propose...celebrate." She smiled. "Oh, come here. I know I've only just met you, but I love this. I love the whole thing. Thank you so much for sharing with me." Chloe smiled sincerely, hugging Jo tight.

***

"Okay, okay. I've definitely got it now, it's perfect," Jo said, pouring them the last of the bottle. "We do need to go to bed now though. I'm glad we moved back over here earlier, if we were still at yours, there's no way we would have been able to arrange it all. Do you think it will go alright?" Jo said seriously.

"I think it will go amazingly. I think it will be utter perfection, and I can't wait for Brooke to witness it all," Chloe said. "You're right though, we need to go to bed. I will sort everything in the morning then knock on for you lot, okay?" she said.

Jo breathed out heavily. "Thanks, you have been incredible. Brooke will be lucky to have you." She smiled sincerely.

Chloe was about to say something, but Jo did the same as she had done to Chloe earlier and put her finger to Chloe's lips. "Shhh, see you in the morning." She kissed her cheek, and locked the door behind her.

Chapter Thirty-Five

Chloe's alarm went off, and she didn't even groan, too excited for what lay ahead. She heard her phone vibrate and picked it up, reading the message notifying her that Joel was outside.

Chloe went to the front door. "Hey, thanks for this," she said, kissing Joel on the cheek and handing him the bottle of Pink Moet and two champagne flutes.

"No worries gorgeous. See you shortly," he whispered.

"That you will," she winked. Chloe ran back inside and got a quick shower. She got dressed, wearing a pair of short board shorts and a hoodie over the top. She put her flip flops on and grabbed the felt tip pen from her drawer. Locking up and grabbing her surfboard, she left the cabin and knocked on Brooke's door.

"Hey." Brooke opened the door biting her fist, as her eyes did a slow roll over Chloe's athletic body. "You are killing me," she whispered to Chloe.

"Don't know what you mean?" She smirked, undoing her hoodie a little more, exposing more flesh to Brooke.

"Guys, Chlo's here. Are you ready?" Brooke said, shaking her head at Chloe. "You will pay for that," she warned Chloe.

"Can't wait!" She smirked some more. She was in a great mood.

"Hey, you okay?" Jo said, coming out looking like she was going to be sick at any point.

"Hey, why don't we go on? She may move faster if she thinks we've left without her?" Chloe said to Brooke.

"Good thinking, batman," Brooke said. "We'll be five minutes behind you." She smiled.

Chloe and Jo walked off quickly. Chloe looked behind her to make sure they were out of sight. "Come on, run with me," she said.

"Really? You're holding a huge bloody surf board," Jo said astonished.

Chloe laughed. "I know, come on."

"You're bloody insane," Jo said, as they reached the beach. Chloe stuffed her board in the sand and turned to Jo.

"Here you go," she handed her a miniature of tequila.

"Are you kidding, do you know what time it is?"

"Of course I do. In fact, it's more night than morning. It's Dutch courage. Take it or leave it, but give me your hand," Chloe said.

Chloe finished as Jo was finishing the drink. "What do you think?" she smiled, clearly impressed with her handiwork.

Jo laughed. "Ha, Chloe, it's perfect." She smiled.

"Shit they're here, come on. Remember, keep your hand open. The sun is already coming up so you won't have to wait long," Chloe kissed Jo on the cheek. "Good luck, buddy." She smiled.

The four of them went and sat with Joel as the sun started to rise. They were all chatting normally as the sky began to change. The sun rose with different tones of blues to the light pinks, corals, and oranges that it was slowly portraying now. Joel asked the girls if they wanted to try surfing, and brought out a couple of boards, planting them sideways alongside each other. He discreetly put the bottle of champagne and two glasses beside them, out of view of Kate.

Joel finished what he had to do and got himself out of the way, returning to the shop doorway, calling Brooke and Chloe over to him.

"What's up with him?" Brooke asked Chloe.

"No idea, let's go and find out."

"Really?"

"Yes, it could be important," Chloe said, walking over and looking back over to Kate and Jo.

***

"You okay? You seem quiet," Kate said to Jo.

"Yeah, just thinking."

"Why? What about?"

"Erm, something that Brooke told me last night about what Maria had done. Just got to me, I guess."

"What do you mean? What did she say?"

"Oh don't worry, I'll tell you later." Hell, what was she thinking? "So, I brought some champagne to continue her birthday celebrations." She smiled, and poured the drink from the side. Did you bring your camera? You're better than I am at taking pics. Oh, we should get a pic of the champagne in the sunrise," Jo said, smiling to Kate.

"Oh yes, that would be a cool idea for a photo," Kate said smiling, loving any good photo opportunity.

"Ooohhh, actually, have you ever seen when they do the hearts with your hands with the sunrise in the background?" Jo said smiling.

"Yes, I know like this?" Kate said. "Oh, look its gorgeous, take a pic of it please?" she said.

"Well, how about you do one part and I do the other?" Jo smiled shyly, kissing Kate's nose.

***

"What are we doing here, when they are there? With champagne no less, watching the sunrise?" Brooke said agitated.

"Just be patient and quiet for god's sake and watch," Chloe said.

Brooke looked between Chloe and Joel, who seemed to be watching her friends more than the sunrise.

***

"I love it. Just like our hearts, joined together." Katie smiled sheepishly. "I love you, do you know that?"

"I know that," she said, kissing her softly. "Okay, let's do it then." They put their opposite hands together, forming a heart. The perfect heart as it was half of both of them, Jo thought. They manoeuvred it so that the sunrise over the sea and the pinks and oranges were all visible within it. Kate took a couple of photos. "Oh my gosh, it's beautiful," Kate said, showing it to Jo. We should have it on a canvas. "It is baby, as are you," Jo said turning, moving her half of the heart over to face her palm to Katie.

She watched Kate's facial expressions, as Kate read the words, 'will you marry me?' across her palm, going from concentration as she read the words - then reread the words - to realisation as she understood the situation - to Jo's complete and utter satisfaction and elation. At that point, Jo handed her a glass of pink champagne, raising the glass so the stem was level with Kates eyes.

She took the glass and spotted it, the sparkle in the bottom of the glass. Kate screamed, and quite possibly woke up the entire island of Anglesey, Jo thought. She tipped the champagne out through her hand and collected the ring. Then jumped on Jo and kissed her incessantly, unable to stop, the ultimate ecstasy passing through their bodies.

"Get it now?" Chloe looked at Brooke with tears in her eyes.

"She proposed? Jo Jo proposed? To my Katie? My Jo Jo and Katie bubbles are getting married?" Brooke said to her, crying.

"Yes...," Chloe said confused. "Your Jo Jo and Katie...erm bubbles, are getting married." Before she had a chance to finish the sentence, she was being dragged across the beach with Brooke's shrills piercing through her. She dove on her two best friends, screaming and crying, and kissing them both, with hyperactive actions.

"Congratulations, congratulations, congratulations," she was saying over and over.

"Brooke, shall we let them get up," Chloe said taking in the picture, bearing a resemblance of a child jumping excitedly over their parents on Christmas morning.

"Sorry, sorry," she got up, lifting her friends up with her. "Let me see, let me see," she said, grabbing Kate's hand.

"Oh my God, it's so beautiful," Brooke said, completely filled with emotion. "I can't believe you didn't tell me?" Brooke looked up to Jo questioningly. "And, am I mistaken or did you actually tell this one?" Brooke said, pointing to Chloe, who was blushing now.

"I did. And not only did I tell her, but this beautiful little heart pretty much came up with all of this and planned it all for me, with this other little one," Jo said, with her arms around both Chloe and Joel.

Chloe couldn't believe she had just told them all that, looking at her completely aghast.

"I will caveat that with, whilst I am a romantic and know what my beautiful wife to be likes, I also know that she is the most romantic soul on earth. And whilst I think I could have come up with something special, it would never have held weight with this one. We don't keep secrets from each other and actually, I wouldn't ever want her to believe this was me when it was all you. I cannot thank you enough. You truly are the most kind-hearted person I've ever been fortunate enough to have met," Jo said sincerely. "Same to you, Joel. Thank you both so much. So before this one throws anymore thirty-pound champers away, Joel, I don't suppose you have three plastic cups or mugs over there do you?" Jo said.

"Yes, I'll find something," he said delightfully. "Hey ladies, out of interest, what's your favourite colours?" he smiled, asking Jo and Kate.

"Why?" Kate asked quizzically.

"Ah. Now that's for me to know and you to find out." He grinned his beautiful smile, which accentuated his perfectly formed square jaw line.

"Mine's Azul," Jo said.

"Really? You can't just say pink or yellow," Kate rolled her eyes. "Well, technically it depends on what you're referring to. However, I am confident you will not tell me. I would normally say black, but I am not in a very 'black' mood now, it seems. So I will go with another favourite of coral." She smiled.

***

"I still can't believe it," Brooke was saying, shaking her head. She was so completely moved by the morning's events, and actually touched that Chloe had assisted her friend, *and* kept it quiet.

"Yes, so you keep saying," Jo laughed. "And before you say again, yes, Chloe knew, yes Chloe helped, yes it was all Chloe's idea. And nobody else knew, bar both sets of parents," she said, smirking.

"No need to be rude," Brooke said, still laughing.

"Hey guys, I need to get off. I need a shower and have to go shopping," Chloe said.

"You're coming back though right? We need to celebrate my engagement," Kate said concerned.

"Seriously, I don't think I need to crash your whole weekend."

"Chloe, you are part of this *and* us now. Regardless of what happens with you two when we aren't looking…"

"Kate!!" Brooke and Jo shouted.

"Let me guess, *still* too soon?" she rolled her eyes. "Anyways, regardless of anything else, you are part of this. You made this all happen and I won't take no for an answer. I don't give up that easily." She pointed to Brooke and herself.

"This is true," Brooke confirmed.

"So whilst I may be a bit high maintenance at times and one helluva romantic, I'm clearly pissing you all off trying to force you two together. But in my defence, it is only because you are so completely made for each other. The fact is you are both so bloody stubborn with the

298

whole 'fear' aspect and too dumb to realise it yet. I will wholeheartedly say despite any of that, and I may get punched now. But if, and I will caveat this statement with a very BIG if. If Maria and Paula had done all of this, equally I would want them to be a part of this with us. So for once I am not going to try and be a 'meddling mother hen', but will genuinely, from the bottom of my heart, ask you to please come back and celebrate this spectacularly, wondrous, astoundingly, extraordinarily breath-taking perfect day with us. Which was in a large part thanks to you," Kate said sincerely.

"I'd love to. For the record, I was only going to shower and go shopping for the Sunday lunch this little lady wants to cook you." Chloe smirked, pointing to Brooke. "But seriously, awesome to see you grovel." She kissed Kate on her cheek and walked to the door.

"I'll get you for that! Brooke can't cook, so how is she making lunch?" Kate said.

Brooke followed Chloe to the door, advising her friends that she would discuss the lunch situation in a few moments.

"Are you sure I can't come with you?" she said. She could feel that it was more of a plea and was hoping Chloe wouldn't notice. But truth be told, they had spent so much time together. Aside from sleeping in their own beds, they hadn't been apart.

"Really? Well if you insist, I love shower sex." Chloe smirked.

"Oh my God, Chloe." She slapped her side, blushing furiously.

"Ouch, what's that for? I said I'm going for a shower, and your response was 'can I come with you?' Why do I get hit?" She was still smirking.

"It will be much worse if you continue with that," Brooke said.

"Hmmm? Hot shower sex, and then spanking? How very Christian Grey!" she laughed, her eyes sparkling.

"Right, out. Go, get the beef and make sure the shower is cold for Christ sakes."

"Regardless of level of temperature, nothing's going to get these dirty thoughts out of my mind now, just saying! I will be as quick as I can, but I am ninety-nine percent sure my shower will take a while. Because I need to relieve um…let's say some stresses." She looked back at Brooke raising an eyebrow, watching her simply stand there in utter disbelief.

At last she had got the control back, she thought as she headed off.

***

Brooke opened the door to find Joel. "Hey you, what's up?" she asked. "You wanna come in?"

"No thanks, it's just a quick one. This is for Jo and Kate. I made it for them," he smiled genuinely.

"Thanks so much," Brooke said, walking back inside and giving them the papered gift. Jo opened it and found a hand carved mini surfboard. One half was coral the other half was Azul, connected in the middle by a love heart in which he had carved 'she said yes'. "Oh my God, this is beautiful," the two women gushed, thankful to the genuinely beautiful man.

<u>Chapter Thirty-Six</u>

Chloe was watching Brooke, who was concentrating implicitly. "So, you always this much of a perfectionist?" she asked amusingly.

"Piss off," Brooke reprimanded her without looking up.

"I'm pretty sure when I met you, you didn't swear?" she laughed, pinching a carrot.

"Okay, just add a little soda water to the mixture and then leave it like that," Chloe instructed.

"Soda water? In Yorkshire puddings?" She put down the spoon looking confused. "Are you messing with me?" she said.

"No, of course I'm not, silly! It helps to raise them and makes them a little bit crispier. It's my mum's secret ingredient, and you can't ever challenge a northerner when it comes to Yorkshire puddings. Do you not remember how amazing they were last week?" She smiled to Brooke.

"Hmm, yes. Oh, they were divine. How exciting that I will be making those today," Brooke said excitably. "Are we good then? Can we join the two lovebirds?" Brooke asked, leaning against the side and looking out to her friends still completely smitten over the morning's events.

"Nearly, now we need to make a special cocktail." Chloe smiled a wickedly evil grin.

"Is that a euphemism?" Brooke asked confused.

"Are you always this sex obsessed?"

"Excuse me? You were the one th…," Brooke looked back around to check they were out of earshot. She whispered closer to Chloe while shooting her an evil look. "You were the one who was talking about DIY'ing in the shower earlier. Not me."

Chloe couldn't kerb her grin. She wished she wasn't so easy to wind up. Chloe leaned forward, only millimetres from Brooke's face, and whispered equally as quiet. "I think you'll find the reason I had to 'DIY' as you put it, was because you started talking about sex in the shower and spanking." She smirked.

Brooke was blushing heavily, and had no control over it. She was enjoying the banter with her, but again, she wouldn't let her know that though. Brooke could feel the fear in the pit of her stomach as the realisation kicked in that she was enjoying the banter and not running scared. She couldn't think about that now, so she'd have to put it away for later.

***

"I just don't know what the big deal is. That's all. It's a helping hand, and it always works in the movies," Kate whined to Jo.

"Baby, I love your romantic side, I truly do. I love that you want people to have what we do, and I think you're completely right. I agree they are totally falling in love, but there are times and places to lend a helping hand. And in reality, do you think if we split up tomorrow after all this time, considering they were together much longer than us…do you really think that you are going to want to jump into a relationship with someone right away? You have to have time to heal.

Maybe sleep with them, yes? But enter into what you
have just lost, all you've known for most of your adult
life? Baby, if we push this, we are going to put so much
pressure on them both that it will all fall apart. This has
all happened without us, so how about we allow the
universe to work its magic, and watch it unfold, however
it plays out. Then you and I concentrate on our long and
wonderful life together?" Jo said, kissing her fiancée's
lips lovingly.

"You are so cute, and smart," Kate said, kissing each
one of Jo's hands.

***

"Okay, shake, shake, shake a shake it," Brooke was
singing as she shook the cocktail shaker, dancing around
the room.

Chloe was watching Brooke intently. She *was*
infectious, as Chloe had realised time and time again.

"Stop looking at my breasts," Brooke warned,
ignoring Chloe.

"You're jumping around like a bloody lunatic and
your chest is bouncing, very nicely may I add, all over
the place. I'm a lesbian and you are thrusting your breasts
in my face, so get real, girl! And I think the cocktail is
sufficiently shaken," Chloe said.

Brooke sugared the rims of the glasses and shared
the cocktail out between the four. "So, are you staying
and drinking today? Or do you have to leave?"

"Nope, I'm here for the day. I will get up and leave
around 7ish, which will get me into work on time if I get
ready here. Is that okay?" Chloe asked seriously, cutting
the fruit up into slices to put into the drinks.

"Yes, of course." Brooke smiled, watching Chloe's steady hand. "Will you be back on Thursday or Friday?" she said, gently placing the slices Chloe had cut, onto the rim of the glass.

"Actually, I won't be. It's Em's hen do this weekend, so we have a quiet one with us three on Friday, and then Saturday is the actual event. So, I'll be pretty much fit for nothing on Sunday. Is the following weekend your final weekend, or do you have one more?" she said, smiling lightly.

"Oh, yes of course. I remember them saying, that will be great fun. You'll be a hit walking around with the penis necklaces around your neck," she said expressionlessly.

Chloe felt the pain rip through her once more. She didn't know if it was the not seeing her for a full week or the hurt on Brooke's face, but she couldn't face that right now, not with the girls outside. "Come on, these are ready," she said, taking two glasses and walking out to the girls.

***

"This dinner is smelling amazing, Brookie. I hope it tastes as good as it smells. Do you have plans for your birthday?" Kate said.

"Oh, nothing. I've celebrated this weekend, so I'm just going to get up, go for a surf, and maybe go shopping and treat myself to some bits. It's been a while since I've done that. And then just relax I suppose," Brooke said solemnly.

"What? Please tell me you are kidding? If you have no plans and are going to be here alone, why don't you just come home with us tomorrow? If you want to come back you can, but if not, just cut your stay short," Kate said concerned, looking between Chloe and Brooke.

"Kate, I'm a big girl now. The last thing I want it is to be back in Oxford. I'd rather be here alone. I'm going to go and check on the food," she said, walking off.

"Wh…"

"Kate, do not even start that sentence. Chloe has her own life also. She isn't Brooke's babysitter, so you can't put this on her," Jo said, cutting Kate short.

"Guys, have some faith in me. She will enjoy her birthday," Chloe said, smiling slightly and following Brooke.

"What the hell does that mean?" Kate whispered to Jo. "I don't like this, Jo."

"It will be fine. Chloe will pull out all the stops if today was anything to go by. Just leave them to it," she said. "She would never put Brooke in a situation which could leave her feeling rubbish, that much I'm confident in."

Brooke and Chloe skirted around the issue at hand, then finished dinner off together before serving up dessert. "These Yorkshires are incredible, and this is twice now. However, this week I've contributed…well, around ninety-eight percent so it's all on me," Brooke said. "Just saying." She smiled, very proud of herself.

"Brooke this is incredible. I can't believe you did all this. The Yorkshire puddings are wonderful, so tasty and crispy. and perfectly raised. I love it all! And FYI, you have no excuse now when you get back home. You will be having us over to cook like this," Kate said to her, missing the look between Chloe and Brooke, realizing that they would be on opposite ends of the country in a few short weeks.

***

"Seriously, it was so lovely to meet you. We hope you will come down to visit. You have given us so much, and it's been wonderful that you were a part of that," Jo said, hugging Chloe tightly. They each said their goodbyes. Each hugging, kissing and wishing safe journeys home the following morning, before Jo pulled Kate inside, leaving Chloe and Brooke on the doorstep. Brooke shut the door behind them.

"Thanks for this weekend. It was incredibly sweet of you to do all of that for me," Brooke said, looking out into the distance.

"You want me to come back for your birthday? I'll try and get the day off?" Chloe blurted out.

"God, no. I'm fine. Don't listen to them. Anyways, thanks for everything, Chloe." Brooke smiled shyly. She couldn't pinpoint the exact point when things had changed, the point that she didn't actually want to let her go now. Maybe it was the awareness that she could potentially not see her again? Maybe it was the connection with her friends? Maybe everything she did to ensure her best friends had the most beautiful and memorable experience ever? She didn't know. What she did know was…she was here in front of this beautiful, incredible woman. Inches away from her, with those incredibly stunning green eyes looking at her. Looking at her in that way, Brooke thought. The way where she looks up through her eyelashes. Brooke didn't think she'd ever get that look out of her head, she was so incredibly beautiful.

"I guess I should go," Chloe said.

"Sure. Please send my love and best wishes to Emily and say hi to your friends. It's late, and you should sleep," Brooke sighed.

"I will. That will mean a lot to them. Good night, Brooke Davis. Thank you for yet another amazing weekend." She smiled, and reluctantly started down the steps.

"Chloe?"

"Yes," she blurted, turning and looking at Brooke desperately, yearning with anticipation and hope.

"Will I ever see you again?"

Chloe held onto the railing, realizing this was more to steady herself than anything else. She took in a deep breath, closing her eyes. Sighing lightly, she turned around and walked back to Brooke. Taking her face in each of her hands, she gently stroked her thumbs across Brooke's cheeks, noticing the woman closing her eyes as she did so. God she was beautiful.

"On a scale of one to ten, how much do you think I'm a floozy?" Chloe smirked.

"Excuse me?" Brooke said, surprised by the words from her mouth in this touching moment, before noticing the wider smirk on Chloe's face and went with it. "An eleven it seems," she said pointedly.

"So, do you really think I'm gonna walk out of your life without at least getting one...," Chloe stopped, and considered which route to take. *Hell, you only live once.* She was going to go for it! Lightly grabbing Brooke's hair, and pulling her head to one side and lightly kissed her neck and continued the sentence. "Steamy." Stopping again, taking the utmost pleasure of the control she was currently holding, pulling her hair back further still gently, she then kissed her windpipe. "Hot," she continued, lightly biting her chin, luxuriating in the gasps that Brooke was relinquishing. "Shower," she said, pushing Brooke up against the wall with some force, and kissing her more passionately than they had currently embraced.

Brooke had no self-control, and she couldn't stop herself seemingly when it came to the crunch. She couldn't remember a time having ever been so out of sorts, and so caught up in the moment and oh God, this kiss was every unspoken word they had ever failed to utter. This was an earth shattering, firework-worthy kiss, and Brooke knew that the moment she let go, she would let go forever. So for now, she was simply going to refuse to let go! At least she hoped she could…

Chapter Thirty-Seven

Brooke was roaming the caravan, not fully used to the emptiness from everyone leaving yesterday. It had been the best weekend, and she was so glad the girls all clicked so well. Smiling to herself as she recollected the antics over the weekend, it had taken her two trips to the bins to get rid of the bottles alone, and she was now ready for a bit of a detox. Luckily, she had the opportunity to get plenty of surfing and running in over the last two days.

Making a sandwich for her dinner, she lay on the sofa, watching the soaps and spending a while googling caravan sites near to her home. Each time she saw something she liked, there was always the negatives which outweighed it. Why was that? It wasn't close to the beach. It wasn't pretty enough. They didn't get sunsets. They didn't get sunrises. There was a long list it seemed, and she couldn't move away from why that was the case. She googled the site she was currently on and searched to see if there were any vans here. Brooke looked into both the static caravans and cabins. But she couldn't really justify paying that level of money, when in reality she didn't know how frequently she could get up here given the distance. This was stupid, and she was being stupid for even considering the site. Additionally, she didn't want to acknowledge or even think about the reason she was considering buying one here.

Brooke decided to go for another run, before coming home and crashing. She needed to clear her head, plus she didn't want to think about tomorrow. Kate had been texting her to check up and ask what she was doing the following day. In reality, Brooke didn't really feel up for much. It was just another number after all, so what if it was 'allegedly' a big day? It wasn't not like she had anyone these days, and she was more than confident that Maria wouldn't even give her a second thought. Interestingly though, she wasn't that fussed on that fact any longer.

***

Brooke had pushed herself hard, and hadn't really gave enough time to let the sandwich digest, which had made her feel a little sick. She loved that feeling of running the troubles away. She always loved to run, allowing her mind to wander off, having little daydreams. The problem was, each daydream started leading to the same thing which she wasn't particularly happy about. This caused her to start started running harder and faster to get rid of those little '*happy*' thoughts.

After Brooke got home and showered, she got into a pair of Calvin Klein boxer shorts and a Hooters vest she wore around the house. The vest was from a holiday where Maria insisted they visited a Hooters restaurant. They were her comfy clothes and cool, which was ideal at this moment given the run she had just returned from. Taking her book and being well aware it was far too early to be in bed, she figured she'd read for a while and then have an early night. Maybe she would get up and see Joel for the sun rise in the morning. *That would be a good way to start my 30th birthday,* she thought, smiling widely.

Chapter Thirty-Eight

Brooke woke startled, her heart was beating way too fast and she couldn't control her breathing. Was someone in the van? She steadied her breathing trying to listen carefully, hearing another bang. However, this time she realised it was not so much a bang but a knock on the door. Checking her alarm, it was 12:01 a.m. *What the hell?* She unlocked her phone and pressed 999, keeping her thumb hovering over the green call button, in case she needed to call the police for backup. She ran through in her mind all of the self-defence moves she could think of in case they were required. Jesus, she was talking like she was at work. She was in the middle of nowhere, and pretty sure if it was a murderer, she would be dead by the time anyone arrived. Switching on the light to the kitchen and living room, she called, "hello," through the door. God she wished she had her gun with her. Caravan doors weren't safe at all. You had to open it outwards, which basically meant that the outsider would always have the advantage on the strength and power. Your only option was to pull it in. There was no answer to her call, so she would just have to go with it. She opened the door slightly and couldn't see anyone there. She saw the light fading on her phone and tapped it before it could lock. Opening the door a little further, she called out *hello* again before noticing her chair in front of the door. She pushed the door open further, noticing the chair with a giant fluffy teddy bear holding a single red rose. The teddy had a sweater on with the words 'happy birthday' across them.

Her heart was still beating ridiculously fast and she didn't know how to control it. "Joel? Joel? Where are you?" Brooke was quietly calling. What was happening? Why had he just disappeared? This could only be him, forced to do it by Chloe, just like his help with the proposal.

"Joel?" Chloe said, walking out from behind the car.

"Chloe?" Brooke said, confused.

"Yes. Why the hell would it be Joel though?" she asked, standing in front of Brooke, who unfortunately for Chloe, was wearing quite possibly the best outfit she had ever seen her in. She looked cute with her freshly woken look. Her hair was a little messy. But the piece de resistance was most definitely the light grey checked Calvin Klein boxers, which accentuated her long defined legs, and a black low cut Hooters vest.

"Hello? You're making me feel like I need to go change, the way you are looking at me," Brooke said, leaning up against the door. "So, what are you doing? Why are you back? And why did you feel the need to scare the crap out of me for the second time in a matter of days?" Brooke said, folding her arms.

"Umm, firstly, I need to do this." Chloe walked forward, and face to face with Brooke, she smirked before unfolding her arms. "Do not fold your arms if you want me to not look at you like a piece of meat," she said, raising an eyebrow. "Okay, right, first question..., I was trying to surprise you with a teddy and a rose. To answer your second question, it's your birthday, that's why I'm here. Last question, I didn't actually mean to scare you either time. Things make more sense in my head when I plan them," she said, smiling. "So, can we bring the things in and go inside properly now before we get told off for making such a racket?" Chloe said questioningly.

Brooke's head was swimming with information because she said she wasn't going to be here. And she was here, no less at midnight, the turn of her actual birthday. With gifts? And romantic gestures? "Yes, sorry of course," Brooke said, walking past Chloe and moving the chair back into its correct positioning before picking up the teddy and the single rose. She walked back in and locked the door behind them, smelling the rose. "So what's in the bag?" Brooke said, trying to be nosey and look in it.

"Excuse me… never you mind," Chloe snarled, putting her arm out to stop Brooke from snooping, stopping as she realised she had grazed her breast. "Shit, sorry, um I…um, sorry I didn't mean to do that," she said, feeling herself blushing profusely.

Brooke was smirking at Chloe who was clearly very embarrassed by touching her. "Violating a member of the constabulary, probably a pretty stupid crime to commit," she said, looking intently at Chloe.

"Piss off, I didn't mean it. You know that. Play nicely, Brookie, or you won't get any birthday treats," Chloe said, trying to ignore the smirking and control that Brooke seemed to be taking a hold of again. Brooke hadn't been anything like that when they'd first met, but she had definitely had a major transitional change in the last few weeks.

Brooke was loving having the control. Whilst she loved Chloe having taken total control on Sunday night before she left; she was craving taking the reins again. Brooke figured this would allow her to not overthink about what she should or shouldn't be doing, which strictly, was never going to be the case right now. But for now, she would just forget about that and deal with the ramifications later.

Brooke walked slowly over to where Chloe was standing. "So, what exactly were you thinking for my birthday treats?" she said, backing Chloe against the cupboard.

Chloe could feel her breathing increasing, however, she could also notice Brooke's chest quickening. "You shouldn't start something you aren't going to finish, Davis." Chloe smirked.

Brooke pushed herself up against Chloe, so there was no space between them. "Is that a threat, Casey? Don't avoid my question. What are you planning on treating me to for my birthday?" Brooke quizzed.

Chloe smirked as she didn't let Brooke's innuendo go unnoticed. "Well what would you like me to treat you to?" Chloe smirked.

"I will make you pay, if you keep ignoring my questions," Brooke responded.

"Is that a promise? Well, I don't know how much more you can make me pay when you are semi naked in the best outfit on the planet, pressed against my very conscious and um, somewhat frustrated body," she said, holding her thumb and forefinger very close together. "So crack on, do your best lady," she said seriously, with a glint in her eye.

"Really? That's how you want to play it?" Brooke said. "Well, if that's how you want to play it, I guess first and foremost, I'll move away from your *very conscious, somewhat frustrated'* body then," she finished, moving back.

"No, no, here you go, you win. I have champagne and chocolates, and the teddy and a rose. Additionally, I have a few more surprises for you, but not until tomorrow. However, if you are going to actively torture me, I will happily refrain from giving you anything and go back home, right now," Chloe said, smirking.

"All sounds splendid, and I thought you were here for nothing more than to give me a little birthday kiss?" Brooke said, taking the step back in to close the space between them again.

"Do you want a birthday kiss?"

"Do you always answer a question with a question?"

"Does it frustrate you that I answer a question with question?" Chloe challenged, smirking now.

"Oh, you definitely frustrate me!"

"So, you want a birthday kiss then huh?" Chloe asked again.

"I...think I may want a birthday kiss," she whispered.

Chloe held up the teddy she had bought for Brooke's birthday. "Question is, from me or him?" she asked comically.

Chloe was killing Brooke. She was so het up, and scarily, she was turned on to hell. "Well, it's a difficult one, Chlo. He's far cuter than you are." She smiled. "For the love of God, will you just come here?" Brooke pulled Chloe in by the top of her sweater and kissed her softly. She had given up on trying to fight the fact she shouldn't be kissing Chloe, and for the first time, just let go. She pulled back and looked at Chloe,. "Bloody hell, talk about making a girl work for it." Brooke smiled slightly. She put her arms around Chloe's neck, feeling the fear bubble inside her, and choosing to ignore it. "So, you actually came all the way up here to surprise me on my actual birthday? You did that for me?" Brooke asked sincerely, twisting a strand of Chloe's long, dark hair in her hand.

"It's not really too far from where I live," Chloe blushed. "Plus, I wasn't gonna leave you alone on your thirtieth, and I kinda promised your friends that I would give you a good birthday," she said again.

"Kate and Jo asked you to do this?" she said, snapping.

"God no, I was always doing this. Kate said they didn't want you alone, and I merely told them to have some faith in me. I was never going to leave you alone. I was never going to not be here on your thirtieth," Chloe said, blushing.

"Why would you do that for me?" Brooke shook her head.

"I think you know the answer to that, Brooke," she said sincerely, placing a piece of blonde hair behind her ear. "Happy thirtieth birthday, you," she said, pulling Brooke's head closer and meeting her lips. Chloe's tongue found Brooke's and danced together as they shared a slow kiss. It was the first kiss they had shared where Chloe could fully feel all of the meaning and emotion that she had been trying to conceal all these weeks. She pulled back and looked into Brooke's eyes, noticing the tear fall slowly down her cheek.

"Hey. Hey, come here. What's the matter?" Chloe whispered, pulling Brooke in and holding her tightly. "What's wrong? Why are you crying? It's your birthday." Chloe kissed her head delicately, stroking her back, pulling her close again. "Brooke, please? Talk to me? You're scaring me," Chloe pleaded.

"I just can't believe that you have done all this…again. For me? That you have gone to all of that trouble for me. Tonight, and at the weekend. Nobody has ever done anything so thoughtful, kind, and considerate. I just don't know what to say. I don't know how to compute all of this, and I don't know why anybody would do that for me," she said, sniffing a little.

"Sweetie, you are an amazing woman. You are warm, kind, caring, intelligent, funny, loving, generous, silly, gorgeous, super-hot, and sexy as hell in CK briefs and a hooters vest. The list is not exhaustive by any means, and these are merely a small number of the many wonderful things about you. But you have suffered some rubbish recently, and that's made you doubt the truly amazing woman you are. So yeah, I have done it because, despite all efforts to avoid it, I am crazy attracted to you. But in most part, I did it because you deserve it. You are…my word, amazing and truly wonderful. So yeah, you do deserve it, you deserve it more than anybody," Chloe said truthfully.

Brooke was terrified for what she was about to say. This woman was too much. She'd never heard such beautiful things said about her aside from parents, and she'd never had someone do anything like all the things that Chloe had done recently for her.

"What are you thinking?" Chloe smiled, stroking her face softly.

"That you're amazing, and that I want you to take me to bed," Brooke said, looking intently into her eyes.

"Brooke, I didn't do any of thi…"

"Shut up and take me to bed," Brooke repeated.

***

Chloe walked into the bedroom, holding Brooke's hand. She turned to face her and tried to speak, but couldn't get the words out. Her breathing was erratic, and in this moment she couldn't stop herself. She knew she had to. She knew if she didn't, she was…to put it bluntly, royally screwed, with no pun intended.

"Do you not want this?" Brooke asked, embarrassed.

Chloe felt terrible that she had made Brooke feel this way after everything she had been through already. She was losing complete control, because whilst she was aware of the pain she would feel if she did this, it wasn't even close to the yearning and aching her body was having over the opportunity of making love to this beautiful woman. "I've never wanted anything more, Brooke. But I'm concerned that you are not ready. Are you absolutely sure about this?"

"I was absolutely sure when you kissed me the way you did on Sunday night. And spoke of hot, steamy showers," Brooke said, moving Chloe's hair to the side and gently kissing down her neck, generating a slight groan from Chloe.

Chloe finally opened her eyes, looking directly into Brooke's. "You have no idea how much I have dreamt about this moment," she said, running her index finger slowly from Brooke's temple all the way down the outline of her face. She stopped at her chin and gently brushed her thumb over her lips. "You are the most beautiful woman I have ever met, you know that?" Chloe said sincerely.

Brooke leaned towards the light switch to turn out the lights.

Chloe reached her hand with her own and stopped her, causing Brooke to look back concerned. "Brooke, I want to make love to you, every part of you. Because to me, every part of you is beautiful. Please let me see all of you?" Chloe pleaded, aware that the scar was an issue for Brooke and unsure how she would react. In that moment she could see the fear in Brooke's face, reflective of a 'rabbit in headlights'. "Trust me, baby girl," Chloe whispered, slowly lacing her fingers through Brooke's and pulling them away from the light switch. She lifted the hand and kissed it softly, still maintaining eye contact.

Chloe held Brooke's face in her hands, gently stroking her cheeks with her thumbs. "It's okay, it'll be okay, I promise," Chloe whispered, before lowering her hands to the bottom of Brooke's vest. She stroked her waist with her fingers, lifting her top slightly before looking up to Brooke for acknowledgement.

Brooke felt completely exposed, but Chloe's eyes were soft and loving, and in this moment she had never felt safer. It terrified the hell out of her. She took in a deep breath, closing her eyes slightly. She lowered her own hands to meet Chloe's, and very slightly lifted to give the confirmation that Chloe required. The expression on Chloe's face was all the evidence she needed that she had done the right thing. She leaned in and kissed Chloe, this time filled with passion and force...this time, the kiss was fuelled with the burdening desire that was overwhelming her.

Chloe groaned into the kiss, touched at Brooke's trust in her. She was really going to do this she thought. Rightly or wrongly, she was going to go through with this and deal with the consequences later. But for now, she was desperate to appreciate every part of her body, and enjoy every moment of it.

Chloe pulled Brooke's top off slowly, maintaining eye contact the entire time. "You okay?" she whispered, kissing her neck softly, eliciting a number of groans from the woman. Chloe gasped as she slowly took in her body. "You are so incredibly beautiful," she said, slowly laying her onto the bed, and straddling Brooke. She pushed her thick blonde hair to one side. It was so soft, lifting it slightly and allowing it to slope through her fingers. "Your beauty terrifies me; you know that?" Chloe said, kissing Brooke's neck.

Brooke was groaning in pleasure as her kisses worked their way down her neck. "No, I don't quite know what you mean, but I don't care. Just continue what you are doing to me," she groaned again.

Chloe kissed further down her neck, working slower with each kiss that got closer to her breasts. "You really do have an incredible body," she sighed into another kiss at the top of Brooke's breast. "My God, you have amazing breasts," she declared. Kissing further down, she raised herself up and cupped Brooke, revelling in the pertness. She grazed her nipple with her thumb, causing further groans from Brooke. Chloe smirked at Brooke. "Hmm, sensitive area? Oh, I'm going to enjoy this now," Chloe said.

"Cheeky," she gasped, as she felt Chloe's mouth close in around her nipple.

Chloe gasped herself as she felt Brooke's nipple rise to attention, gently biting the area and circling her tongue slowly, before picking up the pace and flicking faster and harder over the area. Chloe was loving the effect it was having on Brooke, who was groaning harder and louder now. Chloe moved over to the other breast, replicating the actions, once more eliciting deep groans of pleasure from Brooke.

Chloe lifted herself up and scratched her nails gently down Brooke's tummy, tracing it with kisses. She kissed around the rim of her boxers all the way around, slowly following with her forefinger slightly under the material. She kissed all the way around the side of her mid-section, to the base of the scar, looking up immediately to Brooke to ensure she was okay. Her eyes were already desperately searching Chloe's and the area. Chloe grabbed her hand and gently kissed the back of her fingers. She slowly crawled up the bed to face Brooke, gently stroking the backs of her fingers over her cheek. "You have no idea how completely beautiful you are, please don't be afraid of me or of the scar. It's part of you, and you are incredible. It's who you are, but it shouldn't define you. It's a scar and you should be proud of it. You should be proud of the fact that you took a bad person out and you lived to tell the tale," Chloe whispered. She softly kissed her lips before continuing to kiss all the way down her body again to where she left off. Chloe gently lifted Brooke and traced the outline of the scar, kissing each part of it. She wanted to appreciate every part of her, including the scar, but didn't want to overdo to the extent that she made Brooke feel uncomfortable.

Chloe kissed back around the rim of her boxers, then placed her fingers under the rim as she felt her fingers begin to shake.

"You okay?" Brooke whispered, watching Chloe's chest heaving heavily and her hands trembling.

"Seemingly, nervous. Very unlike me." She smiled, breathing heavily.

"Do you want to stop?" Brooke asked reluctantly.

"That's the stupidest thing you've asked me since I met you." She smiled. "I've got no intention of stopping, unless you ask me to. I'm not nervous because of not wanting it, I'm nervous because I can't remember wanting something so desperately, that it's terrifying me." She smiled sincerely, looking down at Brooke's body. "I love your body," she said, eyes roaming each part of her. She slowly pulled the boxer shorts down and unravelled the remainder, gasping as she took in her naked body.

Chloe kissed her waist all the way around to her side, gently nibbling the area as she got a playful giggle from Brooke. "Hmmm, lil bit ticklish are we?" she murmured, replicating the act and hearing more giggles, thankful she was relaxing. Chloe kissed and gently bit down her legs, moving around to her inner thigh. She slowly ran her tongue the length of her inner thigh, and delighted in the groans of pleasure coming from Brooke. She moved around closer to where she needed to be and stopped, taking her in, and teasing her a little as she smirked up to Brooke. She found Brooke's hand and laced her fingers through her own, watching her emanating delight. Chloe ran her tongue between her lips, hearing and feeling Brooke's body react to the touch, elated when she realised how ready Brooke was for her. Chloe ran her tongue softly over her swollen clitoris, feeling Brooke's body rise to the touch, provoking her to put more pressure on the area as she heard Brooke gasp and groan heavily. Chloe moved down further, running her tongue between her lips, slowly and gently pushing her tongue into her centre, tasting her sweet taste. Chloe felt Brooke's grip tighten as she was pushing her tongue deeper inside, feeling Brooke's body rise to allow Chloe to enter further inside her. She could hear and feel Brooke's breathing becoming erratic, and the groans become louder and faster. She brought her free hand down and pushed her thumb back onto her swollen sensitive area, and pushed her tongue in deeper and faster. She was filling Brooke and could feel how wet she was becoming. Chloe lifted her bottom up so she could get deeper and push further inside her, applying more pressure. She could feel Brooke was close to releasing and hitting a state of ecstasy as she felt Brooke's grip tighten around her. Her spare hand left the pillow she had been holding onto tightly before grabbing Chloe's head, and pushing her in deeper as wave over wave released from her.

***

Chloe made her way back up to where Brooke was. "Hey you."

"Hmm," Brooke groaned, unable to say anything more whilst she was waiting for her body to come back down. A few minutes later, she finally turned on her side to face Chloe. "So…haven't done that for a while," she said shyly.

"I'm glad I could accommodate, especially on such a special occasion." Chloe smiled, and pushed her hair behind her ear.

"Oh, you most definitely accommodated. However, I am a little concerned as to how exactly you are still fully clothed?" she said, manoeuvring the cover to pull over her.

"Please don't? I don't know if I told you, but you have the most incredible body. I *love* your body," she whispered. "And the reason I am still clothed is because…I don't know if I told you, but you were wearing the sexiest outfit known to man? Which left very little to the imagination, hence the urgency to get you undressed." She smirked, running her thumb over her nipple.

"Easy, tiger. That will not end well." She smirked, grabbing hold of Chloe's fingers. "Okay, so if I'm staying like this, it's only fair you are not lay next to me fully clothed." Brooke smirked back at Chloe.

"I can't see that me touching you is going to end any way, *other* than well, personally. Do you fancy opening that bottle of champagne to celebrate, or is it too late? Alternatively, I can go home if you want to crash," Chloe asked, concerned at her presumption.

"You are not going anywhere outside of this van this evening. I can assure you of that right now. As long as you don't have to be up too early, then yes, I wouldn't mind a glass of champagne. However, I have one birthday request," Brooke said, sardonically.

"Oh dear God, this sounds concerning."

"On the contrary, it's anything but concerning," she added.

"Go on, what's this request? And I will clearly state on the record, it is only a request because I am not guaranteeing I will be doing it," Chloe said, leaning down and kissing Brooke's erect nipple.

"My word, you can tell you have been floosying about for years. You certainly know what you're doing with that tongue of yours," she said.

"You haven't seen anything yet." She smirked. "Anyways lady, that's not very nice, when I have come all the way over to surprise you at the exact point you turned thirty," she said, pushing out her bottom lip and crossing her arms across her chest.

"Get over yourself," Brooke laughed, throwing the teddy bear at her.

"Again, you're mean. Right, I'll go get the champers," Chloe said, getting off the bed.

"No, no," Brooke grabbed Chloe and pulled her back on the bed. "You my lovely, need to take your clothes off before you go anywhere," she said, smiling widely.

"Is that your request?"

"Yup, sure is. So come on, don't make the birthday girl wait, or do you need a helping hand?"

"And what if I don't honour said request?"

"Then I'll just do it for you."

"Well that sounds like much more fun." Chloe smirked.

Brooke rolled over and straddled Chloe. "See, the problem with that is, I like the control and I'm a huge tease. So now, as a result of you disobeying me, there are consequences to pay!" Brooke smirked. She looked down as she slowly eased Chloe's top up a little, revealing that perfectly toned and tanned midriff that taunted Brooke in ways she refused to engage in.

"Oh really? Wow, quite the control freak aren't we? So, how exactly am I going to get punished then, Detective Davis?" she asked playfully, running her finger down Brooke's neck, all the way down the centre of her body.

"Only on occasion. Namely, when people are naughty, and need somebody to keep them in check." She smirked, grabbing Chloe's finger as she lifted it up to her mouth, circling her tongue around the tip of it. She didn't let it go unnoticed that Chloe's breathing was becoming more rapid. "Well, Casey, it's not good. See now, I'm going to have to tease you…, and with that, you aren't allowed to touch. Did you know insubordination is a very serious offence? And by defying authority and refusing to obey orders, well this has now resulted in me having no choice but to punish you. So, as I nicely sit here…relaxing as I straddle you naked… may I add? I'm going to slowly undress you, and hugely take my time…garment…by…garment," she purred. "As I appreciate and relish every part of you. But, you need to remember, Casey. If you try to touch, kiss, feel…hmmm even look, you will really pay then." She raised her eyebrow to Chloe and kissed down her neck, raising both hands above her head and holding them in place there.

Chloe looked down between the two women's bodies. Brooke's incredibly beautiful and naked body alongside her own, partially, naked body…this woman was too much, but she was right, and Brooke was well aware of it. Chloe was desperate to touch her…her body actually ached for the physical contact. "Okay, okay, I give in. I'm sorry, I need to touch you. So lemme go? I'll get undressed then go and get the champers? Then I can assure you I will be touching you…again…*and* again, *and* most probably again." She grinned.

"Well, that was easy," Brooke said, as she kissed her lips and rolled off her. "Go on then, make my birthday dreams come true," she added.

Chloe got up and took her bra off first, undoing the belt to her jeans next. She saw Brooke watching her intently, and could see desire in her eyes and wanted to play with her a little. "You okay there, Davis? Good view? You want to see more?" Chloe smirked.

"Chloe Casey, stop fucking with me and get those jeans off before I make you pay."

"You're very aggressive with all this making me pay malarkey," Chloe said. "See, I'm not so sure you can make me pay anymore, because from that glazed look in your eyes, I can see how much you want me to take the jeans off. So maybe I will wait...hmmm...until I get back?" she laughed.

"But it's my birthday?" she said sadly.

"Ohhhh, no...no way," she stopped, pointing her finger to Brooke, trying to contain the smile creeping up. "Play fair, you can't pull the puppy dog eyes on me. No, *No,* Brookie," Chloe said, looking away. *For God's sake*, she sighed and turned her back to the bed, unbuckling the belt to her jeans and slowly sliding them down her body.

Brooke couldn't take her eyes off Chloe. She was wearing a Victoria's Secret, red lace underwear set which perfectly complimented her toned and olive skin. The French knickers sat perfectly across her toned bottom, and Brooke couldn't stop looking at her. She was sexy as hell, and surfing certainly looked after that body. Brooke watched Chloe slowly turn around. She looked amazing from behind, but incredible from the front. And at that point, Brooke could feel the loss of control suddenly leave her body. "You look good enough to eat." Brooke smirked at Chloe.

"Really!" she said sarcastically.

"Dunno what you mean? But this is more than okay. I don't think I will ever forget this vision, it's that okay!" she grinned. Brooke's demeanour changed, and she suddenly became very serious. "You are gorgeous, you know that?" she said, still unable to move her eyes off of Chloe's body. "And red looks fabulous on you...just saying. I think you should come over here and let me take a closer look," she added, raising her eyebrows.

"Champagne first," she laughed, slowly walking out. *Slow* enough to allow Brooke time to enjoy the view.

"You're mine when you get that sexy little butt back in here," Brooke shouted after her.

"Yeah, yeah, promises, promises," Chloe shouted back after her, causing them both to laugh.

Brooke slid herself down her bed and covered her face with the pillow...*what are you getting yourself into?* She sighed, but was unable to stop the smile creeping up over her face, thinking it *was* her birthday after all.

Chapter Thirty-Nine

Chloe returned, holding a bag, a bottle of champagne in an ice bucket, and a couple of glasses.

"What's in the bag?" Brooke questioned.

"Patience is a virtue, my sweet. I am sure I have told you this on numerous occasions already," she said, sitting down on the bed and pouring a drink into their glasses. She rummaged in the bag, moving things about and pulling out two wrapped presents and a Tupperware box.

Chloe handed a glass of champagne to Brooke and wished her a happy birthday once more. She leaned in and kissed her, gently biting her lip. She pulled back and looked into her eyes, "I think you are incredibly beautiful, and I hope you know that."

"Well, you have told me once or twice tonight," she said, smiling.

Chloe loved when her smile reached her eyes. She couldn't remember ever seeing such honesty and authenticity behind a smile before, outside of children.

"You have made my birthday perfect. Better than perfect in fact, thank you so much." Brooke smiled sincerely.

"Well, it's still early into it, so technically it's only just beginning. Here you are. They are only a couple of small things, so please don't get excited," she said, handing her a couple of gifts. "I just wanted to give you something that you could open. Oh, and I made these for you," she said, handing her a box filled with chocolate covered strawberries.

"Oh, wow, these look amazing." She bit into one, moaning with delight. "Wow, here," she said, feeding Chloe the remainder of the chocolate covered strawberry. "I can't believe you did all of this for me. I am so incredibly touched. But you really didn't have to. Especially not get me gifts, too. I mean really, this is more than enough," she said, tracing a finger down the side of her body paying particular attention to the underwear set. "And don't think that hiding that body hasn't gone unnoticed."

Chloe smiled. "Come on, open your gifts," she said, jumping up onto her knees, excitably.

Brooke was studying Chloe attentively, noticing the excitement overtaking her because of the gifts. Seemingly, she appeared to be more excited by the giving than she'd ever witnessed before, and that was an entirely different approach for Brooke to witness. "So, can I guess?" she said, shaking the gift next to her ear. "Hmmm, is it a photo of you in that underwear set?" she laughed.

"You are embarrassing me, keep going on about it?" she said, covering her body with the duvet and smiling.

Brooke opened the smallest gift first, and read the packaging. "Board wax." She smiled.

"The most important part for a board," Chloe said, "it's only a little something as I told you."

"I love it, it's so cool. Who'd have thought a month ago I would own a surfboard and surfboard wax?" She smiled.

Chloe pushed her the next gift, and Brooke opened it to see a '*beginners guide to cooking, cook book*'. She loved that Chloe was so thoughtful. "I love it, thank you so much. I can make you something before I leave." She smiled enthusiastically.

"How about for tonight, we just enjoy this?" she said, pointing to the two of them. "And...forget about everything else? Fear? Worry? Leaving? Exes?" Chloe said, sighing.

"That sounds like a good plan." As Brooke put the gifts on the floor and turned to face Chloe, she picked a piece of ice out of the bucket, smirking as she met her eyes. Brooke held out the ice cube above her breasts raising an eyebrow slightly. "For now...I *need* you," she said, sucking the ice cube a little, allowing the coldness to cool her lips. "I need to *kiss* you...," she stopped as she kissed her neck, relinquishing a groan at the coldness of her lips. "To *tease* you...," she continued as she rolled the ice cube down the centre of her chest, mesmerised as Chloe's back arched at the power of her execution. "*Touch* you...," she added, as she ever so gently grazed the back of her index finger of the lace hiding her nipple. "and... *taste* you...," she purred, lowering the ice cube once more and running it over the top of her chest, before she used her tongue to lick the remnants of the ice cube. Brooke was fiercely aroused and loved the groans that Chloe was emanating right now. She lazily opened her eyes before taking hold of Brooke's hand.

"We have one slight problem with that gorgeous."

Brooke looked up from where her eyes had been residing...lightly cupping the red laced breast, she softly grazed her thumb over it again. "Yeah, and what's that exactly?" she asked Chloe.

Chloe rolled Brooke back over and mounted her. "That I am nowhere near done with you yet," she said, pushing with a little force, evoking a slight scream from Brooke.

***

Chloe enveloped the beautiful woman, their legs entwined as she tried to bring Brooke back down, and allow both of them to even out their erratic breathing. It appeared Chloe couldn't get enough of Brooke. It was so late, and Brooke was adamant she couldn't physically take anymore, but she was desperate to physically be with her, again and again.

"I can't believe you are still in your underwear set," Brooke mustered, as she got closer to Chloe, making shapes on her tummy.

"Well what do you expect? Seemingly, I couldn't get enough of you. I was *compelled* to pleasure you, apparently on numerous occasions," she giggled.

"Cheeky. I know! You are *such* a selfish lover for the record," she said as she looked up smirking and pulled Chloe in for another soft kiss. She couldn't erase the thoughts from her mind that she loved this. That this felt so right and it could never be. She could kiss this girl forever though, and loved the soft, warm tongue that played with her own when they kissed. She loved the way they both had a love for biting each other's bottom lips through the kiss. Shit, she was an amazing kisser and an amazing lover, and Brooke was now officially screwed. No less, thirty and screwed she thought, ignoring the negativity and deepening her kiss with Chloe anyway.

Chapter Forty

Chloe woke up disorientated at first as the sun was gleaming in to the room on her face. She looked around and took in the blonde hair partially across her chest and across the pillow, the soft curve of her jaw silently resting on her shoulder. Brooke was...simply put, stunning, Chloe thought. She gently stroked the side of her face, terrified of how deep she was already in. Unfortunately, every part of that was magnified as she looked down and watched her sleep. Chloe sighed and gently moved Brooke, trying desperately not to disturb her. She got up and threw on a t-shirt of Brooke's, quietly shutting the door behind her as she went off on her birthday mission.

Chloe smiled as she arranged the plate, "Davis, you are gross," she said to the silence of the kitchen. Pouring the fresh squeezed OJ into a glass, she grabbed the bag and made her way back to the bedroom.

Brooke stirred and looked up while rubbing her eyes/ "Hey, what are you doing?" she said groggily. "Cute t-shirt, it looks good on you." She smirked. "So what have you been up to now, sexy?"

"Ahh you know, just wanting to make sure that my favourite neighbour has the best day ever." She smiled and kissed Brooke, as she placed the tray on the bed before her.

"Well, I think you already did that when you...Erm," Brooke stopped, looking embarrassed, but noticing the sincerity in Chloe's eyes. "When you rocked my world four times last night," she blushed. "FYI, I'm loving this on you," she pulled the bottom of the grey t-shirt that Chloe was wearing, slightly grazing her inner thigh, causing them both to flinch and blush.

"Come on, before this gets cold," she said.

"Okay, so what do we have here? Another rose." She winked. "Wow, I do feel special. Or was that your dastardly plan all along? To get into my knickers with roses." She bumped Chloe's shoulder.

"By your own admission, I think I did that four times last night with only one rose, so apparently not." She poked her tongue out in jest to Brooke. "Okay, so we have one single rose for one beautiful lady, we have one fresh OJ for the lady that loves OJ, and last but not least…for the most beautiful, but the grossest girl ever, we have...Drum roll please…," Chloe laughed and lifted the lid off the plate. "The piece de résistance, is I do believe your favourite. Bacon and maple syrup and pancakes and sugar." She smiled.

"Oh my God you didn't? Ohh, you did? You are quickly becoming my actual dream woman." She smiled.

"Watch out world, Davis will be proposing next." Chloe smirked.

"You cannot offend me, nor even get a reaction from me in any way, shape ,or form when it comes to this meal. I am going to be happy, stay happy, and embrace the first meal of my thirties," she groaned as she took a bite. "Seriously, you have to taste this. Please?" Brooke pleaded. "For me?"

"No way, that's gross."

"Please, pretty please? Come on, you have to. I will do anything," Brooke tried again, raising her eyebrows.

"You know, Davis, that's a pretty loaded statement." She raised an eyebrow back.

"I don't care, that's just how good this is. Anyways, shut up and let me enjoy my favourite meal. You are so sex obsessed," Brooke said.

"Yes, you are soooo right on that one. However, I will caveat that with the fact that you are the one who is making me sex obsessed, just so you know. Okay, stop being greedy and let me have some of this odd ensemble. I'm on a promise to get anything I want if I try it, so why the hell not?" Chloe giggled.

Brooke put all the ingredients onto the fork and offered it to Chloe.

"Brooke, I think that is the least romantic feeding of someone I have ever seen," she said between mouthfuls, and wiping her mouth. "And FYI, that's grosser than it looks," she said, taking a mouthful of her OJ. "So, last two gifts I'm afraid, and then we can do whatever you want today." Chloe laid down on her side facing Brooke, revealing the red panties peeking out from the bottom of the top.

"Really?" Brooke raised her eyebrows, looking down at the lacy Victoria's secret French knickers. "Well that's a no brainer." She winked and took another mouthful. "You really shouldn't have got me anything else, you have done far too much," she sighed.

"Hey, how about you let me be the decider of that? Open," Chloe said, handing her the birthday card.

Brooke opened the card and read the words. She noticed that Chloe had beautiful handwriting, realising she'd never seen what her writing looked like before. She put it on the bedside table and kissed her quickly.

Holding up the two gifts sitting in front of her. "Any preference?" Brooke asked.

S.L. Gape

"Yes. This one first, then that one. They are both only small things. Well this one is actually a homemade gift, a bit retro, and somewhat sad, I'm afraid." She smiled. Brooke opened the CD she had made. "I figured you probably have a CD player in your car and it could keep you company when you drive home, or are just on the road. It's homemade, and the first song is Shania Twain's, *You're Still The One,* as I know you said it was one of your favourites a few weeks back. And then, just some…well, some other similar type ones." She smiled shyly.

"Chloe, I can't believe you have done this? This is incredible," she said honestly. "There is a CD player in the lounge, so we can put it on later and listen to it together."

Brooke opened the next gift, revealing a small square box. She looked at Chloe questioningly before she lifted the lid, and in the box she saw a beautiful three-part intertwining silver bangle. "Oh my gosh, it's beautiful. I love it. Chloe this is all far too much. I'm so grateful, but this is far too much. I couldn't accept this," she said to Chloe truthfully.

"You kinda don't get the idea behind birthday presents do you? I think it shall fit, but let me know. I can change it for a smaller size if it's too big. Additionally, you can't not accept it, it's tailored to you. Look inside each bangle," Chloe said to her, blushing.

Brooke turned the first bangle around and found the inscription, *be thankful for yesterday's lessons.* She turned the second, following the same pattern and she read *be honoured for today's achievements.* Finding the last inscription, she read *be excited for tomorrow's adventures.*

336

Be thankful for yesterday's lessons,
Be honoured for today's achievements,
Be excited for tomorrow's adventures.

What beautiful words. She loved how thoughtful this woman was.

Brooke looked up at Chloe with tears in her eyes, and Chloe instantly pulled her into an embrace. "Hey, what's up? It was supposed to be a nice gift."

"It is. It, so, *so* is. It's beautiful, it's perfect, I don't deserve it, and I don't think I have ever had anything so incredible. You are beautiful and incredible. Thank you. I promise, I am happy. I'm sorry, I know I keep repeating myself, but I cannot believe you have done all of this for me," Brooke confirmed.

"You aren't supposed to be crying though," Chloe said, looking at her intently and stroking her face.

"I know, I know. They're tears of happiness though." Brooke smiled.

"I'll accept that then. Does it fit?"

Brooke put the intertwined bangles on her wrist, smiling widely. "It fits perfectly, it's perfect, Chloe," she said. "Thank you so very much," she added, pulling her arm to get her up off the bed.

"Are you sure? I can exchange it if not. Or change the size? Whichever you prefer," Chloe added concerned.

Brooke put her arms around Chloe's neck, stroking her hair slightly. "There's not a chance in a million years that I'm exchanging it. I adore it. It's so perfectly me and my jewellery style, added to that I love the words more than anything. They are so apt and so incredibly perfect right now. It's perfectly beautiful and a perfect fit...I...," She stopped, unsure if she was brave enough to continue. Breathing in deeply, she said, "Ummm...just kinda like

I'm feeling you are right now." Brooke looked deep into her eyes and prayed that Chloe would feel the same ease and lack of fear that she was somehow getting lost in. Brooke was feeling oddly courageous and unafraid, and was praying that Chloe was feeling some if not all of this too. Once again, she leaned in and kissed her deeply, finding her tongue with her own, before slowly sliding down her knickers. They continued their kiss, getting deeper and more meaningful as Brooke softly grazed the perfectly smooth area which had been hidden by those beautiful briefs all night, causing a loud groan from herself.

Brooke pulled away for a very brief moment as she lifted her own t-shirt over Chloe's head, and then threw it on the bed before returning to their kiss. Brooke lightly outlined the trace of her nipple through the bra before unknowingly unclasping the enticing lingerie.

Brooke looked at her for a few moments, admiring her beauty. "For the record, in my opinion, you are pretty damn amazing," Brooke whispered gently, running her fingers over Chloe's suntanned skin. She pushed her long dark hair out of the way and gently kissed down her neck and collarbone, hearing the gasps and light moans coming from her.

Brooke pulled her hand, leading her to the bathroom. She switched the shower on and returned to their kiss, hearing Chloe mumble something and leaning back, looking at her confused. "Excuse me?" she asked.

"Sorry, caught up in that kiss. I said what are you doing?"

"Kissing you?"

"Funny girl," she threw her eyes up to the shower, and deepened the kiss, realising that she needed to stop talking.

"Well I do believe I owe you a hot, steamy shower and maybe an orgasm or two," she smirked, pulling her inside the cubicle and shutting the door behind them.

"Bit cosy isn't it?"

"*And?* That's wrong because? Now, shut the hell up and kiss me," she said, pulling Chloe closer and lightly grazing her bottom with her nails. The water was powerfully flowing over their bodies, as Chloe pushed Brooke against the wall, deepening their kiss once again. She allowed Brooke to finally roam her body freely. Brooke kissed Chloe's neck, up her shoulder and then down her windpipe. She slowly turned Chloe around, moving her hair out of the way and kissing down her neck from behind. "God, you're beautiful," Brooke whispered in her ear. Brooke kissed all the way down her spine, feeling the water rushing over their bodies. She reached her lower back and gently bit the top of her bottom, eliciting more gasps. Brooke began the ascent once more, kissing all the way up her spine. She kissed over her shoulder bone and gently bit the top of her shoulder, before moving her hand around the front to her stomach and scraping her nails up her tummy. She stopped at the base of her breast, gently cupping it as she applied some pressure to her erect nipple. Brooke pulled Chloe's wet hair back slightly, bringing her head back to rest slightly on Brooke's own shoulder. Then she kissed her neck as her spare hand reached down past her soft skin and grazed her fingers between her lips.

Chloe gasped and felt her knees buckle at Brooke's careful touch. She was resting her head on Brooke's shoulder and turned her head to face her, finding her mouth and kissing her as Brooke's fingers found her sensitive region. Chloe could sense that it would take no time at all before she was thrown into a sense of euphoria, as the experienced fingers were moving faster and harder over her swollen area. Chloe reached her arm around Brooke's head, keeping their kiss intense and fuelled with passion and desire as her body was slowly climbing to a state of release. Chloe's lips were sore as she deepened the kiss further, tongues rushing frantically together. Brooke took Chloe's nipple between her thumb and forefinger and applied more pressure, as she listened to the groans that were coming from both women. Brooke could feel Chloe was on the edge, quickening and hardening her movements, tightening her grip around Chloe and feeling the waves release over her.

Brooke held Chloe in her arms in the same position, whilst she waited for her to come back down. Chloe had one arm wrapped around her neck, and one pushed against the shower cubicle. Her head rested against Brooke's shoulder, with the water continuing to rush over them both.

Chloe finally came around and turned to face Brooke, resting her forehead against hers. There were no words spoken, they just stayed there for a while and enjoyed the moment.

***

"Well, that was all a bit unplanned," Chloe said, smirking to Brooke as they lay on the bed together, following the heated shower.

"Hmm hmm, although, I'm still not so sure that this wasn't all a ploy to have your wicked way with me." She smirked, and kissed Chloe's hand.

"How very dare you? I was just merely being the kind, caring neighbour," Chloe said, raising an eyebrow.

"You know, I shouldn't make my life out to sound like the whole 'woe is me', and I really shouldn't make Maria out to be this Godawful woman, because in reality, she wasn't completely awful. And truth be known, I would have and could have left at any point. But whether she didn't care, or whether other things were more important I don't know. But in nine years she never did an ounce of what you have done for me over the last week. And this…," she stopped and held her new bangle, twisting it and looking at the inscriptions distantly. "This is the most beautiful and thought provoking thing I have ever received," Brooke said, pulling up the cover around them and snuggling into Chloe.

"Brooke, I can't talk about what I do and don't want, nor can I talk about what will or won't happen. However, what I will say is, in my opinion, you deserve everything in the world. Personally, I don't think I've done anything that's above and beyond, because honestly, this is no big deal to me. I guess it's just who I am, and I don't want to make that sound like you're not worthy, because you have no idea how incorrect that is. But this is natural to me. I *would* do this. I would think this is all normal, and reflective of how someone should act. So as I said, I don't want to overthink stuff. I want to enjoy today as much as what I have enjoyed every minute since one minute past midnight last night, and hopefully ensure that one of the coolest people I have ever met has the best thirtieth birthday ever," she said, smiling widely.

"Thank you. You really are wonderful. Okay, no more talk like that. So, what does having the best birthday ever involve?" Brooke smirked.

"Ohhh, lots and lots," Chloe raised an eyebrow.

"Really? Care to elaborate?" Brooke leaned in closer, whispering.

"Okay, no more whispering. It turns me on to fuck, and we won't leave bed otherwise," Chloe said sternly.

"And what if I don't want to leave bed? You said this was my day," Brooke said seriously.

Chloe looked back at her, moving a strand of blonde hair from her face. "Well is that what you want, princess?"

"Okay, so I don't mind you calling me princess when it's in a nice lovey way, but when you are just being condescending, I'm going to smack your ass," Brooke said.

Chloe leaned in close to Brooke. "You promise?" She kissed her lips quickly. "You didn't answer my question."

"I thought I made it quite clear, that's what I want."

"Very demanding, Miss Davis. Okay, well you settle with your book and give me fifteen minutes okay?"

"Why? What are you doing now? Where are you going?" Brooke asked, looking concerned.

Chloe placed her hands on Brooke's face, stroking slightly. "Trust me beautiful," she said winking, before leaving.

"Ermm, one question?" Brooke said seriously.

"Yes? What?"

"Are you going to put on any clothes? I mean not that I'm complaining. Like, O…M…G...not… at...all. But you know, if you're leaving you may want to?"

Brooke smirked. "FYI, I'm gonna caveat that with, when you return it's back to nothing. It's my day after all."

"You are very, very demanding lady, you know that?"

"Yes, I do! That's what you like about me though."

Chloe raised an eyebrow before throwing on last night's t-shirt of Brooke's and leaving the room, shutting the door behind her.

<u>Chapter Forty-One</u>

Chloe peeped her head around the door. "Shut your eyes."

"Bloody hell, I thought you had left? I hope you have a big mac there. I've waited so long," Brooke said.

"You want a big mac? God, you are so bloody high maintenance. I can assure you, I am not brave enough to go out in a t-shirt with no underwear on just to get you a McDonalds. But if you want one, as it's your birthday, I will happily go get you one. But clearly, I need to get dressed first." She pointed out. "Now for Christ's sake, shut your eyes," Chloe snapped.

Brooke closed her eyes, muttering *grumpy* under her breath. She threw the cover over her head, sighing loudly.

"You know for a thirty-year-old, you sure act like a petulant child at times," Chloe said, bringing everything into the room.

Brooke couldn't stop the wide smile over her face. "Whatever, old lady," she giggled.

***

Chloe threw the t-shirt back off and got under the bottom end of the cover, crawling her way up Brooke's body, kissing all the way up until she reached her face. "Hey, sexy lady. Miss me?" She smiled, smirking to Brooke.

Brooke felt the fear overcome her once again, but fought against it. "I did. Now come and kiss me please.

It's my birthday, and I was hoping I would get at least six an hour."

"That's one every ten minutes. You know that right?"

"I know, but I thought I was worth it." She sniffed, feigning sadness.

"I can give you that, now shut up and move. It's too damn hot and there's no air to breathe under this duvet," she said, kissing her passionately before leaving the enclosed space. "Okay, enough, enough. Right, lady, you said you wanted to stay in bed all day, so we have…snacks," she said, holding up bags of crisps, chocolates and sweets. "We have drinks," she added, lifting the cool box lid showing cans of diet coke and wine. "Lastly, we have movies and TV shows, and well whatever we want really." She pointed to the laptop placed on top of the chest of drawers facing the bed. Now, I don't think I have forgotten anything, but please, princess, do share if you disagree." She smirked, pulling the laptop onto her lap.

"You really have thought of everything haven't you? You're not just a pretty face and hot body after all."

"Charming! So what do you fancy watching then? Chick flick? Horror? L word? Cartoon? Porn? What?" Chloe asked, looking over at her seriously.

"Porn? Really? You are so kinky," Brooke laughed, grabbing a coke from the cool box. "I think we'd give them a run for their money, personally," she said, raising her eyebrows. "Let's put the L word back on. It's easy watching, we have both seen it before, so if we, um…get side-tracked it won't really matter," she said, raising an eyebrow.

"My gosh you really are a sexual deviant aren't you?"

"Hardly, it's just been a bloody long time. Plus, it's my birthday. So I figure if any day is *just,* then today is certainly it. I don't know if you are aware, but it is my thirtieth after all," she said, winking to Chloe. "Additionally, as you are busy this weekend, I'm guessing you probably have to leave tonight or very early tomorrow and won't be coming back. *Then*, even if you do come back next weekend, I have my friend here all weekend, so I won't get a chance and...," Brooke scratched her head, sighing. "Erm, well the next week, I'll be gone...back home. So yeah, I would actually quite like to get side-tracked a few more times," she said sombrely.

"Okay, a couple things. Firstly, we are going to have a good day. It's only lunchtime, and if you would like to stay in bed all day and have sex, I for one am not complaining. And...well, more than happy to oblige. However, no more talk of that. As I said earlier, let's just enjoy this...enjoy your birthday. Secondly, about this weekend. Well I wasn't lying, it is Emily's hen do this weekend, so you're right I have to leave. But not until tomorrow. And...well...wow...this is harder than I figured," she sighed.

"What's wrong? Why is it hard?" Brooke asked confused.

"Well, don't feel obligated or anything. I mean, if it's too much, then don't worry, I get it. It was just a thought. Ya know put it out there...," she said awkwardly.

"What? Come on, just say it?" Brooke said confused.

"Well, I was wondering if you fancied coming to mine this weekend. I have a couple of meetings tomorrow morning, but will be able to get back after lunch. And we can go for lunch, maybe movies. I don't know, whatever you fancy. Then Emily said she was okay with you coming on Saturday. I just needed to check because of places and deposits etc. But she has had a couple people drop out and said more the merrier. She would also love for you to come on Friday. It will just be the three of us, well four with you, and then you can come back on Monday. I figured it may be a nice little break for you from here. But um, it's no big deal if you don't want to? Or feel uncomfortable. That's fine, it was just an idea," Chloe said, fidgeting with the ring pull on her diet coke and taking a long breath.

"Jesus, you barely took a breath in that sentence. Do you think it's weird?" Brooke asked.

Chloe pondered on the question before she responded. "Honestly, I dunno. I guess no weirder than what we have spent the last twelve hours doing. I suppose it's not so much weird, it's more...scary...and probably stupid," she sighed.

"Stupid how? Stupid because of me? Or stupid because of asking?" Brooke asked inquisitively.

Chloe smiled softly, turning on her side to face Brooke. "Actually, neither. Stupid because, it's just another step closer to me getting hurt," she said sadly. "But honestly, I know I can't do anything about that now, and I know I have gone too far. So to answer to your question. No, I don't think it's stupid to ask you, and I don't think it's stupid for you to come and enjoy the weekend. I think it's stupid that I'm terrified of getting hurt and terrified of liking someone for anything more than some fun. Yet I have gone and done all of this, and already really like you. When I was desperately trying to avoid that happening, I go and do things like this…," she said stopping. "Like, come up here to surprise you. Probably spent far too much time with you and kissed you. Which for the record I've loved. Made love to you. Which again, *loved* that. So with every fibre of me that's telling me to run, screaming for the hills, I keep U-turning and coming straight back to the centre of the fear. So honestly, I would love for you to come this weekend, more so now that this could be the only time left to spend with you. So there you go, all on the table for you," she sighed, looking into the computer, pulling up the L word.

Brooke knew exactly what Chloe was talking about. Like Chloe, she knew that she should run in the opposite direction to prevent any further hurt, but she couldn't stop herself. Worse still, when she could hear Chloe feeling so exposed and putting it all on the line, *she* also had no control over herself any longer. It was like this protective mechanism inside of her just clicked and she wanted to grab her and tell her it was all going to be okay. But of course it wasn't, and how could it be? "So, can you maybe take me out when you get back from work to buy an outfit? I didn't really plan for any kind of special events like this, so I don't really have that part of my wardrobe with me." She smiled, turning on her side to face her.

"You sure?" She smiled widely. "Of course I'll take you shopping. Jesus, I'll buy you an outfit," she said excitably, and jumped over, pulling her in tight.

"Chlo, thanks for the offer, but I have money. I don't need you to buy me something, okay? I do need to ask you something serious though." She stopped, looking deep into her eyes.

"Erm, okay sure. What's the matter?" she asked, confused and concerned.

Brooke sighed heavily, "I'm sorry. I have no right to ask or accuse this, but I just need to know. I can't help it, but my head is still a bit messed up. I am still questioning everything, and I can't deal with it all again. So, I'm sorry if I offend or hurt you now. But at least if I know, I can assess it and know what to deal with," she said sadly.

"Right, um, okay? I'm not going to lie, now I'm concerned. But as I said, if you don't want to come, I don't want to make you feel uncomfortable."

"Is your ex, the um…the girl that broke your heart; the girl that put you off relationships. Will she be there?" she wanted to kick herself for sounding so insecure and stupid.

"What? Sarah? Erm? Unlikely, considering she lives on the other side of the world now and isn't friends with my friends. Why? Is that what you wanted to ask me? I'm lost. Where'd that come from?"

Brooke sighed heavily, putting her head in her hands. "Why? Why did you ask me? I didn't know if you just wanted someone to show up with. I'm sorry, I'm sorry. I sound pathetic. I know I do, but is that why you asked me?"

"Oh my God, come here. Please? *Please* come here? You have no idea, no, no…gosh NO. We haven't seen or spoken in years, and they wouldn't invite her because of me. Jesus if she was going, I would never have asked you. I can't believe you would even think that. In your defence, I appreciate that we don't really know each other so well, and for that I understand your concerns. There's nothing more to it," Chloe said, taking a deep breath. "There's nothing more to it, than…honestly, I just don't want to go a weekend without seeing you, especially on your birthday weekend. I know that's all too much, but that's the only reason why. I'll just start the show from here," she said embarrassed, and pressed play on a random episode of L word before putting it back on the chest of drawers. Chloe was suddenly feeling like she'd made a mistake in asking her. Maybe the whole thing had been a mistake, she thought. It was very clear that Brooke wasn't ready for any of this, that it was still far too soon. And she may have just completely broken the both of them all over again by coming here last night, she thought distantly.

"Will you get me please?" Brooke asked quietly.

"Huh?"

"Get me…please? Just here?" she pointed to Chloe's side under her arm, where there was space for Brooke to snuggle into.

Chloe smiled softly. "Come here, silly," she said, pulling Brooke in close, and kissing the top of her head as they settled in to watch the TV show.

Chapter Forty-Two

"I'm so glad I gave you the postcode. When those Lorries passed us on the motorway, I was thinking, there is no way she is going to keep up now," Chloe said, giggling as they pulled into her drive.

"Nice place," Brooke said, looking up to the house.

"I guess no better than yours," she said simply. "Um, where you lived. Sorry," she blushed.

"So you should be. I'm homeless remember?" Brooke banged into her shoulder.

"Well, I have a couple of spare rooms." Chloe smirked. "Although, if yesterday was anything to go by I don't think my body could cope," she added, shaking her head.

"That's because you're too old these days and can't handle the pace with us young whipper snappers." Brooke winked, following her towards the door.

"You're a cheeky little shit and will be sleeping in the garage if you carry on like that."

"You wouldn't dare. You couldn't resist me if you tried."

"Oh, little miss confident now, aren't we? Right. Shut the hell up, I have work. You knock yourself out and make yourself at home. Call me if you want to go anywhere and I will either direct you, or I can give you one of the girls' numbers. They may be able to come with you," Chloe said, kissing her and running out of the house, leaving Brooke there unsure of what to do.

***

Brooke heard the doorbell and suddenly didn't feel so relaxed any longer. She was feeling uncomfortable at the further intrusion on Chloe's friends. She grabbed hold of her beer bottle, and nervously listened to the greetings.

"Hey you," Emily squealed. "Thank you so much for coming." She smiled and hugged Brooke tightly.

"*Really?* I'm totally intruding…again." Brooke squirmed.

"Shut up, you idiot. We're all super happy you are here. Plus, we're pretty sure she's drunk or high or something. Who wouldn't want to see that?" Nat said, pulling Brooke in tight.

"Natalie, she's a bloody cop. And FYI, when the hell have I ever, *ever* got high? And double FYI, Brooke, I am not just saying this for your benefit," Emily said hitting Nat.

"So, *so* easy." Nat winked. "Like her, I'm happy you came over." She smiled sincerely. "How's everything going though, you feeling any better?"

Brooke relaxed a little and smiled. "Yes, I'm good. Very good in fact, thanks, Nat. How are you?" she said, feeling much more relaxed and noticing Chloe's soft and sincere smile from across the room.

***

The evening was spent with laughs, funny stories, drinks and great food. Brooke was completely relaxed now, albeit after about seven bottles of champagne. But at no point did she feel uncomfortable or out of place. In fact, she felt no different to last weekend with Chloe and her own friends. The girls were all so friendly and welcoming, and this was an entirely new dynamic for her.

It was after two, and Emily had been putting them back like they were going out of fashion. Nat was laughing at the state she was in and Carla, surprise-surprise, didn't look like she'd touched a drop all night. Chloe eventually made the girls go home, concerned that Emily would ruin her hen party the following day. They were being picked up at nine a.m. for their little jaunt to Blackpool for the day. The only place where twenty-six women ranging from eighteen to seventy-six ,wearing flashing penis necklaces, would fit in.

"Hey…so two things," Nat said, pulling Brooke to one side. "You were pretty cool when we first met," she said, pointing her finger to Brooke and hiccupping. "Excuse me. But you seem loads better now, and you really are a cool woman. I'm glad you came this weekend, and clearly so is she, and that's the other thing. I'm sorry if I came across rude when we first met. I didn't do it intentionally, because I liked you a lot. Sorry, I sound like I'm hitting on you now. But my point…hmm I had a point…what was I saying?" she asked Brooke, confused. "Oh yeah, that was it. Well, I could tell you were in a pretty bad way. And I know that Chlo is so afraid of getting in a relationship to avoid getting hurt again, and I didn't want her to try and jump into bed with you and hurt you more. So I was actually looking out for you, not her," Nat said, hugging her tightly. "You are awesome, please stay in touch. I'm sorry, I'm drunk."

"So, she's the type that just wants to prove a point? Pull someone because she shouldn't? Like for a game? Another mark on the bedpost and fuck off? Is that it?" Brooke said pointedly to Natalie.

"Woah, come here. Listen to me. No, that really, really isn't it. She's my best mate, that isn't her at all. Her ex, Sarah, fucked her big time. She gave everything to Sarah and when she screwed her over, she then vowed never to do so again. She put everything into work and her business, and didn't look back. She dates, yes. She has sex, also yes, occasionally. But when she sees people could potentially get attached, she walks away. She does that so that people don't get hurt. Chloe is the kindest, most thoughtful person you'll ever meet, and she would never purposely hurt anyone. But she was struck by you, I could see it. I could also see that if she got too close to you, and the realisation kicked in that she was following the same path, she may scare herself too much and just run. She isn't a game player, Brooke, I'll promise you that. I could tell that she really liked you though, and I would have done anything to protect you both," Nat said seriously.

"Would have? Past tense?" Brooke asked.

Natalie laughed at Brooke. "Yeah baby, because the looks that you two have been throwing each other all night," she paused, holding her hands up in defeat, "is way out of my control now. The universe has taken over, and honestly...," she stopped and looked around, before whispering. "Although, you guys would totally disagree with me that you are both to the point of no return. It actually looks good on you both, and you both seem happy. On that note, I'm leaving. I love you like one of these knuckle heads, I really do." She kissed her head, and walked away before Brooke could say anything else.

***

"So, have I pissed you off or was it Natalie?" Chloe sighed, aware that since they all left Brooke had barely spoken to her. She had seen Nat push her into the corner and figured she'd said something to piss Brooke off.

"Huh?" Brooke said, looking up to Chloe standing in the doorway, as she changed into her pyjamas.

"You heard me, Brooke. Someone's pissed you off. If it's me, I'd rather you just say so," she sighed, rubbing her temples.

"Nobody's pissed me off at all. I've had a wonderful evening."

"Right, of course," she said, sighing again, wondering where it had all gone wrong. Why was it so tremendously different at her home, opposed to Anglesey? "Good night then, I'll wake you up at eight a.m., unless you've changed your mind about coming?" Chloe said, walking out of her spare bedroom and leaving Brooke to it.

"What the fuck?" Brooke said to herself. She followed Chloe into her bedroom and into her en suite. "Really? *Really*? You are doing this? I have just said I'm fine, so what's your problem?"

"My problem? You were fine, then Nat said something and you've gone all weird. You aren't talking, you deny there's a problem, and then you go to the spare room."

"You put me in the spare room," Brooke responded, ever so slightly more reactive than she wanted to have been.

"I was being polite. I didn't think you'd actually sleep in there," Chloe shouted back, grabbing the sides of her sink. "What did Nat say to you?" she turned around facing Brooke, folding her arms.

"It doesn't matter," Brooke said solemnly.

"It matters to me."

"You two were a couple weren't you?"

"What? What do you mean? Well clearly, I know what you mean. *No*, we were never a couple. Where did that come from?" Chloe said, walking towards her. "I'm sorry, it's no excuse, but clearly we've all had too much to drink. I just figured this weekend would be very different to how it's already started. Tonight…it was going so well, and I know Nat doesn't approve or whatever, but I love my friends. God I love them so much. But all night I've done nothing but wait for them to leave so we could be together again, and not in a sexual way, just in a normal way," Chloe said. "Normal…bloody hell, I don't even know what normal looks like any more," she said, shaking her head. "Look, I'm sorry. I'm shit at this, it appears. You should go to sleep. It's late and…well…it's late," she sighed, walking past Brooke into her room and taking off her shirt. She sat on her bed wondering where it had all gone wrong.

Brooke came and sat next to Chloe, taking her hand in her own. "We aren't very good at this are we?" she sighed.

"I think we keep overthinking everything maybe?" Chloe responded.

"You know, Nat didn't say anything negative about you, just that you run from things that get serious. I think maybe she was insinuating that we have feelings for one another."

"What?" Chloe snarled, shaking her head.

Brooke looked at her for a while, her head swimming with what Natalie had told her not so long ago. And how Chloe was reacting. Did she want anything more? Was she just playing her? Natalie was adamant that she wouldn't mess about with her, but what if that wasn't true? What if the fear got the better of her? What if all she wanted was another notch on the bedpost? A different notch? Because she was damaged goods? Brooke sighed, so confused at this moment. "I'm sorry, Chloe, I should go to bed, I'm sorry…"

Chapter Forty-Three

Chloe woke up feeling a bit groggy. *Did we actually drink seven bottles of champagne?* She thought. She smiled, rolling over to the other side of the bed. She opened her eyes searching the empty space, as she had suddenly recalled the final aspects of the previous evening, sighing heavily.

Chloe hated fighting, especially in circumstances like this. She knew she had very little time with Brooke before she returned to the opposite end of the country, and her life. Why the fuck did Nat have to get involved? She got that she liked Brooke and was just looking out for her, but Chloe had never allowed herself to get this far before bailing. And truth be known, she was already aware it was far too late. There was absolutely no going back now, and one way or another Chloe didn't want it to be the end of it. She placed her hand on her beating chest as the realization set in that Chloe had actually already fallen for the woman. She couldn't determine quite when and where it had happened. But she needed to apologize for her actions last night, for being so reactive, and go back to how perfect things had been twenty-four hours prior.

Chloe jumped out of bed, feeling the pain from the copious amounts of alcohol the night before and jogged to the door. She stopped still, and ran back to her en suite as she poorly brushed her teeth and mouth washed, before quickly making her way back to her spare room.

Chloe knocked on the door, opening it and smiling widely. A smile which soon faded as she saw the bed made and a folded piece of paper on the pillow. Brooke was gone. She didn't know when or where, but the emptiness of her contents made it clear that she had packed her belongings and left.

Chloe sat down on the bed and opened the folded piece of paper, as she read the words before her.

I'm so very sorry. I just can't do this. Bx

And that was all she wrote…

<u>Chapter Forty-Four</u>

"You did what?" Kate snapped.

"Baby, calm down. Brookie, start again at the beginning," Jo said calmly, holding each one of Brooke's hands.

Brooke went through the whole story to Kate and Jo, filling them in on every aspect, from the first kiss all the way to leaving her. She hadn't left anything out, even down to the love making. Albeit, not in quite as much detail though. Brooke told them about the surprise at one minute past midnight on her birthday. She told them about her request to go back to Chloe's house for the hen do, where she had had a wonderful evening until the conversation with Natalie. That caused a niggling in her head all night in the spare room, which of course resulted in the six a.m. dash. The dash that consisted of sneaking out, driving back to the van, collecting her belongings and running…running as fast as she could. Not passing go, not collecting two hundred dollars. And better still, not getting hurt.

"What the *hell*? Are you actually insane?" Kate shouted.

"Kate, go. Now. Leave it, okay?" Jo snapped, and pointed to the door.

"Brooke, you sure you know what you're doing?" Jo said seriously.

Brooke stayed silent, looking at Jo. Moments passed and Jo left her until she was ready to respond. "Yes I'm sure," she said dejectedly.

Jo was worried about her friend, but she knew she couldn't push it. These things needed to be addressed by the people involved, and ultimately, that was up to Brooke now. She squeezed Brooke's hand. "Okay, Hun. Okay," Jo said, smiling lightly.

***

"Well you do what you want. I'm not just ignoring this, because that isn't a good plan. I'm being no part of this, seriously, Jo. Jesus, she is more destroyed than Maria. How can you seriously think this is a good idea?" Kate spat to her girlfriend, not giving her a chance to respond before continuing on her rampage once more. "Seriously, there's no way I'm just sitting back and letting this go. You do your thing and I'll do mine, but Jo, do not touch my computer. I mean it, don't touch it. If she doesn't see sense with this, then she really is screwed," Kate said, picking up her handbag and leaving the house.

Jo sighed heavily. Kate couldn't listen to reason in situations like this…ever, but she had to love her for the love and compassion she showed to others. Jo did as Kate asked and left the computer screen on in view as she left the study and shouted upstairs. "Brooke, I'm going to work. Kate will be back shortly. We'll see you this evening." She hadn't heard much from her for nigh on a week. Had they not both been regularly checking up on her, she'd have been concerned for her welfare. This was really not what she needed on top of everything else this last year. Jo really hoped this worked. If it didn't, she was completely unsure of what would happen to Brooke, she thought sadly. She closed all the doors downstairs and left the study open, before leaving for work.

Chapter Forty-Five

Brooke lay on the bed, ignoring the resounding words running through her head. Kate wasn't happy *at all*, and in most part because she thought Brooke had fucked up. Bollox to Kate, bollox to them all. None of them knew. Brooke knew though, since Natalie made it clear that she was only in for a notch. She told herself this again and again, ignoring the doubts in her mind. Chloe didn't want more. Chloe just wanted an out of towner, and she probably saw them all the time. And probably screwed them all the time. *No way*, not her. She wasn't going to succumb to Chloe…to her kind words, her grand romantic gestures, her cooking lessons, her presents, her lips, her love making skills. "Stop it Brooke!" she said to herself. Jumping off the bed, she wasn't going to mope again. She knew what she needed to do. Chloe may not have been what she needed and may have hurt her, but she was thankful to her for one thing…she had pointed her in the right direction of life.

Brooke got herself a coffee and went into the study. She needed to contact HR to discuss moving forward, and had no intention of going through Maria. She would speak directly to HR. Brooke sighed as she looked at the picture of Jo and Kate on Anglesey beach, when they had just got engaged. They were holding the ring with the sunrise behind them, grinning like nothing she'd ever seen before, causing the thoughts of the place, and Chloe, to come flooding back all over again. She swallowed back the lump in her throat and moved the mouse to remove the screensaver and bring the computer back to life, noticing Kate's Facebook page opened at the messages page.

"*Chloe Casey*," She said to herself. "You're friends with Chloe Casey, are you fucking kidding me? What the hell is wrong with my *friends*?" she said disgustedly.

Brooke read the message on the screen. "Kate, thank you, I love you for it. But she's made it clear. She doesn't want me and nobody can force her. Nothing is in our favour. Say hi to Jo for me." She turned away and shut the lid, walking into the kitchen again. Her breathing was heavy and erratic as she tried to ignore the words from Chloe. '*Nothing is in our favour*'. Why was Kate doing this? She'd told her what Nat had said. Why were her friends betraying her? She poured a glass of wine. It wasn't the greatest idea she'd ever had at 11a.m., but she felt that it was warranted right now. Brooke was still ignoring the words that were constantly replaying in her mind, and getting more and more frustrated with her friends…*and* their betrayal. How could they do this to her? No, they were not going to do this to her, she needed to know what her friends were saying about her.

Brooke took her glass then walked back and retrieved the entire bottle. She made her way back to the study and opened the computer once again. Scrolling down the lengthy email chain she went back to the very beginning and began reading.

***

"Hey gorgeous, you still mad at me?" Jo said, kissing her fiancée.

"I wasn't mad at you. I just don't want her to miss out on something that has the potential to be what she is totally deserving of. I'm sorry I went all crazy on you, you know what I'm like. We just have different approaches, that's all. I get the logic behind the whole stopping and waiting, but I know her baby. And she doesn't compute like you do. She has had far too many kicks whilst she's been down. More importantly, she's been down for such a long time. She will be petrified and she'll be more inclined to push everything into another project and ignore it...all in a bid to protect herself. We could see what they had. Baby, we could see it before they even could. So I can't wait for her to realize when it's too late, and Chloe has either moved on or dug herself deeper into the whole avoidance thing again. It may not work. In reality I'm quickly beginning to think it won't, but I had to have one last shot at making her see sense before it's too late. I'm sorry I was a cow," Kate said sadly, leaning into Jo.

"When you give me a whole speech like that, how can I possibly think you're a cow? I love you, and I love everything about you. Come on, I said you'd be back earlier than this, we best go and see what's going on in there today," Jo said anxiously.

Jo and Kate walked into their house and looked around the hallway. "Well I'm guessing your theory didn't work, considering the only door open is the kitchen?" Jo said to Kate.

Kate sighed. "Great! Well as I said, I'm quickly realizing it's too late, it's gone. Maybe it just wasn't meant to be," she said sadly, walking to the kitchen to make a drink for them both.

"Baby, I told you, we can't force it," Jo said softly, taking Kate's hand. "I'm sorry, angel. I love you," she said about to kiss her, upon hearing the whimpers coming from outside the kitchen door. They both looked to each other, before quickly making their way out the kitchen to follow the sounds to the study. As they opened the door, they found their friend laying on the floor in the foetal position, sobbing quietly.

"Hey, hey, what's happened? Baby, come here." Jo dropped to the floor and pulled her close, with Kate joining her on the other side snuggling into her, looking confused to her girlfriend. Kate turned around and noticed the computer open to the Facebook messages and Chloe's messages opened. Alongside that, she noticed the empty bottle of wine, as she turned back to Jo and shot her eyes behind her so that Jo could see the picture before them.

Jo rolled her eyes, stroking Brooke's head softly. "Come up, sweetie. What's the matter? Talk to us?"

Jo and Kate had no understanding of the sobs filling their room. It was clearly a very big mistake asking her to talk, as it was resembling of a sobbing child. Brooke was talking, but unfortunately for them, the words were coming through uncontrollable sobs, so neither of them could understand. "Okay, baby, just calm down, calm down. And then talk to us. Okay?" Jo soothed.

***

Finally, Brooke had managed to compose herself a little. She was still laying in Jo's arms, finally trying to steady her deep breathing. "She was all in," she said sadly. "I *think* maybe, she was all in. And everyone knew it, but us…*Everyone* knew it, but us. But she did. She knew it too, and despite not wanting to get hurt or get in a relationship again, she did it anyway. She put herself on the line for me. Like, she thought I may have *actually* been worth it…I think? And everyone knew but me," she sobbed once more.

Katie moved around, laying on Jo too, turning to face Brooke. "Baby, you are worth it, you've always been worth it. And she knew that, Brookie,…Chlo knew that. But I think you knew this was happening, too. In your heart of hearts, you knew, too. In here, you really knew," Kate soothed, touching Brooke's heart with her own hand. "You were maybe just too scared to admit it, which is okay, baby. That's okay too, and that's normal after all you've been through. Nobody would want to rush or even consider anything with what you have been through. But you can't run, Brookie. When a door opens for you, you can't just ignore it," Kate said, stroking her hair softly.

Jo's heart swelled, as she loved her fiancée more than anything. As much as she wasn't the most impatient person, she was the most warm-hearted woman she knew. She stroked her hair softly, looking down and smiling at her lover.

***

Brooke woke up the next morning barely able to see. Her eyes were swollen, which instantly worried her, causing her mind to go into overtime. Had she been kidnapped? What had happened? Why couldn't she see? She was claustrophobic and couldn't move, and forced her eyes open through the pain and looked around her, still half asleep. She thought she was at work, but something had gone wrong, and now she had been caught out. Her mind was still a few steps behind of the last ten months.

"Hey you okay?" Jo said.

She looked over and made out Jo. "Hey, where am I?" She stopped, remembering the last twelve hours. Sighing and laying her head back on the pillow, then looking to the other side, she saw Kate stirring. She recalled the floor sobs, and how her two best friends had made her go to bed with them so they could look after her, forcing her to be in the middle of them, which explained the claustrophobia.

"How you feeling?" Jo asked again.

Brooke's heart started racing...her head became overly heated, and the pain in her chest increased and tightened. She could feel her breathing become erratic, as she could feel the panic attack start. Worse still, how the hell could she control it when she didn't know what the cause was anymore?

"Brookie, Brookie, look at me, look at...me," she heard Kate shouting. "Calm down. Calm your breathing, you can fight this. Come on, you can do this, you have always been able to do this, sweetie. You *can* do this. Count to ten, baby. Come on, don't let it take you. You aren't having a heart attack, this is just a panic attack, caused by all the recent upset. Come on, Brooke," Kate was holding her face tightly, working with her to eventually allow the panic attack to subside.

Brooke breathed heavily, trying to make sense of everything last night. She looked over at Kate and kissed her gently, "I love you, thank you so much," she said, allowing the tears to fall down her cheeks.

Brooke turned to Jo. "Thank you, too. I love you both so much. You know that. And I genuinely don't know where I would be without you both," she said solemnly.

"We love you, too. But if you have any feelings towards anybody outside of this room, then you shouldn't be here, you know that right?" Jo stated it firmly, looking at her girlfriend and winking, allowing her to realise that Jo was on board with her approach at last.

Brooke looked at Jo seriously, before turning to Kate, who half smiled. Brooke thought back to what she was planning before she went to the computer. She smiled to them both, and got up, kissing Kate and Jo on the cheeks, telling them both that she loved them as she left.

***

Brooke was on google, researching what she needed to find, desperately ignoring how stupid she was being. She recalled a couple of months earlier when she was in Brighton, doing a similar thing. Finding what she needed and submitting the details, she sighed heavily, as the fears and concerns ran through her mind. "Fuck, Brooke. Are you really doing this? What if it all goes wrong? What if you do all this for nothing? Maria will ensure you never work again." She had absolutely zero faith in what she was about to do, but yet she still wanted to do it. She *had* to do it, she needed to. Mitch had left and she would be with a new partner, which no doubt her new boss would most likely just fuck her over with any way she could, *just* because she could.

Brooke pushed back the thoughts of the morning's doings and didn't allow herself to reconsider anything. She looked at the station in front of her and sighed heavily. Nothing she had ever done was even slightly as close to this scale of ridiculousness. Why was she even considering it? Why? Because, what did she have to lose? For once she was doing something for her, and if it didn't work out and fell apart at her feet, at least she knew she tried.

Brooke walked out of her car with confidence, as the woman went after what she wanted.

"Detective Davis? You're back?" the familiar voice said.

Brooke inwardly cringed at Maria's voice, having not seen her since the morning they broke up, and she turned around to face her ex. "Hi, Maria," Brooke said confidently. "Can I talk to you please?" she said, still trying to control her breathing.

<u>Chapter Forty-Six</u>

Brooke left the room, finally allowing her breathing to do what she had been purposefully preventing it from doing…becoming erratic. "I'll come back to you? *I'll come back to you*? What had she done?" she lowered her head between her legs and held it in her hands.

She found Jo's number and pressed call.

"Hey? What's going on?" Jo asked concerned.

"What have I done? I can't do this. Jo, what if I've lost my job? She's my boss."

"Babes, only you know what's right for you. Ignore what anybody else thinks. If this is what your heart is telling you, then…," Jo paused. "Go for it. Babes, you can't be on the sick forever. You would have eventually been forced to do something about it. Do what *you* want for a change, and we'll love you always. Don't stop fighting until you have a definitive answer," she said quietly.

Brooke allowed the tears to fall once more. "I have to go," she said sombrely.

Chapter Forty-Seven

Brooke sat in the corner of the bar, sipping her glass of champagne, as she pondered the past couple of weeks' events. Maria had come through in the end, and it had only taken one shitty text threatening to go to Paula and tell her to consider why exactly Maria wouldn't let go of her. Blimey, if only she'd realized years ago what a vindictive cow that woman could actually be. Either way, it was done now. She no longer had to fret about being on long term sick and the consequences when she returned. Brooke smiled lightly as she thought back to the look on Maria's face when Mitch and herself stood in front of her and invited her to their leaving do. She was absolutely stunned that the pair who hated her more than anyone else, had asked her, still causing her to giggle a little. She had shown up and bought them both a drink, thanking them for their hard work, commitment and dedication to the force and the team. Then she politely left the team to their night, celebrating and saying their goodbyes to their colleagues.

Brooke was brought out of her thoughts as she heard the door open, each time hearing the bell go off, feeling her heart drop. This time though, she could see the reflection in the picture above the facing seat. At last she was about to face her destiny.

***

Chloe walked into the bar where her client, Mrs. Smith, had said she would be seated. She couldn't believe she was about to sell another piece. After everything that had happened with Brooke, she had completely thrown herself in to work again. She had spent a bit of time at the cabin, which fortunately or unfortunately, feeling the loss of the woman, just spurred her on all that more. And now, one of her most recent pieces had been seen and had had an offer put on it. She made her way to the corner table, to the woman sat with her back to her.

"Hi, Mrs Smith?" Chloe said, holding her hand to her buyer.

Brooke stood up, holding her hand out, smiling sadly.

Chloe went to speak, but couldn't get the words out. She suddenly felt like she had been punched, before turning to walk away.

"Please, Chlo. Please don't leave. It isn't a set up. I am a genuine buyer," Brooke said quietly.

Chloe weighed up how desperately she needed or wanted the sale, and it was neither. Firstly, she didn't need to sell her soul. Secondly, her business and her very own paintings were doing exceptionally well. Her heart was heavy and she didn't know if she could deal with this right now.

"I hope you don't mind, I have ordered some champagne, but there is no insinuation there. I came to see you at work last week and I saw the painting. I don't want to assume it's me, but I think it may be. Irrespective of that, it's everything I remember and loved, so I stand by my words. I wasn't a 'hoax' buyer. Here is the cheque for the picture, I do believe it was two thousand, seven hundred. I've made it out to you for that amount, however, if I need to make it out to your business, I can do that. I have my cheque book here with me now," she said, anxiously grabbing her cheque book from her bag. Chloe looked tired, and Brooke wondered if it was her who had done that to her. "There's more I would like to say, but I don't want to push it, and I don't believe I'm in a position to push you. So I'm going to make it easy on you. I need the bathroom, because it's been a very long day. If you are here when I return, I will tell…I…" She stopped, taking a deep breath and trying again, pushing back the swell in her throat. "Well, I will say what I want to say. If you are not, I will leave you alone to…to, umm…move on in your life," Brooke said, fighting back all the emotion ruling her body right now as she turned and left the table.

***

Brooke walked out of the bathroom and her heart sank as she saw the empty seat before her. She wasn't surprised. Honestly, how could she be? She sat back down, happy that she was facing the wall once again. Brooke allowed the tears to fall as she silently sipped the champagne and retrieved her phone. What was she going to do now? She couldn't very well blame Chloe. Maybe she would come around with time? She considered desperately. She thought of the painting that day at her gallery. At least she had the very first addition for her new home she thought, as she looked at the picture of a blonde haired woman sitting on a surfboard, legs hanging in the water and watching the sunrise. Brooke saw the glass placed on the table before her and looked up to the owner.

"So...I kind of went a bit overboard with the champers at Emily's hen do following the umm...well you know, you leaving and that, so I really can't face it for a while," she said, holding up her glass. "So I went and got a vodka instead," Chloe said, sitting down. "So? You said you had something to say?" Chloe said sadly.

Brooke was dancing for joy inside, but could see the hurt and pain behind Chloe's eyes. How the hell could she have done this to the most amazing woman she had ever met? Brooke wiped her eyes before speaking. "Sorry," she said trying to compose herself. "I thought you'd left." She breathed in deeply before she began speaking again. Brooke started by apologizing for hurting her, and after that she began at the beginning and told her everything. From the conversation with Natalie, the argument with Chloe, the fear of it all, the rushing out, the leaving without a goodbye, all the way to the parts Chloe hadn't been party to. She told of the decision to go and speak to HR about her job, which resulted in falling upon Kate's Facebook page...which she had since learned was all a ploy, to get her to see sense. She told her about finding and reading the messages and pretty much everything leading up to the point she had left Kate and Jo's house earlier that morning.

Chloe stayed silent, nursing her vodka and giving nothing away.

Brooke took a large gulp of her champagne and leaned into her bag pulling out a manila folder. She looked up, offering a small smile to an expressionless Chloe. "So I'm going back to work," she smiled gently, stroking the folder.

Chloe looked surprised, but also looked genuinely pleased for Brooke. "Wow, I'm...that's incredible...I'm made up for you. That's a huge step, and an incredible thing to have overcome," she said, kerbing her enthusiasm a little. "When? And what happened? They didn't force you, did they?" Chloe asked concerned.

"No, they didn't," Brooke said with a slight smile, feeling her heart swell at the concern of the woman. "It was totally my request. Don't get me wrong, it wasn't easy with her. Maria was not really willing to help, and resulted in me having to be a bit of a bitch and threaten her new found love and relationship. But anyways, it worked out for the best. And I'm hoping it will be very soon, I'm just waiting for it to be approved." She nodded slowly, playing with the rim of her glass.

"That's amazing, seriously. I'm really happy for you," she said sincerely.

"Thank you, genuinely that means a lot. I'm nervous as hell because, well it's been a while and I'm concerned with everything that happened and stuff. But I'm trying to be positive," she said, looking back up to Chloe.

"Brooke, you have come so far in your career for your age, so you are clearly very good at it. You have been through an incredibly difficult time, more than most could manage, So anyone would feel this way. Just don't put too much pressure on yourself and take it easy. Utilize Mitch as much as you can, and don't let her antagonize you, and I'm sure you will be fine," she said, moving her hand towards Brooke's, before realizing what she was doing and quickly snatching it away.

"Well, no chance of her antagonizing me because she won't be my boss anymore, and Mitch is moving to Canada in a week," she said, smiling slightly. "Normally they aren't so keen on transfers, but it's not like she wants me there. And HR has pretty much confirmed it's a certainty," she said nonchalantly, as she took a long sip of her drink and kept her gaze away from Chloe's confused glare.

"*Transfers*? What do you mean, your boss doesn't want you? You mean Maria? Has your ex forced you out?" Chloe spat.

"No, Maria has not forced me out. However, I did have to go and ask permission of her first. I pretty much blackmailed my boss that I would take her to HR following our 'little conversation'. Then I said to her that if she didn't approve it and put in a good word, I would text Paula and ask her why Maria was so against making me leaving her station. That obviously made her more than happy to approve my request. Additionally, HR is okay about it too, and actually agreed that the change maybe exactly what I need to move forward. So if all is well and good, I'll be transferring to the South Yorkshire Police Department in a week or two."

"South Yorkshire? But…what do you mean? You can't commute down south, that's here?" Chloe asked, confused.

"Hmmm hmmm…additionally, I hope you don't mind, but I really liked your village when I stayed. So I've just rented a place there. I'm sorry if that sounds a bit '*stalkerish*' but, well I'm not so great when it comes to adapting to change. And as I said, I loved your village. I figured it may make the move a little easier, to somewhere I know and like. But if it's a problem, you may want to let me know sooner rather than later, as I'm moving in on Monday." Brooke turned the manila folder and opened it to her. "Here, you want to see some pictures of the place I'm renting?" she said, showing her them.

"Wha…what?" Chloe said, eyeing her confused.

"I know I've been a fool, Chloe, and I don't know what else to say other than I'm sorry. I know I'm an idiot, and I know I'm terrified, but I'm more terrified of losing you. You're perfect to me, and you'll always be perfect to me. I love you, and I know that's probably obscene given the short period of time we've known each other, but it's true and …I was wondering," she stopped, her breathing quickening once again. "Well, I was hoping you may let me take you out on an official date?" Brooke said seriously, unable to look at her for fear of rejection.

Chloe looked at Brooke seriously, completely confused by everything she had just said. She was weighing it all up, unable to comprehend what was happening. Chloe stood up. "Thanks for buying the art Brooke. I'm not really sure what you want me to say. It's just all…" She stopped, sighing heavily. "All a bit too much. I…I just need the bathroom," Chloe said, leaving the table.

<u>Chapter Forty-Eight</u>

Brooke was trying to control the breathing and hold back the tears that were threatening to appear once more. It wasn't supposed to end this way. She could hear Jo and Kate in her head saying fight it. *If it's love, fight it,* she thought. She stood up in search of Chloe. She couldn't give up this easily, she just needed to fight harder and make her see how much she meant to her.

Brooke walked into the bathroom and saw Chloe, holding onto the sink with tears rolling in succession down her cheeks. She moved quickly towards her, but Chloe stepped back and put her arms out to stop Brooke from coming closer.

"You were wrong ya know? When you said last week that Sarah was the love of my life. She was in my mind at one time, but she isn't anymore. I need to return to work, Brooke," she said, sighing. She reached the bathroom door and looked around at Brooke, sheer desperation, anguish and fear filling her face. That was when the realisation set in that she couldn't live without this woman. Chloe opened the door, "Pick me up tomorrow at seven," Chloe said, smiling slightly and leaving her there with those final words playing back to her.

Brooke turned around to face her reflection in the mirror. She couldn't help but relish in the stupidly wide smile crossing her entire face. She pulled out her phone and sent a group text to Kate and Jo, *I just walked through that open door ;) xxxxx*, and left the pub.

379

<u>Epilogue</u>

"This is obscene. What sort of sodding idiot chooses to live in this climate? It's colder than flipping Iceland," Chloe said, shivering as she walked outside, passing the lodge sign with welcome to Alberta, Canada on it.

"Are you going to moan this much forever?" Brooke asked, dragging the suitcase. "This is my best friend remember? And FYI, you were the one that was talking about opening the little cozy restaurant that offered authentic British roast dinners, remember? What was it *'let them ole men mosey on down with their little women'*?" Brooke laughed, as she pulled the key out to their log cabin. "My boy is thrilled to be here, remember? And all loved up with some Canadian girl. Which, for the record, you cannot be rude to this evening about the coldness of the country," Brooke said, smiling as she opened the door, immediately feeling the heat spill out.

They walked through the door and took in the beauty of what would be their home for the next couple of weeks. Chloe went and lit the fire in their lounge before checking out the beautiful huge kitchen, appreciating the huge AGA. "Come look at this," Brooke said, pulling her hand to the kitchen back door and showing her the hot tub on the balcony, looking out over the frozen lake before them.

"Oh my God, it's beautiful. I can't wait to get you naked in there." She smirked, wrapping her arms around her girlfriend from behind and softly kissing her neck.

"You are such a pervert." She pushed her playfully. "Come on," she said, walking back inside, going to the door next to the bathroom and seeing a cosy indoor sauna. "Ooohhh, we need to use that at least once a day," Chloe said excitably.

"Oh yes, that's a given. Okay, now the piece de resistance." Brooke pulled Chloe to their bedroom, which looked phenomenal in the photos. It had four poster beds, private balconies looking onto the lake, and their own private fire place. She was just about to open the door, when Chloe put her hand on hers. She softly kissed her lips and said, "for you my baby," before pushing it open. Brooke turned to Chloe, who was smirking as she watched the look of surprise as the heat and light radiated upon opening the door. Brooke looked back to the room and walked over to see what was on the bed.

Chloe saw Brooke's face glow with the candles lighting up the room, and sidestepped to observe the recognition as it hit. Why had she not thought to take a picture at this point? She would have loved to have been able to capture that look and keep it forever.

Brooke stepped closer to the bed noticing the...easily, 30 candles lighting up the room, before noticing the rose petals, surrounded by the candles on the bed, spelling out the words 'Marry me?'. She couldn't control her heart, nor her emotions as the tears fell. "What? How? When? We've been together this whole time. How did you do this? Really? Is this for me?" she asked all manner of questions.

"It's amazing how incredibly romantic the Canadians are," Chloe whispered, grabbing Brooke to her, not wanting to give anything further away.

"Really? You are really doing this?" Brooke asked.

Chloe pulled out a box from her pocket. "So I know you're not really a fan of the whole 'one knee thing', but I was kinda hoping you'd be a fan of this?" she said, pointing out the scene before her. "And this?" she said, opening the box to a small diamond ring, encrusted with aquamarine stones on the outskirts.

"Oh my God, baby, I love it," Brooke cried.

"Well, I know you aren't a big diamond fan, and I figured the aquamarine stones may be memorable to the surf and sea...you know, how we met?" she said shyly.

"Oh my God, you are perfect, you are my perfect girl. I love you, baby, I love you," Brooke said, fitting her finger with the ring and pulling Chloe in to a tight embrace.

***

"Seriously, I cannot believe you propose in the most perfectly romantic setting, with the most perfect ring, and then drag me out? That's just mean." Brooke stomped through the snow, looking at her ring once again.

"Baby girl, we're visiting your best friend. We're in Alberta to see your best friend, and these plans have been set for weeks. We cannot ditch him on the only night he's off, when we have two weeks together....Just because I have proposed." Chloe smirked.

"Just...*just*? Seriously? Just becau...," Brooke said walking through the restaurant door.

"Yay!" the screams began, startling Brooke.

"What the h..." Brooke looked around, taking stock of everything before her. She was unsure when she had grabbed onto Chloe, who was pretty much holding her up right now.

"What? Did you do all this for me?" Brooke asked Chloe, still holding on to her. She looked confused as she noticed a big table with Mitch, and assumingly his new girlfriend, Jo, Kate, Natalie, Emily and her husband John, and Carla all sitting there.

"Baby girl, it wasn't too hard to get your friends to come for a holiday to Canada." She winked. "I figured Jo owed me one, and I thought you may want to celebrate with them as well," Chloe said, kissing her girlfriend.

"I cannot believe how amazing you are. You truly surprise me every day and make me feel like the richest woman alive, to call you mine. I can't wait to spend the rest of my life with you, Chloe," she said sincerely. "In other news, Carla may not be so happy about Mitch's new girlfriend, and she'll end up getting herself in trouble for sure," she said, kissing her girlfriend's hand and pulling her to their friends.

"Of course I know that, but he'll be fine. He can look after himself," Chloe laughed. "I love you with all my heart, angel. To me, you are true perfection," Chloe said, leaning in and kissing her fiancée.

<u>About the Author</u>

S.L. Gape is 36 years old and enjoys writing, cooking, travelling and photography. She lives in Cheshire with her partner Jen, and currently splits her time between writing and her day job as a Regional HR advisor.

She gets a lot of inspiration from travelling and her experience as a holiday rep for seven years, where she was lucky enough to have lived and worked in Spain, Greece, Bahamas, Egypt and Lapland. Whilst she has only been writing for a year, she find it a tremendous stress release for her job, and loves to live through the escapism.

Follow her on Twitter: @louise_7uk and Facebook: S.L. Gape

Other Titles Available From
Triplicity Publishing

Blue Ice Landing by KA Moll. Coy is a beautiful blonde with a southern accent and a successful practice as a physician assistant. She has a comfortable home, good friends, and a loving family. She's also a widow, carrying a burden of responsibility for her wife's untimely death. Coby is a woman with secrets. She's estranged from her family, a recovering alcoholic, and alone because she's convinced that she's unlovable. When she loses her job as a heavy equipment operator, she'll accept one that'll force her to step way outside her comfort zone. When Coy quits her job to accept a position in Antarctica, her path will cross with Coby's. Their attraction to one another will be immediate, and despite their differences, it won't be long before they fall in love. But for these two, with all their baggage, will love be enough?

Never Quit by Graysen Morgen. Two years after stepping away from the action as a Coast Guard Rescue Swimmer to become an instructor, Finley finds herself in charge of the most difficult class of cadets she's ever faced, while also juggling the taxing demands of having a home life with her partner Nicole, and their fifteen year old daughter. Jordy Ross gave up everything, dropping out of college, and leaving her family behind, to join the Coast Guard and become a rescue swimmer cadet. The extreme training tests her fitness level, pushing her mentally and physically further than she's ever been in her life, but it's the aggressive competition between her and another female cadet that proves to be the most challenging.

For a Moment's Indiscretion by KA Moll. With ten years of marriage under their belt, Zane and Jaina are coasting. The little things they used to do for one another have fallen by the wayside. They've gotten busy with life. They've forgotten to nurture their love and relationship. Even soul mates can stumble on hard times and have marital difficulties. Enter Amelia, a new faculty member in Jaina's building. She's new in town, young, and very pretty. When an argument with Zane causes Jaina to storm out angry, she reaches out to Amelia. Of course, she seizes the opportunity. And for a moment of indiscretion, Jaina could lose everything.

Never Let Go by Graysen Morgen. For Coast Guard Rescue Swimmer, Finley Morris, life is good. She loves her job, is well respected by her peers, and has been given an opportunity to take her career to the next level. The only thing missing is the love of her life, who walked out, taking their daughter with her, seven years earlier. When Finley gets a call from her ex, saying their teenage daughter is coming to spend the summer with her, she's floored. While spending more time with her daughter, whom she doesn't get to see often, and learning to be a full-time parent, Finley quickly realizes she has not, and will never, let go of what is important.

Pursuit by Joan L. Anderson. Claire is a workaholic attorney who flies to Paris to lick her wounds after being dumped by her girlfriend of seventeen years. On the plane she chats with the young woman sitting next to her, and when they land the woman is inexplicably detained in Customs. Claire is surprised when she later runs into the woman in the city. They agree to meet for breakfast the next morning, but when the woman doesn't show up Claire goes to her hotel and makes a horrifying discovery. She soon finds herself ensnared in a web of intrigue and international terrorism, becoming the target of a high stakes game of cat and mouse through the streets of Paris.

Wrecked by Sydney Canyon. To most people, the *Duchess* is a myth formed by old pirates tales, but to Reid Cavanaugh, a Caribbean island bum and one of the best divers and treasure hunters in the world, it's a real, seventeenth century pirate ship—the holy grail of underwater treasure hunting. Reid uses the same cunning tactics she always has before setting out to find the lost ship. However, she is forced to bring her business partner's daughter along as collateral this time because he doesn't trust her. Neither woman is thrilled, but being cooped up on a small dive boat for days, forces them to get know each other quickly.

Arson by Austen Thorne. Madison Drake is a detective for the Stetson Beach Police Department. The last thing she wants to do is show a new detective the ropes, especially when a fire investigation becomes arson to cover up a murder. Madison butts heads with Tara, her trainee, deals with sarcasm from Nic, her ex-girlfriend who is a patrol officer, and finds calm in the chaos of police work with Jamie, her best friend who is the county medical examiner. Arson is the first of many in a series of novella episodes surrounding the fictional Stetson Beach Police Department and Detective Madison Drake.

Change of Heart by KA Moll. Courtney Holloman is a woman at the top of her game. She's successful, wealthy, and a highly sought after Washington lobbyist. She has money, her job, booze, and nothing else. In quiet moments, against her will, her mind drifts back to her days in high school and to all that she gave up. Jack Camdon is a complex woman, and yet not at all. She is also a woman who has never moved beyond the sudden and unexplained departure of her high school sweetheart, her lover, and her soul mate. When circumstances bring Courtney back to town two decades later, their paths will cross. Will it be too late?

Mommies (Bridal Series book 3) by Graysen Morgen. Britton and her wife Daphne have been married for a year and a half and are happy with their life, until Britton's mother hounds her to find out why her sister Bridget hasn't decided to have children yet. This prompts Daphne to bring up the big subject of having kids of their own with Britton. Britton hadn't really thought much about having kids, but her love for Daphne makes her see life and their future together in a whole new way when they decide to become mommies.

Haunting Love by K.A. Moll. Anna Crestwood was raised in the strict beliefs of a religious sect nestled in the foothills of the Smoky Mountains. She's a lesbian with a ton of baggage—fearful, guilty, and alone. Very few things would compel her to leave the familiar. The job offer of a lifetime is one of them. Gabe Garst is a police officer. She's also a powerful medium. Her work with juvenile delinquents and ghosts is all that keeps her going. Inside she's dead, certain that her capacity to love is buried six feet under. Anna and Gabe's paths cross. Their attraction is immediate, but they hold back until all hope seems lost.

Rapture & Rogue by Sydney Canyon. Taren Rauley is happy and in a good relationship, until the one person she thought she'd never see again comes back into her life. She struggles to keep the past from colliding with the present as old feelings she thought were dead and gone, begin to haunt her. In college, Gianna Revisi was a mastermind, ring-leading, crime boss. Now, she has a great life and spends her time running Rapture and Rogue, the two establishments she built from the ground up. The last person she ever expects to see walk into one of them, is the girl who walked out on her, breaking her heart five years ago.

Second Chance by Sydney Canyon. After an attack on her convoy, Marine Corps Staff Sergeant, Darien Hollister, must learn to live without her sight. When an experimental procedure allows her to see again, Darien is torn, knowing someone had to die in order for this to happen.

She embarks on a journey to personally thank the donor's family, but is too stunned to tell them the truth. Mixed emotions stir inside of her as she slowly gets to the know the people that feel like so much more than strangers to her. When the truth finally comes out, Darien walks away, taking the second chance that she's been given to go back to the only life she's ever known, but she's not the only one with a second chance at life.

Meant to Be by Graysen Morgen. Brandt is about to walk down the aisle with her girlfriend, when an unexpected chain of events turns her world upside down, causing her to question the last three years of her life. A chance encounter sparks a mix of rage and excitement that she has never felt before. Summer is living life and following her dreams, all the while, harboring a huge secret that could ruin her career. She believes that some things are better kept in the dark, until she has her third run-in with a woman she had hoped to never see again, and gives into temptation. Brandt and Summer start believing everything happens for a reason as they learn the true meaning of meant to be.

Coming Home by Graysen Morgen. After tragedy derails TJ Abernathy's life, she packs up her three year old son and heads back to Pennsylvania to live with her grandmother on the family farm. TJ picks back up where she left off eight years earlier, tending to the fruit and nut tree orchard, while learning her grandmother's secret trade. Soon, TJ's high school sweetheart and the same girl who broke her heart, comes back into her life, threatening to steal it away once again. As the weeks turn into months and tragedy strikes again, TJ realizes coming home was the best thing she could've ever done.

Special Assignment by Austen Thorne. Secret Service Agent Parker Meeks has her hands full when she gets her new assignment, protecting a Congressman's teenage daughter, who has had threats made on her life and been whisked away to a Christian boarding school under an alias to finish out her senior year. Parker is fine with the assignment, until she finds out she has to go undercover as a Canon Priest. The last thing Parker expects to find is a beautiful, art history teacher, who is intrigued by her in more ways than one.

Miracle at Christmas by Sydney Canyon. A Modern Twist on the Classic Scrooge Story. Dylan is a power-hungry lawyer who pushed away everything good in her life to become the best defense attorney in the, often winning the worst cases and keeping anyone with enough money out of jail. She's visited on Christmas Eve by her deceased law partner, who threatens her with a life in hell like his own, if she doesn't change her path. During the course of the night, she is taken on a journey through her past, present, and future with three very different spirits.

Bella Vita by Sydney Canyon. Brady is the First Officer of the crew on the Bella Vita, a luxury charter yacht in the Caribbean. She enjoys the laidback island lifestyle, and is accustomed to high profile guests, but when a U.S. Senator charters the yacht as a gift to his beautiful twin daughters who have just graduated from college and a few of their friends, she literally has her hands full.

Brides (Bridal Series book 2) by Graysen Morgen. Britton Prescott is dating the love of her life, Daphne Attwood, after a few tumultuous events that happened to unravel at her sister's wedding reception, seven months earlier. She's happy with the way things are, but immense pressure from her family and friends to take the next step, nearly sends her back to the single life. The idea of a long engagement and simple wedding are thrown out the window, as both families take over, rushing Britton and Daphne to the altar in a matter of weeks.

Cypress Lake by Graysen Morgen. The small town of Cypress Lake is rocked when one murder after another happens. Dani Ricketts, the Chief Deputy for the Cypress Lake Sheriff's Office, realizes the murders are linked. She's surprised when the girl that broke her heart in high school has not only returned home, but she's also Dani's only suspect. Kristen Malone has come back to Cypress Lake to put the past behind her so that she can move on with her life. Seeing Dani Ricketts again throws her off-guard, nearly derailing her plans to finally rid herself and her family of Cypress Lake.

Crashing Waves by Graysen Morgen. After a tragic accident, Pro Surfer, Rory Eden, spends her days hiding in the surf and snowboard manufacturing company that she built from the ground up, while living her life as a shell of the person that she once was. Rory's world is turned upside when a young surfer pursues her, asking for the one thing she can't do. Adler Troy and Dr. Cason Macauley from Graysen Morgen's bestselling novel: *Falling Snow*, make an appearance in this romantic adventure about life, love, and letting go.

Bridesmaid of Honor (Bridal Series book 1) by Graysen Morgen. Britton Prescott's best friend is getting married and she's the maid of honor. As if that isn't enough to deal with, Britton's sister announces she's getting married in the same month and her maid of honor is her best friend Daphne, the same woman who has tormented Britton for years. Britton has to suck it up and play nice, instead of scratching her eyes out, because she and Daphne are in both weddings. Everyone is counting on them to behave like adults.

Falling Snow by Graysen Morgen. Dr. Cason Macauley, a high-speed trauma surgeon from Denver meets Adler Troy, a professional snowboarder and sparks fly. The last thing Cason wants is a relationship and Adler doesn't realize what's right in front of her until it's gone, but will it be too late?

Fate vs. Destiny by Graysen Morgen. Logan Greer devotes her life to investigating plane crashes for the National Transportation Safety Board. Brooke McCabe is an investigator with the Federal Aviation Association who literally flies by the seat of her pants. When Logan gets tangled in head games with both women will she choose fate or destiny?

Just Me by Graysen Morgen. Wild child Ian Wiley has to grow up and take the reins of the hundred year old family business when tragedy strikes. Cassidy Harland is a little surprised that she came within an inch of picking up a gorgeous stranger in a bar and is shocked to find out that stranger is the new head of her company.

Love Loss Revenge by Graysen Morgen. Rian Casey is an FBI Agent working the biggest case of her career and madly in love with her girlfriend. Her world is turned upside when tragedy strikes. Heartbroken, she tries to rebuild her life. When she discovers the truth behind what really happened that awful night she decides justice isn't good enough, and vows revenge on everyone involved.

Natural Instinct by Graysen Morgen. Chandler Scott is a Marine Biologist who keeps her private life private. Corey Joslen is intrigued by Chandler from the moment she meets her. Chandler is forced to finally open her life up to Corey. It backfires in Corey's face and sends her running. Will either woman learn to trust her natural instinct?

Secluded Heart by Graysen Morgen. Chase Leery is an overworked cardiac surgeon with a group of best friends that have an opinion and a reason for everything. When she meets a new artist named Remy Sheridan at her best friend's art gallery she is captivated by the reclusive woman. When Chase finds out why Remy is so sheltered will she put her career on the line to help her or is it too difficult to love someone with a secluded heart?

In Love, at War by Graysen Morgen. Charley Hayes is in the Army Air Force and stationed at Ford Island in Pearl Harbor. She is the commanding officer of her own female-only service squadron and doing the one thing she loves most, repairing airplanes. Life is good for Charley, until the day she finds herself falling in love while fighting for her life as her country is thrown haphazardly into World War II. Can she survive being in love and at war?

Fast Pitch by Graysen Morgen. Graham Cahill is a senior in college and the catcher and captain of the softball team. Despite being an all-star pitcher, Bailey Michaels is young and arrogant. Graham and Bailey are forced to get to know each other off the field in order to learn to work together on the field. Will the extra time pay off or will it drive a nail through the team?

Submerged by Graysen Morgen. Assistant District Attorney Layne Carmichael had no idea that the sexy woman she took home from a local bar for a one night stand would turn out to be someone she would be prosecuting months later. Scooter is a Naval Officer on a submarine who changes women like she changes uniforms. When she is accused of a heinous crime she is shocked to see her latest conquest sitting across from her as the prosecuting attorney.

Vow of Solitude by Austen Thorne. Detective Jordan Denali is in a fight for her life against the ghosts from her past and a Serial Killer taunting her with his every move. She lives a life of solitude and plans to keep it that way. When Callie Marceau, a curious Medical Examiner, decides she wants in on the biggest case of her career, as well as, Jordan's life, Jordan is powerless to stop her.

Igniting Temptation by Sydney Canyon. Mackenzie Trotter is the Head of Pediatrics at the local hospital. Her life takes a rather unexpected turn when she meets a flirtatious, beautiful fire fighter. Both women soon discover it doesn't take much to ignite temptation.

One Night by Sydney Canyon. While on a business trip, Caylen Jarrett spends an amazing night with a beautiful stripper. Months later, she is shocked and confused when that same woman re-enters her life. The fact that this stranger could destroy her career doesn't bother her. C.J. is more terrified of the feelings this

S.L. Gape

woman stirs in her. Could she have fallen in love in one night and not even known it?

Fine by Sydney Canyon. Collin Anderson hides behind a façade, pretending everything is fine. Her workaholic wife and best friend are both oblivious as she goes on an emotional journey, battling a potentially hereditary disease that her mother has been diagnosed with. The only person who knows what is really going on, is Collin's doctor. The same doctor, who is an acquaintance that she's always been attracted to, and who has a partner of her own.

Shadow's Eyes by Sydney Canyon. Tyler McCain is the owner of a large ranch that breeds and sells different types of horses. She isn't exactly thrilled when a Hollywood movie producer shows up wanting to film his latest movie on her property. Reegan Delsol is an up and coming actress who has everything going for her when she lands the lead role in a new film, but there one small problem that could blow the entire picture.

Light Reading: A Collection of Novellas by Sydney Canyon. Four of Sydney Canyon's novellas together in one book, including the bestsellers Shadow's Eyes and One Night.

Visit us at www.tri-pub.com

www.ingramcontent.com/pod-product-compliance
Lightning Source LLC
Chambersburg PA
CBHW051547250626
47157CB00001B/224